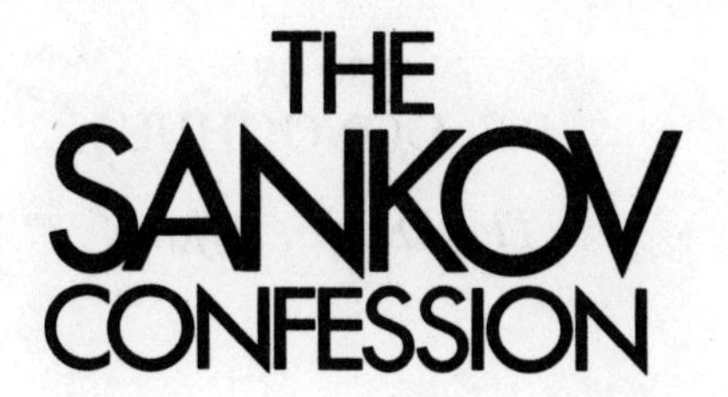
THE
SANKOV
CONFESSION

ALSO BY

P.S. DONOGHUE

The Dublin Affair

THE SANKOV CONFESSION

A Novel by

P.S. DONOGHUE

DONALD I. FINE, INC.

New York

 Published in the United States of America by Donald I. Fine, Inc. and in Canada by General Publishing Company Limited.

Library of Congress Cataloging-in-Publication Data

Donoghue, P.S.
The Sankov confession / by P.S. Donoghue.
p.cm.
ISBN 1-55611-161-4
I. Title.
PS3554.0538S26 1989
813'.54—dc20 89-45439
CIP

Manufactured in the United States of America
10 9 8 7 6 5 4 3 2 1

DESIGNED BY IRVING PERKINS ASSOCIATES

This novel is a work of fiction. Names, characters, places and incidents are either the product of the author's imagination or are used fictitiously. Any resemblance to actual events, locales, organizations or persons, living or dead, is entirely coincidental and beyond the intent of either the author or publisher.

This book is for Austin Dairing
and Hollis Fleming,
with their father's love.

"Once you start looking inward and trying to find the mole, you do an awful lot of damage to yourself and your organization."

William Webster
*Director of The Central Intelligence Agency**

". . . the discipline of counterintelligence theory demands rigorous examination of every potential suspect when penetration by a ruthless and hostile intelligence service is suspected."

Mask of Treachery
John Costello

**Newsweek*, Oct. 12, 1987

BOOK ONE

ONE

Washington

As the Staff meeting broke up I drained the last of my coffee, stubbed out my cigarette and stood up. My watch showed four o'clock. The meeting had lasted an hour, and as I often did I marveled at the way ten minutes' worth of business could be expanded by a factor of six. Probably, I thought, because officers with insufficient work loads seized opportunities such as this to talk excessively and thus amplify their importance in the eyes and ears of their peers.

The discussion had to do with a possible contamination of Rome acquisition operations, and a remedial consensus was solicited by the new chief of our Counter Intelligence Staff, Herb Porter. The others were filing out when Porter caught my eye and crooked a finger. I stopped by his chair.

"Brent," he said, "you didn't have much to say."

"Like you," I said, "I'm new to this line of work. The old hands are gone. Without experienced guidance all we can do is spit in the wind and hope."

"I don't want to screw this up," he mused. "Should we really set up an entrapment for our own man? Suppose Jeffers is innocent?"

"Then he's a fool and ought to be yanked tomorrow. His source stopped being productive three months ago and it took a junior reports officer to notice that what we've been getting from the guy is low-level garbage. At minimum Jeffers warrants low marks for laziness. He should at least stay on top of his source, squeeze him for usable stuff."

"Well, I agree," he said thoughtfully. "Of course the Sovs may have concluded that they're getting disinformation from this particular agent."

"Despite the four-man team that fabricates it, not to mention the people at DIA and the FBI who coordinate every scrap before it's passed."

Porter sighed. "I've only run two double agents and both times they were trashed by the Opposition, so I'm not much of an expert. What do you recommend?"

"Watchful waiting plus temporarily enhancing the quality of what Jeffers is given to pass along. Send an Eyes Only to the Rome chief and lay out our concerns."

"How about bugging Jeffers' safehouse—where he meets the source?"

"Do it," I said, "if it can be done without Jeffers' knowledge."

"Which means sending a team from here." He paused, looked out of the window toward the distant Potomac River. "Well . . . maybe . . ." His voice trailed off. "Thanks, Brent. Have a drink later? Upstairs?"

"I'd like to," I said, "but I've got an appointment on the Hill."

"Senate barracudas, eh? We'll try again."

I nodded. Porter had two grades on me and was entitled to drink and dine among the maharajahs in the Senior Officers' Mess. I was never entirely comfortable in someone else's club, so declining was easy. Besides, I'd scheduled an interview session with the Bulgarian defector who'd walked into the Stockholm Embassy requesting asylum five months ago and was drying up prematurely. I had a personal interest in "Mr. Walker"—as we called defectors generically—because this one had been part of the KGB operation that burned me out of Moscow. A co-opted *agent provocateur.* I didn't hold it against him—he was doing his job—but he should be a much better source on UDBA—Bulgarian intelligence—and KGB covert ops than he'd proved. Walker was holding back and the growing assumption was that he was a plant. If so we'd toss him back to the Sovs and let it be understood circuitously that he'd cooperatively spilled his guts. Good-bye, Walker.

Porter had put me on the evaluation committee and I was to have a go at Filip Sankov after dinner when he was relaxed and not expecting to be interrogated.

As I left the conference room Porter's secretary said, "Mr. Graves, your secretary called with a message from the British Embassy."

"Mountjoy?"

"I don't know—here's the number." She handed me a message chit.

"Thanks," I said, and went into the corridor. The number wasn't Peter Mountjoy's Embassy Office, but his Georgetown home. I hadn't seen Peter or Lainey in over two weeks, so maybe they were asking me over for drinks. Peter was the MI-6 liaison man in Washington, and his wife, Ghislaine, was a talented French-born artist. Lainey was talented in other ways, as I'd learned in Paris after my wife moved out and moved in with one Raoul Boucher a senior official of the French Foreign Ministry.

We had a therapeutic relationship that was never going anywhere except bed, and we enjoyed each other's company. We spoke French together, enjoyed French cuisine and were as discreet about our relationship as was possible in Washington's incestuous social circle.

I closed my office door, sat down and dialed on my outside line.

Lainey answered; her voice was instantly recognizable. Her speech was British upper class with the faintest possible accenting of Parisian French, and her use of American idiom was far more facile than her husband's. I said, "Brent here. Peter want me?"

She laughed lightly. "I do hope not. Actually, *I* want you, luv."

"Uh—can we talk?"

"You sound like the late Joan Rivers. Yes, we can talk. I'm just back from ferrying Peter out to Dulles. He had to make a courier run to Bermuda, back tomorrow. Will you come by for dinner—and such?"

"Ah . . . yes, with pleasure, but I have appointments before and after."

"What a shame—I'd planned on your staying the night."

"Well, I will, but I may not get back until fairly late." I looked at my desk clock. "I'm on my way to the Senate, probably see you around six. Okay?"

"I'm excited."

"Don't start without me."

I hung up and my secretary buzzed over the intercom. "Mr. Pierson from the General Counsel's office will meet you at the Russell Building."

"Good, now call Dorsey Jerrault's office and tell him I'm on my way." Dorsey was my personal attorney and a very high-priced one. An ex-Rhodes Scholar and two-term Congressman from New Jersey, he knew his way around Washington and the Congress which was why the firm he joined paid him a rumored three-fourths of a million dollars a year. He would bill me at least a thousand dollars for the Senate hour with me, but for me the psychic benefits were worth it.

My secretary said she'd close the file safes and see me tomorrow. I got hat, raincoat and umbrella from the stand and left for the elevator.

Below, I showed my laminated pass at the guard barrier and tucked it inside my wallet. Outside the main door I opened my umbrella against a slanting rain and trod fifty yards through puddles to my numbered parking slot. I keyed off the intruder alarm in my Porsche, folded my umbrella and slid under the wheel. Rain beat drearily against the windshield. At least I was leaving early enough to miss the angry snarl of home-bound cars on Memorial Parkway.

My windshield decal got me waved through the exit gate and I turned east toward Highway Bridge across the Potomac. Four thirty and streetlights were showing along Independence Avenue. I steered for the Senate underground parking entrance, and when a

Capitol policeman stopped me, I tapped the windshield decal. He shrugged and let me coast down the ramp.

I edged along rows of large expensive cars, found the slot I was looking for and steered my stubby Porsche into it. Senator Marigney of Rhode Island had left that morning on a junket to Scandinavia and wouldn't be back for a couple of weeks. So I was saving ten dollars' parking plus the aggravation of walking three blocks in the downpour, and Marigney would never know.

After opening my umbrella I propped it atop the hood to dry, left my hat on the seat and walked to the elevator.

On the third floor I spotted the Committee Room. Dorsey Jerrault was nearby, chatting amiably with Sam Pierson. Both were lawyers, but with different interests in me. Pierson was there to listen and report to the Director's Office. Dorsey was there to protect me.

I shook hands with both men, we commented on the typically lousy spring weather and Pierson murmured that Toby Gerard, the Oversight Committee's Assistant Counsel, was waiting.

"Then let's get it over with," I said, and opened the door. They filed past me, and as I pulled off my raincoat I saw the customary long table, filled ashtrays, emptied styrofoam cups, yellow legal tablets, glass of pencils, maze of mike and recorder wires and two stenos. Tobias Gerard, Esquire, sat at the far end.

He was a long-faced young man with excessively long hair—to cover encroaching baldness—who copped a lot of TV time by looking sage and letting stand-up interviewers do most of the talking. He wore a white-on-white shirt with French cuffs, gray vest and a Phi Bete key. He leaned back languidly in his chair, eyes half closed, hands clasped over the vest notch just below the glinting gold key. Amherst and Yale Law, and on the fast track to a lucrative future.

Gerard allowed us to hang our coats before fully opening his eyes. "Gentlemen," he said abruptly, "what have we here?" He consulted a typed sheet. "The witness is—um—Brent Prosser Graves, accompanied by—"

"Samuel Pierson," my appointed escort supplied.

"Ah, yes." He looked upward. "Mr. Jerrault—you're welcome,

of course, but I wasn't notified you'd be present." He glanced at me. "Representing the witness?"

"Exactly." Dorsey made himself comfortable, reached for a mike and scratched it with his thumbnail. One of the stenos grimaced. "It's working, sir," she called.

"Excellent." Dorsey glanced at his watch. "Now, sir, why are we gathered here?"

Gerard frowned slightly. "You weren't advised?"

"I saw no subpoena."

"That's because the Director advised the Committee that none would be necessary—in keeping with his position of complete cooperation."

Pierson nodded brightly. "That's quite right. That's the understanding."

Dorsey regarded him in silence before saying, "Nevertheless, my client is entitled to his basic constitutional rights, sir, and that includes my presence. I gather you propose to ask Mr. Graves certain questions. About what, sir?"

Gerard grimaced. He didn't like being challenged, but Dorsey was a well-known senior member of the D.C. Bar, and Toby had his future to consider—particularly when, in due course, the Bar made judicial recommendations. Swallowing, he said, "Hardly worth your time, Mr. Jerrault, since it has to do with informally clearing up some of the fallout left by the most recent Contra investigation hearings." He turned to the nearest steno. "Swear the witness."

Dorsey said, "I believe Mr. Graves is entitled to 'use immunity.'"

"That may be," said Gerard," but the Committee would have to vote on that. Meanwhile, he enjoys his Fifth Amendment rights, of course."

"To be sure," Dorsey agreed, "as does any common criminal. Now, before my client is sworn I think we should know a bit about your line of questioning."

Reluctantly, Gerard said, "Committee investigators have been informed that Mr. Graves took part in certain activities in Honduras that may lie beyond the bounds of what was authorized by the Congress."

Dorsey looked at me but my face stayed expressionless. "I see," he said quietly, "and who were those informants?"

"Sir, you know that's privileged information. The Committee is not required to reveal its sources. This is not an evidentiary hearing, not a court of law. It's an informal interview."

"Adversarial," Dorsey said smoothly, "for which reason I am advising my client to answer no questions whatever—until he has been granted 'use immunity' by the Committee."

Toby was sitting forward now, face working. "At least," he said, almost pleadingly, "let me get something into the record. I'd appreciate it very much."

I glanced at Pierson and saw him goggling at the Assistant Committee Counsel. Probably the first time Pierson had seen him challenged—and back down.

Dorsey said, "I don't object to that, sir."

After clearing his throat Gerard dictated boiler plate to the stenos: place, time, my name, the names of Jerrault and Pierson. Then he faced me. "Your name is Brent Prosser Graves?"

I looked at Dorsey, who said, "Since you're not sworn you may answer." I said that was my name.

Gerard continued. "And you were born in Zurich, Switzerland, of American parents?"

"My father was American—a metallurgist then employed by Siemens. At the time of my birth my mother was Welsh, a British subject. She became an American citizen some years later."

"Thank you for the correction," Gerard said dryly. "You were educated at schools in Switzerland, England, France and this country. You took the graduate program at Columbia in Russian Language and Studies."

"That's correct."

"Two years in Vietnam with the Army, assigned to the Phoenix Project. After which you were recruited by our national intelligence agency."

"Yes," I said. "CIA."

Gerard picked up another sheet of paper. "According to this classified c.v. your first overseas post was Madrid, under cover. Then a Headquarters assignment during which you married Marilyn Goetz—are you now married, Mr. Graves?"

"She filed for divorce in Paris, but the French courts work slowly."

"I've heard." He penciled a question mark on the sheet. "You were assigned to the Paris Embassy."

I nodded.

"And from there, posted to Moscow."

"Yes." A malicious smile twisted his thin lips. "Where you were p.n.g.'d by the Soviet Government for actions incompatible with your status as a diplomat."

"It was a provocation operation by the KGB," I said, "in reprisal for the arrest of two Soviet spies in New York by the FBI. Anyway, I was under operational alias at the time, and as far as I know the Sovs don't know my true name. If they learn it the leak will come from you people."

There wasn't a lot of red blood in Toby's veins, but enough to color his face. "I resent that," he said, grating his teeth.

"Resent away," I said. "I'm telling it like it is—in front of witnesses."

"Yes," said Dorsey Jerrault, "quite so. Accordingly, I enjoin the Committee to handle this life-threatening information with the greatest prudence and care. If not, we will know where to turn for satisfaction."

Gerard thought it over, clenched his jaws, and I saw a vein bulge in his prominent forehead. After a few moments he looked at the sheet again. "After which, you were assigned to take part in certain clandestine activities in Honduras?"

Dorsey sat forward. "I think," he said deliberately, "my client will be well advised not to respond since it opens into your inquiry."

I said, "I decline to answer the question on advice of counsel."

"Then," said Gerard grimly, "I take it you have reason to fear prosecution."

Before Dorsey could restrain me I said, "It's well known that certain of my colleagues are being prosecuted for alleged violations of Congressional intent. I'm not anxious to join them—okay?"

"Nor will he," Dorsey remarked, as he withdrew a vest-pocket agenda and consulted it. "At such time as the Committee grants my client the customary immunity you may notify me of an appearance date. However, I see that I am presently scheduled for trial in Memphis—representing an old colleague, Congressman Bolten"—he smiled in satisfaction—"after which I am scheduled to travel with the American Bar Association's International Law Committee to Tokyo, London, Moscow, Paris and Copenhagen." He closed the agenda and put it away. "Making me unavailable to represent my client for the next six weeks." He smiled apologetically. "After which period I will be at my client's and your disposal." Slowly, he stood up. "Pleasure, sir."

Gerard's hands opened and closed, opened and closed, as though he were preparing to throttle me. To Pierson he hissed, "Tell your Director this is not my idea of the complete cooperation I was assured."

Pierson got up and went around to the end of the table, bent over and whispered to Gerard, who was staring at me. While he was doing that, I got my coat from the hanger and walked out with Dorsey. Outside the Committee Room I said, "Thanks. Do you think they'll grant me immunity?"

He shook his head. "Gerard's working against a tight schedule, Brent. He's supposed to wind up in three weeks. No way the Committee's going to meet on anything as trivial as an immunity grant."

We shook hands.

Dorsey said, "Besides, you were witness number fifty-seven and I hardly see what you could add to what the Committee already has." He patted my arm. "You won't hear from Gerard again. Depend upon it."

"That's good to know."

"And when you see the Director, give him my regards." He winked at me. "We both come from Glens Falls, you know.

I hadn't known that. But the likelihood of my seeing the Director was minimal. He dealt with Deputy Directors, Assistant Deputy Directors and Staff Chiefs, not with field hands like myself. And if the Director knew anything about me it was that I'd been p.n.g.'d from Moscow, and had refused a Pakistan assignment working with Afghan resistance. Hardly gilt-edged credentials.

I watched Dorsey enter his chauffeured limousine and then I retrieved my car from its borrowed senatorial slot.

Driving up the ramp I reflected that much as I disliked Toby Gerard's liberal, blame-America-first politics, I had to concede that he was a brilliant bastard—dedicated to doing his job, as he saw it, but still a bastard.

The rain was worse and so was the traffic as I crawled along Pennsylvania Avenue, heading for Georgetown and the Mountjoys' Canal Street house.

TWO

Getting where I was going didn't require much individual participation. I felt as though I were on a kid's train in an amusement park where the cars are equally spaced and all you have to do is relax and enjoy the ride.

I wasn't enjoying the ride because I was thinking of Gerard's parting stare. There was malice in it, and I realized that although he hadn't laid a glove on me today there might come a future time when Dorsey won't be around and Toby Gerard could take revenge on me. He wouldn't do it overtly, but he could make things uncomfortable for me at my place of employment through nonentities like Sam Pierson.

I visualized Pierson as a man who'd married in his second year at a third-rate law school, whose wife had odd-jobbed for table groceries and tuition help, a man whose class standing was too low for all but the worst-paying law firms, and who had turned to Civil Service for the security of a federal paycheck and group hospitalization. Sam Pierson was perfect for today's assignment, and a willing foil for the likes of Toby Gerard.

As for Toby, there was a palpable animosity between us. I knew his type too well. During the Vietnam years, while I'd been out in the boonies killing Cong he'd been smoking Thai Stick, demonstrating at the Pentagon and slapping sow shit around draft offices. In different ways we were both Vietnam Vets, but he'd come out of it a lot better than I had. He had foreseen the future and I envied him for that.

My dash clock showed five forty-five. I was due at Lainey's in fifteen minutes, but at the Ellipse traffic loosened up, and by the time I reached Washington Circle I decided to stop at my own place. Lainey had the European's casual attitude toward time and if I wasn't at her door by six, so what? Anyway, I was pretty sure she'd have ordered dinner from Maribelle's, the upscale catering shop on Wisconsin Avenue—two or three gourmet dishes for microwaving while we downed initial drinks. Unlike American girls, she liked to screw first, saying it improved her appetite, so arrival time was not a large problem.

After crossing the bridge over Rock Creek I was on M Street. At Thirty-first I turned north. Near Dumbarton I pulled into my short driveway, and got out. The private drive was one of the main reasons I'd bought the house; most of my neighbors battled for curb space, but I was spared that frantic nightly search.

As I locked the Porsche my front door opened and Salomé stepped out. She was an undocumented Haitian refugee and a willing, reliable worker, accustomed to my odd hours and absences. We got along splendidly.

"Mist' Grave'," she called. "You got a 'brulla I can borry?"

"Sure," I said, opened mine and gave it to her. "See you *demain.*"

"Letter come for you—I took it."

"Thanks." I went in, locked the door behind me and found a large envelope propped up behind the silver mail tray.

It was addressed in old-fashioned script and had arrived registered. From Paris. I knew what it contained before I opened it, but I checked to make sure.

As I read the French legalese I realized that one of Gerard's questions was now answered. The Paris court of the Fourteenth Arrondissement had dissolved the marriage between Marilyn Ruth Goetz and Brent Prosser Graves, and they were, accordingly, free to pursue separate lives and interests.

My mouth was a little dry. I went to the cellarette, poured a double shooter of Black Label and tossed it off, glad that I had things to do that would take my mind off my failed marriage.

I hadn't been married to Marilyn long enough to fall entirely out of love with her. The bitterness I felt—it would pass—came from her deserting me for what my pride would only let me think of as a lesser man. But who can argue with a woman? Especially if she's as cock-struck as Marilyn had to be.

So she was gone. Good riddance, I told myself. In her place I had Lainey. But not really—I shared Lainey with Peter, and that was how it was always going to be.

The thought of a follow-up consolation drink was tempting, but because I didn't want to disappoint Lainey and I needed a clear head for my later chat with Mr. Walker, I put away the bottle.

The divorce decree, I noticed, had been properly authenticated at the Paris Embassy with embossed seal and red ribbon. I went over to the far bookshelf, took down a bound set of Montaigne and opened my combination safe. Before putting in the decree I reviewed the safe's contents: one Heckler & Koch .38 pistol; one HK 9mm pistol, both with homed magazines, spare mags and shoulder holsters; one envelope containing one thousand dollars in cash; one envelope with five thousand Swiss francs; my personal passport, and a passport with my photo in an alias name that had been used for only two trips abroad. I kept those items at home in the event of midnight orders when it would be difficult to locate travel cash, weapons and documentation. To them I added the notarized decree, closed the safe and replaced the volumes to conceal it.

I stripped and tortured myself under a shower so cold that I was still gasping while I shaved.

The Mountjoy abode faced the old C&O Canal and the Towpath, not far from where sightseeing barges tied up for the winter. The path that bordered the canal and led to the house was cobbled, uneven and slick with rain, yielding uncertain footing as I neared the two-story clapboard house. It was painted gray with pink trim and borders. The handmade window panes distorted images on either side.

The paneled door was framed by bull's-eye lanterns and bore a polished brass knocker resembling an eagle in flight. I didn't need to look at the bronze plaque on the nearby clapboard to recall that it had been placed by the Georgetown Preservation Society and bore the date 1791; I was a frequent visitor, often when Peter was home.

I lifted the knocker and let it fall twice. The door opened on my date.

Lainey was wearing a well-stained artist's smock, leather sandals and a perky smile. I removed my dripping hat and said, "Sorry I'm late."

"Pooh—who cares about time? Come in out of the rain." She stood back and I went in. As I pulled off my wet coat I could hear her bolting the door. Careful girl.

Ghislaine Sevier Mountjoy had lively, intelligent eyes, a freckled, cherubic face, snub nose and voluptuous lips. Barely thirty, she had a Botticelli figure and ample breasts. Five-two in her slippered feet, she rose on tiptoes to kiss me, sliding her tongue between my lips. "I've been thinking about you all day," she murmured.

"*All* day?"

"Well, ever since I saw Peter off." She took my hand and drew me toward her atelier. En route we plucked drinks from the sideboard and toasted each other.

The room had started out as a solarium, then three sides had been boarded for privacy, but the overhead remained clear, slanted glass whose transparency provided her with the natural light she needed for painting.

The canvas on her easel was a half-finished portrait of her husband. Wavy blond hair, thin, straight nose and weak chin line. Aristocratic. The oils were still wet, they glistened in the dim light. Lainey cleared space on a sturdy work table and got up on it facing me. As she unbuttoned her smock she said, "I'd like to do *you* some time, Brent."

"Would Peter suspect? I mean—"

"Why should he? You're friends, after all."

Yes, I thought, and he's a better friend to me than I am to him. Having swived his wife on and off over more than two years.

She said, "If it bothers you, turn the easel."

"It doesn't bother me," I said. "What about you?"

She shrugged. "It's only a picture." The smock slipped from her shoulders and she sat naked before me. "Let's do it here," she said. "Like this."

"Won't it be—uncomfortable?"

"I learned how at the Beaux Arts. Believe me, it's good."

I moved toward her, touched her full breasts. "Well," I said doubtfully, "it's certainly worth a try." I kissed taut nipples. Her thighs parted; as often as I'd entered it I was always surprised by the flowering abundance of her bush.

She moved forward to meet me, lifting her derrière and we found each other. Then I was thrusting insatiably, frantically trying to conquer the unconquerable. Lainey moaned, bit my neck and rubbed her breasts against me until in a sudden rush we came. I felt her arms and legs go limp, my knees were dissolving and I leaned forward against her. She gave me a long, luscious, lip-licking kiss and whispered, "Wonderful! Just what I've been needing."

"Me, too"

Lainey eased off the table, gathered up her smock and said, "While I eliminate the evidence, mix a couple of drinks, huh?"

"Gladly." I made it to the living room and found the nearest sofa. Languor after lust. The shower went on—or was it the bidet?—and I could hear her voice chirping happily away at some unfamiliar tune.

Before she returned in an Oriental housecoat I'd replenished our glasses. I touched mine to hers and said, "I'm a single man again."

Her expression changed, became apprehensive. "Congratulations," she said, "though I'll never understand how Marilyn could leave you for that ass Boucher."

"Me neither. Anyway, it's over with. Chin chin."

Absently she drank, then said, "Brent, now that you're free, promise you won't ask me to marry you."

"Would that be a bother?"

"I could never hurt Peter, you see. We're well matched in most ways." Nervously she sipped again.

"Except—"

"Except for, well, you know, bed games."

We'd never discussed the reasons for her extramarital compulsions. I suspected she had other lovers but never inquired. "Peter," I said, "looks perfectly normal to me."

"Well, he is—in a British way." She laughed briefly. "I remember this story from Paris, Brent. A Frenchman is tried for violating a woman's corpse—no, don't make a face, I promise you'll laugh—and his defense was that he didn't know she was dead, he thought she was English."

We both laughed and Lainey said, "Reverse the sexes and you'll get my point."

"I do. 'Nuf said."

She put her arm through mine and we moved into the small kitchen. "Wine's in the fridge," she said. "You still like lobster Thermidor, don't you?"

"Irresistibly."

I uncorked an excellent Chablis from her family's vineyards near Epernay while Lainey set frozen trays in her microwave. She watched me chilling our wine glasses and said, "You didn't promise, Brent."

"You mean—about marriage?"

"If you don't ask me I won't have to struggle with my conscience, and I'm not awfully good at that."

"Then I promise."

She kissed my cheek and hugged me, nearly knocking the glasses from my hand. "That's such a *relief*, dear. Now I can confess that I probably love you and would marry you *if* you insisted. But I have this firm commitment to Peter. You do understand, don't you?"

"Sure," I said. But I didn't. Maybe a Frenchman would, but I wasn't French. Besides, from our first coupling in Paris years ago I'd adopted the position that if there was an infidelity problem it was Lainey's, not mine. And I'd enlarged on that to the point of rationalizing that if she wasn't screwing me she'd be screwing some guy who might pry her away from Peter. So, by limiting his wife's waywardness I was really doing Peter a favor. Keeping his marriage intact, if not entirely whole.

The oven buzzer sounded, and as she turned away I wondered if she was ever troubled with remorse. I'd never seen traces of it. Lainey came across as a happy hedonist guided by the pleasure principle, constrained only by a reasonable dose of caution.

Peter Joule Mountjoy was the younger son of an hereditary peer. His brother had a Commons seat that, eventually, he would leave for Lords. Meanwhile, Peter, out of Winchester and Oxford, was following a respectable if plodding career in Her Majesty's Secret Service. I was fond of him, sometimes thought of him as a younger brother, but in Paris I'd learned that Peter was as conservative in secret operations as he was in his political thinking. He wasn't a risk-taker; I was.

Which is why, I reflected as I moved toward the dining table, I was with his wife instead of alone at the Kennedy Center concert.

If I knew Peter he'd be spending a dull, chaste evening with the Six man in Hamilton, talking shop and British politics, his only known interests in life. Peter, I felt, had been a virgin right up to his wedding night.

Lainey interrupted my reflections saying, "Preoccupied, luv?"

"I had an unusual experience at the Senate. My lawyer told them to stuff it."

She laughed merrily. "That *is* unusual. What did you say?"

"Very little. I left talking to my mouthpiece. Let's eat."

The Thermidor was excellent, as expected. Big white and pink chunks of Maine lobster—not Channel *langouste*—in a marvelous, creamy wine sauce, and alarmingly expensive, as I knew. But both Peter and his wife were independently wealthy, as people in the British Establishment were supposed to be. SIS members who lacked private means were assumed to be vulnerable to monetary enticements by the Opposition. Worse, they could never expect to rise significantly on Whitehall's roster.

Lainey said, "When do you have to leave?"

"Seven-thirty, eight, without rushing us."

"But you'll return?"

"Of course. By eleven."

"I wanted to be sure before I chilled champagne. The bed's already made, fresh sheets and fluffed counterpane. So, you're expected." She leaned across the table and kissed me. The taste of her mouth was pleasant. She said, "Did I ever tell you that Marilyn once made a pass at me?"

"No. Are you sure?" The thought startled me.

"Yes. We were in a Balenciaga fitting room together and Marilyn said she admired my breasts, asked if she could touch them."

"Did you let her?"

Lainey nodded. "I thought she wanted to find out if they're real—they are rather ample, you know."

"I know."

"It was exciting to have her . . . touch me that way. But I wasn't prepared for her kissing me—on the mouth. Not that she was the first—I went to English boarding school—but I'd never thought of her in a sexual way."

"Did it go beyond that?"

"I didn't respond, and that was that. She never made advances again. But I was careful never to be alone with her and chance a reprise."

"Interesting," I said, and drank deeply from my glass. The overture didn't sound like the Marilyn I'd known. "Think she was interested in threesies?"

"I doubt it—that was before you and I became lovers."

"One of life's small mysteries." I filled our glasses and glanced at my watch.

Lainey said, "Brent, have you ever thought you might be in love with me?"

"I've wondered," I admitted, "but there was never any point to it—then or now."

"That's so," she said, "even though we're awfully good together."

I nodded agreement. Lainey served chocolate mousse and espresso, and when we finished it was nearly eight o'clock. She saw me to the door and pressed the key in my palm. "Don't be late, luv." I stepped into the drizzle and heard the door locking behind me.

No matter how the session went with Sankov, I could look forward to a warm bed and a willing body. As I trudged back to where I left my car I thought what a rotten son of a bitch Sankov really was. He'd abandoned his wife and two children to certain reprisals, preferring promised Paradise in the West to the obligations of husband and father.

Worse, he was welshing on the deal he'd made with us, and I was going to make it very painful for him to back out.

So thinking, I drove across Key Bridge and headed west into Virginia where Sankov was maintained in a comfortable safehouse with a Macedonian cook and a complement of armed guards.

THREE

The rain beat steadily on my windshield; even on high the wipers offered clear visibility for no more than fractions of a second. The blacktop was a river shooting ahead of me, and I eased back to forty so I could maintain control.

Big semis sped past, wheels spewing Niagaras across my windows, and docilely I let them have their way. My Porsche purred, the rpms held steady, and if the engine stayed dry I'd be able to get back to Lainey as promised.

Beyond Falls Church I turned south on 495. The Beltway was wider and I found fewer heavy trucks zooming through the night. I stayed on the Beltway's SW quadrant as far as State 350, passed the west entrance to Fort Belvoir and switched onto old US 1 a few miles further on.

Dark nights and heavy rain brought back memories of my childhood home in Zurich. When thunder woke me I'd get out of bed and stand at the windowpane peering out at the pelting rain, glimpsing the towers of the city and the distant mountains as the lightning flashed. If thunder rolled near and I wailed *schweste* Irmi would dry my tears and console me while my parents slept undisturbed.

An Arizonan by birth, my father had left the family's hardscrabble ranch in 1941, enlisted in the Army and fought through Normandy's hedgerows with the 79th Division. Later, manning an antitank gun near Belfort, he was captured by the retreating Wehrmacht. During the confusion of an air raid, Dad escaped and, with two Americans, one British and one Belgian soldier, crossed the mountains and reached Switzerland, where he was interned until VE Day. After the war Dad attended the School of Mines on the GI Bill and transferred to CalTech for advanced work in metallurgy. During his wartime months in Switzerland he had been impressed by Swiss precision manufacture and their advanced knowledge of metallurgy. Bethlehem Steel sent him to Solothurn for hands-on experience in the development and application of superhard metals, and two years later he met my mother during a sightseeing cruise on Lake Geneva. My mother's family, the Prossers of Swansea, had been wiped out by V-bombs toward war's end. Alone, she had gone to Bern for the British Union as a teacher of music and English at the British School. Three months after meeting they were married in Bern, and decided to stay in Switzerland. My father joined the Siemens subsidiary near Zurich and began working with titanium, a metal crucial to America's rocket and space program. In due course he began passing technical reports to our Bern military attaché, although I was unaware of his intelligence activities until after I'd joined the Firm.

David Graves was a handsome, well-built man with a salt-and-pepper mustache, a well-tuned intellect and an immense capacity for affection and humor. He adored my mother and his love was returned in full measure. His death by cancer when I was fourteen devastated her, and though I had wanted to stay with her in our Zurich home she insisted I continue my schooling at Hammersmith, where she visited me on holidays.

Until Dad's death I had not realized the considerable wealth his researches and patents had brought us.

Having suffered through Dust Bowl and Depression as a child,

Dad remained distrustful of American banking throughout his life. He kept his capital in Swiss banks and his investments were entirely Swiss. Royalty payments from his patents went directly to Swiss accounts that my mother and I now shared, and aside from a checking account at the Riggs branch in Georgetown I kept no money in the States.

At sixty, my mother enjoyed good health except for arthritic knees. At home on Sea Island, Georgia, she played piano and bridge with a congenial circle, used her heated Jacuzzi daily and had the services of an excellent cook-maid. I visited her at least four times a year.

Mother had been frank about not caring for Marilyn, whom she found shallow and uninteresting. In retrospect I realized that Dad wouldn't have liked her either, though he would have kept his negative opinion to himself.

So, I was the product of caring parents, tough foreign schooling, an affectionate, intellectual father and a warm-hearted, artistic mother who spoke English with enviable precision.

Considering that background I often wondered why I hadn't made more of myself, but then my mother frequently reminded me that contentment was a gift of the gods.

I couldn't remember being contented since before my father's death. Careless, lackadaisical hours in classes at the Sorbonne, with its politicized student strikes and indifference to excellence, had had their effect on me. Even at Columbia I'd lived day to day, almost hour to hour, with no overall strategic plan for my life.

No ultimate goal, either.

I faced the fact that, unlike my father, I lacked ambition.

I thought back to the way Lainey had reacted to the news of my divorce. She didn't want me to harass her with marriage proposals, but what she didn't know was I'd ruled her out as a potential mate at least two years ago. True, we'd come together in the wake of Marilyn's desertion when I was adrift in Paris and drinking far too much, but though I would always be grateful for Lainey's support and tenderness I'd come to realize that her inclinations were basically promiscuous. And I didn't want to become a miserable cuckold a second time.

Eventually, I knew, our affair would end, whether through Peter's discovery or my being sent abroad. But end it would. Until then I intended to enjoy its physical pleasures—just as Lainey did.

Well south of Woodbridge a sign pointed toward Dumfries and the Quantico Marine Base, where Sankov's first guards had been stationed. Since then his guard force had been civilianized with military retirees who hadn't forgotten how to handle firearms. At Dumfries I turned northwest onto State 234, glad that the rain was slackening, for the two-lane road was slick and poorly lighted.

Eight miles short of Manassas I slowed and began looking for the estate's entrance posterns. Built of fieldstone and cement a hundred years ago, they were washed with rain and looked almost new.

I steered between them, came to a stop at the guardhouse set well back from the entrance and got out my ID. A tall man with a Uzi slung across his dark Sou'wester played his flashlight across my credential and waved me on. I guided the Porsche up an incline and around a twisting road that led to the safehouse's side entrance. I got out and hurried in, halting long enough for the guard to check my ID and pat me down for weapons. Then he unlocked the grilled door and let me in.

I went up three steps to a carpeted hall and stopped at the manned reception desk. The guard recognized me from previous visits and shoved the register book in my direction. I signed the John F. Marston alias I'd used in Moscow, just in case Sankov managed to see the book. I entered 9:02 which was the time according to the desk clock, in the "In" column and asked if Mr. Neville was there.

"He's expecting you, sir." The guard gestured down the lighted corridor to the house chief's office.

As I walked I pulled off hat and raincoat and hung them on a gray metal coatrack, which was obviously GSA issue. Neville's door was heavy oak with an inside bar lock that I heard sliding back after I'd knocked.

Neville was a clinical psychologist who'd turned to that profession after serving in 'Nam with a medical unit. His work name, like mine, was an alias, and he'd been recruited out of a Veterans

Hospital where he'd had unusual success in rousing vets from deep depression by giving them goals to live for.

We shook hands briefly and he went back behind his desk while I sank into a leather-upholstered chair. "While since you've been here," he remarked.

"Hasn't been much reason to come," I said and lighted a cigarette. I dropped my match in an aluminum ash tray. "How's Walker doing? What's his state of mind?"

Prefacing his reply, Neville punched a remote button, and one of four wall-mounted TV monitors came alive. The video camera was looking down on Sankov from a corner position, and it showed him sitting in a chair watching a US sitcom on a large TV screen. Beside his chair was a scatter of books and magazines. The only visible newspaper was *Le Monde*. Neville said, "He reads, watches a lot of TV—we let him see only cable news, the networks would give him a rather biased picture of what's happening in the U.S."

"Is he writing letters? Memoirs?"

"No, and he's displayed no interest in writing anything at all." Neville looked back at me. "That's unusual because after four months the average defector begins to display remorse symptoms: asylum has fallen short of expectations; he begins to wonder about his family's welfare—maybe they could be spared nasty reprisals if he returned and faced the music—which is just fantasy, of course." He sighed. "This Walker is a hard-core True Believer."

"Aren't they all? When was the last time anyone saw an ideological defector?"

He nodded. "Walker's been talking a good deal about his father lately." Grigor Sankov, Neville explained, had been a landholder whose sympathies turned to the plight of the peasants—so much so that Grigor joined the Agrarian Party. When Premier Georgiev was ousted by Czar Boris, Grigor's land was confiscated, which loss turned him into a Communist. After Bulgaria joined the Axis, Grigor fought with the resistance, emerging as a seasoned Party leader. "In 1950, when our Mr. Walker was still a child, Chervenko ruthlessly purged the Party. Grigor had been one of his victims."

"That should have turned the family against Communism," I said.

"Not a viable alternative. Food, lodging, everything is doled out by the Party, you know that."

When Bulgaria joined COMECON and Stalinism relaxed a bit, Grigor was rehabilitated—posthumously. As the son of a wartime resistance fighter and Party leader, Sankov had found his circumstances improving. He became a Young Pioneer and a favored son of the State. He and his mother were brought from Varna to Sofia, and he was entered into the university. The KGB had spotted him when he was in school and relocated him to Moscow for specialized training, then sent back as a UDBA officer. He was a Soviet agent in the Bulgarian Intelligence Service, I remembered. Not a bad deal for a guy who could have ended up digging beets on a *kholkoz.* In fact, he had prospered. With his language abilities and foreign experience he could have been a candidate for UDBA chief—especially since the KGB dictates who gets the top East Bloc jobs.

"I've never fully accepted his stated motive for coming over," Neville said.

"Hell," I said, "he was caught screwing the senior *rezident*'s wife, what more do you need?"

"Maybe he was, maybe not," Neville said, judiciously. "We tried confirming that with narcosynthesis, but it remains arguable."

"The basic point," I said, "is that he's here, and some of us think we'd be better off to unload him."

"That decision should not be hastily reached."

"It hasn't been made," I said. "Yet. That's why I'm here. I'm on the evaluation team." Sankov lifted a small glass and sipped. "Still likes his brandy," I remarked.

"Who doesn't? We limit his alcohol intake to 200 milliliters a day and he's not allowed to accumulate it." He paused. "By the way, that's about a quarter of a—"

"I know," I said. "I was raised on the metric system."

"Sorry." He looked back at the monitor. "Seen enough?"

Nodding, I said, "Is there any chance, *any* chance whatever, that he's been able to communicate with the outside world?"

He thought it over and said, "As a psychologist I don't deal in absolutes, Mr. Marston, but you know the security system here as well as I do: four video cameras in every room of Walker's suite, three of them concealed. Wall mikes, fixture mikes, pressure-sensitive pads . . . windows barred on the outside, covered with sheet-iron inside. No way he can see outside or toss out a message if he could. Two locked security phones our only telephonic contact with the outside—and that to Headquarters. Checkpoints at every entrance, video scanners along the fences plus heat-seeking sensors. Guards equipped with night-vision gear . . ." He clicked off the monitor. Sankov and his room dwindled down to a pinpoint of light. Neville sighed. "The resources of modern technology have been deployed to make sure that intruders can't get in, and Mr. Walker can't get out."

All the recording equipment, mikes and videocameras fed down into a secure room in the basement, where technicians monitored everything Sankov said or did, including his bathroom habits. At his request he'd been supplied with pornographic materials to enhance masturbation fantasies. In Stockholm he hadn't needed them because he'd been humping the *rezident's* young and voluptuous wife.

If his story was to be believed.

The basement monitoring room was where the tape reels and VHS cassettes were stored so that if anyone at Headquarters disputed a transcript the original tape was available for comparison. The materials were computerized and cross-referenced for fast access.

For a few moments I considered the security measures. Then I said, "Nevertheless, that motherfucker Wysinzski managed to slip out a message and next day the Polish ambassador, his staff and four assholes from State showed up demanding his release. Remember that?" I stubbed out my cigarette. We had agreed to Wysinzski's release—unfortunately—because four hours later he was on national and international TV claiming he had been kidnapped and subjected to unspeakable tortures by the *Amerikanski* imperialists, and there was hell to pay all around.

Neville swallowed. "Very well," he said tightly, "but that didn't happen here."

"True."

"Moreover," he said, "Wysinzski managed to develop a carnal relationship with the female cook. He made her his accomplice. So—"

"What about the cook here?"

"She's a dyke," Neville said. "We made sure—very sure—of that."

"Live and learn," I said. "Seems you've covered all the bases. What about the local cops?"

"We told them this is a classified government research facility."

"Do they believe it?"

He smiled. "Why not? Isn't that what it is?"

I got up from my chair. "From the operational point of view a defector's only value is what he knows. If he won't share it he's worthless. We start from that premise and from it everything else derives."

"Including the possibility of termination."

"Definitely."

His face was expressionless as he looked up at me. "You don't like him, do you? Personal animosity, Mr. Marston?"

"Impersonal," I said. "In general I don't like defectors because a man who betrays his own country won't hesitate to betray ours if he thinks it serves his interests."

"Even when he's burned all his bridges"

"They never believe that," I said. "They always think there's a path leading back. It's part of the hope that sustains them."

"And the hostility of interrogators such as yourself."

I shrugged. "I do my job as best I can. Others may criticize..." Turning, I said, "Tell him I'm on my way."

As I left the room I heard Neville speaking on the intercom: "Mr. Walker, you have a visitor. Mr. Marston is here to see you."

I closed the door and went back along the hallway to the staircase. As I climbed to the second floor I reflected that Neville was dealing with life as a rational man, a humanist seeking reassuring answers in a forest of bewildering contradictions. He seemed curiously untouched by actualities, as though he were immune to man's frailties, regarding them with scientific tolerance and amusement. Neville wouldn't have been my ideal choice as Sankov's keeper, but he was the best available.

In the end, old man, I said to myself, we're all dead, and that's an end to philosophy.

The guard sitting outside Sankov's door stiffened as I approached. He got up and stood at attention, military-style. I waited while he unbolted the door.

I didn't knock. I shoved the door inward and spoke to the guard. "If you hear a rumpus, ignore it. But on the slight chance this creep manages to take me, you shoot off his kneecaps. That's an order."

"Yes, sir. Fully understood." He closed the door behind me and I turned to Sankov.

Showdown time.

FOUR

The Bug defector turned and gazed at me. His skin was pale from months of sunlight deprivation and my order to the guard, which he overheard, seemed to make it even paler. Or perhaps it was the contrast to his coal-black hair. "Tube off," I told him, "we have things to discuss."

His fingers touched the remote unit and the big screen went gray. I walked behind his chair, reached over and cupped my right hand under his jaw. Hard. "I've never been a patient man, Fil," I said, "so this is your last chance to purge yourself, come clean."

Despite the hand-vise around his jaw he managed to say, "You won't hurt me. Americans don't do that sort of thing."

"You've been living in a pampered world," I told him, "and it's about to dissolve. I'm not a full-blooded, guilt-laden American, I'm the hyphenated species with only a veneer of respectability—like the one you acquired." I released his jaw and moved around to a chair that faced him.

He felt his jaw and opened his mouth. "I could defeat you in a fair fight."

"What's fair? Anyway, you're out of condition. Your only exercise is pulling your putz."

His cheeks colored slightly, then he sat forward. "You weren't so macho when the KGB grabbed you, Mr. Marston. Why didn't you fight them?"

"Surprised you noticed, Fil. After you stuffed that phoney document in my pocket you ran like a rabbit. Was I supposed to be manly and battle four plainclothes thugs with guns and clubs? Wouldn't have been compatible with my diplomatic status. I went limp—like the peaceniks you guys adore." I shook out a cigarette and lit it. I didn't offer him one. "What was your payoff for setting me up? An hour's free shopping in the GUM store?" I flicked the match at his ashtray. It missed.

He said, "I was following orders. You know that."

"All right. You know it, I know it. And you know a lot of things you've chosen not to divulge to the country that gave you asylum." I exhaled smoke in his direction. "Temporary asylum."

He picked up his brandy glass and emptied it down his gullet. "Temporary? I thought—"

"Temporary," I repeated. "You have visitor status, that's all. You can be repatriated before dawn—if I say the word." That wasn't entirely true, but it was good enough for Sankov.

He said, "I don't know why you people should be dissatisfied with the information I've disclosed. I was only a major, not a big *nomenklatura* man like Shevchenko."

"Shevchenko had his limitations. He never had access to the Illegals register as you have. In two services—KGB and your own."

"Access is very restricted, you must know that. I didn't copy lists and cryptos."

"So we'll go with what you remember—*everything* you remember from Mogadishu, Damascus, Ankara, Moscow and Stockholm. Put yourself in my position, Fil. You wouldn't be satisfied with the political-economic garbage you've passed to our analyst. You'd want names and cryptos, agent commo systems and targets; *rezidentura* pecking order; who's fucking who, who's blackmarketing, who's in danger of recall; in short, who's vulnerable to hostile recruitment." I sucked in smoke and exhaled noisily. "Which imperialist embassies are penetrated—need I go on?"

He thought it over for a while, got up and walked over to a bookshelf for his pack of Marlboro filters. He was tall for a Bug, well-built, and with the kind of nonthreatening good looks that would appeal to embassy spinsters who handle coding and classified pouches.

I didn't have any difficulty analyzing Sankov because we were in the same trade, though I didn't like to recognize it.

"What you've managed to accomplish," I said, "is to give your old friends time to close down their ops and get home. I saw it from the beginning and warned against procrastinating. Unfortunately, I didn't have the final word, so you got away with it. Now I have full authority, Fil. Satisfy me by compensating for the recent past or we'll dump you at the Soviet Embassy."

His face was working now as the reality of his situation sank in.

"What's the practice?" I asked. "Does a returned defector get a last word with his family before they tie on the blindfold? Will Irina be allowed a final wifely kiss?"

He turned away and faced the bookshelves. I flicked my butt at the empty fireplace and wondered how the monitoring techs in the basement rated the scene. I hadn't played it often. Lacking authorized guidelines, I did what I thought he'd probably be doing to me.

Of course, I no longer had a wife. Or any children.

Despite the tension, my mind wandered and I found myself wondering what kind of birth control Lainey was using and if she had ever had to have an abortion. If she conceived by me would she fob the child on Peter? I wrenched my mind back to the present. "You're not saying much, Filip."

Slowly, he turned around, resting his back against the bookshelf. "I have knowledge," he said, "that would be worth more to the West than anything you could possibly imagine."

"I can imagine a lot of things. Indulge me."

"First, we will amend my contract."

"We will? In what way?"

"Are you Catholic?"

"Lutheran, if anything."

"The price is half a million dollars."

I whistled. "Chebrikov might be worth that—but a UDBA major?" Viktor Chebrikov was that year's chairman of the KGB.

He seemed not to have heard me. "Half a million in a Swiss account—yes, I have one—then plastic surgery, new legend documentation and relocation in a country of my choice."

"You need a brain scan," I said. "Your synapses are totally fucked up."

"Don't forget, I had a successful career for years—until that one small indiscretion."

"Small? You're lucky you didn't lose your balls."

"Luck? I moved swiftly, preemptively."

I grunted. "With all the Swedish pussy in Stockholm you had to bang your colonel's wife. Was she that irresistible?"

"Lidiya said if I didn't, she'd tell her husband I tried."

"And she wasn't bad looking, either. But that's the past. My patience is running out. You've named your price . . . in return for what?"

He came over to his TV chair and sat down. "Let us suppose I convinced you that my information is worth my conditions, and more. How many officers in your organization would you have to approach in order to effect the transaction?"

"Three."

"And how broad the area of knowledgeability?"

I considered. Typists, computer registry, Finance. Bloc Ops . . . "A dozen souls, probably more."

"More?" He didn't like it, it wasn't the way his service did things.

"Plus," I said, "some people in Congress."

"Why?"

"Half a million means asking Congress for spending authority. But we're talking fantasy. Let's get back to your full knowledge of Illegals. That's factual stuff."

I didn't feel it prudent to tell him that since 1974 "some people in Congress" meant nearly three hundred Senators, Representatives and staffers. In addition, they'd let wives and children know, plus media pals. Because of the Hughes-Ryan Amendment it was simply impossible to keep significant secrets under wraps for more than a day. For that reason the slogan of the KGB's Washington *rezidentura* was rumored to be "Ask and it shall be given."

But Sankov was right. I couldn't imagine what info of his could be worth half a million . . . unless Gorbachev turned out to be a queen.

Sankov said, "You've blocked your mind against anything I might say, Marston. Because you still resent what happened to you in Moscow."

Partly true, and I had to concede it, but not aloud. "Give me a sample of your wares."

His eyes narrowed as he appraised my intentions. His lips tightened, and he began. "The Pope is Polish, no?"

"So I've heard."

"And a thorn in the side of the Polish People's Republic."

"That's news?"

"Also, the Pope openly supports the anti-State movement called Solidarity, which General Jaruzelski failed initially to suppress."

"But finally accomplished by force. Common knowledge."

He nodded patiently. "It was either that or the Red Army moving in to occupy Poland completely. Orders had been issued. Divisions were mobilized with orders to crush any resistance. Bad for Poland, bad for the USSR—in world opinion."

"World opinion," I sneered, "meaningful as a whore's reputation."

He smiled almost invisibly, then his face sobered. "Believe me, Marston, the bloodless alternative was the better." His face turned away. "In 1968 I was a second-year student at Sofia University and a reservist in an armored regiment. In the dead of an August night I was wakened, told to get into uniform and report to the assembly point. The tanks were already there, engines warming—scores of them, exhaust vapors rising in the still air. In two hours we were on the roads, very bad roads. Six hundred kilometers to Budapest, Marston, a third of the tanks by then disabled. We had very little food and seldom stopped for a hot meal. Not much water, either. I remember how parched my throat was all that long hot week." One finger touched his throat. "None of us knew where we were going, so when we reached Budapest we thought of Warsaw Pact maneuvers. But we stayed there only long enough for provisions. Hungarian tanks joined the formation and we rolled on." His face was bleak. "Where? we wondered. Where? Berlin? We didn't know for another five hundred kilometers—until we rolled into Prague with Soviet armor alongside. Then we knew. I was the tank's corporal gunner. My job was to blow down buildings, barricades, destroy men and women in the street . . ." He swallowed. "Kids. I tried always to find other targets when the sergeant wasn't looking, tried not to kill the kids . . ."

His earnestness had me believing him. This was a side of Sankov I'd never seen, never suspected. A human side.

In a distant voice he said, "Our fraternal forces crushed the Czech mutiny, ended the Prague Spring. Everyone was decorated, bits of colored ribbon from the USSR, from my army, the Hungarians . . ." He shook his head. "I never wore them—ashamed to admit I'd been part of the butchery. Andropov directed, Jaruzelski was a witness. Rather than see it happen to Poland, he bowed, suppressed Solidarity. I think he did the right thing."

"That's one way of looking at it."

"But with the leaders like Walesa, underground or imprisoned, the Pope remained—the Polish Pope, secure within his Vatican City, Vatican State in the heart of Rome." He faced me. "The Polish Pope, Karol Wojtyla, remained a threat to the order and integrity of Jaruzelski's Poland."

"No question," I said. "Are you leading to where I think?"

"Probably, Marston. Quite probably."

"Having told me nothing beyond worldwide presumptions."

"There's more. If I'm to purge myself you must give me time, is that not fair?"

"I'm still listening."

"I could use another brandy."

"Tomorrow. Two hundred milliliters. You'll enjoy it more."

"Very well." He seemed to pull himself together. "The previous Pope, Albino Luciani, who named himself John Paul I, enjoyed a very short papacy, you recall?"

"Something like a month."

"At a time when the Vatican's finances were being investigated."

"Such as the Banco Ambrosiano."

"The tip of a dark, deep iceberg, Marston. But that was only part of what faced that Pope. John Paul I was a humble man, a man of the people—a country priest, incorruptible. He was not of the Curia, the Vatican ruling clique, and a number of them felt threatened by him, by the reforms he'd hinted at, liberalizing church doctrine, entertaining the concepts of divorce and artificial birth control . . ." His lips twisted. "Equivalent to suggesting capitalism to the Presidium of the Supreme Soviet. Totally unthinkable. So, among the Curia intriguers a hidden conspiracy developed. The unwanted Pope was found dead in his bed, though only three days before, his lifelong physician had pronounced him in perfect health."

"And you're going to tell me he was killed. Why would anyone pay you half a million for repeating an old rumor?"

He shook his head. "You don't understand—yet. This is prologue. But John Paul I *was* murdered, poisoned by priests who followed orders. There was no known autopsy, the body was embalmed and quickly buried. Thus the threat he represented to the Curia was liquidated.

"A month later the Polish Pope was chosen, John Paul II, who represented no threat to the Curia; for them he meant business as usual—an American phrase I've always liked, by the way. Coolidge? Hoover?"

I said, "If there was no autopsy, how—?"

"But there was. State secrets can't long be hidden from the KGB. Poison was found. Ergo—"

"Ergo," I said, "you're telling me a tale that can't be proved. For all I know you fabricated it while enjoying life at taxpayer's expense."

"Possible," he conceded, "but I have no talent for fiction."

"Just a large talent for evasion." My mouth was dry. I wanted a drink more than Sankov did. "Even as a Lutheran," I said, "I find it hard to believe that in today's Vatican the old Borgia solutions prevail."

"Why should they not? The Vatican is a state, and you surely realize that every state rules first through myth, then fraud and ultimately force."

"That's dialectic dogma."

"Also historical truth."

"Go on."

He didn't like my skepticism, but I was tiring of personal memories and dredged-up Vatican politics. Now we were back to Poland, whose compassionate dictator had chosen to garrote his people rather than see it done by his Soviet masters. For that Jaruzelski probably thought he should have got the Nobel Peace Prize; instead, the anti-State conspirator, Lech Walesa, got it.

Sankov said, "You understand that the KGB has sources within the Vatican—penetrations developed and inserted long ago."

"Cardinal Rossinol among them. The 'Red Cardinal.'"

"And others. The Polish Pope has never moved against them, so they are satisfied to have him remain. The supporters of his predecessor are mild men, indecisive, incapable of concerting an assassination against the incumbent Pope, who draws neither deep loyalty nor fanatical hostility from within the Curia. The hard opposition to Wojtyla came from outside—Warsaw and Moscow—and the decision was made to liquidate him in a fashion that was not traceable."

I said, "Where was the decision taken?"

"In the Kremlin's secret Defense Council. Eliminating Pope John Paul II was deemed necessary because for four years Jaruzelski had proven incapable of dealing with him. Accordingly, instructions were issued to GRU and KGB to locate and prepare assassins with no Communist connections or background. The eventual revelations of Oswald's past became a formidable problem for the Kremlin to overcome; nevertheless, it was accomplished. Since Oswald, the KGB's foreign assassins have been limited to those of fanatical right-wing orientation."

"My organization understands that," I said. "You're talking about Ali Agca, the crazy Turk."

"Mehmet Ali Agca. When the Defense Council's orders were disseminated I was in Ankara, working in the Bulgarian Embassy for UDBA—and the KGB. Ali was a criminal terrorist, incarcerated for a series of violent crimes. His political orientation was diffuse, but it was not Communist. His escape from prison was publicized and came to my attention." He went over to the bookshelf and I saw him writing on a small sheet of note paper. When he returned to his chair I said, "This is beginning to sound interesting."

"I thought it might. Within a short time Ali Agca was located, given refuge and evaluated for suitability as a candidate for the assassination of John Paul II. Mehmet Ali Agca passed the screening and was recruited for the task. Elsewhere, two other candidates were recruited to complete the assassination team, a man and a woman."

I leaned toward him. "Who recruited Ali Agca?"

He didn't reply at once. Then he spoke barely audibly. "For the present I must withhold that information, Marston." But he cupped his hand in a way that hid the piece of paper from the room's four video cameras. He let me glimpse it.

On it he had printed: Filip Sankov.

FIVE

Even though I'd begun to anticipate the revelation, it jolted me when it came.

Sankov casually crumpled the paper and slid it in a trouser pocket. He had shared the critical information with me, not with the room's mikes and cameras. Probably to give me a negotiating edge. I said, "There was always a known Bulgarian connection, but in the Italian courts it was never proved."

"There was a notable lack of enthusiasm on the part of Italian authorities to dig deeply into the matter. The Christian Democratic government wanted amicable relations with Bulgaria and the Soviet Union, and their task was eased by the Vatican influence I've already mentioned."

"You know identities?"

"Two. Moreover, the Italian government had Ali Agca, did they not? Why look for others? And Agca played his role well—confessing and recanting, shouting his mission was divinely inspired, implicating others who proved to be innocent . . . By the time he was convicted and sentenced he had lost all credibility. With Agca behind bars the world turned to other things." He smiled thinly, "The Pope even forgave his would-be killer."

"Well," I said, "he's the Pope, and I suppose he felt he was setting a good example of Christian charity. But if the Pope was seen by the Kremlin and Jaruzelski as a monstrous threat in 1981, why wasn't a second strike laid on to rid them of that troublesome priest?"

"I can't say—I've speculated that another attempt, successful or not, would have solidified world suspicion concerning Kremlin culpability. But the idea was undoubtedly considered within the Defense Council. Besides, John Paul II soon became interested in rapprochement with the East, with improving State-Church relations in the Socialist countries."

"Making him more tolerable to the Kremlin. What else?"

"Ali Agca knows more of the truth than he ever told, more than he should have been permitted to learn."

"Such as?"

"Before being dispatched he was advised that arrangements had been made whereby Carabinieri guards would be so deployed as to make his escape easy—after the shooting. Those arrangements had been made through Vatican figures I am prepared to name. In truth, though, the Carabinieri formation accompanying the Pope through St. Peter's Square had been designed to permit the escape not of Ali Agca, but of someone else."

"You'll name him?"

He lit a cigarette and inhaled deeply. "You saw films of the assassination attempt?"

"Of course. Mass confusion."

"As anticipated. Members of the assassination team formed a diamond around the *campagnola*, the Pope's vehicle. Castor, the woman, was positioned ahead of the Pope. Pollux, to his left. Nestor—Ali Agca—to the right. Ajax was close behind."

"That's four," I said. "You told me it was a three-man hit team."

Exhaling, he nodded. "Ajax was not assigned to kill the Pope. His responsibility that day was to kill the Pope's assassin, close his—or her—mouth forever, then melt away."

"Sort of a Jack Ruby," I suggested. "Who was Ajax?"

Sankov tapped ash from his cigarette and smiled almost lasciviously. Leaning forward he whispered in my ear. One word: "Me."

For a while I stared at him. His tale had come together finally in a logical synthesis. Except for one thing. "But you didn't kill Ali Agca."

"Review the film," he said, "and you'll see that Nestor kept on firing. The additional shots gave guards and others a few seconds to crowd around the Pope as a shield. Agca was shielded, too." He shook his head. "A massive failure, Marston."

"Fortunately for the Pope."

"Yes."

"What about Castor and Pollux? What did they do?"

"The scheme was that whichever of the three had the best opportunity was to shoot the Pope. Hearing a gunshot, the others were immediately to leave St. Peter's Square, get rid of their weapons and proceed to designated points for pickup. Castor to Milano, Pollux to Venice. There they expected to receive the balance of their rewards."

"Instead they were liquidated."

"Of course. I knew airports, railroad and bus stations would be watched, so I left Rome in a rental car. I drove as far as Bologna and took the Rapido to Trieste. You can imagine my state of mind during all those solitary hours. Ali Agca had failed to kill the Pope and I was going to be held responsible for the failure of an operation directed by the Defense Council itself. I thought first of defecting, then of killing myself."

"Why didn't you?"

"Where there's life there's hope. Understand, I *wanted* to believe I could explain failure in a way that would mitigate the punishment I expected. I reasoned that the KGB's first impulse would be to liquidate me, so when I reached Belgrade I went to my own embassy and told the Bulgarian ambassador a cover story. He approached the Soviet ambassador, who sent the KGB *rezident* to interview me. It was a grueling experience, Marston, far worse than anything I've faced these past few months. In the end, he made his report to Moscow Center, including a demand by the Bulgarian ambassador that I be given fair treatment in Moscow. Otherwise, the Bulgarian ambassador would not permit me to leave the embassy."

"He had balls, that ambassador of yours."

"Yes. He had also been a comrade of my father's in the anti-Nazi resistance. He refused to see the son executed as the father was."

"So—what happened?"

"In Moscow I underwent nine weeks of interrogation by KGB and investigators from the Defense Council. It was . . . highly unpleasant, but in the end I wasn't harmed. I was restricted to Moscow, assigned to the internal KGB section that surveys and compromises foreigners. I had the languages, you see, as the women do, the 'sparrows' who bed down with foreigners in rooms with hidden cameras. My sentence was demotion and two years' probation. Compromising you was one of my first jobs."

"How did the KGB identify me as an intelligence officer?"

He smiled. "Very simply. Through the 'sparrows' who had the Marine guards give them access to your embassy's secret files. After Zamyatin and Kilenko were arrested in New York you were chosen for expulsion in reprisal." He exhaled slowly. "I don't suppose it advanced your career."

"No," I said, "it didn't. Which is why I'm here instead of in the field, where I could be useful."

"Perhaps," he said, "this discussion of ours will mark a turning point in your career—if you are successful in presenting my petition."

I took a deep breath. "We need to cover a few more points. Who were Pollux and Castor?"

"Castor was a young Shiite woman from Lebanon, whose family had been destroyed by Christian militia. She was motivated by hatred for anything Christian, and welcomed an opportunity to strike down the head of the largest Christian church. Her name was Fenis Kevorkian. As for Pollux he was a Maltese who had been imprisoned and banished for anticlerical acts that included wounding a priest during mass. Yosif Postiko. A fanatical agnostic, and unbalanced."

"Like the other two."

He nodded. "All three, of course, were expendable, but only Ali Agca survived."

"Why hasn't he talked? Told the whole truth?"

"After his first outbursts he was told privately that the lives of his family, his mother, brothers and sisters depended on his silence." Sankov paused. "As long as he is in prison and holds his tongue Ali Agca will be allowed to live. Of course, if he should ever be freed he will meet with an 'accident.' A fatal one."

"Clearing the books."

"Precisely."

I got up and went over to the empty, smoke-blackened fireplace. Staring at it I said, "The primary value of your story is in its exploitation. You'll have to go public, Filip, but not until everything you've told me has been checked and triple-checked. You'll spend a lot of time on the polygraph and you'll see as many interrogators as the KGB threw at you in Moscow. If your story is true, the world ought to hear it and learn that the Kremlin sponsored Ali Agca's attempt to assassinate the Pope."

"I understand that and I am prepared to fulfill my part of the bargain."

"Including public appearances?"

"Yes."

"And full cooperation in identifying Illegals?"

"I'll toss them in," he said with a wry smile, "for free. You've paid for them."

I turned back to him. "All right. As soon as I leave you're to begin writing down the full story, leaving out nothing. Name every name, including the Vatican officials who helped set up the Pope." I paused. "Both Popes."

"Bear in mind, Marston, that what I learned about John Paul I's murder was hearsay. Masons, Mafia, Opus Dei and bankers were said to be involved, but I can't be specific about their names. I heard that six men outside the clergy were implicated. One supposedly hanged himself, another died of apparent heart failure, one is in prison for banking crimes and three are refugees, hiding in South America."

"They're secondary to the main tale," I said, "so leave that till later." I looked at my watch. "Considering the number of people I have to see tomorrow, the meetings and the slowness of decision-making I doubt I'll come back until tomorrow night. By then you'll have written a complete confession and we'll go over it together. You have to satisfy me fully before I lay my career on the line."

"I understand. Is your Director Catholic?"

"I don't know."

"Casey was, and Colby. So was McCone. And General Donovan, of course, your legendary founder. Catholics won't want to hear about Vatican intrigues, they'll be hard to convince." He grimaced. "From now on, Marston, my life is in your hands. Tell only those officials who *must* know my story to make the decision."

"You're safe here, Filip."

"Am I? James Angleton went to his grave believing a KGB mole had penetrated the top levels of your organization."

"And tore the place apart with his allegations. It was an obsession."

"But never disproved."

"Who knows? That was before my time, at a level far above me. But no one discounts the possibility."

"Good. Because if my willingness to talk becomes known to—let us say enemies—my life will be endangered." He paused. "And yours."

It was ten o'clock when I left Sankov, but I didn't leave the safehouse. Instead, I went down to the basement and entered the secure room. The technician was a small man with a reddish mustache. He was drinking coffee and watching Sankov's image on four video screens. After I told him what I wanted he plugged a computer terminal into Visual Research at Headquaters. I sat down at the terminal and punched in Europe, Italy, Rome, Pope John Paul II and the date May 13, 1981. For good measure I added St. Peter's Square. I sat back and waited.

Within three minutes the screen showed a long panoramic shot of St. Peter's Square as the Pope's vehicle began crossing through the huge crowd. The lens zoomed to a medium shot of the Pope waving and blessing the crowd. Around his vehicle marched Swiss Guards with pikes and Carabinieri in their plumed hats. I froze the frame and tried to spot Sankov behind the entourage, but the only face I recognized was the Pope's. Sankov would have to point out Castor and Pollux, as well as his own location. I let the tape roll on, and suddenly saw an arm and a pistol pointing at the Pope. John Paul II clutched his chest and fell back in his chair. Immediately guards and the crowd closed around him. The vehicle moved ahead, accelerating, and I saw a tight nucleus of people wrestling Ali Agca to the ground. Then the camera followed the Pope's departure. The crowd opened to let the Popemobile pass, then closed in behind like a great wave. The screen went blank.

There would be much more footage in Research files, closeups of the action, stills of Mehmet Ali Agca, but without Sankov's guidance there was no point in watching it all. I would have to have a complete video tape prepared, a VCR installed in Sankov's room and let him watch the scenes and begin to authenticate his story.

I turned off the computer terminal, stood up and stretched.

"Coffee? Just made some," the tech said.

"Thanks, I could use it."

He went over to the big urn, drew a mug and gave it to me black. It was hot and good; it would help me driving back to the District. After swallowing I said, "During the hour Walker and I talked, how much got through to you?"

"Very little. I kept the audio low"—he gestured at a small FM receiver—"so I could hear the Kennedy Center concert." He sat down in his padded chair and squinted up at me. "Why?"

"Because what went on is ultrasecret."

"Who says so?"

"I do, and I have classification authority. Take out that cassette and give it to me. I'll sign for it."

"Mr. Neville reviews every tape."

"He won't review this one. Do it."

He reached for the intercom to buzz Neville, but I pushed away the box. "Don't buck me, little man, or you'll wind up in the Nicaraguan jungle taping Sandinista broadcasts."

His mustache twitched. He got up, went over to his big VCR, ejected the cassette and handed it to me. Then he inserted a new VHS cassette. The one in my hand was designated Walker: 193. The tech shoved a clipboard at me and I scribbled a receipt, signing as John F. Marston. He didn't look at it. I slid the cassette in my pocket. "Is there parallel video feed to Headquarters?"

"There is—on request."

I tapped the cassette. "So this is the only recording."

"That's it."

"It better be," I told him, "and as for Neville, keep your mouth shut." On the monitor screens Sankov was pulling a chair up to his writing table. On it was a lined tablet, pencils and pens. The tech said, "It just come to me where I seen your face—in the papers. When you were kicked out of Moscow. Sloppy."

"You've got a good memory, but this is one night to forget. When does your relief come on?"

"Midnight."

"Tell him nothing. *Capeesh*?"

"Got it—*Mister* Marston."

I left the room, slammed the door behind me and took the stairs. Neville came out of his office and met me in the hallway. "How'd it go?"

"I gave Walker a project to complete. He's not to be disturbed until I come back tomorrow."

"When?"

"Late."

He walked me to the door. "Not a bad fellow, is he?"

"He's a graduate of the KGB's charm school, pleasant when he wants to be but the veneer is very thin. Scratch it and the bedrock shows."

Neville said, "My goodness, you *are* hostile to Walker."

"There's more than an even chance he's here on a pollution mission—to upset the Firm's tranquility, bog us unendingly in trying to find answers to unanswerable questions."

"Like Belenko."

"Something like that." Sergei Belenko had come over from Cairo just after JFK's assassination, when questions were being raised about Oswald's sponsorship. Belenko testified to the Warren Commission that his position in the KGB would have made him aware if Oswald was an agent. Belenko swore he wasn't. Despite certain evidence to the contrary the Warren Commission believed, Belenko's access. They *wanted* to believe him, and so did the Johnson Administration; the alternative would have been unthinkable. Half the Firm believed Belenko was an authentic defector whose arrival was coincidental and whose denials were credible; the other half figured Belenko as a plant bearing a specific disinformation message that conveniently got the KGB off the Kennedy hook. I'd never seen Belenko's interrogation transcripts—they were sealed for fifty years—so I had no opinion. I knew only that the controversy surrounding him caused profound animosity and discord within the Firm. No real consensus had ever been reached. Probably never would be.

I couldn't discount the possibility that Sankov was another Belenko, and there would be months of debate about his confession. I said so.

Neville said, "Well, I certainly hope not."

"By the way, whatever happened to Belenko?"

"I heard he was killed in a car accident in Colorado."

"Figures."

"It stopped raining, but I imagine the roads are plenty wet. Take it easy."

Outside, I said good night to the guard and walked to the Porsche. There was no rain, but in its place a thick drifting mist.

The postern guard passed me through, and I turned on to Route 234, driving back toward Washington.

Traffic had thinned and my fog lamps helped with the mist. I crossed Key Bridge at eleven o'clock and parked two blocks north of the Canal. Then I walked down and over to the Mountjoys' gray-pink dwelling.

Through the distorted pane I could see a lighted table lamp in the living room—a signal that Lainey was alone and I was welcome. Using her key I went in, and bolted the door. I got out the

VHS cassette and took it to the shelves that held their library of VHS tapes. The spine of one was labled *Skiing—Val d'Isère.* I labled mine *Skiing—Gstaad* and fitted it among others on the shelf. Then I took off my hat and raincoat and carried them upstairs.

Lainey was asleep in the big bed. I set the digital alarm for six, undressed and got in beside her. I tried snuggling up against her, but felt something hard poking my hip. It was her vibrator. The minx hadn't waited for me, and now she was deep in postorgasmic slumber.

Just as well, I thought. Our preprandial quickie was plenty satisfying and I felt drained from my session with Sankov.

He had detoured me from my original objective of squeezing the last gram of CI information from him into a revelation with cataclysmic implications. I found myself half-wishing he'd laid it on someone else—someone with more seniority and experience in navigating the Firm's labyrinth without loss of blood. Lainey's bottom moved back against me, but it wasn't an overture. She slept on. The contact relaxed my body but my mind was still churning, racing along like a driverless car. Sankov was concerned about his safety and he had reason to be, considering the KGB's long record of bloody reprisals. But I felt—hoped—his warning to me was excessive. I didn't feel in personal danger, hadn't since 'Nam. A certain amount of caution was prudent, but if it escalated into an obsession it was demoralizing, paralyzing.

The last time I looked at the clock, its red numerals showed 1:26AM . All that time my brain had been reviewing Sankov's confession.

Tomorrow, I told myself, was going to be one hellacious bitch of a day, and with that internal observation I finally fell asleep.

SIX

Having no work schedule Lainey usually slept late. When the alarm wakened me I shut it off quickly, pulled on Peter's bathrobe and went down to the kitchen. My hostess had readied the percolator, so I turned it on and found juice in the refrigerator. I poured coffee in two cups and carried one to the night table nearest Lainey's outstretched arm. The other I took into the bathroom, where I used Peter's lather and a spare razor. Rinsed, the face that stared back at me from the steamed mirror was square-set rather than oblong; brown-black hair, a thin bleached scar at the hairline. Close-set ears, nose-bridge widened where bone had surrendered after repeated smashing by hockey pucks and sticks. Capped frontal teeth, too perfect and a shade too white for nature. Lainey thought my pupils were sometimes gray, sometimes brown. Today the whites were bloodshot. It was my face, mine for better or worse. I rinsed Peter's brush and razor and set them back where he'd left them yesterday morning.

I showered, and as I was dressing, Lainey woke, saw me and

the coffee, and smiled lazily. "When did you come back?"

"At the appointed hour." I went over and kissed her forehead. Her hands clasped around my neck, and she whispered, "Apologies, Brent. Make up for it now?"

"Rain check," I said, and tweaked an exposed nipple.

"Ouch! Don't *do* that!"

"Drink your coffee and stop complaining."

"I don't know when we can be together again—Peter's due back sometime today. I suppose he'll go to the Embassy first but I never know."

"Just as well, I've got a full schedule today—and probably tonight."

She squinted at me. "Another girl?"

"Only the *complaisante* Salomé."

"You're dreadful. I'll call you."

"Dinner was great."

Her tongue outlined her lips. "So were the *hors d'oeuvres.*"

I kissed her again and took my coffee cup downstairs. In the kitchen I carefully washed and dried it, and set it on the china shelf. Peter wouldn't like coming across two used coffee cups; he drank only tea.

I went into the living room and began walking toward the cassette shelves, then decided to leave Sankov's tape cached for the time being. The fewer who saw it the better, I thought. If I couldn't make a verbal case for Sankov, the video recording would be useful.

As I walked back along the Canal I saw a pack of morning joggers following the Towpath. Last night's mist had cleared, but the sky was gray and unpromising, puddles hadn't drained away.

When I reached the building I parked as usual and went in for early breakfast in the big cafeteria. The choice was limited, but how can you improve on fresh eggs, bacon and hot blueberry muffins? I bought a paper from the vending machine and was scanning depressing reports from Lebanon, when one of my shopmates strolled over with his breakfast tray. "Mind if I join you, Brent?"

"He'p 'sef," I managed through a mouthful of buttered muffin, and he sat down across from me. I continued reading the first page. Selwyn Bates had a bland, pleasant face and a luxurious blond mustache. He was a nowhere guy, a time-serving leech who fastened on anyone who might provide a few drops of gossip. His current job was winnowing old files, and I'd heard he was to be passed along to the Staff Historical Section after the next personnel meeting. Few ever got fired, just transferred around; office space and amenities reduced with each transfer.

It was the Firm's way of gradually creating nonpersons, and sometimes it worked.

He said, "Marvelous concert last night. Von Karajan was never in better form. You there?"

"Had tickets but something came up." Sankov.

"Too bad. Thinking of another foreign assignment? Your penance about over?"

"Haven't heard."

"Nothing? I mean—well, aren't you pushing for a worthwhile slot?"

"I hear Recife's opening up."

"Re—"His delicate nose wrinkled. "I'm positive you can do better than that, Brent."

"Never dispute my betters," I said and drank coffee. "Early lesson from a stern, demanding pater. Solid precept, too." Setting my paper aside I started gulping my breakfast to escape this dreary conversation.

Selwyn blathered on about dual divorces in which two ops officers were exchanging marital partners. Someone had told him the training farm was turning into a brothel, with heavy drinking after field sessions and orgies after dark. I said it sounded unlikely to me and pushed back my chair.

"Let's have lunch one day soon, Brent. My club."

"What club is that, Selwyn?" I knew perfectly well his club was the Cosmos before he said it, because he dropped the name at every opportunity, frequently adding that his father and grandfather before him were members. I supposed that was why Selwyn had been accepted at an early age. Picking up my tray I said, "Porter's running me raw these days, but when things slack off I'll give you a call."

"Yes, yes, do that." He smiled, pleased. Not eight o'clock and I'd made his day. I carried tray and unread paper toward the exit.

Herb Porter's secretary was just opening his file safes when I went in. "Put me down," I said, "for the earliest possible appointment with your boss. I'm not kidding, Betty. Ultraurgent."

She peered at me through thick lenses. "About what, Brent?"

"The Bug defector. Last night he told me some astonishing things. I'll be in my office. Waiting."

"I'll tell Mr. Porter."

As I walked down the hall I remembered Selwyn Bates' tale about the dual marital exchange. Too bad, I thought, that Peter Mountjoy hadn't lusted after Marilyn in Paris. Then I could have taken Lainey and everyone would have been happy. But straight-arrow Peter Lainey would never have succumbed to Marilyn even if she'd egged him on. So, why even contemplate it? The past was past, irrecoverable, irreconcilable. I had to deal with today and tomorrow.

As I went to my office it occurred to me that I might be developing some kind of post-divorce syndrome. An oppressive feeling of abandonment, finality, of a chapter that couldn't be rewritten.

And ever since Lainey told me about the fitting-room episode, I'd been looking at Marilyn from different perspectives. While we were married I hadn't thought her capable of taking a lover, but she had. And making overtures to Lainey . . . ? I was coming to realize I'd never really known or understood my wife. On the other hand, how well had she understood me? How hard had she tried to mesh our characters? Blend our lives into the mythic Unity of Marriage?

Too late now to dwell on it, but if I did I ought to visit Psychological Services and talk it through with a shrink, a real one. Not Neville, Sankov's house-father and senior prefect.

Before my secretary, Mrs. Talman, arrived, I read the first three pages of the paper and the editorial section, none of which gave me any satisfaction. There seemed only minimal connection between what was actually happening in the world and correspondents' descriptions of those events.

The section courier brought me the morning's General Intelligence Bulletin, and I began reading it. Mrs. Talman came in, shed her precautionary raincoat and placed her umbrella in the stand. She straightened her skirt, fluffed her hair and greeted me. "Care for coffee now?"

"Later, thanks." Like most working wives she had daily family concerns to contend with. Her husband was an auditor at Commerce and between them they had one car and two apparently sickly children. Between getting them to doctors' appointments, picking up prescription medicines, doing family marketing, preparing two daily meals and keeping the car in running order, Gertrude Talman didn't seem to have a lot of time to attend to work. But she was an accurate typist, followed instructions well, was usually agreeable and tight-mouthed as a mummy. Compensating qualities.

When she brought in the overnight intercepts I said, "I've petitioned Porter's office for a priority appointment and I'm waiting for that."

She nodded. "Any dictation?"

I shook my head.

"Then if you don't mind I'll make some personal calls—on the outside line."

I scanned the intercept traffic, but because I wasn't in Positive Ops they didn't relate to me. I put both classified bulletins in my Out box and thought about Filip Sankov. After a while I started making a list on a ruled yellow pad, the way lawyers do.

One column listed Sankov's four demands: half a million, cosmetic surgery, new docs, relocation. I made a parallel column listing his trade goods: Sov/Bug Illegals; Vatican chicanery—John Pauls I & II; Agca recruitment & training; assassination plans—Nestor, Pollux, Castor & Ajax; scope of Agca's knowledge; Carabinieri positioning; evasion plans including death of Agca; Fil's escape route; Bug Emb/Belgrade. Bug Ambassador's protection; KGB grilling; Fil's punishment . . .

The phone rang and Mrs. Talman answered. As an afterthought I wrote down: Jeffers—Rome. The intercom speaker squawked the news that the chief would see me now. I picked up my pad and strode down an antiseptic corridor to Herb's office.

He was signing a stack of cables when I went in. Looking up he said, "Something hot, eh? How long'll it take?"

"Last night it took me an hour, but I'll condense."

He got up, handed signed cables to his secretary and said, "No calls." We sat on the leather sofa before which coffee service had been set on the low mahogany table. Herb poured and sugared. I took mine black.

While he was adding condensed milk to his cup, I said, "First off, two things: Sankov may have been dispatched here on a pollution mission, but I doubt it. Second, he's worried for his safety, and when you've heard what he conveyed I think you'll agree it's a reasonable concern. He's insistent his info be very carefully limited."

He nodded. "I'm listening. If necessary I'll enforce a Bigot list. Go on, Brent. I'm due at COPS' meeting in half an hour." COPS being Merle Crosby, the agency's Chief of Operations.

Porter was a tall, rangy man with sandy hair and a mind good enough for Fulbright study twenty years previous. He was well-liked at stations where he served, and he loved action ops as much as I did, maybe more. Neither of us adored staff duties. That much we had in common.

I gave him a reasonably succinct account of my first confrontational minutes with Sankov, then segued into Sankov's revelations. As I talked, Herb's interest grew; the coffee was forgotten.

When I finished I noticed that I'd taken thirteen minutes. Herb sat back and said, "Holy cow! I guess you realize what this means?"

"A major exposure of the Kremlin—trying to kill the Pope."

He ran a hand through his hair, shook himself. "And we just lucked into it." *We?* I thought . . .

Herb said, "Any thoughts how we should proceed?"

"I've got Sankov committing his confession to paper—in his own hand—should be ready tonight when I go back. Today, I see two parallel lines to follow. You inform COPS and brief the Director. I'll launch computer retrieval to check out Sankov's stories from the names, dates and places he's supplied—there'll be more from him tomorrow."

He stared up at the ceiling. "If we could just mobilize those

Western Europe Catholics into a solid anti-Communist front, the foreign policy benefits would be . . . incalculable." He warmed to the subject. "Imagine converting those worker priest assholes and liberation theologians from Marxism. Dammit, Brent, this is a once-in-a-century chance to fuck the Kremlin!"

"Sankov could be the key, the moving force."

His face sobered. "Suppose he doesn't check out—that it's all *desinformatsiya?*"

"Then COPS and the Director can't possibly oppose us dumping him, so it's a plus either way."

"Let's reprise that action." He got up and went over to his terminal console. I suggested what to punch in, and presently we were watching what I'd viewed in the safehouse basement.

"Jesus," Herb exclaimed, "happened fast, didn't it?" He ran back the tape to where the crowd was crushing in just after the shooting. "No wonder Sankov couldn't fire at Ali. Which one is he, by the way?"

"He'll show us, plus the other two assassins."

"Too bad they were forcibly retired—it would be nice to have their testimony buttressing Sankov's."

"The only thing Agca doesn't know is he was scheduled for a bullet."

He turned off the terminal and came back to the sofa. "Think Sankov could persuade Agca to talk?"

"Only if his family's security could be guaranteed to Agca's satisfaction. That's a big op in itself."

"But not insuperable." He sipped from the cooled cup. "Damn, Brent, this is *big*. I've never hit on something this size before."

"Yeah. But let's restrain enthusiasm until after checkout."

He looked around the office. "Your entire session was videorecorded?"

"Routinely."

"I'll want to see it when there's time. Audio tapes good quality?"

Shit! I'd forgotten them. That little tech bastard had held out. I said, "I haven't checked them."

"Your secretary know anything?"

"No."

"Keep it that way." He glanced at his watch. "Two minutes. I don't want any part of your interview fed here from the safehouse. Too damn many people will become knowledgeable and the *Post* will print a lead story before we've had time to vet Sankov. Then Congress . . ." His eyes rolled upward. "Jesus, we'll have those assholes around here thicker'n fleas on Lincoln's dog."

I looked down at my pad. "There may be a useful job Jeffers could do without knowing why."

"Name it."

"He's covered as a free-lance feature writer—occasionally even gets things published in British rags that pay farthings and tuppence. I'd like to have him review the whole Ali Agca *schmier*—what happened that day, what Agca said then and in subsequent confessions. Also transcripts of all court proceedings, documents that reflect Italian investigations of the people Agca falsely accused. Vatican reaction . . . In short, everything that's available in Rome. Details Sankov can't possibly have been able to acquire but which can passively support or demolish his story."

"Draft the cable and I'll get it out." He paused. "After I've gotten COPS' reaction." Over the intercom his secretary reminded him of the imminent meeting. As Porter started out he said, "I've been trying to find something for Selwyn Bates to do. You know him?"

"Somewhat. He belongs to Cosmos."

"He speaks Italian, too. Think he could help support Fred Jeffers?"

"Like the iceberg supported the Titanic."

Porter grinned. "Fuck'im. We'll talk later." He went out and I followed. Porter had the coordinated stride of an athlete; at Amherst, he was a standout in basketball, a sport I didn't know much about. But I knew he'd seen Airborne service in Korea and come out with two Purple Hearts, a Silver Star, a stiff elbow, a shot-up lung and a prohibition against smoking. There were other guys like that around, but none more gung-ho for the Firm than Herb Porter. Working for him was almost the only thing that made my penitential position tolerable.

Mrs. Talman was still warming the outside phone when I passed her desk and sat down at mine. On my pad I drafted a cable to Rome Station for Jeffers. I used no privacy indicator to avoid anyone thinking the assignment was particularly special and worthy of water-cooler broadcast.

I waited until my secretary finished her personal call then asked her to type the cable for Herb's release.

Air conditioning kept Computer Central's underground area at a steady sixty-five degrees, so most of the techs and programmers wore jackets or sweaters with long-sleeved shirts or blouses. There were a lot of Kleenex boxes on desks, and sinus trouble was a continuing work force complaint. I went over to the section that served CI Staff and found the deputy section chief in her cubicle—the chief was off somewhere at a conference; they usually were.

Ms. Joyce Ritter was a seemingly intelligent young officer. Wheaton or Holyoke, I guessed. I liked her because she paid attention to what I was saying and didn't ask me to repeat. That was unusual enough to warrant a Merit Award, and I said so.

She smiled cheerily. "That's a nice compliment, Mr. Graves."

"Are you married?"

"No, but I have a boyfriend."

"Rats. The likely ones are always spoken for. Now, how long is this historical survey likely to take? Offhand?"

Her lips pursed thoughtfully. "Offhand—let's see, those requirements again. Umm . . ." Her pencil made scratchy sounds. "I'll set up the program myself, and run it—though I can't promise positive results. The computer only retrieves inputs. And if the inputs aren't there—"

"—the outputs can't come out. I understand. How long?"

"Offhand? Four-thirty."

"Today?"

She nodded. "Just don't expect much Vatican internal, okay?"

"Okay. The product is ultrasecret, special handling, no mention. Me and you, no third parties."

"Understood. I'll bring up the printout myself." She actually blushed. "In a plain brown wrapper."

"Perfect. I'll be waiting."

I stopped by the Italian Desk for a few words with Jay Catini. He was a handsome, olive-skinned man with carefully trimmed black hair, an aquiline nose, manicured nails and Gucci loafers. His family was prominent in the San Francisco produce trade and was said to have substantial equity in at least one Vegas casino. It was also rumored that a cousin and an uncle were doing federal time for union finagling and tax evasion. It wasn't held against Jay at the Firm because most of us didn't care much for unions or the IRS.

On the wall behind his desk hung inscribed photos of Tony Bennett and Ol' Blue Eyes. Jay was well connected. He said, "If you've come to flail me about Fred Jeffers I surrender, Brent. I've kept him afloat out of compassion. He's got a seriously retarded kid, you know."

"I didn't know."

"Fred can handle the medical costs in Rome, but back here he can't. So—"

"If the Firm can tolerate alcoholic station chiefs and neurotic wives," I said, "Jeffers deserves equal consideration. You wouldn't mind if he was given some productive work?"

"I'd welcome it. Anything in mind?"

"Herb Porter has—you'll probably coordinate the cable today."

Jay sighed in relief. "It'll ease my conscience."

"Where were you in 1981?"

"Rome Station—my second daughter was born then."

"So you were on hand when the Pope was shot."

"Definitely. Big file search for traces on that nut Agca, close work with Italian Military Intelligence, reports from the prosecutors' office, janissaries flocking in from all points of the globe—a very tense and disorganized period, Brent. Lucky you weren't there."

"Vatican contact?"

"Had to be, but that was all above my piffling level. The Vat's interest was paramount, of course, and we were trying to help out, however feebly."

"Meaning the Station didn't have much to add to what was generally known."

He nodded.

"Was the Vatican contact passing anything to the Station?"

"Word of mouth, but very little. The reports were confined to a special channel."

"Are they retrievable?"

"Probably not without Director authorization. I wouldn't even know where to look. Mind telling me what this is all about?"

"Just an idea of Herb's."

Jay sat back and looked at the ceiling. "An immense effort was made to link Ali Agca to Bloc Intelligence via the Bug connection—you know, that Bulgarian Airlines guy he implicated. But nothing ever came of it. Or the search for alleged accomplices who were supposed to shoot the Pope if Agca failed. In the end, Agca was in prison, Italian justice had been done and the Vatican seemed satisfied. By then the Station was sick of the whole thing and we went back to our usual pursuits."

I said, "I got the idea Herb wants the whole story on paper in coherent form."

"Why?"

"So he can point to it as an accomplishment during his watch. I assume we have high-level Catholic contacts around Washington?"

"Sure. At Catholic University, Georgetown U. and of course the Papal Nunciature. Now and then I take cakes and wine to a Monsignor who was at the Vatican when I was in Rome. Good guy, wasting away at Georgetown."

I said, "I'd like his name in case Herb wants an overview from an insider."

"Giuseppe Abelardo. Last year I thought it would be nice to give him a look at the Real America, so my family comped him a Vegas weekend." He got out a personal card engraved on cream-colored parchment and wrote *Msgr. Abelardo* on the back. Below he added: *Feel free to talk to Brent Graves,* and handed me the card.

I had no idea I'd ever need it, but contacts were always good to have.

Jay said, "If you see Joe, tell him we've acquired a vineyard up

Sonoma way. If the wine's any good he'll get a case this fall. A good Old World guinea, Brent—you'll like him."

"Thanks, Jay." I went to my office and found the typed cable on my desk. I initialed as Originator, added Jay's name as Coordinator, and dropped it in my Out box for Herb's release.

When the phone rang I hoped it was Herb; instead, I heard the cheerful voice of Peter Mountjoy. "Brent, just in from Bermuda with a flask of Gosling's for you."

"Welcome back—rum's even more welcome."

"I've called Lainey and we'd like to have you dine with us tonight. Are you free?"

"Wish I were, Peter—maybe later in the week. Anyway, it's time you and Lainey dined with me. Pick a night and let me know."

"Well . . ." his voice was disappointed ". . . I'll be off to Ottawa in a few days, but we'll do it before then."

"Good."

"Incidentally, the Embassy's throwing a big ball two weeks hence to honor the Prime Minister. I'll be in Jamaica and I'd be most awfully grateful if you'd escort Lainey. Black tie or better. Will you?"

"Glad to, Peter," I said, and I really was. Being in public with Lainey always gave me a proud feeling of possession.

"That's a boon. One of those obligatory occasions, you know, and one of us *has* to be there."

"Look forward to it. How was Bermuda?"

"Rainy."

"And crowded with Americans."

"Right. Check with you later."

As I hung up I reflected that Peter had unwittingly told me when his wife and I could be together. He should stay home, I thought, and cultivate his own fields just as the Bible recommended.

Mrs. Talman buzzed and said Mr. Porter was on the secure line. "Brent? Took some doing but COPS is on our team."

"And the Director?"

"In New York addressing a Wall Street bunch. Can't get to him until tomorrow earliest. So we'll proceed as planned."

"The Jeffers cable is ready. I'll see Sankov tonight."

"Guess we're on track. When I think of the implications they overwhelm me. Then I think we might have another Belenko on our hands and I foam at the mouth. Sooner we establish all bona fides the better."

"That's what we're working toward," I said, and told him computer retrieval was underway and I'd have the printout before quitting time.

"I have to give a training lecture later today so I'll overnight at the Farm and see you tomorrow."

Before leaving the office I prepared a short memo to Personnel advising of my changed marital status. Then I drove across the bridge to Georgetown, parked under the Freeway and walked up the hill to M Street. The City Tavern doorman greeted me and marked my arrival. I went down to the Grill and found a seat at the bar. The bartender gave me Black Label on the rocks and a small pitcher of mineral water. I sipped, munched macadamia nuts and consulted the Grill menu, settling on lamb chops and a green salad.

At a corner table I noticed Windsor "Wink" Warren, with Sandy Parton and two fellows dressed like senior State Department types. Wink was one of the Director's boys, a large Southwesterner who affected a hearty backslapping Good Ol' Boy persona to camouflage a shrewd and vicious mind. When I returned from Moscow I'd been subjected to a couple of lengthy sessions with Wink, after which I avoided him as much as possible.

Parton was one of our few Arabists who wasn't at the Beirut conference when our Embassy was truck-bombed to shards; luckily for him his flight from Cairo had been canceled. To fill the immediate leadership void, Sandy had been elevated two ranks and appointed head of Mid East Affairs. He didn't like Arab terrorists, and he didn't get along with the Israelis. Mossad had requested his removal, but the Director backed Sandy, and when the Pollard affair erupted the Director was vindicated for not bowing to pressure. Sandy and his wife had a renovated colonial house in Old Town Alexandria and rode with the Warrenton Hunt. He got up from the table and ambled over to me.

"Join us, Brent? We're having a few drinks, maybe lunch—if we get around to it."

"Thanks, but I'm just taking a fast break."

"Things popping, eh? Maybe we ought to have a coordination session soon."

"Coordinating—what?"

He smiled indulgently. "Any probing of Turkish matters reaches me pretty quickly, Brent. Besides, word in the corridors has it that an alien figure is beginning to influence you unduly."

I popped another macadamia in my mouth and gazed at him innocently. "What alien would that be, Sandy? Peter Mountjoy?"

"Your Bug defector—Sankov. And I don't think it's in our overall interests that you stir dead ashes. Ali Agca is in prison, where everyone trusts he'll rot. There's a treaty at stake, you know, and whether or not there was a Soviet conspiracy at this point is no longer an issue. Leave it at that. Or—" He shrugged and started turning away.

"Or what?"

"There could be unpleasant consequences."

"Who says?"

"A little bird."

"Tell that little bird," I said, "to stick his beak up his ass and fly around in circles."

His face reddened. "I'm under orders, Brent, just like you. Any exhumations, I'm in charge."

"Fine," I told him. "Now zip your fly and go back to your buddies."

He realized he'd fallen for a hoary one, mouthed *Up yours*, and went back to his table. I waved genially at the others and again marveled at the rapidity with which secrets spread around the Agency. Equal to the speed of light.

The waiter said my table was ready and I went to it. So much for Wink and his pals, I thought. If Sankov checked out, they were in for some surprises.

All of them.

SEVEN

I didn't like it that someone as remote as Sandy Parton had learned of my interest in Ali Agca within the space of a few morning hours. The speed of dissemination was scary, but as I drove back along the river I tried to convince myself that Sandy had probably overheard something at the COPS meeting and would keep it to himself. But who else was aware of my investigating the Sankov-Agca connection? And who suddenly wanted Sankov's confession suppressed?

I'd lunched at a small table well away from Parton's merry group; having censured me, he decided to ignore my presence. But he managed to spoil what I anticipated as a tranquil luncheon, and when I got back to my desk I made a note to let Porter know that word was swiftly getting around.

Mrs. Talman had left me a message: Call Mountjoy home, so I dialed and Lainey answered. "Peter phoned you?"

"Yes."

"I couldn't let him know I was already aware you had plans

tonight, but I said I'd work out a date for dinner *chez toi.*"

"Whenever both of you can make it."

"Let's see—he leaves for Canada the morning of the fourteenth. Your place the night before?"

I wrote it on my calendar pad. "Eight o'clock okay?"

"I'm sure it is. And then you'll be with me every night he's away?"

"Of course. Plus his Jamaica absence."

"Brent, I'm enchanted you're escorting me to the Prime Minister's Ball. So much so, I've phoned Paris and asked Givenchy to send over something appropriate for the evening. Isn't it exciting?"

"It is," I said. "What's the date, by the way?"

"Night of the second." I noted it on my calendar.

"Brent, I know dress is optional, but you will come white tie?"

"Anything for you, pet."

"I do depend on you," she said, "for so many things."

"See you the thirteenth, with Peter."

"If not before."

I sat back in my chair. That was three days from now. I wanted to be with Lainey before then, but it was out of the question. Our relationship was developing an intensity I hadn't anticipated. Give it until summer, I thought. By then either Peter or I could be transferred; if not, a decision was going to have to be made. If Lainey was going to stay with her husband I was going to break things off. I wanted her full-time or not at all. The way things were going the relationship resembled an occasional banquet between periods of fasting.

I wondered if British Embassy eyebrows would raise when Lainey arrived with me. Apparently it wasn't a problem to Peter or Lainey, why should it be with me?

Years ago Lainey and I had managed a quiet weekend at Honfleur, and since then we'd never been away together. I decided to invite her to Sea Island while Peter was in Jamaica; we'd call on my mother, whose insights were better than mine. She'd let me know if Lainey passed muster.

I went off to a two-hour review of the Greek political situation, which was dismal. It looked as though, sooner or later, the USG was going to lose airbase and communications facilities throughout Greece. The NSC had asked for covert action suggestions to forestall the threat but I didn't have any. Neither did anyone else. I got back to my office at four o'clock, and there on my desk was a thick, wrapped parcel with my name on it, and the red stamp: Eyes Only.

I opened the computer printout, closed the door and began to read.

At five o'clock I took the printout with me and drove home.

Salomé had prepared a spiced shrimp dish and left it in the microwave for warming. I made myself a pair of drinks, watched cable news and opened a bottle of Chandon white.

After dinner I fitted the printout into a briefcase and drove back across the river into Virginia. I was ready to check Sankov's confession against everything the printout told me.

At Fort Belvoir I had to slow and let an Engineer convoy pass, but I was at the safehouse by nine.

When I entered Sankov's room he flicked off the TV and got up. I saw a thick pile of handwritten pages on his writing table.

He said, "Do we have an agreement?"

"Not until verification's complete." I laid my briefcase on the table.

"When will that be?"

"Soon," I told him. "You've withheld this a long time, Filip, so what's a few more days or weeks?"

He nodded glumly. "I want a change of scene as soon as possible."

I pulled a chair to the table, adjusted the light and began reading Sankov's manuscript. He took his easy chair and picked up a book, Solzhenitsyn's *Cancer Ward.* In his situation, not a big morale builder.

I'd been reading for maybe a quarter of an hour when I heard firecrackers off in the distance. That fourth of July was months away didn't occur to me just then; my mind was immersed in Sankov's Mogadishu ops.

Minutes later I heard a car engine nearing, and if I thought anything at all I supposed it was that a relief guard or tech was arriving.

Then came soft popping sounds below, like champagne being uncorked. I looked around and saw that Sankov had half turned in his chair. He looked at me, then the door. Footsteps neared. Outside there was a louder pop, then another. Sankov stood up and there was fear on his face. "Marston—" he began, and then the door burst inward.

There two men were, both dressed in black *ninja* suits. I could see only their eyes, the silenced machine pistols in their hands. They shot Sankov with rapid bursts. His body pitched backward and I saw his bloody head land in the fireplace.

The bullets hit my chest like a huge fist slamming me backward. I was down and legs crossed over me. For a few seconds, I was numbed by shock and I lay perfectly still. Then the pain started, flooding outward, gripping my body in an excruciating vise. I was dimly aware of movement nearby, heard briefcase leather scraping the table top, and then nothing. Consciousness dwindled into a black hole with no beginning and no end.

It seemed an eon later that I was vomited out of the black void. My nostrils smelled smoke, my ears heard the crackle of rising flames. The assassins were gone. The room windows were sealed, impenetrable. I began crawling toward the open door.

I remember seeing the doorguard's body crumpled in his chair. The hallway was filled with smoke. On knees and elbows, I made it to the staircase but couldn't see anything below because of shooting flame. Despite the pain, I drew my body into a ball and rolled off, tumbling down the burning stairs.

My clothes were on fire. I had to get out. A strong inward draft oriented me to the doorway, and with my last strength I got to my feet and staggered past the dead, sightless guard. I clawed off my burning jacket.

Then I was outside. My knees gave way and I was down, rolling in dew-wet grass. Pain overwhelmed me and again I dropped into that silent, unending void.

I was dying.

BOOK TWO

EIGHT

When I opened my eyes the light around me was very dim. Where were the flames? was my first thought.

I was on my back in bed. A hospital bed. I was thirsty, throat so dry I couldn't swallow. My lips were puffed, leathery. My left arm was taped to a board. I could see a needle, a plastic tube and a bottle inverted in an IV stand. Some kind of clear, lifegiving liquid was feeding into my vein. Gauze bandages covered my face and both hands. My right side felt as if it were encased in cement. The edge of my chin rasped hard plaster.

Pain seemed to focus on my right side; dull, as though suppressed by drugs. I wondered how it would be without drugs. Bad, probably; very bad. I tried moving the lower part of my body, and yelped. I was bandaged like a mummy.

"*Water,*" I croaked.

When nothing happened I closed my eyes. I heard the door open. A woman's voice said, "Here's water. How are you feeling?"

"Alive." I opened my eyes and saw a hand holding a water

glass. Another hand guided the glass straw between my lips. I sucked hard and long, then the straw was withdrawn. I licked my lips. "I needed that—where am I?"

"Safe, in a private clinic."

I swallowed. "Did anyone else—?"

"Survive? I'm afraid not, Mr. Graves." She bent near to check the IV drip rate. ". . . I'm afraid you almost bled to death." She went around to the foot of the bed and made a notation on the clipboard chart. Her face was oval, with regular features. Black hair parted at the crown fell just short of her shoulders. She was wearing a white medical jacket, plastic nameplate pinned to the pocket. When she came back I saw that it read Dr. J.M. Cereza.

"How long have I been here, doctor?"

"Nearly four days. One bullet penetrated your right pec and went through. The other broke your collarbone. You were in emergency surgery for three hours getting your chest wounds repaired. You were burned, too. I guess you know."

"It was that or die where they shot me—and burn anyway."

"Your skin will be pink for a while, but we don't anticipate much permanent scarring."

"My face itches."

"Of course. Your beard keeps growing—we can't prevent that." She had a nice smile that revealed white, even teeth. "I've seen you before, Mr. Graves."

"Where was that?"

"After you came back from Madrid you gave a talk at the Farm about working undercover. I was one of the students."

"But you're a doctor."

"That came later—after I realized my opportunities were limited because I'm a woman. I wanted the kind of operational career you've had, though not that sort of violence. You can have semi-solid food whenever you want."

"What is this place?"

"As I said, it's a private clinic, a small one, with cleared personnel. I'm cleared, too, but not for what happened at the safehouse."

"Have I talked much?"

She shook her head, and hair brushed her face. "You probably realize that a number of people are eager—more than eager—to learn what happened. So far they've got nothing but a body count and some car tracks. Your own car, by the way, was taken back to your house."

Sudden rage gripped me. "Christ, how could it have happened with all those guards and security precautions? It was supposed to be a fortress."

"Probably because no one anticipated a coordinated assault." She took my temperature electronically and recorded it. "Did you see the killers?"

"Eyes only." I remembered those eyes. Quick, alert, searching . . . I shivered.

"I can give you something for pain."

"Why not? Might as well enjoy the perks."

She pinched off the IV tube and fitted a filled hypodermic cylinder onto the needle in my arm. I saw the plunger depress, and in a few moments a feeling of warmth and well-being flowed out from my arm. Pain dissolved. Replacing the IV, she said, "When you feel up to it, Mr. Porter is anxious to see you."

"I'll let you know tomorrow," I mumbled, and drifted into sleep.

Sankov's face stared at me, skin blistered, eye sockets empty, blood gouting down the forehead. Bloated lips parted and words emerged. I couldn't hear them but I knew Sankov was accusing me of allowing the assassins to penetrate and kill him. I tried to shout denials, but my throat was compressed, pinched shut. Soundlessly I tried to explain, trying to wrench words from my throat. As his face faded I reached out. His blood seared my fingers. I stared into nothingness and wept.

An empty ballroom. Two women dancing together to sounds I couldn't hear. They held each other breast to breast, thigh to thigh. I seemed to be drifting above them, couldn't see their faces. They kissed lustfully, looked up defiantly. Marilyn and Lainey. Then Peter was with them, watching. He turned to me. It was my fault. He wanted me to take back my wife so he could have his own. I tried to explain that I was powerless, but he shook his head. Lainey was his, I must find my own woman. The ballroom faded away.

St. Peter's Square, the vast plaza flooded with blood from the Tiber. Shooting, bodies falling. White Guards defending the Winter Palace. Cossack cavalry sweeping through the square, sabers slashing. Massed cannon firing against the charge. Balaklava. By W/T I tried to report the pandemonium to Porter, who said it made no sense, report later. From behind a tree, Charlie fired at me, smashing the transmitter from my hand. I dove into a gulley, covered my head. Automatic weapons fire traversed above me. Two men in dark uniforms, faces masked, firing until their MAC-lls were incandescent. They dropped their weapons and fled. The jungle ignited around me. I tried to crawl from billowing flames, but my strength was gone.

I screamed.

My eyes opened and I saw the room's dark ceiling. My heart was pounding, I was trembling. The woman doctor hurried in, checked the IV flow and took my pulse. She said, "You called out."

"Nightmare, "I said huskily. "Where's the nurse?"

"On a break. I was in the area." She smoothed my pillow. "Bad dream?"

"Nightmare. I was scared out of my skin."

"I'm sorry," she said, and I believed her. She gave me more water to sip. "If you like I'll stay here with you. Read to you . . ."

"Read me newspaper stories of the massacre."

"I'm sorry, they're not . . . available."

I pushed away the water glass. "If they were, would you be allowed to?"

She bent over, bisected her lips with one finger, and I understood. My room was miked. Smoothing my pillow again, she said, "What a silly idea, Mr. Graves. You must avoid considering yourself a prisoner here. Everyone's glad you survived that bloody night; they want you to recover fully, and that's why you must rest and mend."

"Sure," I said, "I understand. Someone will have kept clips for me."

"There is probably," she said, "an entire new file devoted to you at Headquarters. If you ever get the chance to read it, the contents will very likely amaze you."

"Very likely," I said. "Can you give me something to sink me without hallucinations?"

"I think so."

While she was preparing it I felt a chill. Inputs to me were restricted; to some extent, I was a prisoner . . . and the subject of a special new file. Special file, special treatment.

Why?

Did the Firm think I was somehow responsible for the success of the assault team? For the deaths of Sankov and the others? Was that possible? Or was it the other way round: powerful forces had decided to squelch Sankov's confession, eliminating everyone with knowledge of it, including me?

It didn't seem plausible, but then the assault was incredible too.

So why was I still alive?

Easy enough to snuff out my life during or after surgery, any time over the last four days.

If my handicapped brain was still able to reason, the answer was that the Firm—or one of its elements—wanted to find out how much I remembered, and appraise the degree of danger I represented.

Doctor Cereza came in with a small graduated cup partly filled with brownish fluid. As she moved it toward my lips I said, "What is it?"

"What you asked for, sedative plus tranquilizer. Why? Do you think it's poison?"

"I'm not functioning," I said. "Don't know what to think." Slowly I sipped the bitter potion. "The taste alone could kill." I licked my always-dry lips. "What do your initials stand for?"

"Joann Marisol."

"Thanks," I said, "maybe I'll remember that much tomorrow. And thank you, doctor. With your help I think I'll be able to make it out of here." My speech was beginning to slur. I didn't care. Her eyes told me she understood my message. "I hope so."

She said quietly, "And I'm glad you trust me. That's important.

While you're under my care nothing is going to harm you. I promise."

"Believing that," I said, "Should help with the nightmares." The potion was taking over, my body began to relax. My tongue felt heavy, lifeless. Dr. Cereza sat down beside me. I wondered if I was trusting her too quickly and too completely. But what choice did I have?

I looked at her tranquil face, and the last thing I remembered was the depth of her dark brown eyes.

When I woke again she was gone. I had no idea how long I'd been under. I remembered no dreams. External light silhouetted window bars behind the room's heavy curtains, so it must have been daytime. My fifth day of suspended animation. I wondered how long it took a broken collarbone to knit. The other side of it had been broken in a Zurich hockey game, and I thought I remembered being in a cast at least three weeks. This time recovery would probably take longer; a bullet doesn't crack bone neatly, it smashes and chips.

Today, breathing was easier. Stitches closing my right pectoral entry wound were beginning to draw, but I could raise and lower my head with only minimal pain. In a voice too low to be heard beyond the room—but not too low for mike pickup—I said, "Water, I want water." Waited.

Presently a male nurse came in with a glass of water and the usual bent-glass straw. He was a big curly-headed fellow, probably a service medic. "Here you are," he said cheerfully, and helped me drink. I finished the glass and said, "I'd like a consult with the dietitian."

"Hungry? Tell me what you want and I'll check it out."

"I'd rather," I said, "have the dietitian tell me what I'm allowed and I'll choose from that."

He thought it over, said, "Sounds okay," and went out closing the door. But for the doctor's warning I wouldn't have insisted on seeing the dietitian, the point being to be seen by as many clinic personnel as possible. This way it would be more difficult for me to "disappear" without questions being asked. I wanted to see faces. Masks had hidden the killer's faces, and I needed to see faces now. Lots of faces—so I'd know them in the future.

If there was a future.

A woman in white nursing uniform and a green cardigan came in. One hand held a printed form, the other a pencil. Already I'd decided I needed writing materials, but she wasn't the person to ask.

I said, "Who are you?"

"I'm Mrs. Simzak, and I'm so glad you feel up to eating. Soft diet for now, you understand."

"I'm Brent Graves," I said, "in case you didn't know, and I was shot up fairly seriously, but I guess you know about that."

She flushed. "I never inquire the nature of a patient's injuries."

"I suppose I look as though a car accident bashed me up—but it came from bullets plus a bad fire in a house. What can I have for breakfast?"

"Actually, it's midday," she said, giving me my first time clue, "but that's not important to you. Now, you may have oatmeal, Cream of Wheat, milk-toast, eggs boiled or poached, warm or cold milk."

"Oatmeal and brown sugar—or honey." My mother often served Alpine honey with hot cereal. "Two boiled eggs with butter, salt and pepper."

"No pepper, I'm afraid. In a few days, though, assuming your progress continues."

And I'm still alive, I thought. I said I could wait, and saw her leave.

Before the tray arrived, a nurse removed the IV and untaped my arm from the board. She trimmed gauze from my fingertips and helped me hold a spoon.

Flexing my left elbow was painful but I did it a few times, remembering Herb Porter's war wound. I didn't want to talk to anyone but Porter, I told myself, and the doctor had mentioned his name.

As I began eating I realized I was famished. Between the nurse's two arms and my left hand I got down all but one of the two boiled eggs. She cleaned my lips with a pine-scented wipe and said, "You did very well, sir."

"Name's Brent," I told her. "Brent Graves. Call me Brent, and thanks for your help, Miss Bailey."

"Just relax now . . . Brent, try to hold it down. You'll gain strength that much more rapidly."

As she was leaving, Dr. Cereza came in. Her face was tired but she smiled at me. "I'm very pleased you're eating. IV does have its limitations."

"Whatever you gave me last night was just right, doctor. Mind's functioning today. I'm aware of my circumstances—I mean surroundings—thanks to you, and I'm getting to know the folks here. They're treating me good—I mean, well."

Her eyes flashed that she understood my pretended word confusion. She said, "I'm going to remove chest drains today, front and back, assuming there's no infection." Her hand moved up and down my cast. "To make you more comfortable I'll see if we can free your right arm somewhat. Should help your eating."

"After that I'd like to get up for a while. Won't that improve circulation and healing?"

"Depends on your burns," she said, "but it's a good idea." She took my pulse and temperature and recorded them.

"Any chance of a TV with remote control? I'd pay the surcharge gladly."

Matter-of-factly she said, "As hard as you've been working you've probably missed a lot of worthwhile movies, so I've arranged a VCR and about twenty cassettes for you."

Until that moment I'd forgotten the Sankov cassette I cached at the Mountjoy house. Well, it was safe there for whenever I might require it. "Sounds good," I said, "and thanks for being so thoughtful. I'm getting five-star treatment."

"You deserve it." She came around my bedside and peeled back my forehead bandage for a brief look. "Healing nicely. Do you feel up to talking with anyone?"

"Anyone?"

"You know—people who want to know what happened."

"The police, you mean?"

"The Firm, really. For now, everything is being very closely contained. The idea is to keep the assassins from learning anyone survived."

"Officially I'm dead?"

"Not exactly—no casualty lists were published."

"I see. Then my mother isn't in mourning."

"No. You're close to her?"

"Not particularly," I lied, and continued lying for the mike's benefit. "Lives in Surrey with another widow, afraid I haven't seen her in three-four years. As to talking with anyone, first I need to collect my thoughts. Creature of habit, I make notes before talking—eliminates mistakes."

She nodded. "That's quite important. If I can free your right arm enough I'll bring you pencil and paper."

"Then," I said, "tomorrow I should be ready to recount everything."

"I'm going to give you a mild sedative now to ease discomfort when you're taken into Xray and OR and moved around. Okay?"

"Okay."

She made a nearly painless injection into my left buttock, after which I became groggily aware that two orderlies were lifting me onto a gurney. One placed a single layer of gauze over my face without explanation, but I knew it was to prevent me from being identified by people who had no "need to know."

My cast area was Xrayed, then on to the OR. Dr. Cereza's face was masked but for her eyes. Distinctive, unforgettable eyes. "Try to stay relaxed," she instructed, but I gritted my teeth as the table tilted me on my left side. I could feel/hear cutting and snipping. The crushing bite of heavy shears that freed my right forearm to the elbow. As the sedative wore off, pain increased, and I didn't stabilize until I was back in my room. The promised VCR had been installed, with a large TV screen, but too exhausted for entertainment, I slept.

When I woke, it was dark outside, and I was hungry.

In the morning, after another semisolid breakfast, I found a writing pad and three pencils on the bedside table. Clumsily I wrote: *Get a message to Peter Mountjoy, Brit. Embassy MI-6, telling him where I am. Suggest anonymous call.*

I folded it six times and slid it under my left thigh. Then, for effect, I began writing about that fatal night, using twelve sheets of paper.

When I finished, the pile reminded me of Sankov's written confession—taken by his killers or destroyed by fire. I knew they'd taken the computer printout, but my account didn't mention that. I wanted interrogators to believe I'd been too shocked to register details, or else my mind had blocked them out. Feigning disorientation seemed my main hope of leaving the clinic alive.

Toward lunchtime Dr. Cereza came in and looked me over. I said, "Mind checking under my left thigh? Feels like a bed sore developing."

"Possible," she said, and pushed back the sheet. Her fingers encountered the folded paper and she nodded. "I'll take care of it, don't worry. I want you to leave here in good condition." Her hand slid the message into her jacket pocket. "I see you've been making those notes."

"Yes, and I'm ready to go over things with whoever's most interested."

"I'll pass the word."

My lunch tray arrived. I picked at it, thinking about my message to Peter. Would Joann Cereza deliver it to him—or to someone at the Firm? Perhaps she'd been told to develop my trust so I'd confide my plans and suspicions.

If Peter received my message what would he do? I didn't expect him to do anything, really, just be my insurance policy. It would be out of character for him to come to the clinic and demand entrance. What I didn't want Peter to do was talk it over with the Firm's liaison; that could be an error in judgment with unforeseeable consequences to me. Possibly even fatal.

The male orderly took away my tray and told me I had a visitor. I said I'd be glad to see him, and sat back expecting Herb Porter.

The man who came through the doorway wasn't Herb, but the Director's confidant and gofer, Wink Warren. Few people I wanted to see less.

With a strained smile he said, "Brent, mighty glad you're feeling better. Lots to talk about." He sat down and pulled out a small tape recorder. Placing it on my bed table he said, "Mind?"

"Where is Herb Porter?"

"Herb? He's been transferred to Sri Lanka to fill a critical vacancy." He turned on the recorder. "You must have gone through hell, Brent. And to think you survived. The only one." He shook his head in disbelief. "How 'bout that?"

"Well," I said, "it wasn't because the Opposition didn't try. How many killed, by the way?"

He edged closer, the recorder was running. "Near as I recall the killers took out Neville, two techs, two inside guards, a door guard, the gate guard, the K-9 handler and two Alsatians—and, of course, Sankov. Makes nine, doesn't it?"

"Counting me," I said, "nine and a half."

"Right, mustn't ignore you. And now you're going to tell us exactly what happened. Thank God there was a surviving witness."

I sighed. "So, Sal's in a brothel, Pat's in jail and I'm the one to tell the tale."

"That's about the size of it. Talk, pal. I'm all ears."

NINE

"Before we get into the night of the ninth—"

"Tenth. It was the tenth of March, Brent."

"Guess I'm still a little fuzzy. Anyway, have someone stop by my house and pay my maid, will you? And tell her I'm okay. Her name is Salomé Guignan and I owe her one-sixty-five, cash. She'll be grateful, me, too."

"Consider it done." He loosened his bolo tie. "As I get it, you made a breakthrough with Sankov; he was promising big revelations about Ali Agca's try at the Pope back in '81. Said he was part of a Kremlin-instigated plot to extract El Papa from Jaruzelski's side. You told Sankov to write down his confession, and you went back the following night to collect it."

"Right. He asked for a new contract—half a million, relocation . . . I forget what else."

"It'll come to you," he said patiently. "Just ease it out, buddy."

I stayed silent for a while before saying, "Our whole conversation was video-taped and mike-recorded, Wink. You don't have to

+

depend on my recall."

He grimaced. "Unfortunately, the fire melted down everything in that so-called basement vault"

"Ah," I said, "the fire. I remember the fire now. So it destroyed all those records. But Neville told me everything was electronically fed back to Headquarters on closed cable circuit."

"Mostly so. But for some damn reason the tech didn't feed your talk with Sankov, no part of it." He picked at a large upper incisor, probably a piece of macadamia nut.

"Damn! That means you don't have video footage of Sankov's murder."

"That's right, buddy. What we got is you."

Referring to what I'd written, I slowly recounted my arrival at the safehouse, the few words that had passed between Sankov and myself; how I'd brought a computer printout as reference to check the confession against; how I'd begun reading the handwritten pages, heard what sounded like distant firecrackers, then corks popping below.

"They had silencers," he said tensely.

"Sure did on the two guns I saw." I described how the killers kicked in the door and with hardly any hesitation fired at Sankov. "While I was watching, they shot me. I dropped and passed out."

"You see their faces? Think, this is very important."

"I saw their eyes, just their eyes from about twelve feet away. Heads and faces were masked, see? They were wearing what I can only think of as *ninja* outfits."

"Them old-time Jap killers? Know what you mean. Did they say anything? You hear words in any language?"

"All I heard was the door breaking in, the firing."

"You sure? Positive?"

"Wink, I'm telling you the way it was. Not a word was spoken." I laid my notes aside.

He thought it over. "Strange," he said finally, "you'd think they'da said something."

"Why? They were real pros. It was all rehearsed. They knew the safehouse, knew Sankov was there, even which room. They had no reason to talk."

"And Sankov said nothing. You?"

"Even if I'd had time, what was there to say? Don't do it, boys, think of your mothers?"

"And you made no attempt to resist?"

"With what? The guards strip-search every visitor, you know that."

"Yeah, too damn bad they didn't search *those* visitors."

"I figure," I said, "there were four on the hit team. Two took care of the grounds, two killed everyone inside."

"Except you. Had time to wonder why that was, Brent?"

"I've had time to be grateful they weren't more thorough, Wink. Sankov was their target, not me. Everyone else was killed to clear the team's access to him. They dropped me as a precaution against interference. And they were going to burn the place."

"They did a thorough job, too, very thorough. Sankov and the other inside personnel were identified by dental work."

"As I said, I passed out after I was hit, bleeding badly. Smoke and fire roused me. I crawled away, breathing what air there was on the floor, rolled down the stairs and somehow made it outside." I looked down at my bandaged hands. "Woke up here."

"And that's all you remember?"

I nodded slowly. "Won't help the cops much, or the FBI."

"FBI?"

"Federal officers were killed, that brings the Bureau in."

"Everyone killed was Contract."

"Neville?"

"Him, too."

"Well," I said, "I'm a career officer. The attempt on my life gives the Bureau jurisdiction."

"You don't want to press that too hard, pal. The Director is sensitive to turf questions. He regards the Bureau as the camel's nose in the tent—our tent. He appointed me to head the investigation, keeping it in-house."

"And the county police? No homicide investigations?"

"What can they do that we can't, with our worldwide resources?"

"How many multiple murders does the Firm investigate in the

course of a year? Or ever?"

"Just leave it, Brent—decisions have been taken far above your level. Be satisfied you're alive and healing."

I needed to balance resentment against wisdom, so I said, "Okay. I'll play it your way." Thinking: for now. "In retrospect it came off like one of those Miami drug massacres you read about."

"Yeah. How far were you and Porter into your little research project?"

"Barely scratched it. Herb hadn't even had time to establish a Bigot list. Gone with the wind now. And we had great hopes for it."

"Console yourself with the thought that Sankov was probably fabricating to gain big bucks for himself. Wouldn't be the first, would he?"

"By no means." I was tiring and my throat and mouth were dry, but I had a few more things to say. "Any theories how the killers knew where Sankov was?"

"Thought you might help us on that. You talk to any outsiders?"

"No, but guards and techs might have . . . or Neville."

"Neville? What would he break secrecy for?"

"He was a humanist, empathized with Sankov, thought well of him—of course, there's the obvious tattler."

"Who?"

"Sankov himself. Suppose he'd managed to get out a message, a call for help. He'd need time for the working party to organize, so he carefully concocts a story about recruiting Ali Agca, a tale whose implications concentrate our attention, whose details are going to require a lot of checking out. Isn't Sankov the logical culprit?"

"Never suspecting the rescue party would be a hit team, he self-destructed." Warren rubbed the side of his face. "Certainly a viable theory, Brent. Good thinking." He tapped his forehead significantly. "Offhand I don't have the means to challenge it." Or the desire, I thought.

"So," he said, "we'll lay it at the KGB's door. Eventually we may pick up a defector who knows the whole story."

I managed a smile with my damaged lips. "Since I'll be here a while I'd like to have visitors—social friends, you know."

He shut off the recorder and got up. "Fraid that's not in the cards. This place is designated secure. Can't have casuals drifting in and out. Besides, there's your personal security to consider."

"How so? The hit team didn't know my name, no one at the safehouse did."

"Your Porsche was there. They could have traced the tag number."

"Unlikely they'd jot it down when they planned to kill the owner, whoever he was."

"Then you're not worried about a follow-up?"

"Like I'm worried about my next meal. Unless you know more than I do?"

"Hey, you're our sole source. If you're not concerned, neither am I." He tapped the recorder. "Besides, we've got it all here, haven't we?"

"The whole ten yards. Ah, how do I explain my absence, this physical damage?"

He picked up my note pages and folded them into a pocket. "Maybe you were spring-skiing in the Laurentians and banged into a tree."

I held up my bandaged arms. "Snow doesn't burn."

"Say you were smoking in bed at the lodge, your blanket caught fire."

"Very clever," I said. "No one will question it."

He rapped knuckles on my cast and grinned broadly. "One final caution, *bubileh*. Nothing about this to anyone, inside or out. Not a word, not a whisper."

"Gotcha."

He leveled a forefinger at me and raised the thumb. "Stay clean." He walked out.

For a long time I stared at the closed door, hoping I'd convinced him I was a cooperative idiot and no menace to him or anyone else involved in the cover-up. I hadn't expected to be allowed visitors, but not asking might have seemed suspicious.

I grasped the water glass in my left hand and drank deeply, then turned on the VCR. I was watching a dreary Woody Allen comedy when Dr. Cereza came in.

"I hope," she said, "the conversation wasn't too tiring."

"I got a lot off my chest."

She came over and checked under my forehead bandage while holding a hand-printed note before my eyes: *Called your friend but he is in Canada. Sorry. What now?*

As she bent over I whispered, "I'll think of something," but as she began taking my temperature I wondered what it could possibly be. For the present, at least, Wink Warren seemed satisfied I was under control.

Until I could manage to get out, my only friend was Dr. Cereza. I knew she'd tried to contact Peter Mountjoy because I now remembered he was due for that trip to Ottawa—Lainey and I were going to exploit his absence.

Lainey must be wondering what happened to me, why I hadn't kept the dinner date with her and Peter. Wink Warren's cov explanations were fatuous, of course, and I'd have to come up with something more believable. Telling Peter and Lainey the truth would involve them. Dangerously.

I said, "I've got a lot of accumulated sick leave, doctor, and now I've got an opportunity to use it."

"Resting, I hope. Being overly active would be risky."

"I was thinking of reading the entire best-seller list."

"I approve of that." She gestured at the VCR. "You like Woody Allen movies?"

"Visually, but I don't understand them. Probably because I'm not familiar with his milieu."

She began lowering the bed. "Try to walk over to the easy chair. I'll help you."

Left arm over her shoulders, I set my feet on the floor and felt dizzy. She let me rest, then helped me trudge six feet to the chair. By then I was gasping, new pains flashing from different points in my body. Slowly, I eased into the chair. The pain gradually subsided.

She placed the remote VCR gadget in my hand and said, "I'll change the movie if you like."

"I'd rather talk," I said. "You know a good deal about me—tell me about yourself."

After checking her watch she sat down and began to talk. Her family came from Venezuela, her father was a diplomat in Washington, where she was born. There was a coup; he was recalled and disappeared. Her mother, sister and brother stayed in the U.S. "Fortunately," she said, "there were no money problems. My brother went to St. Alban's, my sister and I to Cathedral. Rosa, my sister, was rather—arty. She went to Bennington. I graduated from Georgetown. PolySci major, Biological Science minor."

"Odd combination."

"So everyone said, but those were my inclinations. After leaving the Firm I entered Georgetown Med and got my degree."

"Have you specialized?"

"Trauma and reconstructive surgery—which is why I've been taking care of you."

"I don't think," I said, "I could be in better hands. Older, maybe, not better."

"Thank you, Brent. Saving you was a challenge."

"Which you more than met. I'll always be grateful."

She stood up. "I must go now. Sit there a while, then try walking back unaided. The more walking you manage the sooner you'll be out of here." She paused. "The clothing you wore had to be cut away, but I'll bring whatever you want from home."

"Good idea. Was my billfold saved?"

"It was. Address on your driving license. I don't live far away."

"Alone?"

She flushed. "Yes, if you must know."

"I hope you'll have dinner with me."

"That would be very agreeable—we'll see what happens."

She left then, and I found a comfortable position in my chair. My mind began reviewing what I'd told Wink Warren, trying to reach conclusions about Sankov, the massacre and its cover-up.

I didn't really believe Sankov had summoned a rescue team; possible but not logical. He'd been with UDBA and the KGB long enough to realize there was no road back for him—no safe one—and his security depended upon our good offices.

But I believed what he'd told me about the conspiracy to liquidate the Pope and his role in it. He understood that his testimony, properly exploited, would be of immense value to the West in the continuing struggle for men's minds and loyalties. Exposure of the Kremlin's hand in recruiting and training Ali Agca would go far toward solidifying anti-Communist thinking throughout the Christian world. Herb Porter had perceived that, but Herb was far away.

And I was, in effect, a prisoner in a miked room. Warned not to talk about Sankov and the safehouse slaughter.

Why?

By fortuitous circumstance I had preserved the only record of Sankov's story, his verbal confession to me. I was the only one who knew the videotape existed and where it was cached. At some future time it could be useful to me, but not right now. Spadework had to be done.

The Firm had lost eight employees and a promising defector, and I'd come close to dying, yet there seemed to be no official interest in tracking the murderers. On the contrary, Wink Warren had told me not to press it.

Why?

The Firm had domestic as well as foreign antagonists, but there had to be more than avoiding public embarrassment behind the decision to bury the dead and say nothing. The Firm had been embarrassed before, often by false charges, sometimes by charges that could be substantiated.

When I remembered how casually the killers had shot me and left me to incinerate beside Sankov I was seized with anger and hard resentment. I wanted revenge. I wanted the truth to be known, but I was only one man, and a watched one at that. Until I was on my own turf and free there was nothing I could do.

But I could use recovery time to plan ahead, try to fit together parts of the jigsaw and develop a logical picture.

Assuming the killers were from the KGB was reasonable enough, but why wasn't the Firm trying to find and unmask them? And if not KGB, what power center directed the assault?

The only beneficiaries I could think of were the Vatican conspirators Sankov alleged helped in the the attempt on John Paul II's life.

But how could they have known Sankov was beginning to talk? Before I met Sankov that final time only the Director, Herb Porter, Merle Crosby, the Chief of Operations and myself were supposed to have known anything about Sankov's revelations.

Then Sandy Parton had displayed a degree of knowledge that startled me. *I don't think it's in our overall interests that you stir dead ashes. Ali Agca is in prison . . . no SovBloc conspiracy. Leave it at that. Or . . . there could be very unpleasant consequences.*

I'd already suffered consequences that were highly unpleasant. Had Parton caused them? If he was responsible what was his motivation?

I had to know.

Jay Catini knew that Herb and I had wanted Fred Jeffers to compile an account of the attempt on the Pope and succeeding events. But Jay didn't know Sankov had sparked our interest.

Who else was witting? Not Joyce Ritter, the computer whiz; I'd been careful to compartment her away from Sankov.

My secretary knew nothing of Sankov's revelations—forget her. But other secretaries and paper-processors could have picked up information and passed it along, intentionally or not.

And now Herb Porter was gone. True, he'd been eager to get overseas again, but his departure disturbed me. Coincidence? I hoped it was only that.

The Office of Security personnel knew where Sankov was being kept, and a few high-level officers in Logistics knew because they were responsible for maintaining safehouses and hiring guards.

So my original list of four legitimately witting officers was expanding. I estimated that no fewer than twenty had information about Sankov's location and probably much more.

Someone on the inside had arranged the catastrophe. Identifying that person was worth an intensive large-scale effort. If Wink had fabricated the existence of the investigation, then absolutely nothing was being done.

There was a massive cover-up, and I was damn well going to find out why.

TEN

Over the next week I began some serious walking. Dr. Cereza's visits became less frequent, her explanation being that I was free of infection and well along toward full recovery. After another Xray session—to which I walked escorted by the male orderly—Dr. Cereza said my collarbone was knitting nicely. She cut off the cast, wrapped my shoulder with elastic bandage and devised a comfortable sling. More to limit arm use, she said, than to speed healing. That I'd done so well was a tribute to my physical condition.

New pink skin grew back over burned, peeled patches. My eyebrows were growing back and so was my singed hair.

For the first time in more than two weeks I was allowed to shave—with an electric razor—and two days later Dr. Cereza arrived with departure clothing. "Your maid was very helpful," she said, "and she's been very concerned over your absence."

"Salomé's a jewel. Did anyone bother to pay her?"

"It didn't come up, but let's hope so. You're free to leave, Brent, and I'll drive you home."

"That's a bonus. I'll be dressed in ten minutes."

She opened a sealed envelope and handed me my wallet. The contents looked intact, but the leather smelled of smoke. The smell brought back disagreeable memories.

As we left the clinic I saw no one except the duty nurse and male orderly. Outside the day was clear and unusually bright. Joann helped me get seated in her BMW convertible, and while she was starting the engine I looked at the clinic. It was a compact, two-story brick building with a sign reading:

Medical Associates, P.A.
A Private Clinic

Extraordinarily private, I thought. She steered around the gravel drive, and a mile or so away drove through the small, pleasant town of Leesburg. She said, "If you should feel nauseated I'll pull over."

"Doing fine. The fresh air helps."

"You've been placed on indefinite sick leave, Brent. Go back to the office only when you feel fully up to it."

"That's my intention," I said. "Lots of catching up to do."

"The whole thing's baffling, isn't it? The assault, the cover-up. Have you made anything of it at all?"

"There had to be a leak somewhere—but where?"

"I hope you'll be satisfied to accept your life and recovery and not try to uncover things that could be dangerous."

"Is that an official message?"

"No, entirely personal," she said irritably. "I'm on your side, you know."

"I know." I inhaled deeply, glad that chest pain was mostly gone. "When can we have dinner?"

"Hard to say. I'm on call at three emergency rooms: Sibley, Georgetown and GWU."

"And the clinic."

"Yes. So I can't really maintain a social schedule. That's been a problem. The male friends I've had wouldn't put up with it."

"I might be more understanding."

"Yes, I think you might."

We crossed over the river and it seemed like years since I'd seen the hilly rise of Georgetown at the far side of the bridge. I was going to have a hard time fitting myself back into the life I'd known. Sankov had changed everything.

"You're a brave young woman," I said, "and I don't mean that chauvinistically."

"I know."

"More courage than most men I know."

We were driving up Thirty-First toward my house when she said, "I'm sorry I couldn't reach Peter Mountjoy for you."

"You tried, that's what was important. As things turned out it made no difference." By now Peter was probably home from Ottawa. I needed to square things with Lainey and that wouldn't be easy. Sankov had complicated my life enormously.

She steered into my drive and braked behind my Porsche, got out and opened my door. I asked her in but she said she had a patient waiting at Sibley.

"Can you possibly name an evening for dinner?"

She smiled. "I'll check my calendar and phone you. Best I can do."

"Your best is very good." I didn't want her to leave. I wanted her to come in, see my house with the things I'd collected over the years, photos of my parents, of me as a child . . .

"Well," she said, "good-bye, Brent."

"Good-bye, Joann," I watched her BMW back out and head down the street. Then I went to the door and rang. Salomé must have been watching through curtains, because she opened the door immediately and started to fling her arms around me. But when she noticed the sling she stepped back, alarm in her eyes.

"It's nothing," I said, "don't worry about me."

"Hadda worry, Mist' Grave'. So long away . . ." She dried tears wetting her cheeks. "Ev'thing jus' same here, you see I take good care."

"I know you did." I stepped across the threshold and she closed the door behind me.

I was home.

I was free.

I went to the nearest phone and dialed Lainey.

Her phone rang once before I hung up. Wait a minute.

I unscrewed the receiver mouthpiece and examined diaphragm and magnet, looking for a nickel-sized low-frequency transmitter. There wasn't one. I reassembled the hand set and dialed again.

Four rings and she answered. "Lainey," I said, "I'm home and I want to see you. Can you come?"

"Brent, what on earth? Where have you been?"

"I'm just out of hospital," I told her, "and I want to apologize for missing our dinner. And the Prime Minister's Ball."

"Oh, Brent, I didn't know . . . I'm *so* sorry. I'll drop everything and come. Of course I will."

Salomé left for the M Street market and I poured two glasses of sherry. Then Lainey was impatiently ringing and I let her in.

Staring at me, she touched fingers to her lips. "My God, so pale! And your arm—are you in pain? What happened, in God's name? Tell me all. I'm bursting with questions."

I drew her in, handed her a sherry and led her into the library. When we were seated on the sofa I said, "I took part in a night training exercise—agent infiltration—the plane crashed on takeoff. I got burns, a broken collarbone and ribs."

"Yes . . . I see that." Her voice trembled. "Couldn't you have phoned? So I could visit and cheer you."

"My lungs took a lot of smoke," I said. "I was on pure oxygen for days. And the hospital was far away. Can't say where."

Her hand touched my regenerated lips and eyebrows, the tip of my nose. Chastely she kissed me. "I've missed you so—I called and called. Your office said they knew nothing about you. I was . . . beginning to suspect the worst."

"Well, it wasn't that, just close. Anyway, I'm back and planning to enjoy sick leave."

"I'll help you," she said, snuggling against me. "I really will, Brent. Not having you near . . . well, it was devastating and I realized how much I depend on you."

She was wearing moccasins, bluejeans, a loose-fitting Arran sweater, and her hair was tousled from the wind. I thought she had never looked lovelier or more desirable. I lifted her hand and kissed it. She began to weep.

As I kissed away tears she said chokingly, "So awful . . . not knowing . . . couldn't understand . . . put on a brave face for Peter . . . thinking you *had* to be dead." Passionately she covered my face with kisses. "When Peter got back I begged him to put through an official inquiry, but he said it would be bad form."

"He was right. It would have been . . . embarrassing. But I missed you too, believe me. There were times I wanted you with me more than you could believe. I was so isolated I sometimes felt absolutely lost."

Abruptly she sat back and began pulling off her sweater. "Ah, Brent, why don't you leave it, all of it? You don't need a salary and they haven't treated you very well."

"Why doesn't Peter leave?"

"It's different with the English, you know that." She flung the sweater to the floor. No bra. She pulled my face between her warm breasts. Pressed them against my flesh. "It's expected of him to be in Civil Service and he's not good at anything but what he does." Her whole body shivered as I tasted her nipples in turn. "I want you," she said fiercely. "Can you? I mean . . ."

"I can try," I said, and led her up to my bedroom. As I closed the door she wriggled out of her jeans, pulled off her briefs. I said, "Salomé could come back . . ." and loosened my belt.

"I don't care. If she doesn't know I'm your woman it's time she did. Come here, luv." The tears were gone. Her eyes sparkled with mischief. "Leave everything to me."

She managed things perfectly. Her loving ministrations emptied me of pain and fear, then filled me with euphoria until I felt whole again. We lay side by side, afternoon light penetrating the blinds, moisture glistening on our flesh. Quietly she said, "I've done a lot of rethinking—about myself, about us, and I know I don't want to be with anyone but you. How do you feel about me?"

"You mean more to me than anyone I know, but I can't make your decisions." My collarbone was beginning to throb again. I turned on my left side to ease it. "I have some decisions to make that involve my future. And for the next few weeks I'll be involved in the crash investigation—the pilot wasn't as lucky as I was. And

I'm supposed to have physiotherapy every day."

"I offer myself for that—after nearly losing you." I felt her body shiver against mine.

The telephone rang beside me. I lifted the receiver and heard Wink Warren's voice. "Made it home safe, did you? Just checking, pardner. Take care of yourself, hear? Remember what I said and be very, very careful."

I swallowed hard. "Sure," I said, "mum's the word."

"Gotcha." The line went dead.

Lainey said, "Who was that?"

"Office, inquiring after my welfare."

"Thoughtful."

"Unavoidable." I saw her glance at the bedside clock and sit up. "Time to go," she said, "much as I hate to. But I guess most of your needs are seen to by Salomé. Peter depends on me." She picked up her briefs and stepped into them. "Too much."

She helped me into a bathrobe and I went down with her to retrieve her sweater. We kissed, and at the door she picked up the evening paper and handed it to me. "I'll come back tomorrow," she said, "and we can do anything you want. If you like, I'll drive you into the country . . . or we can just stay here and talk."

"We'll decide tomorrow."

I watched her roll up her sweater collar and thrust her hands into her pockets. Then she was jogging down toward the Canal and I lost sight of her in the next block.

It had been a long time since I'd seen a newspaper. I carried it into the library and eased myself into my customary chair, tired but pleasantly so. I opened the paper and read the first page, feeling I'd been caught in a time-warp, so much had happened in the world while I'd been isolated.

On the second page a short paragraph caught my eye.

> DIPLOMAT KILLED IN TAMIL AMBUSH, Colombo, Sri Lanka. An attaché in the U.S. Embassy was shot to death by Tamil guerrillas at a roadblock in the Batticaloa district, according to Government forces fighting the Tamil separatist movement. Herbert V. Porter, who arrived in Colombo less than two weeks ago, was ambushed in his car by a guerrilla

band that fled the scene of the attack. According to the U.S. Embassy, Mr. Porter, 54, was a native of Maryland, where his wife and three children reside. The Sri Lankan Government vowed to . . .

But I couldn't read on. My eyes were opaque with tears. Herb dead. I couldn't believe it, he'd been so full of life when I'd last seen him, so eager to exploit Sankov's confession . . .

I got up and walked around the room, unseeing. Was his death sheer happenstance—or planned?

Besides myself he was the only one who knew details of Sankov's confession and understood their implications.

Now he was silenced. Dead. My throat constricted.

Unreasoningly I felt guilty of his death, but where did the answers lie?

The telephone rang, and my neck hairs prickled. I felt a thrill of danger. It rang again. I stared at it as though it were a cobra poised to strike. I didn't move.

The telephone rang, filling my brain with an insane, discordant clangor. I covered my ears with my hands.

It rang . . . rang . . . rang . . .

I fled through the house and out into garden. I leaned against a tree, sounds racking my throat.

Someone knew the *why*. Warren? Parton? Who?

When I could control myself I walked slowly back into the house. Salomé was unpacking her shopping bag in the kitchen. I passed her wordlessly and stood at the living room window, staring at the street.

Ten deaths now, ten blood payments due. I'd resolved that before leaving the clinic.

Finally I was free, able to move according to plan.

In the library I removed Montaigne from the shelf and opened my safe. Everything was there: money, passports, weapons . . . They'd had their chance at me, I told myself, at the safehouse—then the clinic.

It was my turn now.

I pocketed the HK 9mm and locked the safe again, replacing the leather-bound volumes.

Until I had a starting point I'd be stumbling blindly through a dark and dangerous labyrinth. I needed information.

I thought I knew where to begin.

Slowly I climbed the staircase to my bedroom, where I'd shed my clothing. Since Joann Cereza had opened the sealed property envelope I hadn't inventoried my wallet, and I needed to.

It was in a jacket pocket. I sat down and emptied the wallet on my rumpled bed. Calling cards, credit cards, driving license, health card, plastic phone charge card. Sixty-seven dollars in U.S. currency. Two AmEx receipts, my bank account card. Two unused tickets to the Center concert . . .

Everything but my building pass.

I might have thought the plastic badge had melted, but five similar plastic cards had survived, unsinged, unmelted.

Building access had been revoked.

I was on the outside now.

Alone.

ELEVEN

Before going to bed I took the phone off the hook, hoping to rest undisturbed. But my mind kept revolving around Herb's murder and my missing badge until I finally had to down a sleeping pill.

In the morning I went into my storeroom and took out a seldom-used phone-answering machine, plugged it into the circuit and turned it on. I tested the remote accessory that enabled me to play back messages by transmitting through an outside phone.

After breakfast I left the house and walked down to Smyth's Apothecary, where I turned over Dr. Cereza's prescription for muscle relaxants. I didn't need them, but Smyth's had a pay phone.

I dialed my office extension, expecting to hear Mrs. Talman, but an unfamiliar voice answered. I said, "I'd like to speak with Mr. Graves."

"Sorry, sir, he's not on this extension."

"Then, could you give me his extension?"

"Sorry, sir, that's not allowed."

"May I speak with Mrs. Talman?"

"She is no longer at this extension, sir."

"Can you transfer me to her?"

"I don't have that information."

"It's important I reach Mr. Graves. Is anyone there who can help me?"

"Perhaps Mr. Bates could help you?"

"Selwyn Bates?"

"Yes, sir. Shall I connect you?"

"I think not," I said, "but have you any idea how to contact Mr. Graves?"

"I understand he is on extended leave, no referral number."

"Thank you so much." I hung up. The responses hadn't surprised me—except that Bates had taken over my desk. Probably because he was readily available and could be counted on to stay in line. Was it a reflection on my abilities that Bates was filling my slot? What slot was that? I'd become a nonperson overnight.

Still, Bates was dim-witted enough to be of possible use and I'd bear the man in mind.

Another quarter in the slot got me Dorsey Jerrault's secretary. After I identified myself she said Mr. Jerrault was out of the country, not due back for another three to four weeks.

"Oh, I forgot," I said. "Please ask him to call me when he gets back."

"Yes, sir. Is it about the Senate Subcommittee? Mr. Gerard called here several times; apparently you've been away, too."

"Right. Give me Gerard's number and I'll get in touch with him." I wrote it down.

I thought of phoning Jay Catini, but I didn't know his extension and the Firm's switchboard wouldn't give it out—strict phone security and discipline, usually desirable but in my present situation a handicap.

Ms. Ritter, the computer maven who prepared the printout for me, was someone I wanted to talk to—if only to verify that she still existed—but I didn't have her extension either. My guess was she'd been transferred in-house or sent overseas.

Near the prescription counter stood a display of leather billfolds and wallets. I selected one, emptied mine and began transferring the contents to the new one.

Catini's face popped into my mind and I slowly made the connection—he'd given me his personal card and I'd admired the engraved parchment. His card was missing, but I hadn't noticed until now. What had Jay penned on it? An introduction to Monsignor . . . Abelardo, that was it. "Joe," Catini had called him—Giuseppe. I was becoming aware that my brain's ability to recall and synthesize information wasn't what it used to be.

The pharmacist brought my prescription and glanced at my sling. "Hope you'll be feeling better. Car get you?"

"Unfortunately, no. I don't have anyone to sue. Truth is I was drunk and fell downstairs."

He quickly began adding the billfold price to the prescription. "Twenty-four thirteen—no tax on the medicine."

"That's a break." I tossed my old wallet into a trash can behind the counter. I handed him a twenty and a five and he returned the change.

In the phone booth I used another quarter to dial my home telephone. Three rings and the answering machine clicked on. I heard my voice asking callers to leave messages at the sound of the tone. I beeped my accessory at the mouthpiece and heard Peter Mountjoy's voice. He was glad I was back, sorry I'd been injured, and wanted to talk with me.

A second caller left no message.

The third voice was Lainey's saying she'd bought fresh croissants and would bring them as soon as I got home.

I phoned her and said her offer was one I wouldn't think of refusing. She said she needed to soak paint brushes and would be with me soon thereafter.

I rang off and left Smyth's. The pharmacy had been there since before Abe Lincoln, and featured personal service, deliveries and exorbitant prices. But the G'town gentry who patronized Smyth's Apothecary wouldn't be caught dead in Walgreen's cheek by jowl with the plebes.

I expected to be using the pay phone a good bit from now on. If the pharmacist questioned me I'd say my home phone had been disconnected for nonpayment.

My walk to Smyth's and back was only six blocks, but the unaccustomed exertion tired me. When I entered the house I told Salomé that Mrs. Mountjoy would be arriving, and asked her to prepare a tea tray for us. Then I went to the library and picked up last night's paper. The story of Herb's killing seemed to lift off the sheet and burn my eyes like lasers. Much like Uriah the Hittite, Herb had been sent into a battle zone and Tamil Tiger guerrillas had obliged whoever transferred Herb to Sri Lanka. My boss and friend was dead, I couldn't bring him back. All I could do was try to get to the bottom of the conspiracy that had dropped over me like a hunter's net.

Salomé answered the doorbell and presently Lainey came in. Today she was wearing a Gordon plaid skirt, dark blue blazer, knee-length cable socks and tassel shoes, and she looked about nineteen. She bent over to kiss me and said, "Salomé's warming the croissants and I asked for blackberry jam."

"Do we have it?"

She settled herself on the sofa. "Crabtree & Evelyn. Anyway, it's an excuse to be with you. While you were away I couldn't bring myself to finish Peter's portrait, but it's done now."

She seemed ready to dismiss it from the inhabited world, but I said, "What I saw of it looked like a fine representation."

For a few moments neither of us said anything. We were remembering our Beaux Arts-style quickie while Peter's half-done portrait silently watched. Lainey sighed. "You'll see it when you're next over. I've decided it should be my Anniversary gift to my husband."

"He'll appreciate it, I'm sure. Incidentally, Peter phoned and left a message he'd call back."

"Probably about the party we're giving at the Sulgrave next week."

"Do you want me there?"

"I'll perish if you're not."

Salomé brought in the tea tray, croissants under a crisply ironed napkin. As Lainey began pouring I said, "For the sake of appearances perhaps I should bring someone."

"Anyone I know?"

"Just met her—the doctor who saved me." I took a cup and added sugar.

"You've fallen in love with your *doctor?*"

"Hardly. It's just that seeing me with someone other than his wife might quell any suspicions Peter's been entertaining."

She broke a croissant and buttered it for me. "He hasn't any. Jam?"

I nodded. "To people who watch that sort of thing the Mountjoys plus Brent Graves probably look like a *ménage à trois.*"

"Ridiculous. No, *don't* bring her, whoever she is. I'd be wildly jealous and show it." She sipped and her nose wrinkled." The tea steeped far too long. I'll bring some from home and show your maid how it's properly done."

"We'll appreciate that," I said dryly. "Tell me about the P.M.'s Ball—who took you?"

"A chinless young Third Secretary named Aubrey Polk-Fennel—I don't think you've met him. Aubrey plays flute in the Embassy quartet and Ambassador Clinkscale positively dotes on him."

"Sounds like a type to avoid."

"Except that he was perfect for the part. Still, all night I kept thinking you were to have been with me, and wondering where you were—if you were even alive. The entire thing was anguishing. I was so distracted I almost curtseyed when presented to the P.M. Darling, you mustn't *ever* leave me without warning."

"If it's ever without warning it's because of *force majeure.* Besides, my Firm isn't so tidy about things as SIS—we're much larger, you know, and lack the warming sense of family that Peter and his chaps enjoy."

"Marilyn hated it, you know—called it a soulless bureaucracy."

"And she was right." The warm, flaky pastry was delicious.

"Do I detect a sense of disillusion, dear? Are you finally thinking of giving it up?" She touched my sling gently. "You mustn't risk your life any more."

"What would I do to keep busy?"

"We'll think of something. Travel. I'd love to spend every spring in Paris—you didn't give Marilyn your wonderful flat on the Ile

St-Louis?"

"No, it's mine. What else have you in mind?"

"A tiger hunt. Take me on *shikari* before all the tigers are slain for their lovely skins."

"Stag in Scotland, I suppose?"

"Partridge in Spain. Bear in Alaska . . ."

"How come you're suddenly dedicated to blood sports?"

"Not suddenly, dear, my father inoculated me from an early age. It's that Peter shrinks from shooting. You know his great love is taking salmon from the hereditary streams." She licked viscous jam from an index finger and thumb, suggestively.

I said, "And when are we going to do all this?" Knowing well what her reply would be.

"When we're married, of course—before the children come and I still have my figgah. Before you're tempted to take up with doxies." She was looking at me earnestly.

"I seem to remember your enjoining me against offering matrimony."

"That was before I came to my senses, luv. Seventeen days without you, seventeen nights panicked with worry set me to rights. I've been so blind . . . but now I see everything quite clearly."

"There's a third part of the triangle—your husband."

She nodded slowly and soberly. "I've thought about that, about him, a good deal. Peter can be quite dense when he wants to be so there's nothing for it but telling him straight out."

"I suppose that's better than his finding us *in flagrante*. Still, we're getting ahead of ourselves, *ma douce*. For the immediate future, I have a number of serious tasks to accomplish. If I survive and you still want me—"

"Survive—?" She sat back, alarmed.

"Let's stroll in the garden, see how the mums are doing."

Outside, under the budding pear tree we sat on a bench and I took her hands between mine. If the garden was miked I was finished, anyway, but I didn't think it was. "What I'm going to tell you is for you alone. Not even Peter, because he's honor-bound to report back to London, and SIS is a leaky vessel."

"Whatever you're going to say I'm already scared half to death."

"Help me out of the sling and shirt."

When she saw the pink bullet scars she breathed, "*God,*" and closed her eyes. For a moment I thought she was going to faint. Instead she kissed the scars very tenderly, then my lips. "Airplane crashes don't cause bullet wounds."

"No. And I'd rather you not know anything, Lainey. Strange things have happened to people who know less than I do, including assassination. When the phone rang yesterday afternoon it was another warning to keep my mouth shut. I'm lucky to be alive and I want to stay that way. More than that, I don't want you endangered. If I tell you what I know your life will be at risk, and rather than make up a lie I'd much rather say nothing."

Her lips trembled. "But you're going away? Why?"

"There's a deadly conspiracy that has to be rooted out and exposed. If I don't try to do it I'll never find peace with myself. If I succeed there'll be no more danger and we can live together in peace, bring up our children."

Sobbing, she clasped her arms around my neck and rubbed her cheek on mine. "Oh, Brent, I'm so frightened of losing you, of there never being an Us."

"If you can bear with me it's going to be all right."

"Promise?"

"Of course I promise."

She dried her eyes on a small handkerchief. "And the woman doctor—is she involved?"

"She patched me up, that's all. Her name is Cereza. I trust her and I've told you her name in case I should ever need to get a message to you. You'll know it's from me."

"Cereza." She nodded. "I'll trust you and bear up as long as necessary—but I need to be sure you love me, you've never said."

"I do love you." We kissed, and the pact was sealed.

Hand in hand, we walked down as far as M Street, said goodbye, and I turned east toward George Washington University Hospital for my physiotherapy session.

Dr. Cereza wasn't there, but she'd left instructions with an attendant who took me to the hydrotherapy room, and afterward to a weight room where she demonstrated how to exercise my right arm and shoulder. It was painful—I hadn't realized how much the disused tendons had tightened—but I kept at it for the required fifteen minutes. At the end I was covered with perspiration and my jaw muscles were tired from clamping my teeth.

The attendant returned and said, "Very good. Sir, if this time is convenient I'll establish a regular daily schedule for you."

"It's a good time," I said. "Long enough after breakfast that I won't throw up, and far enough from noon that I'll be fit for lunch."

She helped me dry off and get into my shirt and jacket, and replace the sling. Then she handed me a folded message form. Signed *Joann*, it read: *Let's try for tomorrow night. I'll call to confirm.*

The attendant said, "Dr. Cereza is an excellent physician. Everyone enjoys working with her—and her patients."

"I owe her a great deal," I said, and stuck the message in my jacket pocket. Dinner seemed an insignificant payoff for all she'd done.

I left the hospital feeling weak, walked slowly home and lay down to rest. The phone rang, but I ignored it and let the answering machine take over. I thought of Lainey and the life we might have together, of children to be conceived, born and nurtured, the places we might live and enjoy . . .

Then sleep came, restful, healing sleep without torturing, exhausting dreams.

It was midafternoon when I woke. Salomé fed me beef broth, green salad and an array of vitamins and bone-building minerals. I felt a good deal stronger than I was on leaving the hospital, so I walked down to the pharmacy and dialed Peter Mountjoy's extension at the British Embassy. When he answered I said, "Good of you to phone me."

"Well, I'm overjoyed you're back—but Lainey tells me you're ailing. Nothing serious, I trust?"

"Healing nicely, thanks, and looking forward to making up for the failed dinner."

"Yes, of course, but we're giving a small affair at the Sulgrave next Tuesday eve and trust you'll be with us. Black tie. You'll come, Brent?"

"With pleasure. Ah—any special occasion?"

"Anniversary celebration, actually. Seven years of wedlock."

"Well, bully for you both," I said, feeling a pang of conscience as I remembered it might be their last together. "Can you and Lainey dine with me Monday night?"

"I'm sure we can, but I'll check at home and one of us will get back to you. Any case, I'm eager to see you after your long, mysterious absence."

"We'll talk about that." I replaced the receiver and fished for another quarter.

This call was to Georgetown University, and I asked for Monsignor Giuseppe Abelardo.

A quavery voice answered. I gave my name, said I was a friend of Jay Catini's and would like to see him as soon as convenient.

"A friend of Jay's is most welcome. Your name again, please?"

"Brent Graves."

"I could see you after evening devotions—my room is in the religious quarters. If you are not familiar with the campus, any student will be able to direct you. Eight thirty?"

"Thank you, Monsignor."

I walked two blocks to Bonner's liquor store and asked Harry to select his best bottle of Italian wine. "Easy, Mr. Graves," he said, "this Bertani Valpolicella '59 is the choicest in stock." Carefully he picked up a twenty-four ounce bottle and caressed the label. "No price showing because some of my elderly customers have weak hearts. I'll whisper it to you." He did, and I clapped my left hand over my heart.

"Will you accept a second mortgage on my house?"

"Glad to," he chuckled. "Deliver this? I see you got a bum wing."

"Sadly so. You have ecclesiastical trade from the University?"

"Like who?"

"Monsignor Abelardo."

"Fine man. This for him?"

"Indeed it is. I thought you might know his preferences in liqueurs"

"Well, he doesn't have much spending money, so I give him a discount." Harry turned and slowly eyed the shelves. "Last time the Monsignor came in I think he went out with the smaller size Amaretto."

"Deliver the large size along with this heartstopper." I got out my new, odorless wallet, extracted my AmEx card and a calling card. Harry loaned me a pen so I could scrawl *Buon gusto* in the space below my name. He made out the charge ticket and I signed it, affecting shortness of breath. Harry took it delicately and returned the blue slip, crumpling the carbons. "Tell you what—I'll send your purchase to the Monsignor nicely wrapped in a handsome raffia basket. Okay?"

"Okay."

"My wife's got the talent for tasteful wrapping. Me, I know wine and spirit."

"Appreciate it," I said, and left the store.

As I walked away I wondered what would come of my appointment with a Monsignor who was at the Vatican when some of his colleagues conspired to end the life of John Paul II. Abelardo might know something, he might not. And if he remembered anything I didn't already know, would he be willing to share it with me?

I hoped he would. *Faute de mieux*, he was my departure point.

The only one I had.

Moodily I trudged back home.

The one message on my answering machine was a prerecorded sales pitch from a bucket shop specializing in gold futures. I was missing a unique opportunity if I failed to send off a certified check for the company's special shares.

I decided to forego the opportunity, and rewound the tape.

The afternoon paper featured a long article about the ongoing Senate debate over the proposed comprehensive Mutual Non-Agression Treaty with the Soviet Union. Backers advocated it as a good-faith step toward civilizing the Kremlin and taming the

USSR's aggressive tendencies. Opponents called the treaty a Munich-type sellout, arguing that it abandoned linkage and rewarded the USSR for past aggressions, while providing no credible guarantees against further Soviet expansionism.

Sentiment in the Senate Foreign Relations Committee, headed by Senator Frank Connors of Kentucky, was said to be divided, while the White House was exerting extraordinary pressure to gain Senate ratification of the treaty. Network opinion polls showed Eastern respondents favoring the treaty by 53 percent. The heartland opposed ratification by a three-to-two ratio. The West—meaning California—favored ratification by a slim margin.

When the debate began I was in the clinic, so I felt as though I was entering a theater during the second act. All I knew of Connors was that he was a shrewd country liberal in the Sam Ervin mode. He was also Toby Gerard's ultimate boss.

Treaty ratification, I felt, would symbolize the triumph of hope over experience.

I scanned inside pages for Sri Lanka datelines but found nothing further on Herb Porter's murder. Another terrorist victim. Forget him. In death he'd found brief celebrity, a classification I wanted to avoid as long as I possibly could.

I now had a future with Lainey to ponder and had to restrain my wilder impulses. I'd promised caution, and so far I hadn't challenged the Opposition. The scale of my reaction—when I was ready—would define the parameters of battle.

TWELVE

Even at night the Georgetown campus was active. Classrooms were lighted. Graduate and undergraduate students strolled between dorms and libraries, lugging loads of books. I was glad I was long out of the academic milieu. A frocked priest pointed out Monsignor Abelardo's residence hall and I turned into the entrance as the clock tower tolled the half hour.

The door was opened by an elderly man in a collarless black shirt, black trousers and gray felt slippers. He was bald but for a fringe of white hair that hid his ears. His nose was slightly hooked, and his eyes seemed enormous through the refraction of thick, wire-rimmed lenses. His tanned face was deeply lined as a fisherman's might be. "Mr. Graves?"

"Monsignor," I said, and went in. His sitting room was sparsely furnished: two chairs, writing table, small worn sofa, and wall shelves filled with books. A wrapped gift basket stood on the table, beside it two small glasses. Abelardo gestured and said, "Even before arrival you have made yourself welcome. Do sit where you like, Mr. Graves."

I thought he might prefer the softer sofa, so I eased into a hard-backed chair. Monsignor Abelardo undid the basket wrappings and said, "You'll join me in a cordial?"

"With pleasure."

He opened the Amaretto and half-filled the liqueur glasses. I took one with my left hand. Our glasses touched. He said, *"Pace,"* and we sipped.

Looking at my sling he said, "I trust the injury is not serious."

"It was, but I'm recovering."

"The *liquore* is excellent. You are most considerate, Mr. Graves. You exhibit a—how shall I say it?—a form of Old World courtesy seldom encountered in the New." He lifted his glass. "Shall we drink to our absent friend, Jay Catini?"

"By all means." We did. The Monsignor was gazing at me with an expression of bland serenity that reminded me of an ancient tortoise. "Have you seen Jay recently?" he asked.

"Not for . . . more than two weeks."

"I was surprised to learn that he is no longer in Washington."

I sat forward. "He's not?"

"I telephoned his office but met a series of evasions. His wife, Marietta, informed me that Jay had been transferred abroad. Rather suddenly." His gaze was unchanged.

I said, "Sudden transfers have involved several acquaintances at the workplace. So Jay's gone, too. Where, may I ask?"

"Ethiopia—Addis Ababa."

I felt my lips twist. "Overseeing famine relief, no doubt."

"No doubt. You . . . attach significance to Jay's departure."

"I do." I remembered my last conversation with him. Jeffers . . . Ali Agca . . . the futile search for accomplices. That I'd told him nothing of Sankov's confession might spare his life. "About three weeks ago I unexpectedly got involved in a special investigation. I thought Jay might be able to supply a lead or two, a name."

"And he gave you mine."

I nodded.

"Why did you think that Jay—or I—might be able to help you?"

"Because both of you were in Rome on May 13, 1981, and thereafter."

His dark pupils seemed to contract. "May thir—that was when the Turkish assassin shot His Holiness . . ." He got up and added more Amaretto to his glass. "An official inquiry? To what end?"

"Establishing Kremlin sponsorship of the attack."

He returned to the sofa. "Was it not always presumed?"

"I wasn't there, Monsignor. Was it presumed?"

One hand waved briefly, like a flipper. "*Cui bono?* The Kremlin would have benefited the most. I heard it spoken of many times."

"But you were capable of forming an independent judgment."

"I was content to leave judgment to the secular authorities. Are you Catholic, my son?"

"No, and that brings me to the next point, Monsignor. As a Protestant, could I be granted the seal of the Confessional?"

"A priest never inquires the faith of the person beyond the screen. Whatever you choose to tell me, my lips are sealed."

"I make you the same guarantee. Officially, I've been placed on sick leave, but that could change at any time. And I've been warned not to disclose what I know. So far, ten human beings have lost their lives and I want to retain mine."

"Quite naturally. Old and useless as I am, I am not eager to abandon earthly life, though I fear not death."

I told him about our Communist walk-in defector, never mentioning Sankov's name. I summarized Sankov's revelations including the alleged complicity of Vatican figures and described the deadly assault on the safehouse. I told him my hospital room had been miked, and summarized Wink Warren's visit and warnings. I said my building badge had been lifted from my wallet along with Jay's card of introduction. "So I'm not surprised Jay was sent halfway around the world. Anyone with significant knowledge of Walker's confession has been isolated or disposed of."

"You mean—murdered?"

"My chief was abruptly posted to Sri Lanka and killed in a guerrilla ambush."

"Coincidence perhaps?"

"Not to me."

"But you have no proof, Mr. Graves. Walker's confession was consumed in the fire, you say, and all recordings destroyed."

I hesitated, debating whether to tell him about the cassette, and decided I'd gone too far to hold back. "That's the general assumption, but in order to limit knowledgeability I removed the video recording of Walker's confession. I have it in a safe place."

"As a bargaining lever?"

"If it comes to that."

"And what is it you seek—revenge?"

"Revelation, the conspiracies exposed—the one against the life of John Paul II, the other to destroy Walker and eradicate all traces of his confession."

"You believe it credible, then?"

"His assassination, along with eight or nine other men, makes it so. Will you help me, Monsignor?"

"In what way?"

"Tell me who in the Vatican held such hatred for His Holiness that they were willing to advance the plot against his life by conspiring with Communist assassins."

For what seemed like a long time Monsignor Abelardo said nothing, and I saw that he was staring at a wall-set figure of the Virgin. "So long ago," he said finally, in a voice little above a whisper. "I was aware of tendencies, of disreputable, unspeakable words against the Pontiff—of a small clique that set itself against the Vicar's unexpected rigidity . . ." He sighed. "Unworthy of Christ's servants. There were such false priests—I acknowledge it with shame."

"Who were they?"

"Personages within the Holy See, who had turned from the teachings of Our Saviour and embraced secular paths to solve the problems of mankind. They were content to see the Holy Church subordinate to the dictatorship of the proletariat." His voice rose. "To see the Church become an organ of repression, to have its holy purpose perverted by cynical, Godless rulers. A Church whose priests would be little better than employees of the state, spies and informants, destroyers of the True Faith, counselors of submission and obedience, not to Christ, but to the secular state."

His voice echoed through the room. When it faded I said, "Will you name them?"

A prolonged sigh issued from his throat. "Perhaps, perhaps not. I love and respect the institution of our Church. Whatever might be used to diminish its authority is not permissible. But you have raised grave issues, my son, and I must deal with them . . . through prayer and meditation." Rising, he said, "I could wish that you had not laid this burden upon me . . . yet in all matters there is a role for truth."

"Surely," I said, "by now some of the conspirators must have died. What harm—?"

"Even were all gathered in, the problem would still confront me. I am not unsympathetic to your quest, your desire for revelation and justice, but I must search deep within myself."

Slowly I got up, realizing our conversation was ending, "You will do so?"

He nodded. "Do not press me for answers. In God's good time you will have my reply." Removing his spectacles, he polished them absently. Without them Monsignor Abelardo looked even older.

I said, "Jay asked me to tell you his family has bought a California vineyard; if the pressings are satisfactory a case will be sent you."

"A fine man," he said in a distant voice, "and of an interesting family. I will pray that no evil befalls him abroad."

"Please join my prayers with yours." We shook hands and I started out, then hesitated. "Don't call my house, Monsignor. When you want to reach me, ask Harry Bonner to phone me."

"Bonner?" His eyebrows drew together.

I gestured at the raffia basket. "Ask him to convey your thanks for the Valpolicella."

"I understand. Good night, my son."

I had walked to the University, and now as I crossed the front campus I paused before the bronze statue of Georgetown's Jesuit founder. Archbishop John Carroll, 1735–1815. As I moved on, I wondered how that resolute churchman would have answered the questions I put to the Monsignor.

Don't call me, Abelardo had said in effect; I'll call you.

When?

Through quaintly lighted streets, over narrow, uneven walks, I made my way back home.

In the morning I rented a safe deposit box in the Riggs Bank branch at the corner of Wisconsin and M Street. From a pay phone I dialed Lainey, and after six rings I hung up and walked over and down to Canal Street. I slammed the eagle knocker a few times in case she'd been showering, but after she failed to appear I used the key to go in. I took my *Skiing-Gstaad* cassette from the shelf and let myself out. Then I taxied to a Sixteenth Street VCR store and waited while three copies of my videotape were duplicated at high speed. I had the cassettes wrapped for separate mailing, and carried them off in a plastic shopping bag.

My first stop was Jerrault's law office, where his secretary greeted me in the reception room. I handed her one of the wrapped cassettes and asked her to put it in a secure file, saying, I'd convey instructions to Dorsey when he returned.

I taxied back to Georgetown and returned the original cassette to the Mountjoys' library shelf. Then I went to the bank and left a copy in my newly acquired safe deposit box. The fourth tape I set in my wall safe, and was replacing the books when the phone rang. The machine responded until I heard Joann Cereza's voice, and then I cut in. "Are we on for tonight?"

"Everything points that way."

"Let's have cocktails here. Where would you like to have dinner?"

"Do you know the Laurel Brigade Inn in Leesburg? It's a favorite of mine."

"If you'll drive."

"Of course. Five thirty too early?"

"Just right. Incidentally, I'm on my way to physiotherapy.

"How are you feeling?"

"Thanks to you, very much alive."

* * *

The second hospital session was as painful as the first, and after I'd dried off and stopped trembling I phoned Lainey and asked her to lunch with me. She suggested the City Tavern, but I wanted to avoid the likes of Wink and Sandy, so we agreed on Chez François and met there at noon.

We had escargots, sole amandine, a bottle of Pouilly Fuissé '81 and a delicately browned lemon soufflé with coffee.

"Let's see," she said, "we'll be with you Monday night, and you'll join us at the Sulgrave on Tuesday. That's firm?"

"Absolutely."

"Now that we've made our mutual confessions, dear, I want to be with you all the time. When Anniversary toasts are made on Tuesday night I'll be on the verge of tears."

"Stiff upper lip," I advised. "Like the British."

"But I'm not British—I only talk that way. And I certainly don't *think* British. Silent fortitude and bearing-up are not attributes of mine." She looked away. "It would be much more forthright to tell Peter now and cancel the Anniversary party. May I?" She turned to me expectantly.

"Forthright but shortsighted. I've too many things to resolve."

"*Dangerous* things?" Her lips trembled. "*Please* be careful, whatever you have to do, darling."

"Didn't I promise?"

We sipped coffee and after a while she said, "I've been thinking about the Paris flat, Brent. I want to redecorate and refurnish it completely. The lighting is dull and the furniture stodgy. I can bring family pieces from the country, we'll have new drapes and curtains, brighter walls . . . *d'accord?*"

"Whatever you like," I said.

"Nest-building while purging the place of Marilyn reminders."

That settled, Lainey left to keep an appointment with the framer of Peter's portrait. I walked up to Svenska on Wisconsin Avenue and selected a dozen lead-crystal highball glasses, paid with my AmEx card and arranged for giftwrapping and delivery to the Canal Street address.

Probably the last gift I'd be sending the two of them. An

engraved silver dish would have been appropriate for their Anniversary, but when the time came a dozen glasses would be easier to divide.

At home I paid bills, took a nap and shaved. By the time Joann Cereza rang, Salomé had set out the drink tray with hot canapés.

My dinner date was wearing a blue watered-silk dress with a pearl necklace and high-heeled shoes. As she sat across from me she said, "What an attractive place, Brent—for a bachelor."

"It was partly furnished when I bought it. I just added a few things." I made two whiskey sours and turned on an FM easy-listening station. Nothing wrong with Mantovani.

She said, "You don't seem to be suffering post-trauma strain."

"Only at night. The dreams are pretty bad."

"They'll pass. You're a strong man."

Before we left I said, "If you'll humor me, I'd like to have a look at what's left of the place where I was shot."

"Is that wise?"

"Hundreds of people drive past it every day."

We got into her BMW convertible and I gave her directions. With the top up, the small interior space lent a sense of intimacy. Once across the Potomac, she used her mobile phone to call her answering service and say she'd be dining at the Laurel Brigade Inn.

South of Fort Belvoir she said, "What was it like when you were picked up in Moscow, Brent?"

"Unexpected. I was walking about four blocks from the Embassy and noticed a man walking toward me. As we passed, he jammed a paper into my pocket. A trailing car braked and four plainclothesmen piled out and grabbed me. They took me to Levfortovo, put me in an interrogation room and announced I was going to be shot as a spy—unless I cooperated. I said they couldn't do that to a diplomat. They said they could, no one would ever know. They pushed me around, but nothing to mark me up. The whole thing was halfhearted, a performance staged to justify my expulsion. I refused to sign a confession and after six hours they drove me back to the Embassy. Next day a note from the Foreign Ministry said I'd been declared *persona non grata*, so I left Moscow and reported in. Elapsed time five months."

"What kind of a reception were you given?"

"Nothing to warm one's heart. A week's debriefing, a medical checkup and an assignment to Honduras."

"Working with guerrillas?"

"Sorting out logistic problems: inventorying boots, uniforms, weapons, radios, field equipment. My heart wasn't in it. Then the program closed down and I came back for another half-assed assignment—Counterintelligence. I knew less about it than the average typist."

"You sound disillusioned—if not bitter."

"*You* got out, didn't you? Anyway, the whole thing's getting old. I'm viewed with suspicion and my usefulness is ended. A wise man knows when it's time to leave—too many stay on and on." I was thinking of Selwyn Bates.

"And you were almost killed."

I said nothing. I was looking ahead at the roadside for landmarks. "Should be just beyond the next hill," I told her.

Joann eased back on the pedal, and when we glided down the far side of the hill I sat forward, perplexed. "Slow down," I said, and pointed at the entrance posterns. Beyond them there was no guardhouse. The estate grounds were fenced with gleaming chainlink. Where I had expected to see rubble of the fire-destroyed safehouse stood a long building divided into wooden box stalls. Horses grazed in the pasture.

Arched over the fieldstone posterns a sign read: LOUDON STABLES. BOARDING AND INSTRUCTION.

"Bulldozed and built over," I said, hoarsely, and felt a chill run down my spine. "Nothing left to see."

On the road to Leesburg we didn't say much. Joann had her own thoughts, and I was thinking about the Firm's speed in eliminating all traces of the safehouse. No evidence.

As we pulled into the Laurel Brigade's parking area Joann said, "Suppose there's a perfectly innocent explanation, Brent? There are always eager buyers for country real estate. The Firm offered the place for sale and the owner converted it."

"Possible," I said, "but after what I've gone through I don't have much faith in innocence." We left the BMW in one of the few remaining spaces, a dark area thirty or forty yards from the Inn's entrance. The hostess seated us and left our menus. I ordered a rare steak, Joann chose lamb chops and we enjoyed a second round of whiskey sours. I'd always thought of the Inn as a luncheon spot for senior citizens and families with children, but by night the tables were candle-lit, the atmosphere low-key and intimate. During dinner Joann talked about her childhood, the closeness of her family, the shock of her father's disappearance, her struggle through medical school.

Her profession was satisfying, she said, and sufficient reward for all she'd gone through. I classified her as an intelligent, sensitive and dedicated young woman and found myself reluctant to leave when the check arrived.

I paid the cashier with my AmEx card, and we walked outside toward where she'd left her car. Behind me I heard the cashier call, "Your card, sir. You left it."

"Seems I haven't got things anywhere near together," I said.

"You've got a lot on your mind. I'll get the car."

I went to the cashier, thanked her and put the card in my wallet. As I left the Inn I saw Joann get behind the wheel. The interior light showed her fitting key into ignition lock. Then night became day as the car disintegrated in a hellish blast, an incandescent ball of flame surrounding the wreckage. I was momentarily stunned. I started toward the flames but arms held me back. Diners crowded around me; shocked, frightened voices pierced the night. Flames crackled, leaping high above the hedge rows. The nearest car caught fire and a man swore loudly.

I stood, numbly staring at the consuming flames. Tears filled my eyes, overflowed down my cheeks. She wasn't the main target, I was. And because of me she was dead.

But for the cashier's call I'd be dead, too, burnt to a crisp beside her.

Too weak to stand, I sank to my knees, closed my eyes and wept.

BOOK THREE

THIRTEEN

The Loudon County police traced me through my AmEx number on the Inn's charge slip. Lieutenant Timothy Grogan was at my door by ten the next morning. Salomé got me out of bed, and when I'd seen his credentials I let him in. After we were seated in the library he got to the point. "Why didn't you stay around last night, Mr. Graves?"

"I was in shock, Lieutenant, and I didn't know anything that would have . . . helped."

"Isn't that for the police to decide?" He got out his notebook. "Describe your movements after the explosion."

I swallowed. "After fire trucks arrived I walked to the road, found a taxi in Leesburg and came home. With the help of sleeping pills I managed to pass out—until you arrived."

"You felt no sense of obligation to stay around and—"

"What could I do? Joann Cereza was my doctor. Dinner at the Inn was to celebrate my recovery from . . ." I gestured at my arm sling.

"Were you involved with her? Romantically?"

"It was the first time we'd ever been out together." First and last.

"Know anything about her personal life? Boyfriends? She ever mention anyone she feared?"

"We weren't on those terms, Lieutenant. She did surgery at four hospitals. All she ever said to me indicated she had very little private life." I swallowed again. "If any."

"Know her surviving family?"

"They came from Venezuela is all I know. She went to Georgetown . . ." My voice trailed off. I was still groggy from the pills—pills she'd given me. God, I was going to miss her. Number eleven in the body count.

Grogan cleared his throat, looked up as Salomé brought in a coffee tray and poured for us. After adding sugar to his cup he said, "Lived here long?"

"A year."

"According to credit references you're an employee of the Federal Government. What part would that be?"

"The part that occupies that big building on the other side of the river."

"I see. Interesting. Is that generally known?"

"I hope not."

"I'll keep it quiet. Though it does suggest you might have enemies, sir."

"Doesn't everyone?"

"Enemies who would rig dynamite to your car ignition?"

"Wasn't my car, Lieutenant."

"True. But perhaps that wasn't important to them. Who knew where you and the doctor were dining?"

"I had no reason to tell anyone. I don't know who Joann told . . . probably no one."

"Are you married?"

"Divorced." The Opposition must have tapped my phone since I last checked it and overheard our plans to eat at the Laurel Brigade. I'd have to be more careful.

"Are you thinking of bringing the FBI into this? Assault on a federal officer?"

"I wasn't injured. When Joann turned the key I was thirty yards away."

"So the cashier told us. And how she'd called you back." He folded his notebook and put it away in an inside pocket. "Otherwise *you* could be the suspect I'm looking for." He drank the rest of his coffee. "Care to speculate who killed Dr. Cereza, and why?"

"Last night—afterward—I tried to put it together. Came up with nothing."

He laid his card on the coffee table. "No offense, Mr. Graves, but I think you have information you're not willing to share. When you decide to help clear things up, call me."

"If I come across anything I will."

He stood up. "I appreciate you seeing me outside my jurisdiction. Good coffee. Hope your arm shapes up."

"Collarbone." I went with him to the door.

As I watched him walk to his car I thought that if anyone *could* track the killers, Grogan was a good candidate. But no one was going to find them and they would never stand trial.

I was outmatched before I even entered the ring.

Following my usual routine seemed the prudent thing to do. The hospital therapy room reminded me all too keenly of Joann, and when the attendant tried to talk about the doctor's violent death I shook my head mutely, afraid my voice would reveal the sorrow I felt, my fury at her killers.

Although pain had drained me, I didn't rest on the recovery cot. I left the hospital and stood on the sidewalk, wondering what to do. I felt helpless, a bug under a microscope, watched, monitored, my moves predicted.

I had to get away from Washington, make things harder for the Opposition. Try to take charge of my life while preserving it.

Two blocks east of the hospital I noticed a spaghetti house set down in an English basement. I went in and sat at the bar. My hand was still trembling as I lifted a double Black Label. The barlady said, "Care for a menu, sir?"

"Little early for lunch." I sipped a water chaser and downed the rest of my Scotch. I paid, and she said, "Have a good day."

"Always that hope." I went up Pennsylvania Avenue and walked a while, not knowing where I was going. Or caring.

Lunch. Selwyn Bates had mentioned lunching at his club.

He was a creature of habit; perhaps he'd go to the Cosmos today.

I took a taxi to Massachussetts Avenue and strolled over to the Cosmos. Limousines were pulling up at the entrance, depositing members and guests and moving on. A few pedestrians turned in. I recognized one of Dorsey Gerrault's senior partners, a former member of the Appellate Bench. I wished Dorsey were available to counsel me, but his return was weeks away.

As I thought about Dorsey I remembered Tobias Gerard. He was close to Senator Connors, a protégé, I'd heard. Toby and I disliked each other, but as far as I knew his ethics had never been questioned. Dorsey would have told me otherwise.

While I was considering Gerard as a possible confidant I saw Selwyn Bates drive into the club parking area. I crossed the street, and as Selwyn walked back toward the entrance I hailed him. He stopped, stared at me with a blank expression and said, "Brent, Wherever have you been?"

"Here and there. Taking a constitutional at the moment."

Gazing at my arm sling, he came toward me. "How *are* you? Word has it you're hospitalized. What the devil happened? I've taken your place, you know?"

"Have you? Good show."

He glanced uncertainly at the entrance, then back at me. "Feel up to lunch?"

I nodded. "But not here. I'm on sick leave and supposedly *hors de combat*. Wouldn't like colleagues to see me enjoying myself. Let's try the Ritz-Carlton."

"Fine. This *is* a pleasant surprise, Brent."

As we strolled toward the hotel, Selwyn said, "Rotten about Herb Porter."

"Wretched. And unexpected."

"Yes. He was in line for a top job, you know."

We turned in at the hotel and entered its Jockey Club Restaurant. Bates ordered a glass of white wine and said, "Can't get sozzled or stay away from the office too long."

"Glad you're taking my old job seriously."

His forehead crinkled. "Think you'll be replacing me—when you're fit again?"

"Not a chance." I told the waiter I'd have wine, too, and then we ordered lunch.

After a while I said, "What top job was Herb in line for?"

"COPS, no less. He'd have been good, too. Agree?"

"Fantastic." I sipped from my chilled glass. "I don't know Crosby," I said, referring to the incumbent COPS.

"I've met him socially—he's a Cosmos member, of course—but never in line of work. Merle's up there in the stratosphere, rankwise, far beyond range of this mere mortal."

Our veal scallopini arrived and we dug in. After a while I said, "I never got a feel for him. The Firm doesn't circulate c.v.'s."

"Well, he never had a Station, you know. Academic background. Our Director implanted him when he took over. I understand Crosby studied for holy orders at one time, married a former nun."

"So we have to feel that the Church's loss is the Firm's gain."

He nodded. "Crosby keeps close ties to the Church. Handles Catholic liaison—Vatican, Papal Nunciature—I've seen him lunching here with the Nuncio."

"Well," I said, "considering his background, there's surely no one better qualified for the job. I suppose he'll be Director one day."

"Guess so. I've heard he's good with Congress, and that's essential."

"Not like the bad old Cold War days when Dulles either charmed them or told them to go pick raspberries. No, with Congress, it has to be mutual trust and respect," I said unctuously.

He forked marsala over his veal. "After you recover, what are your career plans?"

"None, really. As always, my destiny is in the hands of my betters."

He sipped his wine. "Never heard just how you were injured. Is it permissible to inquire?"

"Well, confidentially, I was down at the Farm for a night exfiltration exercise—Skyhook pickup. The plane came in too damn fast and jerked me up too hard. Shoulder dislocated, ribs bashed when the pilot failed to clear a treetop." I shook my head disgustedly. "They kept me at the Farm's clinic for a while, then brought me home." I finished my wine. "I was asked not to say anything about the foul-up—too embarrassing all 'round. More wine?"

"Why not? Guess I can metabolize a second glass."

"Incidentally, remember me to Mrs. Talman, will you?"

"I would, Brent, but she's no longer around." He paused. "Resigned without notice and took a better-paying slot at Commerce, where her husband works."

"How fortunate," I remarked. "With her husband close by, her productivity should improve. And they can have equal use of the car. Leave it to our all-seeing Government to work out things advantageously for all concerned. Any other changes, transfers, ExLevel promotions?"

"Well, Jay Catini's gone—Addis Ababa, I hear. Probably because he speaks Italian."

"Probably . . . Speaking of Jay and the Rome desk, how's Fred Jeffers doing?"

"Okay, far as I know . . . Why?"

"Last I heard, Fred was under heavy criticism for underproduction, failure to fulfill the established norm. Herb, Jay and I decided he'd do better on a research project we devised. We sent out a cable to that effect. I thought you might know what he's working on."

"Sorry, Brent, don't know a thing." He dabbed at his mouth and looked around to see if he knew anyone among the diners. "Since we're together in a relaxed way, I'm going to ask you a very personal question, and I ask pardon in advance. If you care to answer I might be able to benefit . . . guide myself based on your experience."

"I have few secrets, Selwyn. What's the question?"

He swallowed. "There was a prevalent rumor you'd turned down an assignment to Afghanistan or Pakistan, working with the

Mujaheddin against the Sovs."

"That's true. If you're wondering why, it relates to my short tour in Central America, where I was buried after Moscow. Our Government stopped supporting the troops I was working with and hung them out to dry. Bad faith, Selwyn. I figured the Afghan resistance was next on the abandon list. So, having gone through it once, I said no thanks to a second opportunity."

He thought it over. "I guess it didn't help your career."

"Hardly at all." I didn't want to tell him I'd been sent to the shit job he'd been given; why make him feel lousy?

Uncertainly, he said, "Well . . . thanks for telling me. I appreciate your frankness." I signaled for the check, and while I was paying, Selwyn said, "Next time we'll lunch at my club, Brent. Maybe see each other more frequently."

"I'd like that," I lied, "but I'm signed up for a tendon tightening operation in Boston. Shoulder hasn't responded well and there's a Mass General surgeon who's done a lot of work for the Patriots and the B.C. ball club. Specializes in joint injuries."

"Hope he does right by you." He looked at his wristwatch. "Let me know. Sorry, I've got to move along. Been great. Thanks again. Take care."

"I'll try," I said, and sat there watching him go. I could count on Selwyn Bates spreading word of my forthcoming operation and prolonged recovery, and that suited my plans. Misdirection could provide a substantial advantage for me.

Before leaving the hotel I thought of calling Monsignor Abelardo and asking what progress he'd made through introspection, meditation and divine guidance. I decided not to. He had promised to get back to me with his decision, and I was willing to believe a churchman's vow.

Instead, I used the men's room and stopped at a pay phone to dial the Senate Office Building. The switchboard put me through to Toby Gerard's office, and when I heard his dry voice I identified myself.

"Is Dorsey Jerrault finally available?" he asked.

"Not to me, but this is another matter, Toby. You're in the investigating business and I think I've come up with something you can sink your teeth into. Red meat." I waited a few moments. "If you're interested."

"I'll be interested to hear what you have to say."

"On a fully confidential basis."

"I have no problem with that. Ah . . . just so I'll know what to expect, are you whistle-blowing?"

"Maybe. Pick an empty office and I'll be there in twenty minutes."

He left the phone briefly, returned and gave me a room number. "No stenos, just the two of us, right?"

"You've got it." I hung up, and let the doorman whistle up a taxi.

When I entered the designated meeting room, Toby Gerard was seated at the far end of the table, alone. No recording equipment visible, no notepads.

"Lock the door," he said, "and we won't be bothered."

I did, and walked the length of the table, took the chair directly opposite him. He glanced at my arm sling and said, "No one told me you were injured, Brent. Sorry about that." He produced a pack of cigarettes, offered me one, and when I declined, lit it for himself. "My naturally suspicious mind," he said, "suggests that you're here for a trade-off."

"Am I? Your report's been prepared, Toby, without my testimony. I'm redundant to your investigation."

He smiled briefly. "Dorsey Jerrault is worth whatever you pay him, probably more. Well, it was worth a try, Brent. My cards are on the table and I don't even hold a one-eyed Jack. What's in your hand?"

"Quite a lot," I said, "but before that, a couple of questions. First, you enjoy the confidence of Senator Connors?"

"I flatter myself I do."

"And at the moment you're—between jobs for the Committee?"

"True. Another underemployed lawyer clinging to the Hill."

I opened my wallet and extracted a dollar bill, pushed it toward him. "You are now my attorney," I said, "entitling me to a confidential relationship."

He glanced at the currency. "I don't know that I want to be your attorney, Brent. We're from opposite ends of the political spectrum. You were a warrior, I was peacenik. What do we have in common?"

"Among other things you're cleared for sensitive information—but that's just for openers. What we share is a zeal for truth and justice. That's significant."

He picked up the dollar bill and pocketed it. "Confidentiality is established and I won't breach it—can't without your permission." He flicked ash from his cigarette. "This concerns your present employers, I take it."

"I'll let you be the judge." I wanted a cigarette badly, but even in death Joann's injunction was going to be obeyed.

"Around three weeks ago," I said, "there was an armed assault on a defector safehouse in Virginia. The defector was killed, as were eight guards and safehouse personnel. The house was destroyed by fire. Did you read about it?"

His eyes were bright with interest. "I didn't see the story."

"There wasn't one. Since then, two other deaths have occurred, both related to that massacre."

"How do you know?"

"Because I was there. The sole survivor."

FOURTEEN

The room was utterly silent save for the sound of my voice. I had Toby's full attention. He didn't interrupt with questions but let me tell the entire story—Sankov's revelation and initial efforts to corroborate it, the shooting and burning, my recovery with Joann's help, my miked room, Warren's warnings, Herb Porter's convenient death, the theft of my badge, Joann's murder, my conversation with Abelardo, the transfers of Catini and Gertrude Talman . . . "Both verified," I said, "as recently as lunch today."

Toby Gerard slumped down in his chair, as I imagined he'd done at law school lectures. I poured a glass of water and drank. Finally he breathed, "God almighty! Do you realize the implications of this?"

"No," I said, "I'm sure I don't. Except that it's all connected and it's part of a major cover-up. That bomb wasn't meant for Dr. Cereza alone—I was the primary target."

"Absolutely—I saw that story this morning, read it because my wife and I often have Sunday brunch at the Laurel Brigade Inn."

"Of course," I said, "I *could* have read the account and fabricated everything I've told you."

"We'll discard that straight off. You have copies of the confession tape. How soon can I see it?"

"How soon do you want?"

"Like now." He got up and pulled on his coat.

I drank another glass of water and got to my feet. "The bank is closed, so the most accessible copy is at my place."

"I'll drive you."

On the way to Georgetown, Toby steered through afternoon traffic with purposeful intensity. Crossing the Rock Creek Bridge, he said, "It's obvious that by bulldozing the house's remains and selling the property, the Firm hoped to eliminate any trace of the safehouse. And discredit any witness. But land records seldom lie. Ownership can be traced, and somewhere there will be photographs of the house before it was destroyed . . . You might sketch it for me."

"Sure," I said, "but don't place too much trust in those county files. Anyone able to suppress news coverage of the massacre and fire would have little trouble filching deeds from a county office."

"And you don't know Neville's name."

"Or any of the others. Work names were used at the safehouse—basic precaution."

"And Porter's dead. God!"

"*Sent into the forefront of the hottest battle,*" I quoted.

"Second Samuel," he said, to my surprise. "Yes, I stayed in divinity school until the war was over. I guess that makes you think less of me."

"You weren't the only one," I said. "Every man answers to his own conscience."

"I know," he said. "I know," and said nothing more.

He turned into my drive and we walked to my front door. I rang several times, but Salomé didn't come. I reached under the doormat for my spare key but found nothing. "The maid is probably shopping," I said. "We'll take the back way."

I lifted the garden-gate latch and went to the kitchen door, peered inside.

Salomé lay partway under the kitchen table amid a scattering of vegetables. There was an ugly gash over her temple, a pool of blood under her head.

I kicked the back door open and we rushed in.

The front door slammed.

Toby Gerard phoned for a police ambulance while I gave Salomé mouth-to-mouth resuscitation. Before taking her away on a stretcher a young paramedic said, "Her breathing is strong, and she hasn't lost much blood. These things generally look worse than they are. I'll have the E.R. doctor give you a call when she's stabilized."

"I'll appreciate that, and I'll pay all charges, whatever they are."

After the ambulance whined away, a sergeant from the Seventh Precinct stayed on. He identified himself as Gordon Bream. I told him I was the house owner and employer of the injured woman. He took down our names, and that of Toby Gerard, whom I identified as my attorney. "Guess you scared him, or them, off," he said, "punching the door in like that. Either of you try to follow?"

"I started to," Toby said. "By the time I got to the front door there was no one on the street."

"Too bad. House is pretty much messed up. Maybe we better look it over—for your insurance claim."

I hadn't had time to leave the kitchen, so all of us toured the house. The first thing I noticed was that all pictures had been yanked from the walls, upholstery slit here and there, stuffing pulled out. The dining room chest of drawers was open, but as far as I could tell none of my silver was missing.

"In Georgetown," Sergeant Bream said, "they're generally after table silver and jewels. Usually leave the TVs. I see yours in place."

Upstairs we checked the bedrooms. Mattresses had been overturned and slashed open, bureau and table drawers opened, contents spilled on the floor. Closet clothing had been pulled off hangers, pockets turned inside out. Bream said, "Looking for cash most likely. Probably some crack heads. Anything stolen?"

"So far, nothing."

"But," said Toby, "that's subject to later inventory—when my client is up to it. He's just out of the hospital."

"Noticed the sling. Car smash you?"

"Fell down the stairs." I gestured at them, and we walked down to the library.

Books had been swept from the shelves, baring my wall safe. "Touch nothing," Bream said. "We need to dust for prints." He toed a mallet and cold chisel on the floor. The burglar had managed to chop off the combination dial, but the safe door was shut. I stuck a kitchen match in the crevice and pried, thinking it would open if the lock had been defeated. It stayed firmly in place.

Bream said, "Probably have to torch that open."

"I wouldn't want that—papers inside. Can you recommend a reliable locksmith?"

"Well, we're not supposed to, but I've always heard Bryerson's gives good service. But nothing 'til we've dusted here." With a handkerchief he picked up the telephone and called the D.C. Crime Lab fingerprint unit. After replacing the receiver he said, "Slack day in D.C.—they'll be here within an hour. Then you can call your locksmith."

He walked back to the kitchen and Toby expelled breath. "Like Oliver Hardy used to say—a fine kettle of fish you've gotten me into."

"Aren't we in the same kettle?"

"Looks like. Is the tape in your safe?"

"Should be."

"And that's what they were after?"

I though about it. Since nobody except yourself and Abelardo knows it exists, I think it was a recon raid—see if I had anything relevant."

"It was a damn determined effort." He took out a cigarette, lit it and sat on the slashed sofa. "Two hours ago I was thinking it was time to leave the Committee and cash in at a law firm, then you walked in. Jesus, Brent."

"So you'll stay with the Committee."

"How else can we get to the bottom of this?"

Sergeant Bream came back, shaking his head. "Looks like straight burglary, interrupted in progress. Of course there's bodily assault on the lady, too. They put her down and had the place to themselves while they ransacked it." He looked at me. "When did you leave here?"

"Between ten-thirty and eleven." I didn't tell him he was the second cop to visit me that day.

"So the place was empty except for the lady for as much as four-five hours. Any idea how they got in?"

"I suppose Salomé answered the door," I said, and saw Toby's reproving glance. We both knew they'd entered with my poorly concealed key.

"Then I won't trouble you any longer. I guess you know where the Seventh is—drop by any time you want to amend the complaint."

"Thank you, Sergeant." I walked him to the door.

"Sorry about this," he said, "but with all these street people on drugs the average citizen is bound to become a victim."

I nodded agreement, bolted the door behind him and went back to Toby.

We poured drinks at the sideboard, and steadied our nerves with a second. Toby said, "How are you going to get all this cleaned up?"

"Haven't the first idea." But I thought of Lainey. Maybe she knew someone, a cleaning team that could come in. Or was that up to the insurance company?

It occurred to me that Lainey might have read about Dr. Cereza's death and phoned me—impulsively and unwisely. I went to the answering machine and open the lid.

The message tape was gone.

The burglars and whoever they were working for now knew all my callers. My mouth went dry as I thought of the possible danger to Lainey. Then I remembered she never left her name when she called. The Opposition might have her voice, but no other identification. That made me feel a lot better.

The fingerprint team arrived and began working around the safe. While they were doing it, I phoned Bryerson's and explained the problem. They promised to send someone as soon as they could.

"Next," said Toby, "your insurance company. They'll know what to do."

When I finally got through to the adjuster's office he told me not to touch anything. They'd want photographs of the damage, and he'd be over before five.

Toby said, "I don't think you should stay here tonight."

"I'll manage."

When the locksmith arrived I set him to changing door locks while the forensic team finished up in the library. The leader said, "These tools yours?"

"No."

"We'll take them as evidence. I guess you know that safe's beyond repair."

"And badly located," I said. "Came with the house. I don't think I'll replace it."

He summoned his partner and they left. The locksmith came and said, "Ready for the safe?"

"Any time."

He handed me keys to the new locks and went to his truck for a toolbox. The insurance adjuster arrived with an instant camera and began nosing around the house, snapping flash shots here and there. He took Toby's name and that of Sergeant Bream and said he'd pick up a copy of the police report at the Seventh Precinct. "Meanwhile," he said, "you're entitled to temporary lodging at a hotel. Meals, too."

"That's nice. I'm new to all this. Do I get replacement furnishings? Who takes care of cleaning and straightening up?"

"I'll have men here in the morning. They'll remove what's destroyed and damaged, bring back replacements maybe the same day." He smiled. "Let's hope, huh?" He gave me a form to sign, and departed. While the locksmith was banging away at the safe Toby and I withdrew to stiffen our drinks. Presently the locksmith called that the safe door was open. I peered into it while he was writing out my bill. I paid and thanked him, and when he was gone, I began clearing out the contents.

The VHS cassette was there, still wrapped and undamaged. I handed it to Toby. Next I took out my personal emergency items, passports, money envelopes, divorce decree and finally the remaining HK pistol and magazines.

Toby said, "You have a license for that?"

"Standard government permit, good in all fifty states."

He tapped the cassette. "Unless I can be of help here, I'm going to take this home and watch it." He glanced at the telephone. "I'd call you except . . . Better you call me later from somewhere else."

"What time?"

"Seven?"

I nodded and he downed the last of his drink. "I've been trying to plot a secure course of action. I'd like to fill the Senator in right away."

"From what I read the Senator's heavily embroiled in the Soviet treaty hearings. I'd rather you approached him when he's disengaged . . . and when there's more of a package to show him."

"I guess you're right. The hearings could go on for another month or so. He's got lobbyists, pro and con, beating down his door." He glanced at me. "I suppose you're against the Mutual Non-Aggression Treaty."

"As written, it's a crock of shit."

"Hmm."

"Toby, let's drop it. Is the Senator close to the Church?"

"His wife drags him to Mass occasionally. Knows some local church dignitaries."

"But he's not especially close to—let's say Vatican affairs."

"Not that I know of. Is it important?"

"There's a Church connection to all this, Toby. I'm hoping Monsignor Abelardo will tell me what he knows—and only me."

He nodded thoughtfully. "The Senator visits Ireland every year or so, makes ritual pronouncements in favor of Irish freedom and the IRA, but I've never thought he was emotionally involved. Besides, his state isn't markedly Catholic." He lighted another cigarette. "What I can't come to grips with is the Firm's role in all this. Is it the whole organization or a few crazies trying to suppress Sankov's confession, and ordering all the killing?"

"I can't unravel it either. That's why I turned to you. I don't have subpoena powers—the Committee does."

He said, "You're in serious danger, Brent. I can arrange to have U.S. Marshals guard you."

"And restrict my movements?" I shook my head. "In a safehouse I could be pinpointed—like Sankov. Thanks, but I think safety lies in flight."

"Where to?" His expression became concerned.

"When I get there I'll let you know."

"Damn, Brent, I need you here. You're the key to all this."

"Hey, I'm not backing out, just taking refuge. When you really need me I'll come back."

He stared at the Sankov cassette and I sensed his conflicting emotions.

I got my checkbook from the litter of my desk drawer, sat down and wrote out a check to Salomé Guignan for $5,000. Handing it to Toby, I said, "D.C. General is out of your way, but I'd appreciate your leaving this with my maid. Tell her I'm deeply sorry about what happened, and not to worry about the house. She's not to come back until she's fully recovered. And leave her your card, Toby. Be her contact until things straighten out." If they ever do, I thought.

Toby folded the check in his billfold. "Your house insurance will help with her hospital bills, you know."

"I want her to have this for now. Make sure she gets first-rate attention, private room, TV, the works."

"Glad to. And you'll call me around seven?"

I repeated that I would, and went with him to his car. We shook hands without saying anything more and I watched him back down and drive away. Events had dissolved any antagonism that was left over from the hearing. I felt I could depend on Toby Gerard.

At my desk I sketched the safehouse as well as I could remember it: two stories, four windows on each floor, chimneys at both ends of the house. I indicated where the entrance guardhouse had been, added a few more details and folded the sheet into an envelope that I addressed to Toby's Senate office.

Near Smyth's Apothecary I dropped the letter in a mailbox and continued on to Canal Street, hoping to find the Mountjoys at home.

FIFTEEN

Peter gripped my left hand warmly. "Brent! What a pleasant surprise. I was beginning to think our paths might never cross again. Lainey, Brent's here," he called.

She emerged from the kitchen, bussed me on the cheek and said, "We were just having drinks. Scotch for you?"

"Please. I came because I couldn't call—phone busted." I told them about the burglary—a sanitized version—and they listened in horror. Peter said, "I really must install a security system here, I've postponed too long. And being away so much, I'll feel better knowing that Lainey's safe."

"Good idea," I said. "The Towpath brings all kinds."

Lainey mixed our drinks—mine with ice—and we sat in the living room. Peter lifted his glass. "Destruction to our enemies, perdition to your thieves." We drank to that, and he said, "We've a spare bed, you know, and you're more than welcome to it." Without looking at Lainey I said I'd prefer sleeping at home while things straightened out. Peter said, "I'd want to do the same,

Brent. Anyway, the offer's there. Now tell me how you got bashed up."

I repeated the Skyhook story and Peter accepted it, saying he hoped the Firm was paying my medical bills. I said that part was taken care of and I was in better shape than Salomé.

"Poor dear," Lainey said. "I think I should visit her, try to cheer her up."

"That would be most kind. Particularly since I'll have to be away for a month or so. Repair surgery in Boston." I saw Lainey's face tighten.

"Then you'll miss our party," Peter said.

"Afraid so—but I'll be with you in spirit." The liquor warmed me and I began to relax for the first time in many hours. It was good to be with friends. I felt close to Peter, much closer to his wife. "While I'm away, feel free to use my car—or the house for that matter. Cars and houses need to be used."

Peter nodded. "Strange that nothing was stolen."

"I had money in the safe, but they hadn't broken into it when I arrived. The police put it down to drug addicts." I sipped from my glass. Unless Lainey mentioned Dr. Cereza, I wasn't going to. But I found myself gazing at the cassette shelves. As long as the Opposition didn't know my cassette was there, the Mountjoys were safe.

Unless they had discovered my romance with Lainey.

The glow of a table lamp outlined Peter's youthful, aristocratic profile, and I reflected that he looked not unlike Leslie Howard in *The Petrified Forest*. I felt an urge to tell him about Sankov and the killings, but confiding in MI-6 was out of the question. That knowledge would only endanger Peter without improving my prospects of survival.

And I had Lainey to think of. Preserve and protect.

She said, "I was just tossing salad, Brent. You'll share dinner with us?"

"With pleasure."

Peter stretched out his long legs. "How pleasant to spend an evening at home, no traveling, no diplomatic fuss to suffer through."

We drank to that, then Lainey set the dining table, produced a large salad bowl, and Peter uncorked wine. After dinner I took my leave, and Lainey's handclasp was especially firm. "How soon are you off?" she asked tightly.

"Day or so."

Standing beside his wife, Peter said, "You'll let us know how the operation goes, of course?"

"Of course."

"We'll miss you," Lainey said, and left the doorway.

Peter smiled indulgently. "Sometimes I think she worries about you as much as she worries about me. Take care of yourself."

"You, too."

I walked to Smyth's and telephoned Monsignor Abelardo's room. No answer. I was about to leave when I remembered Toby Gerard. The phone book showed an address in Cleveland Park. I dialed and Toby answered. He was excited. "Fantastic stuff, Brent. God, what an absolute goldmine that tape is! You, Sankov, the whole thing . . . the Senator will go ape when he sees it!"

"Eventually. The point is, you're now a believer."

"The tape clinches everything you told me."

"Except the killings."

"We'll develop that. I can't believe nine corpses can be disposed of with no record, no witnesses."

"Hope you're right," I said. "Did you see Salomé?"

"Yes, and she's more than grateful. Doc said she'll be able to leave in four or five days."

"Take care of her, will you?"

"Glad to. She's good people, Brent."

I said, "Wherever I go, I'll stay in touch."

"I'll count on it."

I left Smyth's and continued on to my house. As I turned in at the walk I glanced at my Porsche and remembered I'd offered it to Peter and Lainey. So it was my responsibility to make sure it was clean. Only twenty-four hours ago I'd seen Joann's BMW blow to bits, and the memory pierced like arrows.

I unlocked my front door, found a flashlight in closet storage and started back to my car. Then I realized I'd need both hands and arms, so I went to the medicine cabinet and swallowed a muscle relaxant pill and a Darvocet capsule to suppress pain. I went to the Porsche.

A streetlight gave some illumination, but not enough for my purpose. Without touching the body I shined my flash into the interior, back and front, peered into the exhaust pipe, deep as the light could penetrate and lay down on my back.

Wriggling slowly under the chassis, I checked the frame for trembler bombs, changing position until I had examined the entire underside. Nothing that shouldn't be there.

Bending over the engine hood, I played the light up and down the closure crack, saw something that reflected back. It was down near the handle lift, a very thin line that glinted under the light. I switched off the flashlight and returned to my storage closet. From my few household tools I selected a needle-nose wirecutter and went back to the Porsche.

Sweat dripped from my face. Should I phone the D.C. bomb squad or investigate alone? Whether or not a bomb was found, the police would ask questions. Questions I was unprepared to answer. Moreover, I had had enough police attention for one day—for a lifetime. I wiped perspiration from my face, and with the light in one hand, the cutter in the other, I very slowly lifted the engine cover. Half an inch was all I needed. Carefully, I fitted the wire-cutter's nose into the space until its sharp edges were around the line. Then I closed them and felt the line seperate.

I was still alive.

I sat back and wet dry lips. I could feel my shirt clinging to my body. I sucked in air, waited while my pulse stopped pounding and raised the metal cover until I could see inside.

My pliers had severed a nylon fishing line. It trailed to the engine block, where it ended in a spring detonator.

The detonator was wired into four taped sticks of dynamite.

Another detonator was wired to a spark plug and grounded on the engine block. Fail-safe. Lifting the engine cover would have blown the dynamite. Turning the ignition key would have done the same. Twin roads to hell.

My pulse was pounding again. Bending forward, I snipped the electrical connections and lifted out the bomb. I pulled out both detonators and disarmed the spring exploder. In my hands I had two detonators and four sticks of dynamite. What to do with them? Without detonators the dynamite was inert. I could toss it into the river to disintegrate harmlessly. The copper detonator tubes would last longer, much longer.

I heard approaching footsteps and dropped the engine cover. I concealed the dynamite in my sling and looked around.

A middle-aged couple was strolling a mustard-color terrier. A Dandie Dinmont. "Nice evening" the man said as they passed.

"Splendid," I said. "Makes one glad to be alive."

With a neighborly wave of the hand he walked on.

I took my lethal equipment into the house, placed everything on a side-slashed cushion and made myself a drink. Then I bolted the front door and stepped around the strewn vegetables to make sure the kitchen door was locked.

Back in the library I sat down and thought about watching cable news. But I had the bomb to dispose of. I looked up at the ransacked bookshelves, and saw the safe door slanting open.

I gazed at the dynamite and the detonators and had an idea.

On the kitchen table I cut one of the brick-colored sticks in half and inserted a detonator in the open end. I laid it on the safe bottom and rigged it to the spring exploder, using nylon remnant line to fix it to the safe door. I closed the safe and wiped fingerprint powder from the surface.

I estimated that the half-stick would take out the shelves, the safe and whoever opened the door. I went down into my unfinished basement, filled a bucket with water and dropped the remaining dynamite in it. I placed the copper detonator in a Mason jar and covered it with tile-cleaning acid. When it began to bubble I walked away.

In the kitchen I perked extra-strong coffee and carried percolator and cup upstairs. I had a hard and painful time boosting the mattress onto the bed frame and arranging the covers. That accomplished, I moved a night table against the wall, disconnected the lamp cord, closed my bedroom door and wrapped the lamp cord end around the door handle.

Two traps set. Downstairs lights off. I shoved the chaise-longue over the hinge side of the door, poured a cup of coffee and turned off the ceiling light. I made myself comfortable on the chaise, flashlight by my left hand, 9mm pistol under my right.

The combination of pills, liquor and letdown made me feel utterly exhausted. I yawned and closed my eyes.

Waiting.

Glass tinkled.

A delicate sound, like wind chimes, came from below.

My clock showed 2:13. I tensed, sat forward and listened.

Nothing.

Then the slight creaking of my front door. My pulse raced, throat tightened. Someone was in the house.

My left hand closed around the flashlight, my right gripped the HK's knurled handle.

I sat perfectly still.

Stairs creaked as risers took body weight. Perspiration oozed down my face. The burglar/bomber had returned to finish his assignment.

I'd thought he would.

My night vision was good. I could see the outline of everything in the room: the bed, the lamp on the night table, even the wire that tied it to the door.

Soft steps in the hall. I heard the door handle turn. I held my breath, expecting the lamp to crash onto the floor, but the door didn't open far enough. Suddenly a flashlight beam traversed the room, settled on the long, manlike bulge I'd arranged under the bed blanket. I was watching the flashlight. Beside it appeared the long, silenced snout of a gun barrel. It popped twice, lifting slightly each time. The hunched ridge on the bed shuddered with each impact. Gun and flashlight thrust inward, the door swung wide and the lamp shattered on the floor.

My flashlight beam caught the intruder's face as he stared down at the smashed lamp. Trying to shield his eyes from my light, he stepped back, raising his revolver.

I shot him. He yelled in pain and clutched his side.

I shot him again—in the thigh. He howled and fell back on the bed. His revolver clattered to the floor. I was off the chaise and moving toward his gun when the house seemed to rattle from its foundations. I felt the floor move before I heard the stunning blast. Through the echo came a choked scream, then nothing.

Except the moaning of the man on my bed.

I turned on the ceiling light and shielded my eyes against the blaze. Smoke. The stench of cordite drifted into the room. The man's right hand clutched his dark jogging suit below the ribcage where blood was spreading outward. His other hand covered the entrance wound in his thigh. He wasn't going anywhere.

I kicked his revolver under the bed and went downstairs. The smoke was thicker as I neared the library, the sharp stench of cordite pierced my nostrils. I played the flashlight beam around the room.

Tendrils of smoke drifted from the bulging safe. Its steel shell had focused the explosive force on the door and blown it off. Shelves hung askew from the walls, fire-singed books glowed with firefly dots. The other three walls were spattered as though a madman had flung red paint around the walls.

I slanted the flashlight beam downward and saw the source of the stains.

A man lay there, feet toward the bookshelves. Like his wounded partner, he was wearing running shoes and a dark jogging suit. The upper part of the suit was charred, right arm missing. The man's head had been flattened as though run over by a tank. There were no discernible features, just a pulpy mass of gore. The steel door had slammed his face with the dynamite's focused force. The rancid odor of scorched blood almost made me vomit, but I forced myself to kneel beside the corpse and search it.

No wallet, no dog tags. Nothing but a silenced revolver protruding from a thigh pocket. I worked it out and held it by the silencer under the light. A very nice Czech piece, a nearly silent killer.

I went to the sideboard and poured a stiff drink. As I swallowed it I summed things up. I had a corpse in the library and a badly wounded man in my bedroom. Together they had assaulted my maid and torn my house apart—maybe only one of them had done it. But I was willing to give odds that they were part of the hit team that killed Sankov, shot me and destroyed the safehouse along with eight other men.

And they were probably the ones who rigged Joann Cereza's car—and mine—with dynamite.

Both deserved to die.

One had.

I went into the library and saw that the smashed grandfather clock had stopped at 2:16. My wristwatch showed 2:21. I moved the clock minute hand ahead to 2:37. I could adjust it later if the bedroom assassin toughed it out.

As I walked up the staircase I wondered how long I could delay phoning the Seventh Precinct. For all I knew some neighbor had already called fire and police.

But the night was still. No whining sirens, no hook-and-ladder claxons coming my way.

In the bedroom I found my would-be killer on the floor. Face down, he'd been trying to crawl toward the door.

He saw my feet and tried to point the revolver in his hand. I stepped on his wrist, toed the revolver away.

"Go ahead," I said, "keep crawling. If you can make it to the street you're home free."

Hate-filled eyes stared up at me. He said nothing, and I didn't think he understood. In Russian I repeated my offer, and this time his eyes showed he got the message.

Continuing in Russian, I said, "But before I let you try, comrade, you must answer questions."

"Help," he said breathily, "I need a doctor, a hospital."

"You do," I agreed, "and it's possible I might send for help. But not just now. What's your name?"

He spat at my shoe. I wiped it on his dark hair. "Who sent you?"

He cursed me.

I bent over and pressed his carotid. Pulse weak. A lot of his blood had soaked into bedsheets and carpet. I said, "I hoped you would come back. I expected one and got two. But forget your comrade. A booby-trap finished him—the dynamite you rigged in my car. That leaves you. We start with your name."

No reaction. Both my bullets had exited, leaving bloody holes by one kidney and the back of a thigh. That was a break—for me. No bullets, no ballistic proof which gun had shot him.

I could see small punctures in the far wall, one a yard above the other. Those 160-grainers were nothing to fool with.

I went down to my storage closet and brought back a can of spackling paste and a spatula I'd used to repair wall nail-holes. The assassin watched me while I filled both bullet holes and leveled the paste, feathering the edges until both patches were level with the wall. In an hour they'd dry.

I returned paste and spatula to the closet and went back to the bedroom. He had managed to move another two feet toward the hallway. "Long way to go," I said, "and you've barely begun. I don't think you're going to make it that way, comrade. So you have two choices—talk, and I'll call a doctor, or say nothing and bleed to death." I lighted a cigarette, inhaled deeply and blew smoke across him. "You could live to smoke another cigarette, drink vodka, make love, eat a good meal . . . up to you."

He groaned. I said, "I have all the time in the world, comrade. You have very little. What's it to be?"

His head turned and I saw his lips begin to move.

SIXTEEN

"Vodka," he croaked.

His face was so pale I decided to grant his request. So I brought up the Smirnoff bottle, uncapped it and let him suck the open end. When I withdrew it his tongue licked his lips.

"Talk," I said. "Who are you?"

He coughed twice before saying, "Pavel . . . Naumov." I knew his chest was filling with blood.

"Who sent you?"

He coughed again, his entire body shaking. "Vasileyev," he husked.

"Who is Vasileyev?"

He lay there still and silent. After a while he whispered, "Sankov."

"You killed Sankov. Shot me."

"Da."

"Who ordered it?"

"Vas . . ." was all he could get out. I peeled back an eyelid.

The eyeball was colorless, capillaries drained of blood. I had thought of a doctor to keep him alive—for a thousand dollars—but even though the doctor had been with the Firm I couldn't count on his silence . . . No, *because* he'd been with the Firm.

His tongue curled out. I wet it with vodka. "*Talk.*"

"Ilya," he whispered. "Rome."

"Ilya Vasileyev is in Rome?"

"*Nyet.*"

"Why was it ordered?"

"Help me," he gasped.

I realized he was slipping away. I bent over. "Why was it done? *Why?*"

"Treaty." His eyelids fluttered, his body went slack. I pressed the carotid hard and felt no pulse. Assassin Pavel Naumov was gone, his last word *treaty*. Was the Mutual Non-Aggression Treaty what he meant? Was he lying? How could he know?

I had no time to ponder it. Carefully I went through his pockets, found a keyring from a car rental agency in Baltimore. On the ring was a miniature license plate—Maryland, with tag numbers. No other ID. He'd brought nothing but the Czech revolver on the floor. Professional.

Standing, I looked around the room. Much to accomplish and very little time. My watch showed 2:38. I bent over and grasped Naumov's wrists, started pulling him toward the staircase, but the pain in my shoulder made me stop, gasping. I swallowed another Darvocet, picked up his revolver and carried it down to the library, where I exchanged it for the safecracker's. I fitted the unfired weapon into Naumov's pocket and closed the flap. Then I pulled the body downstairs and went to the laundry room. Carrying a gallon jug of Clorox, I went back to my bedroom, poured it on carpet bloodstains. I gathered bloody sheets from the bed, soaked the mattress with Clorox and stuffed sheets in the washing machine. I filled it with water, detergent, the rest of the Clorox and started the cycle.

From my closet I took a small overnight bag and put my emergency items in it: money, passports, HK .38 and spare magazines. I ejected the magazine from the 9mm I'd used against Pavel

Naumov and replaced it with a full one. Then I stowed the bag in my closet and went downstairs.

Before leaving the house I looked around and listened, but at close to 3:00 A.M. there was no traffic. No surveillance I was aware of. I walked up Thirty-first, searching for the assassins' car, found it four blocks away, near the entrance to Montrose Park. I drove the Dodge back to my house and parked in the drive.

That was easy, the rest was much harder.

I had to drag Naumov's body from the house and prop it on the passenger side while thinking a patrol car or a neighbor would come by. Finally I had the corpse upright. I drove back to where I'd found the car and wiped my prints from it. Half pulling, half dragging, I got Pavel Naumov behind the wheel, dropped the keys between his feet and closed the door, wiping prints from the handle.

It was now three o'clock. I walked back to my house wiping sweat from my face.

Inside, I got my bag from the closet, shoved the mattress off the frame and pushed the chaise-longue back to its normal position. I carried percolator and coffee cup down to the kitchen and left them by the sink.

Finally, I turned off the remaining lights and walked outside.

From the street I looked back at my house, wondering if I would ever see it again—or live there. At that moment it seemed unlikely.

As I walked toward M Street I carried my bag in my left hand. The shoulder had begun swelling, but it was too late to go back for pain capsules. I set my teeth and walked on.

Two taxis were waiting outside a discotheque. I got into one and rode to the bus station. A bus was leaving for Philadelphia, so I bought a ticket and had time to get a packet of Aspirins from the vending machine. At the water fountain I swallowed four pills and got on the bus, taking a window seat toward the rear.

After a while the bus pulled out and headed north on I-95. The Aspirins were helping ease pain, and I wasn't moving as I had been for the previous hour.

Within the next few hours police would find Pavel Naumov's body, and by noon someone—the postman or the insurance cleanup crew—would notice my broken window, try raising me and report to the police. In the library they would find a burglar killed while blowing my safe, a body dressed like the other one and a silenced revolver with two empty shells. Conclusion: The safecracker had shot Naumov. Why? To avoid splitting the safe's contents with his partner.

I was barely conscious of the Baltimore stop, and when the bus pulled into the Philadelphia station the driver shook me awake. I taxied to the airport and bought a ticket to Savannah, checking my bag through to avoid security inspection.

At the snack bar I ate a BLT, downed two cups of coffee and got aboard the plane. From Savannah I took a bus to Brunswick and a taxi across the long causeway to Sea Island.

By noon I was knocking on my mother's door.

She saw how tired I was, asked no questions, gave me some of her arthritis pain pills and pulled back the covers of the guest room bed.

When I woke it was dark and I could hear television voices in the living room. I needed shaving gear and new clothing, but I could buy them in the morning. I took a shower and got into pajamas I kept there.

Mother was drowsing in her comfortable chair. I kissed her forehead, she woke and we embraced.

"I made you a good Swiss potato salad," she said, "and there is knackwurst, ham, black bread and cold beer—in case you're hungry."

I said I was, and let her set it out on the table for me.

She sat with me while I ate, sipping her tea and asking about life in Washington. I told her it was pretty much the same until recently, and that Marilyn and I were finally free of each other. With a touch of acerbity Mother said, "I never felt she took her committment very seriously. Much better she's free to go her own way."

"Just how I feel," I said, but my feelings were more complicated than that.

"Are you running from something, Brent?"

I said I was, but I'd done nothing wrong.

"It never occurred to me that you had."

"If you should ever be asked, I'd like you to say I came here twenty-four hours earlier, that I stayed here last night."

"Of course. How long can you stay?"

I said my collarbone was broken in a fall and needed time to recuperate. I told her my house had been burglarized and my maid injured, that I'd thought it well to leave while house damage was being repaired.

"Is that true?"

"Mostly."

"Whatever you are involved in must be serious."

"I have dangerous knowledge that I can't share with you. Too many people have lost their lives. Yours is too precious." I raised her hand and kissed it. The hand that had first touched me, the hand that had cared for me so many years. I felt an inner swelling of love for my mother.

When I'd wiped my plate clean she cleared the table and left my dishes in the kitchen. "Emma will take care of things tomorrow."

I'd forgotten about the housekeeper. "She'll know I wasn't here yesterday."

"No, son, it was her day off. I'll simply say you arrived yesterday. Now, shall we play Scrabble?"

As usual, Mother defeated me handily. We played until after ten, her customary bedtime. I needed to call Toby Gerard and Lainey, but not from Mother's phone. That, too, would have to wait until morning.

After we'd said good night I got my Black Label from the cupboard where she kept it, poured a triple shot and carried my glass into the garden. The night air was cool and pleasant. A breeze carried the sweet scent of honeysuckle to my nostrils.

The garden was surrounded by tall spreading oaks, their branches hung with Spanish moss that always reminded me of dead men's beards. A sea breeze rustled the tops of tall Australian pines. The moon came from behind clouds, illuminating the peaceful setting in such contrast to the bloody violence I'd left behind.

I missed Lainey, wanted her with me, but as I thought of her I had to accept the likelihood that I would never see her again. At least she would have my Anniversary present as a reminder of her *amour Americain*, Brent Graves.

It seemed so long ago that I'd thought of bringing her to Sea Island while Peter was away. I still wanted her to meet my mother and I felt that Mother would accept Lainey as a considerable improvement over my former wife.

Thoughts of Marilyn reminded me of my Paris apartment almost in the shadows of Notre Dame. We had lived there happily, I'd thought, and now that I was a bachelor it could serve as my hiding place, a refuge from the Opposition.

I felt a chill from the ocean breeze, went back inside and got into bed. As I warmed up I felt for a while that I was a child again in the security of our Zurich home.

After breakfast I spent half an hour in the Jacuzzi, letting warm jets play over my injuries. Then I drove Mother's Datsun down Sea Island Drive to the village. The pharmacy sold me shaving equipment and gave me a pocketful of change. From a pay phone I called Toby Gerard's office, but he was out and I left neither name or message.

Lainey was home, however, nearly sobbing in relief at the sound of my voice. She had read in the morning paper of the burglary/death at my house and my unexplained absence, and feared I had been kidnapped, killed or both. I said, "What happened decided me I'd overstayed my luck, so I got out."

"Are you in Boston? Can I come to you?" she asked plaintively.

"Not safe," I said, "and for God's sake don't tell anybody I called. I'm recovering in a safe spot and I'll phone you when I can."

"You—won't forget me?"

"How could I? I love you."

"I love you more than anything or anyone." Her voice quavered and I hung up.

I walked a block to a men's clothing store and selected a suit, slacks, jacket, shirts, underwear, shoes and other accoutrements.

The place was overpriced, but so was everything on Sea Island. It had, after all, been founded as a millionaires' retreat, and though it had been open to the public for many years, the original premise was carefully maintained.

At a stereo shop I bought a medium-size ghetto blaster and locked my packages in the Datsun's trunk. I dialed Toby Gerard again, and this time I heard his worried voice. "God, I'm glad you're alive. I read about it and went to your house, fearing the worst."

"Who would have thought they'd come back?"

"*They?* Only one body—"

My mistake. I said, "Just a manner of speech. I mean he. The explosion woke me, I went downstairs, saw the damage, the corpse and got the hell out."

"I think the police are looking for you."

"Why? Do they think I blew my opened safe and killed the burglar? Hell with them. I'm not coming back."

I thought his legalistic tendencies might make him urge me to cooperate, but instead he said, "Ah . . . you probably don't know about Father Abelardo."

"Monsignor Abelardo? What about him?"

"It appears he spent the evening out at Catholic University—a bad part of town. Walking to the bus stop he was mugged, neck broken."

I felt like yanking the phone from the wall. When I could control my voice I said, "Any witnesses?"

"None. The bus driver noticed his body on the sidewalk."

The phone was silent for a while, until he said, "Are you okay?"

"I guess so. I'm safe where I am, Toby, and mending. Is the cassette secure?"

"In my file safe here. No one has the combination. Brent, how did they get on to the Monsignor?"

I explained about Jay Catini's introduction card, taken from my wallet with my badge. I would never know whether Abelardo's reflection and meditation were leading him toward me—or toward a complicity of silence. Now his silence was eternal. Another dead end. Toby said, "Is there anything I can do?"

"Just marshal the facts and decide on your approach to Senator Connors. And look into the owners of the safehouse."

"I'll get on that. You were going to sketch it for me."

"In the mail," I told him, and hung up. Enough bad news for the day, for the year. A kindly, elderly priest was dead because of me. No, I hadn't killed him—the Opposition had. I wasn't going to share their guilt. Not for killing Abelardo, not for murdering Herb Porter and Joann.

I drove to a deserted stretch of beach and walked across gentle dunes. Some had been carved voluptuously by the wind; others were etched sharply in Taliesin geometry. Crawling seagrass and stubby palmettoes topped the shoreward slopes. Spiny yuccas looked like green porcupines. The tide was low; gray rollers sulked offshore. Gulls hung cawing in the wind. A low-flying chevron of brown pelicans beat northward parallel to shore. Smoke from a hull-down ship stained the far horizon.

I was alone with my thoughts.

Yesterday's events had forced me to strike back, and I'd taken the lives of two men—not sensate men, but trained animals, precision killers who deserved to die. Two lives scored against their dozen taken.

A beginning.

Pavel Naumov had told me much less than I'd hoped for. A name: Ilya Vasileyev. And an allusion: Rome.

Was Vasileyev the Rome *rezident?* If so, would he have had sufficient time to deploy Naumov's hit team? Or was Vasileyev a U.S.-based Illegal, burrowed deep within our country's fabric, but available on short notice to dispatch a deadly mission?

Rome? Of course, Rome—that was where it all began.

If I'd understood Naumov's meaning, the pending treaty was the reason for those KGB "active measures." The Kremlin wanted it ratified. Sankov's confession, had it surfaced, would have inflamed public opinion and eroded Senate support. Another reason to silence anyone in the know.

After a while my head cleared. I drove back home and found Emma and mother in the kitchen cleaning fresh shrimp for luncheon salad.

Watching them at their workaday task reminded me how far I'd been flung from sanity, reality. I sat down and began peeling pink, sweet-scented shrimp. Mother kissed my cheek and all was well—for the time being.

SEVENTEEN

That evening Mother and I dined in the opulent surroundings of The Cloisters. The *maître d'* led us to her favorite table, bowed and said he was delighted to see her son again. Mother glowed with pride.

She glowed anyway, having that soft and ageless English complexion. She dressed smartly, her hair was perfectly coiffed, and at sixty she would be a catch for any mature and sensible man. Having met several of her escorts and bridge partners, I realized that remaining single was her decision. It suited her.

We shared escargots, a rack and saddle of lamb *garni* and a robust Beaujolais that brought color to my mother's cheeks. When I mentioned it, she laughed and said, "I really shouldn't indulge myself, but how often do I have the pleasure of my son's company?"

"Not often enough for me."

We talked about the old days in Zurich, my schooling there, and after a while she said, "Did your father ever mention why we chose Hammersmith for you? To perfect your English, of course, but the reason was a sentimental one. Viscount Montgomery's headquarters was in the school, and much of the Normandy invasion was planned there."

"I remember the plaques and inscriptions."

"Your father admired Monty—overmuch in my opinion—but there it was. So you became a St. Paul's boy."

"Except for the food, it was a good place to study."

Mother laughed. "I had to marry your father to learn the pleasures of French and Italian cuisine. It changed my life forever."

I added a small amount of wine to her glass. She sipped and gazed at me. "I've been wondering—now that you're free—what are your plans, Brent. A fresh start? Marrying someone . . . compatible?"

"Both—once I'm out of this briar patch I stumbled into."

"I'm glad. Do you remember your father's—our—old friend, Walther Brock?"

"Of course. From Zurich."

She nodded. "It occurs to me that Walther could be of help to you in many ways. He worked for your father as a young scientist, became a professor and later an adviser to the Federal Council. In case you've forgotten, I believe that Switzerland regards you as having dual citizenship. So you could work there if you chose."

"At what? I speak a few languages, know a bit about foreign affairs. Not much to recommend me."

"Perhaps one of the international bodies could use your abilities."

"Worth thinking about," I replied, "and thanks for the suggestion."

People at a nearby table were waving at Mother. She nodded in their direction and said, "It's my Thursday night backgammon group. Would you mind terribly if I joined them?"

"Not at all."

"Then take the car, they'll see me home."

We went to their table and I was introduced around. After leaving them I walked through the lobby, found a phone booth and dialed my home

Guardedly a voice answered. Sergeant Bream.

"Keeping late hours, Sergeant?"

"Ay, it's you, Mr. Graves. I was hoping you'd get in touch."

"Lately the traffic through my house has been pretty heavy. I hardly know who to expect next. Are you house-sitting or did someone blow up the rest of my house?"

"Frankly, I've just been poking around. Are you—nearby?"

"No, I had a thorough scare. That explosion, seeing the dead man in my library . . . I couldn't take any more. Besides, my shoulder needs more treatment, so I'm at an orthopedic clinic. Safe and sound."

"Mind specifying where?"

"I do. My nerves are all frazzled. I need peace, quiet and medical attention. All I can tell you is that the explosion shook me out of a sound sleep, I saw the results and took off."

"Happen to recall the time?"

"Something before three."

"Yes, that's when the big clock stopped. Clumsy safecracker, eh?"

"Fatally. Could you identify him?"

"We're trying to establish that through prints and what's left of the dental work. I suppose he was looking for money in your safe."

"Probably. But as you know, I removed everything of value. Closed the safe door. Looked like hell hanging open."

"Ironic," he said. "The curious thing is the safe seems to have been blown from inside. After looking it over I began wondering whether a man with your military background might not know how to booby-trap it."

"Even if I knew," I said, "I understand that sort of thing would be illegal."

"Extremely. Even if your maid saw her attacker, this fellow's face was beyond recognition, so it would be hard to establish any kind of connection with the first attack."

"Made me want to throw up. Well, not that it will do anyone any good, but it would be nice if you could identify the burglar. Just for the record."

"That's all it amounts to. Death by misadventure. Well, when you're back this way we'll have to post a special guard around your home—save everyone time and money."

I was about to agree when he said, "You forgot to tell me you were with Dr. Cereza when her car was bombed."

"I wasn't with her," I said, "or I'd be dead, too."

"I think you know what I mean."

"I already talked with a man from the county sheriff's office and made a statement. It had nothing to do with the burglaries."

"Sure of that?"

"If you can find a connection," I said, "I'd be glad to hear about it. What's the weather like in Washington?"

"Cloudy, rainy."

"Same up here," I said, and rang off.

I didn't mind Bream poking around the ruins of my library. He'd seen what there was to see and drawn his own conclusions. Thinking I'd booby-trapped the safe and proving it were two different things, and he knew it.

I started Mother's Datsun and drove home.

Knowing I'd be alone for a couple of hours while Mother trimmed the suckers, I unwrapped my new portable stereo and placed it on the kitchen table. Opening the back, I examined the wiring and placement of the twin speakers. I brought my two semiautomatic pistols to the table and placed them Yin-Yang style to determine how best to fit them in. I began removing one of the speakers, cut here and there with razor and scissors and made space for my weapons plus a spare magazine for each. The kitchen's bag-and-string cupboard produced styrofoam that I trimmed to keep my ordnance from rattling. I inserted four D-cell batteries and turned on the radio. It blared like a lost calf. I switched it off, taped my contraband tightly to the interior and replaced the back.

The radio was now three pounds heavier than it was supposed to be, but I didn't plan on having anyone else carry it. I set it on my night table and listened to an FM station while writing a two-page letter to Toby Gerard.

I told him about the two killers and how I'd liquidated them. I gave him the names of Pavel Naumov and Ilya Vasileyev and suggested his facilities for tracing them were better than mine, which were nonexistent. I said I was trying to get myself in shape so I could begin working things out in Europe. In Europe I had friends unconnected to the Firm, and to stay alive I was going to have to use them. I asked Toby to advance any necessary funds to Salomé against later reimbursement.

The letter, I thought, should reach him at home tomorrow.

After that I drove across the causeway to Brunswick and mailed the letter at the post office.

In the morning I was examined by an orthopedist recommended by my mother. While Xrays were drying, he drummed on my torso and prodded the two pink scars. "Not often I see bullet wounds, Mr. Graves. These look fairly recent. Robber shoot you?"

"Actually, the culprit was a jealous husband—bad timing on my part." I sat up and put on my shirt. "I agreed not to prosecute and he promised not to beat his wife."

"Fancy tale," he said, "and highly unlikely." A nurse hung my Xrays on a lighted screen and he studied them thoughtfully. "I'd say you're doing nicely. Good calcium formation. Couple of unassimilated bone chips, but I doubt they'll trouble you until you reach your mother's age. Keep wearing that sling a while. Want some pain pills?"

I said I'd appreciate them, and he wrote out a prescription for Tylenol plus codeine. "You should swim as many lengths as you can every day," he said. "At home, use a soup can as a dumbell, up, down, in, out." He demonstrated. "Deep heat, too," he added. "I know your mother uses heat pads for her knees."

I paid cash rather than try to invoke the Firm's health insurance and drove to the Cloisters, where mother enjoyed resident privileges. The pool was warm, but stretching out my right arm full-length to swim the crawl caused instant pain. I settled for sedate side-stroking, stayed in for nearly an hour and bought a New York *Times* to read while drying in the sun.

It contained a short obituary of Monsignor Guiseppe Abelardo, S.J., ascribing his death to street robbery. I knew better but I wasn't going to write a letter to the editor.

A story on the treaty, datelined Washington, provided excerpts from testimony before Senator Connors' Committee. Witnesses advocating ratification were mostly from the Eastern Seaboard, while opponents came largely from the Midwest and Northwest.

Opponents termed the treaty a sellout; advocates proclaimed it a necessity for world peace.

Over the rest of my stay at Sea Island I called Lainey twice. I sensed that she was becoming frightened and discouraged, and I felt that she was slipping away. I rationalized it on the grounds that she didn't know the causes—only the deadly effects—of the situation I was involved in and was letting herself be overwhelmed by inexplicable events.

Some day I might be able to tell her the whole story, but for the present only Toby Gerard could know.

I phoned him at night, at home. He had found no traces of the man who called himself Pavel Naumov, but Ilya Vasileyev was a longtime KGB operator both Legal and Illegal, which in itself was unusual. Early known assignments had been in Helsinki, Copenhagen, and Cairo. In 1981—Ali Agca's year—Vasileyev surfaced in Rome as a Third Secretary, participating in ongoing discussions with the Vatican concerning the position of the Church within the Socialist Bloc. Vasileyev's principal Vatican contact was believed to be Rossinol, the "Red Cardinal."

After Rome, Vasileyev disappeared into the maw of the KGB in Moscow, emerging two years later as First Secretary in London, only to be p.n.g.'d along with a hundred other named intelligence agents when the Thatcher Government began reducing the number of Soviet spies as a necessary step in putting Britain's internal defenses in order.

After a brief recuperative interval, Vasileyev appeared at UN Headquarters in New York, covered as a personnel officer for the World Health Organization. The FBI identified Vasileyev as the officer controlling an FBI penetration agent as well as two CIA specialists in the satellite intelligence field. All three traitors were tried, convicted and imprisoned.

Before Vasileyev was publicly named as their controller, he disappeared from New York and was noticed by Special Branch in Ireland in contact with leaders of the IRA's Marxist faction. He slipped away before he could be deported, and three months later was appointed by the USSR to a senior position at UNESCO headquarters in Paris.

"He's been there for almost a year," Toby said, "so it doesn't seem likely he could have directed Naumov's assault on the safe-house, Dr. Cereza or you."

"Distance means nothing. He could have activated the hit team from any part of the world with a simple radio message delivered by cut-out."

He sighed. "Of course. I never much believed in Soviet conspiracies until you came into my office that afternoon. But I'm learning."

"You didn't ask for that background information directly, did you?"

"At least give me *some* credit, Brent! I had an assistant go to Pentagon Congressional Liaison. The Pentagon asked the Firm and the FBI. The take came to me." He paused. "If you haven't been reading the *Post*, the D.C. police finally made a connection between the corpse in your house and the corpse in the car. They seem satisfied one shot the other before being blown up. Clever, Brent. No identification, no Soviet connection."

"I didn't expect any. What's happening with the Treaty?"

"There's no groundswell of public opinion either way. The Senator presides daily, but he's tiring and I think he'll lose patience fairly soon and call for Committee vote. By then I should have enough material to present to him."

As for trying to establish the recent owners of the safehouse estate, he was making scant progress. "Documents are missing, Brent, as you predicted. But several real estate agents have photos of the place in their files, so we know it existed as you sketched it."

"All right, I think you've covered the Soviet side as much as possible for now. It's our own side that bothers me—how Sankov and I were boxed; who converted me into a nonperson. Without running it through the Firm, you might be able to get Warren, Crosby and Parton under a microscope."

"I've met the first two, but—"

"Parton's head of Mid-East ops, learned I was interested in Ali Agca and warned me off. Ten hours later I was shot and Sankov was dead." I grunted. "I should have listened to him."

"I'll go as far as I can without exposing myself."

"This will be my last contact from here. I'll mail you my next location."

It wasn't easy to leave Mother, but she accepted the necessity of my departure and drove me to the Brunswick bus station. At my request she had withdrawn ten thousand dollars from our joint account, enough to keep me going for a while without my having to visit a correspondent bank.

I rode a bus to Atlanta and flew from there to Nassau. A BA flight landed me at Gatwick, where I used my alias passport to enter Britain. During the entire trip the ghetto-blaster seldom left my hand. Because it was scanned from top down, my two pistols were never noticed.

In London I booked a compartment on the boat train to Calais and Paris, reaching the City of Light less than twenty-four hours after leaving Sea Island.

French Customs and Immigration formalities were accomplished on the train with hardly a glance at my radio. So at the Gare St.-Lazare I went directly to the cab rank and rode to my apartment building on the Ile St.-Louis.

After paying the driver I stood for a few moments to gaze at Notre Dame Cathedral, then down at the muddy Seine before entering the concierge's street-level apartment.

She was out, but a key to my apartment was hanging on the board. I took it and rode the grille-sided elevator to the quatrième étage. I unlocked my door, expecting dimness and the moldy odor that breeds in disuse.

Instead, the curtains were open and the air fresh, except for a slight scent of cooking. I put down bag and radio.

I'd expected the apartment to be empty.

But it wasn't.

Very quietly, I took a pistol out of the radio, cocked it and listened.

I heard footsteps approaching.

EIGHTEEN

"Brent!" The shout came from my right. I whirled into combat crouch, pistol covering the bedroom corridor.

"Please—*please* don't shoot me!" Marilyn's voice.

I expelled pent-up breath, lowered the pistol and saw her come toward me, one short step at a time. Her face was ashen, eyes wide with fear. I stood erect. "People get killed being in the wrong place at the wrong time. What are you doing here?"

Gaze fixed on the pistol, she said, "You didn't come back to kill me?"

I set the pistol's safety and placed it on the nearby table. "There was a time when I considered it, but that was long ago. What are you doing here?"

With nervous fingers she began undoing pink plastic curlers. It was a gesture I remembered from the past. She'd always seemed to be putting on curlers, wearing them or removing them from her brown hair. She was wearing cut-off jeans and a halter top. Fluffy slippers. She said, "This is our apartment. You weren't here, and I thought you wouldn't mind."

"Wrong. *My* apartment. I'm here and I do mind. What happened to Raoul's love nest?"

"He—well, I'm not going to go into details, but it didn't work out. I—I left him two weeks ago."

"So he chose career and family over the gullible *Américaine*, did he? I believe I made that prophecy at the time you left me."

She shrugged. "I've been—unlucky."

"You were never cut out for living abroad, Marilyn. Go back to Pottstown and marry that hardware store clerk you were always telling me about—the handsome fellow who plucked your cherry when you were sixteen. Harold. The one you couldn't forget."

"You're cruel, Brent, vengeful."

"Character deficit," I said. "I'm moving in, you're moving out."

"But—where will I go?"

"Pottstown."

She chewed her lower lip, another trait I remembered without much warmth. "Then you got the divorce notice?"

"Yes. Looked very official. We're divorced."

"How long are you going to stay here?"

"Forever, as far as you're concerned. Pack, and I'll get a taxi."

She looked around desperately. "Can't we work out some—arrangement? I really need to stay."

"I really need to be alone, Marilyn. Besides, the broads I'll be bringing here might get turned off when they realize my ex-wife is hanging around."

"I don't have any money."

"That's because you've only been working on your back. Didn't Raoul come up with a handsome allowance for you? Or was food and drink all he could manage?"

Her gaze was resentful, bitter. I said, "Sensitive, understanding Raoul, forever available for concerts, ballet, bezique—"

"Well, you were always at the Embassy or traveling."

"My job, Marilyn, and you understood it when we got married. Did that give you license to fuck the first Frog who blew in your ear?"

"You're crude!"

"Always was." But as I considered her rationale I recognized the similarities with my situation. Peter wasn't around much for Lainey, but I was—sensitive and understanding . . . My moral perch collapsed. Raoul and I canceled each other out.

"All right," I said. "Stay tonight, but tomorrow you're gone. I'll give you money for hotel and a ticket home."

"But I want to live in Paris."

"You can't work here without papers, you know that."

"You could get me a job with the Firm."

"I'm unemployed." I took the plunge: "Also, I'm wanted in the States for heinous crimes. So you're better off—and safer—away from me."

Her eyes narrowed. "What crimes, Brent?"

"Too numerous to list."

"I don't believe you—it's your way of frightening me off."

I shrugged, picked up my suitcase and pistol. "Think I'm carrying iron for ballast?" I walked down the corridor and stopped at the master bedroom. Clothing was draped here and there, bed unmade. I went past it to the second bedroom. I opened windows to void the musty smell and began unpacking.

Between hair gunk and cosmetics there was hardly space on the bathroom shelves for my shaving kit, but I managed. I turned on the shower and waited for the water to warm. After a while I found Marilyn at the kitchen table, staring into space. "What's with the water heater?" I asked.

"No one's paid the gas bill."

"Great." I took a cold shower and shaved with equally cold water, nicking my chin in the process.

I stared at my face. Eyes bloodshot, bags under my eyes, taut muscles. I had hoped never to see my ex-wife again and now she was on my hands. Castoff and helpless. *Shit*!

I put on a clean shirt and bag-rumpled clothing. Marilyn had combed out her hair and was wearing a light blue dress with a single strand of pearls. I remembered buying them for her one holiday weekend in Madrid.

"Anything in the fridge?"

"Some cheese and lettuce . . . I bought bread this morning."

I gave her a twenty-dollar bill. "The restaurant will change this for francs. Buy some food. Meat, vegetables, bread, butter, milk . . ."

"Wine?"

"Chablis—Epernay."

"Chateau Sevier, I suppose. Been seeing Lainey in Washington?"

"The Mountjoys live in Georgetown," I said, "so we're practically neighbors. And if you can find the concierge, give her money to pay the gas bill. Phone working?"

"No."

"Same story, eh? After you've brought back the groceries I'll give you ticket money. There's a travel agency by the Hotel de Ville."

"I remember," she said, and her face softened. We'd used the place often for jaunts when we were married—another time, a lost era. Its final service to me would be getting Marilyn out of France.

She tucked the bill into a small pocket. "You're so tense, so curt."

"I'm a hunted man. And hungry."

After she left I made a mental note to get the door lock changed. I didn't want her trooping back wet and bedraggled at midnight. Or Raoul, to whom she might have given a key. I could live without seeing either of them again.

The refrigerator seemed larger than it was because it was so empty. There was a hacked-at block of Gruyère and a brownish head of lettuce, an open jar of olives, another of sweet gherkins. Marilyn had never been much of a housekeeper, but then she never had to be. Not with at least one servant to cook and keep our households tidy. Well, she'd have to get serious now if she was going to straighten out her life.

As I closed the refrigerator door I thought of Salomé and hoped she was out of the hospital and fully recovered.

I stashed my weapons in a cache I'd kept secret from Marilyn and tuned my dismembered radio to one of the Channel pirate stations. Good music flooded the room: Lou Rawls singing "Masquerade," with the orchestra supplying muted strings to a pulsing tropical rhythm. I looked around the big room and remembered an old couplet:

Paris, tu n'as pas changé, mon vieux.
Paris, tu n'as pas changé—tant mieux!

Whatever my reasons for returning, it was great to be back.

While Marilyn was at the travel agency I prepared food, I was eating when she returned. She looked enviously at my plate until I said, "Plenty for you."

As she served herself she said, "I could have done this for you, you know."

"Didn't want to wait." Marilyn had difficulty boiling rice. She sat down across from me and said, "I have the ticket and almost a hundred dollars change."

"Use it for the hotel. When's your flight?"

"Day after tomorrow. I paid the gas bill but there won't be gas until tomorrow." She laid down her fork. "Brent, are you sure you don't want me to stay?"

"Positive. Let's just break clean without wringing it out all over again. You've had your fling and I'm used to living alone."

"I'm not."

"Things don't usually work out the way we want." I got another wineglass and filled it for her. "By the way, there's no reward for me—in case you thought of cashing in."

"I'd *never* do a thing like that. You know me better."

"I thought I did . . . once."

We finished our meal in silence. I let Marilyn do the dishes while I went out for cigarettes. For a time I strolled along the Seine. A barge passed almost silently under the Pont Marie. Lightoliers illumined the *quais*, acacias were budding. I smoked and walked past closed bookstalls where I'd bought some of my most prized books, recalling that my library needed restocking and refurbishing after the blast. The night air was cool and misty and there were few patrons at the sidewalk tables where I stopped for a *fine café*. The coffee-brandy warmed and relaxed me and I realized that I was very tired. I went back to the apartment and found Marilyn reading a magazine. I said good night to her and went to bed.

An hour or so later I felt her slip beneath the covers, press her cool body against mine. "Brent," she whispered, "we could try again. Won't you forgive me?"

"You're forgiven."

"Don't you want me?"

"It's over, Marilyn, long over. We're better off apart."

I heard her soft sobbing until I went back to sleep.

In the morning I found her packing in the larger bedroom. She glanced at me and said nothing. For a moment I studied her face; straight nose, heavy dark eyebrows, severe mouth, and wondered how I ever could have found her features irresistible.

After breakfast I got Marilyn's suitcases downstairs and tipped the concierge to call a taxi. On the sidewalk my ex-wife and I looked at each other until the taxi drew up. I watched it drive away.

Final ending to a long chapter, I told myself, found the concierge and asked to have my locks changed.

"Madame is not returning?"

"Madame is no longer my madame. *Nous sommes divorcées.*"

"Ah, m'sieu, quelle domage. Je regrettete."

"Moi aussi," I lied. In France abandoned husbands were supposed to suffer most. The concierge approved my misery and let me use her telephone.

My first call was to Freddy de Mortain, an old companion from Sorbonne days who had joined SDECE.* While at Paris station I had seen Freddy socially and professionally, and found him on the phone still amiable and close-mouthed. He said he was glad to hear from me and when could we get together? I named Le Bosfor, a bistro on the Left Bank, and we met there an hour later.

After preliminary updatings and health and welfare inquiries, I told Freddy I was interested in a Soviet agent at UNESCO named Ilya Vasileyev. Freddy stroked his pencil mustache and said he'd seen him here and there. "Close to fifty and handsome for a Russki. Passable manners. One of your cases?"

**Service de Documentation Extérieure et de Contre-Espionnage*, the French foreign intelligence service.

"Outside normal channels. The station's not to know I'm here."

"Interesting. How can I be of help?"

"Get into whatever surveillance reports you can find and let me know where Vasileyev lives, his daily routine, the agents he services." I sipped from my demitasse. "I left Washington unexpectedly, no time to get alias documentation. How's the trade in American passports?"

"Brisk. Try the Cité Universitaire area. I don't know the going price."

"Is Françoise well?"

"Yes, and talking about a fourth child, would you believe it? Three is entirely respectable—we replace ourselves and provide one to rebuild the nation's gene bank. I've asked for a Washington posting to distract her mind."

"You'll find Peter and Ghislaine Mountjoy there."

"Ah, yes, the fair Ghislaine." He nodded approvingly. "Does Peter wear his horns docilely?"

I stared at him until he said, "Come, Brent, everyone knew you found consolation with Madame de Mountjoy after your spouse took up with Boucher. It was the year's most discussed secret romance. Still flowering?"

"Somewhat."

"*Alors*, I congratulate you on being practically monogamous. As my sainted mother advised me in my youth: "Freddy—she said—you can't screw them all. Choose two or three compatibles and remain faithful to them.'"

"Freddy, I don't believe your mother ever gave you any such counsel."

"If she didn't articulate it I'm sure those were her sentiments."

For a while we discussed French politics, and Freddy invited me to dine *en famille*. I said I was working underground, low profile, and we would have lunch together when he had the information I needed.

Near the Gare d'Austerlitz I bought old blue-jeans, a well-scarred leather jacket, worn jogging shoes and a beret. Then I took a taxi to the Cité Universitaire and cruised the cafés until I spotted a student whose size and coloring was reasonably close to mine. I bought him a cognac and offered two hundred dollars for his passport. He wanted four, we settled on three and he went off to get it from his room.

Raymond Claude Lazare was a Canadian citizen born in Brandon, Manitoba, near Winnipeg, he told me, and said he would hold off reporting his passport stolen for at least a month. After that he would need a replacement for a trip planned to Corfu. "Now that I have the funds," he said cheerfully. We shook hands and I went back to my apartment.

The concierge volunteered her niece to clean my place once or twice a week and do laundry. I said once would be enough, and paid in advance. "I require tranquility while recovering from the shock of Madame's defection," I said, "and I neither expect visitors nor want them. Anyone inquiring for me is to be told you know nothing of me, but you will retain messages for me should I appear."

"*Entendu.*" I gave her a hundred-franc grautity, she took it appreciatively and said she sympathized with my plight. My request would be honored, and a locksmith would attend to my doors before day's end.

I changed into my newly purchased second-hand clothing and set out by Métro for a documentation expert I knew of via some former agents.

I found M. Pasquier's printing shop on a narrow street near Butte de Montmartre. At first he protested that he lacked the expertise to alter my passport *(C'est un métier spécialisé)* but when I mentioned Stolsky and Marescu he beckoned me to the rear of his shop. Amid clanking presses and the pungent smell of ink he photographed me, and fingered the Canadian passport thoughtfully. "Four hundred francs seem not unreasonable, *m'sieu.*"

"Three hundred is sufficient," I told him. "No seals to reproduce, no calligraphy to be altered. A simple photographic substitution."

He shrugged. "Very well, three hundred—and twenty francs."

"Ten."

We shook hands. The passport was to be ready by seven.

I strolled two blocks to l'Auberge du Coucou, ordered a démi-carafe of house wine and a cut of rare lamb *jardinière.*

Though I'd taken both Marilyn and Lainey—separately—to the Coucou on a number of occasions, the waiter failed to recognize me in my scruffy working-class garb, and that pleased me. The restaurant's location was unique for Montmartre—Sacré-Coeur over my left shoulder, Paris spread out before me with the Eiffel Tower's spire poking toward the clouds, the solid gray bulk of Notre Dame, the Tour d'Argent. A fiddle and accordian began playing in the nearby Place du Tertre. I finished my meal, drained the last of the wine, and took the Métro home.

A note under my door told me I had had a caller.

A man.

NINETEEN

From the concierge's description I decided the visitor had been Raoul Boucher, and hoped he wouldn't find Marilyn before she left for the States. She would be far better off leading a life she was prepared for than hanging on in Paris dependent on her keeper's whims.

In my absence the apartment had been tidied up, sheets changed, dishes washed and put where they belonged. My shoulder ached, so I took a pain pill and napped through the afternoon.

At seven I collected my Canadian passport from Pasquier and mailed my location to Toby Gerard. Then I telephoned Freddy de Mortain and asked if he'd come up with anything.

He said material was still coming in and I should phone his office midmorning. He remarked that Claudine, his sister-in-law, had broken up with her husband and was available whenever I wanted a dinner partner. I remembered Claudine as an outdoorsy woman with a crepe neck from too many windy wanderings and a face that bore a fixed expression of concern—the result of her husband's flagrant infidelities. I thanked Freddy for the thought and reminded him I was in Paris strictly on business.

Besides, I missed Lainey.

I rode the Métro to the Place de l'Opera and bought a ticket to Roland Petit's ballet *Le Jeune Homme et La Morte*, had a *coupe* of champagne at intermission and left around eleven.

After a late breakfast I phoned Freddie and we met later at a brasserie on St. Germain near the Deux Magots. He produced an envelope containing a dozen Xeroxed pages and said, "All we have on Vasileyev. From the DST." The French internal security service.

"Is he a DST active target?"

Freddy shrugged. "Active, probably, but not sustained. From the reports, I judge that Vasileyev is surveilled when watchers are available."

"Phone tap?"

"Why bother? The Russian would assume so. Look, Vasileyev puts in a brief daily appearance at the UNESCO *palais* and disappears into this city of four million souls—many of them law abiding—and who is to say what he does? Of one thing, though, I am sure—the female listed as his wife, Katya Vasileyeva, on the Diplomatic Register is not the "wife' who was with him in Rome, Cairo or Copenhagen. More likely this Katya is his cipher clerk. She frequently visits the Soviet Embassy even though she is not listed as an employee. They live in a handsome building on the Boulevard Haussmann—my God, the allowances these UNESCO bureaucrats draw! And when Vasileyev entertains, it is at some four- or five-star restaurant—without his wife."

"She's probably a country girl lacking city manners and French."

"No doubt." He sipped from his cup, sighed. "Ay, Brent, how unrewarding is our profession, *hein?* The Russkis do as they will and we are powerless to prevent it. Despite myself I become apathetic. This distresses Françoise, who redoubles her demands that I join her family's *bureau* at the Bourse. Yet I feel I was not cut out to be a broker."

"You have the necessary cynicism and suspicion."

"Perhaps too much." He glanced at his watch. "I have a meeting to attend—it concerns tribal agitation in Nouvelle Calédonie. What to do? We of the committee meet, discuss, argue, and do nothing. More empires are lost by procrastination than through feats of arms. You know that."

"Also that I owe you a splendid lunch. Prunier's tomorrow—noon?"

"If possible I will be there." We shook hands. He went down the street and I paid the bill.

A large, comfortable-looking tour bus drove slowly toward the church of St-Germain-des-Pres, paused for photo-taking and deposited its occupants in front of the Deux Magots so they could savor the Hemingway ambiance for a quarter of an hour before the bus moved on.

I moved on, too, taking Freddy's envelope to the apartment, where I studied its contents carefully. Before burning the reports I cut out Vasileyev's passport photo and wrote down his apartment address.

After sundown I stood in front of Ilya Vasileyev's building, scanning *Paris-Match* until I saw him get out of a taxi and walk into the entrance. His topcoat was well tailored, he wore a fawn-colored hat and matching gloves. His shoes had the Italianate line, in contrast to the blunt-toed model Khrushchev once banged at the UN, and I appraised my target as something of a dandy.

I needed leverage on him, a compelling edge, but his "wife" was insufficient. He might sleep with the woman but the deep ties of love weren't there. Threats against her life would not move him. I needed more.

Blackmailing? Trapping him would require long and intensive surveillance, and I had a shortage of time and no reliable surveillants.

Moodily I strolled along Haussmann to Boulevard Malesherbes and turned into a small, attractively lighted, two-star restaurant named La Victoire. This century the French were notably short of victories, so I didn't ask the *maître* to specify which one the restaurant memorialized. It was enough that the Gallic spirit was alive and on display.

After ordering a *dêmi* red and consulting the limited menu I thought further about Vasileyev. Killing him would be simple enough—and accomplish nothing. I needed him alive and cooperative, I told myself, and then I remembered another Sorbonne schoolmate, Louis-Robert Cassegrain.

Raised in French Algeria, Louis-Robert had been evacuated to Metropolitan France with thousands more *pieds-noirs* and entered the Sorbonne with the Algerian émigré contingent. He was a witty and resourceful young man, deeply involved in the black market and general knavery. It allowed him to live well and, occasionally, attend classes at the Faculté.

I hadn't seen him since my Embassy assignment, by which time he owned a prosperous restaurant on the Rue de Rennes bordering the Latin Quarter. Name . . .? Le Poilu Piquet.

Having mentally resurrected an old and potentially useful contact, I relaxed and enjoyed pepper steak with blanched asparagus and *petit pois*. Table lights were soft, muted conversation came from adjoining tables and I decided that La Victoire was worth another visit.

Entering the Métro at the Madeleine, I rode under the river to the Luxembourg stop and walked through sparsely lighted streets to Le Poilu Piquet. There was a good crowd in the dining room and the waiters appeared skilled and attentive. The *maître* told me that M. Cassegrain was expected presently, and showed me to the bar. I smoked a cigarette, listened to canned Algerian music and sipped *fine* until Louis-Robert grabbed me from behind and pulled me into his office.

After we'd exchanged family data and lamented the interval between meetings I said, "Are you still of the *métier*"

He offered me a long, thin Upmann cigar, I declined and he lit one for himself. He exhaled and said, "Except for not paying taxes to this *sale* government I've been completely honest for at least four years. However," he continued, "I can't help it when old companions refresh themselves at my establishment, now can I?"

"It would be churlish to turn them away."

"And unwise." He eyed me speculatively. "You've been back how long?"

"Two days."

"And you are still employed by that not-so-secret government organization?"

"I was ejected," I told him. "They found fault with me."

"Petty minds." He opened a cupboard and brought out a bottle of Napoleon brandy. He poured it into two small snifters, reverently warmed them over an alcohol flame. "To free, untrammeled enterprise," he said, and we drank to that.

"Now" said Louis-Robert, "I judge you've dined, or I would order a pressed duck for which you would trade your favorite mistress. Dining aside, how may I serve you?"

I said that a certain Soviet official had made life uncomfortable for me in Washington and that I had located him in Paris. I described my desire to question this individual in private and explained that I lacked the means to effect such an interrogation.

Carefully Louis-Robert tipped ash from his Upmann into a black onyx receptacle and gazed at the result. "My late father," he said, "was a member of l'Armée Secrète. He and his associates—until they were compromised and executed—carried on a counter-campaign of terrorism and torture against the emissaries of De Gaulle. They were familiar with Annamese methods of persuading recalcitrants to divulge their complete knowledge of any subject and they employed them unhesitatingly. My father told me this before he was shot, and enjoined me against half-measures. "All or nothing, *mon fils,'* he told me. "Never embark upon something for which you lack *tripes* to finish. The Gaullists are exemplary in that regard, which is why you find me in a death-cell rather than strolling the Champs-Elysées wearing a *boutonièrre* and selecting from among chic pedestrian *poules.'* Brent, *cher ami*, I took those paternal words to heart, how could I not? This *sale Russe* offends you, has offended you, and that is impermissible." He leaned forward angrily. "We will move against him without delay."

I wrote down Vasileyev's address and placed his photograph on the notepaper. Louis-Robert nodded. "Among my past *copains* are a number of burly, aggressive men who have even less love for the Russians than I. Does this Vasileyev go about with bodyguards?"

"No."

"Then three *copains* should be sufficient."

I got out my wallet, but he shook his head. "Think how many breakfasts and luncheons you bought an impoverished Algerian exile. Consider the accommodation a slight repayment. It will be my pleasure to oversee all that is required. Depend upon me."

I wrote down my apartment address, said I lacked a telephone and suggested he communicate by *pneumatique* or messenger. "The fellow reached his apartment building about seven o'clock and is said to be a creature of habit."

He held the photo between thumb and forefinger and blew smoke across it. "After this *type* has expelled all knowledge, what is to become of him?"

I shrugged. We gazed silently at each other, and Louis-Robert drew a forefinger across his gullet.

"Assuming," I said, "the *copains* remain equally silent."

"*Ça va sans dire.* Now, to more cheerful matters. You are alone in Paris, a distressing state of affairs. Perhaps a young and lovely companion to unfetter your mind and rid your system of accumulated venom?"

"You're too generous, Louis-Robert, but I'm lately out of hospital and incapable of giving a good account of myself. Perhaps after my faculties are fully restored."

"I understand completely." He looked at his watch. "At eleven a bevy of voluptuous Algeriennes will dance and sing for customers. Will you linger and enjoy a sip of wine?"

"It's close to my bedtime," I said. "I'm tempted but I must call it a night."

We embraced as Frenchmen do and he walked me to the exit. His chauffeur drove me home, and while I was waiting for sleep to come I thought that I had the basics out of the way and had accomplished a good deal in a surprisingly short time.

Knowing Louis-Robert, I fully expected word within the next twenty-four hours.

His summons came in twenty-two.

TWENTY

The Algerian beside me drove the VW minivan with verve and abandon. He was a stocky, bearded man with dark brown skin and large gnarled hands. The crest of his dark curly hair was topped by a black leather skullcap embroidered with Arabic designs in bright colors. As he leaned forward, the hilt of a knife protruded from his trouser belt, and I wondered if it had helped persuade Vasileyev to surrender.

Our direction was generally northeast, out Rue LaFayette between the Gare du Nord and the Gare de l'Est. Short of the Stalingrad intersection he turned hard right to run parallel with the canal, and a block later, sharp left onto Rue Louis Blanc. Slowing, the driver dimmed headlights and entered a narrow cobbled lane, pulled into what looked like a junkyard of rusting auto bodies and braked near a grilled entrance door. He turned off lights and engine.

We got out and he led me down three trash-littered steps, whistled several dissonant notes, and the inner door opened. Louis-

Robert greeted me and unlocked the grille door. I stood in darkness until the doors closed, then Louis-Robert turned on a pencil flash and guided us deeper into the musty cellar. We passed through two dark rooms with packed earth floors and into a third that was paved and brilliantly lighted. In shadows by the wall stood two muscular men.

The cone of light showed a small wooden table bearing a hypodermic syringe and a corked bottle. A few feet away a coatless man was tied in a high-backed wooden chair. His ankles were bound to chair legs, arms secured behind the chair back. His head hung forward, chin touching breastbone, but I could see a leather strap circling his neck. The strap was drawn through two slits in the chair back and ended in a looped stick to form a garrote.

Louis-Robert handed me a black mask and I put it on.

The purpose of a mask was to encourage a subject to believe he might be freed. If he saw interrogators' faces he would understand that whether or not he talked he was not going to survive.

From behind, a hand reached over the chair and clenched the subject's hair, jerking the head back against the wood. Now I could see his face.

His eyes were wide with terror, his mouth open. Spittle drooled down the corners of his mouth. The pale flesh of his face was unmarked. The set of the eyes, the high, angled cheekbones and the flattish nose were those of Ilya Vasileyev.

And the slim, pointed Italian shoes.

He gasped noisily as his chest expanded to suck in great volumes of air. Behind him a masked Algerian tightened the garrote. Vasileyev's throat veins thickened and purpled and his chest arched forward as his body fought for air. Then the upturned face dropped and his eyes glazed. The garrote loosened and the unconscious man breathed short, harsh intakes.

Louis-Robert said, "I think he's softened sufficiently. With your permission I will withdraw and attend my business while *les copains* remain at your disposition."

We shook hands, I thanked him and Louis-Robert left the interrogation chamber for the outside world.

I drew up a chair in front of Vasileyev and reached for the

corked bottle. I took out the cork and sniffed gasoline. Injected, it was said to produce immediate, intolerable pain. Sixty years ago it was a Cheka favorite in the dungeons of the Lubyanka. I said, "What has he had to say?"

One of the Algerians, a man much larger than my driver, said, "He admits to being a member of the Soviet secret service with the rank of lieutenant-colonel. His current assignment is to charm the Parisian élite, spot influential members for recruitment."

"Very well," I said, "I will talk with him in Russian," and slapped Vasileyev's face. His head rolled and his eyes opened. Seeing my masked face, he yelled.

"Before you leave here," I told him, "we will have discussed a number of things. Your involvement with the attempt on the Pope's life, your friends in the Vatican and Mehmet Ali Agca. The particular responsibilities of the Bulgarian KGB agent, Filip Sankov, and the circumstances of his death. Your direction of the assault team that included Pavel Naumov and the manner by which you were able to obtain information on Sankov's location and intentions—"

"*Water,*" he gasped.

I gestured toward the wall and in a few moments a cup was handed to me. I guided it to Vasileyev's lips and dribbled water into his mouth. Some of it flowed down his torn shirtfront.

"Talk," I said.

Words bubbled from his mouth, fused into a torrent that overtook and flooded my analytical processes. I didn't interrupt because the small instrument in my jacket pocket was recording it all.

Yes, he had been Sankov's controller in Rome, responsible for directing the assassination. Cardinal Rossinol had been an eager ally, placing three trusted priests under Vasileyev's orders. They were Petucci, Goyitia, and Marmolli. They had arranged the positioning of Swiss Guards and Carabinieri to make the Pope vulnerable to Sankov's three assassins and aid their escape.

He confirmed that, in addition to Agca, the other two were Yosif Postiko and Fenis Kevorkian. I gave him more water to drink and said, "After Sankov defected, what action was to be taken?"

"Sankov was to be found and liquidated. And every person who could have heard his story."

"How was he located?"

Vasileyev breathed deeply. "It is public knowledge that our Washington Embassy can overhear whatever telephone or radio communications it selects. The process is highly technical. I have no technical training but I know it involves computers, lasers and microwave intercepts."

I said, "They can't intercept messages that go by secure lines." I was thinking of the system between the safehouse and Headquarters.

"I think so."

"I think," I said, "that your embassy had other help—from inside. An agent of yours in the safehouse or at Headquarters."

"I don't know."

"We'll examine that. Now, having located Sankov, what determined the need and timing of his liquidation?"

"He was revealing the plot against the Pope."

"And—?"

He swallowed hard. "That had to be kept secret from the world."

"Because of the Mutual Non-Aggression Treaty? Wasn't that what determined everything?"

"Yes," he grated. "The Soviet leadership wants it above everything."

"Returning to the identity of the insiders who informed the *rezidentura* and obliterated evidence of the safehouse massacre—who were they?"

"I said I don't know. Each of us knew only a part of the whole."

"I think you know a great deal." Slowly I filled the hypodermic syringe with gasoline, scratched the needle against the flesh of his forearm. Vasileyev winced, looked the other way, neck muscles straining. I sank the tip of the needle into his flesh. Even though I didn't inject gasoline, he jerked and strained to free his arm. One of the Algerians twisted the leather strap, yanking his head back. His face reddened and the neck veins bulged. I nodded and the garrote loosened. In a low voice the Algerian said, "How is he doing?"

"Pas mal," I said, then in Russian to Vasileyev, "I know that an insider was and is involved. Since the assault, another four persons have been fingered and three killed. Naumov was the action agent but his information came from inside. I ask again, who provided it?"

"I don't know."

I pressed the syringe plunger, sending three drops of gasoline into the Russian's arm. He screeched in pain. Flesh around the needle tip swelled and reddened. Vasileyev groaned and thumped his shoes on the concrete floor. The pain must be agonizing, I thought, otherwise why would the Cheka have used this method?

Finally Vasileyev quieted down. His face was red and glistening with perspiration. His breathing was irregular, stertorous. "Once again," I said, "who was it?"

"A code name," he managed chokingly, "is all I ever heard."

"The name."

He licked his lips, stared at the needle in his forearm and spoke one word: "Apollo."

"Apollo is the penetration agent, the informer?"

From his throat issued a hoarse rattle. His head lolled to one side and his body shuddered. I gripped his chin, slapped his cheek, but there was no reaction. His eyes stared beyond me, unfocused. From his right nostril what looked like a bright red worm crawled down his lip, reached his chin. I pressed the carotid artery. There was no pulse. I looked at my three helpers and stood up.

"Fini." I said. *"Mort."* A foul smell rose from his body as death relaxed the excretory muscles.

I put aside the hypodermic syringe, knowing I hadn't injected enough to kill Vasileyev. It didn't make any difference because the Algerians would have terminated him anyway. I felt I'd learned as much as I could before his heart gave out. One of the men began untying the cords, another removed the neck strap. I wondered how often the chair had served the same purpose, and for whom. It was probably a relic of the Algerian war that had torn France apart.

The third man said, "Did you get what you wanted?"

"Almost everything. And the body?"

"Leave that to us."

"Thank you for your help."

"It is our pleasure to do whatever M. Cassegrain requires."

I left the lighted room and retraced my steps to the exit doors, confident the Algerians knew how to dispose of bodies from past experience.

I turned the key unlocking the metal grille, pushed open the outside door and stepped into fresh air.

As I took the concrete steps I realized I was not alone.

Moonlight revealed three figures standing near the minivan, one a woman. I thought they were the Algerians' companions until I saw the glint of a pistol pointing at me. A man said in gutturally accented French, "Put up your hands and turn around."

For a moment I hoped the three *copains* would come to my rescue, but they were far away, behind three sets of doors, and my captor had spoken softly.

From the DST reports I recognized the woman's face: Vasileyev's "wife," Katya.

As I stood there I felt the sudden sharp prick of a needle behind my left thigh. I gasped, the pain vanished, but my leg felt frozen. The chill spread upward, reached my heart and lungs, blinded me.

As sometimes happens in moments of stress an aberrant thought flashed across my mind; I recalled that it was the Eve of St-Jules.

I shivered uncontrollably, my knees dissolved and I dropped into nothingness.

BOOK FOUR

TWENTY-ONE

I existed in darkness, silence and occasional motion. My body sensed a prolonged journey. There were times when I felt suspended in a still, inky lake. Sometimes the blackness would lighten, become charcoal gray, then total darkness would prevail.

Infrequently I heard sounds, not sounds that conveyed meaning other than that they might be human voices. It was like a speech recording played so slowly that everything was almost below bass register. Occasionally, in contrast, the recording speeded up into a sequence of high-pitched, distorted squeals. Those sequences amused me and I would try to imitate what I heard. I did so automatically, as though bidden to, and when the impulse drained away I floated again in dark, endless silence.

Sometimes I wondered if I were dead.

Years passed. Joyless years of self-criticism, humility and penance. They left me without bodily strength, without the ability to summon conscious thought. I was being punished and the punishment was just. I couldn't recall individual sins but I accepted their totality and knew I deserved all that was visited on me. Purgatory and expiation.

As in a vision, I saw the gray towers of Georgetown, the intricately carved façade of Notre Dame, the church of St-Germain-des-Pres, thought I heard the chanting of celebrants. I saw the vast plaza of St. Peter's, a crowd surging around the body of a murdered Pope.

Monsignor Abelardo—was he there? Had he worn his wire-rimmed lenses? Was the aging prelate one of the conspirators? Was that the truth that stopped his tongue?

Around me blackness began to dissolve, became grainy; clouds formed, light showing among them until it penetrated everywhere and destroyed the darkness.

My eyes were open. They stared at a wall.

My body lay under a sheet. I tried to move my toes and saw the fabric pucker. Beside my thighs my hands opened and closed. I tried to swallow, but my mouth and throat were desert dry. My tongue felt thick. The taste was unpleasant, chemical. Desert borax? I closed my eyelids and opened them, turned my head.

The room was windowless, air came from a ceiling grate. There was water on a table near my hand. I reached for it, but my arm trembled uncontrollably and I rested to gather strength.

Other than my bed and the small table there was no furniture in the room. The door was painted the same color as the walls, but it was metal-faced, a Judas-window at eye level. I wondered if I was back in Dr. Cereza's clinic. No, that was Virginia, and I was in Paris.

My last conscious memories were of Paris. Logically I could not be in Virginia. I tried to reach the water pitcher but the effort was beyond me. I wept over my helplessness.

The door opened, a nurse came in. She was bulky, blonde, a face so Slavic it seemed carved from sugar beet. In Russian she said, "Are you hungry?"

"Thirsty."

She tilted the pitcher, poured into a chipped metal cup, helped me drink. I drank two cups of water and collapsed on the bed. My stomach gurgled. I turned my face on the pillow and my beard rasped it. I touched my chin and felt an unaccustomed growth.

Perhaps a week's growth.

That long since they had taken me. After Vasileyev's death. I wondered why I was still alive.

The nurse swabbed my arm, pierced a glass ampule and drew its clear fluid into a hypodermic syringe. I remembered the gasoline syringe and shivered. She said, "This will clear your mind, make you feel better."

I looked down at my left arm. It looked mosquito bitten—at least a dozen punctures. I lacked strength to resist the nurse. She found a vein and injected the fluid. Warmth spread outward. Heroin? Had they made me an addict? My whole body warmed, mucous membranes moistened. Fear vanished, euphoria flooded my mind. I was beginning to feel hungry. I licked my lips and said, "Where am I?"

"Leningrad."

"And this—? Prison?"

"A special clinic."

For the mentally disturbed, I decided, and why not? Some of my fantasies had been hideous, maniacal . . . but at least I knew they were dreams. I breathed deeply and the nurse took my pulse rate, felt my forehead. I said, "I could use some food."

She opened the door, went out and locked the door.

I tried sitting up but immediately was dizzy.

Leningrad. *Leningrad?* Why should I doubt it?

I closed my eyes, rested. After a while the door opened and the nurse brought a bowl of soup. Some kind of meat in the broth, potatoes, turnips . . . She propped me up and helped me take some soup. It lacked salt but I ate all of it. She took the crockery bowl, metal spoon, and left. The ceiling light went out.

I slept.

When I woke the light was on. How long had I slept? Minutes? Hours? Days? The chemical taste had left my mouth. I sat up and found myself no longer dizzy from effort. My strength had begun to return. I tried to walk to the commode but my legs were too weak. I crawled to it, evacuated, crawled back to bed.

The Judas-window opened, slid shut. The light went out.

I slept.

On awakening I found the light on, a chair in the room. For a while I sat on the edge of the bed, dangling my legs, raising and lowering my feet, exercising the muscles. Then I tottered to the chair and sat down. The nurse brought a cordless electric razor and helped guide it over my face. German make, Braun.

She had brought fresh pajamas, too. I changed into them, glad to be out of the others with their rancid smell. I wondered if I was to be kept prisoner forever. General Grigorenko had spent five years in psychiatric wards while his keepers tried to persuade him he was insane.

What would my keepers do?

Part of psychiatric manipulation involved making the subject lose track of time, confusing and disorienting him. Instilling a feeling of hopelessness.

I was confused and partly disoriented, but not entirely without hope. They could have killed me in the junkyard but they hadn't. Instead I'd been transported to a special clinic and kept alive.

As Filip Sankov had been isolated and maintained.

So he could answer questions, divulge his knowledge of secret things.

Undoubtedly that was why I was alive, and my mind was clearing.

My evidence was that I was able to recall three figures who had waited for me outside the place where Vasileyev died. One was his live-in, Katya.

Katya was my nurse.

No one knew I'd made the connection, and it was useful to me because it was a secret worth concealing. I knew something my captors didn't know.

Either Katya had made the plane trip with me to Leningrad or I was still in Paris. She was the link, and I could build on that knowledge.

Wherever I was I had to escape. They would expect me to try. I needed three things: rest, food and exercise. Like Joyce's requirements of silence, exile and cunning. I needed the last of his three as well.

I wondered what my inevitable interrogator would ask, and what secrets I would feel obligated to retain. Were there any? Had not at least some of my superiors become my adversaries? Who transferred Catini and sent Herb Porter to his death? Who suppressed public accounting for the massacre, leveled the safehouse like Carthage, tapped my phone and barred me from the workplace?

Apollo, Vasileyev had told me with his dying breath. Unless he lied, Apollo was the penetration agent. Who was Apollo? Was he the agent Angleton had spent twenty years of his life pursuing?

It had become fashionable to dismiss James Angleton as a fanatic; obsessed, burdened like Quixote with hallucinations. I couldn't judge other than empirically. Only a highly placed mole could have done the things I knew about. There was no other explanation.

Perhaps my interrogators would unwittingly provide a clue, a hint I could enlarge up on, develop into a name, a face.

Without warning my light was extinguished.

Sleepy-time for the patient. It might be night, might not.

I wondered if they knew my name.

I could judge the passage of time only by the growth of my beard. Meals came irregularly, and solid food gradually replaced soups and mush. Russian food, sausage, turnips, potatoes, greens, a chunk of pork. I ate everything and strength returned. I slept too much, but there was nothing to read, nothing to occupy my mind. With a pencil stub I could have written passages from Gogol and Tolstoy, played solitary tick-tack-toe. But there was no pencil stub, no paper except for the few daily toilet tissues I was allotted.

I sat in the chair and did aerobics, stopping when the Judas-window opened. I lifted the chair with two hands, then with one. Did squats, sit-ups, hand-stands and push-ups. I was stronger. My head was clear. I remembered everything.

One morning, I woke abruptly. The door opened and a man entered. The door closed behind him. He was a well-built man, slightly taller than I. His face was square-set, a Mongol cast to his eyes. He wore a well-tailored army uniform piped in blue—the color of the KGB. Shoulder pips ranked him as a Major General.

"Off your bed," he snapped in Russian. "Stand when a senior officer enters." He sat down in my chair and watched while I climbed off the bed and stood at a semblance of attention.

"That's better. My name is Kostikov. Boris Kostikov."

I said nothing. He unbuttoned a pocket flap and got out a package of cigarettes, Rossiyas. "Smoke?"

"Yes."

"Yes, *sir.*"

"Yes, *sir,*" I said humbly and took a cigarette. He lighted it for me. We inhaled and exhaled together. He looked at his cigarette then at me. "Your name?"

"Lazare," I said. "Raymond Claude Lazare. Sir."

He smiled lazily. "You think I'm a fool? That name is a passport name. It is not even the name you went by in Moscow. Do you remember that name?"

"No . . . sir."

"You were known as William Purdey. William Harris Purdey. Do you remember now?"

"I haven't been well," I said, and gestured at the bed. "The dreams . . . I've been confused."

He unfolded a sheet of paper and showed me a reproduction of the carnet issued me in Moscow by the Soviet Foreign Ministry. It showed my face, the name William Harris Purdey. Kostikov barked, "Do you deny it?"

"I'm tired of standing." I sat on the bed.

"On your feet!"

I blew smoke in his direction. "Fuck you, Boris."

His face stiffened, colored. He shot to his feet. "Damn you, obey orders or you'll be punished!"

"I've been punished, Boris. I'm *being* punished, can't you see that? I must have deserved it—or am I insane? Is that why I'm in a special clinic?" I sniffled miserably.

"Who told you that?" he roared.

"My nurse said so when I woke up. I'm in Leningrad in a special psychiatric clinic and I'm being punished." I smiled a simpleton's smile. "Good cigarette. I missed smoking. That was part of my punishment." I anchored my hands around one knee and rocked back and forth.

General Kostikov stared at me and sat down again.

I said, "If you're here to take complaints, I haven't any. The food is good, the air is clean and the commode works. But I would like some reading material. Could I have the poems of Robert Service? *Pravda? Izvestia? Krokodil?* Any of them will do and I'll be much happier. It will help me remember to always say "sir' to you." I drew deeply on my cigarette. "Boris, sir."

His eyes narrowed. "You're putting on an act."

I pointed at my arm's injection marks. "Drugs made me the way I am. I don't remember things, so I don't think too much about the past. Tell me about the past, Boris. Sir. Or should I say 'Sir Boris'?"

He got to his feet and stared at me. "I'll be back. When you decide to stop this foolishness."

As he opened the door I called, "Don't forget newspapers."

He shot me a sneer and the door slammed shut. I was still smoking, still rocking back and forth when the Judas-window opened, then closed.

So ended my first session with General Boris Kostikov of the KGB.

One shave and three meals later, he returned.

Before he settled into the chair I said, "I want to see the chaplain."

"The—what?"

"Chaplain. To attend my spiritual needs."

"Why?"

"I have much to confess."

"Ah, then you are ashamed of your past life."

"Deeply. What I remember puzzles me. I thought the chaplain could help me sort it out."

"I'll consider your request."

"Did you consider my request for newspapers? Why didn't you

bring them? You're not cooperating in my treatment, Boris, sir. Did you bring cigarettes, sir?"

Irritably, he gave me one, lit it and sat down. "Let's dispense with nonsense. You're as sane as I am, so—"

"Then you were treated, too?" I smiled conspiratorially. "One can't become sane unless one is treated. Correct? Sir?"

"That's generally so," he said acidly, "but I was never treated here."

"*Ipso facto* you must be insane. You can stay here with me, Boris, sir. I'd like company. Will you send the chaplain?"

"The chaplain . . ." he waved a hand " . . . went to visit his family in—"

"That's a good thing about Orthodox priests," I murmured. "They don't have to be celibate like Catholic priests. Like the Pope."

"What made you think of the Pope?"

"He's a big religious leader and he's celibate. He requires his priests to refrain from sex." I drew deeply on my cigarette. "I guess Rasputin set the standard for Orthodox priests."

He glared at me. "Forget Rasputin."

"I liked it when John Barrymore drowned him in the river. There were ice floes and—"

"I said no more Rasputin. What do you have to tell the chaplain? Why not tell me?"

"You're an army officer, Boris, sir. Not a man of the cloth." I peered at his lapels. "That's not chaplain insignia."

"No, it's not," he said gruffly. "I'll see about a chaplain for you. Meanwhile—"

"—*and* newspapers. Paris had many papers—I guess you know that. Every day in the cafés I read them."

"Meanwhile, we must begin frank discussions. I ask questions, you answer them."

I said, "I'm ashamed to be in pajamas when you're dressed in that gorgeous uniform, sir. If I can't have a uniform I want my clothes. Then I could feel comfortable talking with you. Are you Ukrainian? Great Russian? Tatar? Uzbek? I like to know who I'm talking to."

"I'm Muscovite," he said, "and that is enough for you to know."

"Stalin was Georgian," I said thoughtfully, "and very proud of it. Moscow has old women sweeping snow from icy streets. As a Muscovite are you proud of that?"

His face reddened. "In the Soviet Union there is work for everyone."

"And a good thing, too. Sir." I lay back on my bed and blew smoke rings at the ceiling. "I left my vitamins in Paris. I need vitamins, Boris, sir. Can I have them?"

"The doctor will determine your needs."

"I enjoy a tossed salad from time to time—endive, artichokes, tomatoes—in Paris I ate quite well."

"How long were you in Paris?"

"I don't know. Years, I suppose, sir. I was a student at the Sorbonne and I worked nights as a waiter. The food and tips were good. Anyone could live well that way. Some of my friends begged from tourists in the Latin Quarter, but I was raised not to beg. Work or starve, sir, my father told me."

His gaze traveled around the room. "You have been well treated here, you haven't worked and you haven't starved."

"I didn't ask to come here, sir—or did I? I don't remember." I let another smoke ring drift upward.

Kostikov said, "I am tiring of your pretense."

"Give me my clothing."

"If I do that, will you talk—sensibly?"

I nodded, and beamed happily. "Your cigarettes taste better than Gauloises. I can forego wine if I have cigarettes."

He laid his pack on the foot of my bed. "Where did you learn Russian?"

"At my mother's knee. She was a Dukhobor. Many Russians came to Canada after the Revolution. Alaska used to belong to Russia. Did you know that?"

He stood up, dropped his cigarette on the floor and ground it under his shoe. "I am going to consider your requests." He walked to the door, and as he opened it I called, "Salad. With Russian dressing. Sir."

In a little while the nurse—Katya—brought in my clothing, less my shoes. Nothing had been washed or cleaned, and it all smelled stale. I thanked her and got dressed, putting on the old felt slippers she'd left me. Clothing was a step in the right direction. My wallet was missing, of course, along with Lazare's passport. I hadn't expected it to survive close scrutiny, but neither had I expected to fall into KGB hands.

How the hell had they known where Vasileyev was taken?

Either the Algerians had been uncharacteristically loosemouthed, or the snatch had been less than clean. I wondered what had happened to them—and the corpse of Vasileyev. Perhaps Kostikov would tell me.

When he returned he brought a pack of Marlboros, copies of *Pravda* and *Izvestia*—both old and shopworn. A second chair was brought in and we sat facing each other, smoking.

Finally, Kostikov said, "No more cowshit, eh? You were Purdey who became Lazare with a stolen passport. Who are you now?"

"Certain people called me Marston."

"Why?"

"It was the name given me."

"By the AIS?"

"I don't remember. Vitamins can help me remember."

He smiled tolerantly. "You think to avoid questioning and prolong your life by playing the fool. Was that part of your training?"

"I was taught to answer questions truthfully. Unless they were too—personal."

He said, "You know, I could send you to a severe regime camp tomorrow and no one would ever know your fate."

"*You* would know," I said, "and it would weigh on your conscience."

He grunted. "Impudent, too." He brought out my miniature tape recorder and displayed it. "No one has listened to Vasileyev's interrogation but myself. That permits us a margin for negotiation."

"What are we negotiating?"

"Your life."

TWENTY-TWO

I drew deeply on my cigarette. "If we're negotiating my life let's get on with it."

Kostikov nodded in satisfaction. "It would have been better for everyone concerned if Filip Sankov had not gone over to your people, the AIS—but he did, and that piece of history cannot be rewritten even by the Kremlin's expert revisionists. Of course, he was a fool to be caught with the wife of his chief, but Bulgarians are not noted for common sense. Sankov's prick ruled him, not his head." He got up and gripped the chair back with both hands. "As you probably know the KGB is closed to all but native-born Soviet citizens. For Sankov an exception was made because of his language facility and his father's rehabilitation. After training, he was for several years our window into the UDBA, and he served us well. There were even plans to position him to head UDBA, which required shaking up."

He exhaled smoke without removing the cigarette from his lips. "Following Sankov's defection, the usual decision was taken to locate and liquidate him. Because Ilya Vasileyev had been in charge of the project to liquidate Pope John Paul II, he was charged with silencing Sankov. The mission was urgent because of what Sankov could reveal concerning the secret Defense Council's decision to eliminate the Pope. You know from Vasileyev"—he tapped my tape recorder—"how we discovered Sankov's whereabouts. Vasileyev left Paris secretly, met his *spetznialny* team in New York, and directed their assault on the safehouse." He gestured at my right shoulder. "Your wounds confirm you were present."

"The only survivor."

"You were fortunate." He drew on his cigarette. "As was Vasileyev's custom, he exceeded instructions—only Sankov should have died. Instead—how many others?"

"Nine dead," I said, "and two dogs."

"His report reached me without delay and I understood ramifications that Vasileyev could not. Instead of a single surgical elimination he had conducted a massacre—and like a maniac, burned the safehouse in an insane attempt to conceal his excesses." He grunted. "I can imagine the scene when fire engines arrived with the police. So what was intended as routine execution of a traitor turned into wholesale slaughter marked by a raging fire." His expression was sour. "Thanks to Ilya Vasileyev." He looked at the ceiling and shook his head disgustedly. "That madman had no understanding of what our country was trying to accomplish in yours—the Mutual Non-Aggression Treaty, so long a goal of the Politburo and the Council of Ministers. Silencing Sankov was compatible with that goal, indeed essential if the American public was to accept the Treaty. Vasileyev assured us that everyone who had knowledge of Sankov's confession was eliminated that night, and he returned to his post in Paris. However, we were shortly to learn that one John F. Marston had been interrogating Sankov in depth and had survived the massacre. Yes, we have Sankov's handwritten confession filed safely away, along with the computer material you assembled."

"I was sure," I said, "it hadn't burned. Like all the video and audiotapes."

"We were going to recall Vasileyev for punishment, but the section responsible for him was afraid he would defect and reveal everything he knew. If he did that, the entire effort to silence Sankov would have been wasted—because Vasileyev was Sankov's chief and knew far more than the Bulgarian was ever told. So, a decision was taken to allow Vasileyev to complete his Paris assignment, live the good life, eat those rich, fattening meals, and hope his heart trouble would terminate him before he returned to Moscow." He ground out the cigarette on the floor and lighted another. "Meanwhile, there remained a problem to resolve, the problem posed by the only man fully aware of Sankov's confession." He eyed me and a thin smile formed on his lips. "Brent P. Graves."

My heart was pounding, but I tried to keep my face expressionless. "Well," I said, "unmasked at last. By whom I wonder?"

"By an agent long in place, an agent never called upon except in extreme emergency. And this situation—your continued existence—was evaluated as critical. So that agent's assistance was invoked." He glanced at the tape recorder again.

I said, "Apollo."

"Apollo," he repeated. "Apollo sanitized files and transferred personnel to eliminate any exposure of the conspiracy to assassinate the Pope."

"And he told the *spetznialny* how to locate and destroy me."

Kostikov nodded. "They came close to succeeding, Graves, but you were too clever. You destroyed them both, did you not?"

"I did," I said, "without a moment's remorse. Naumov lingered long enough to give me Vasileyev's name. Who was his partner?"

"The man who blew himself up? Chekalov—something like that, it's not important, he's dead." He gazed down at the tips of his polished shoes. "Vasileyev might be alive today but for his carelessness. You see, he had lived so long in the West that he began to think of himself as part of the scenery. He forgot conspiratorial discipline—and was easily captured by your men."

I stubbed out my cigarette and watched the dying spiral of smoke. "I've been wondering about that. How was he located? By chance?"

"Not entirely. The woman who lived with him, his office wife, obeyed the rules of *konspiratsiya*. Every evening she watched from the window to make sure he entered their building safely. That was part of her duties, Graves, because she was charged with the security of the SK—Sovietskaya Kolonia—in Paris. When she saw Vasileyev kidnapped, she quickly followed and reported the situation."

"And I walked into your arms," I said glumly. "After that—?"

"The Algerians were shot and Vasileyev's body removed."

"I'm sorry about the Algerians. Vasileyev"—I shrugged—"had it coming."

He nodded slowly. "His end was foreordained. Death by firing squad, or some frozen labor camp. But by hastening his death, Graves, you spared us some difficulty. The KGB never likes to have its officers examined and tried by civil authority; we prefer to discipline our own."

"For what it's worth, I didn't kill Vasileyev."

"Autopsy bears you out. He died of two things that occurred almost simultaneously—cerebral aneurism and heart failure. Probably brought on by the stress of interrogation, but latent physical defects doomed him in any case. I stress that because I want you to understand I don't hold Vasileyev's death against you."

"What about Naumov and Chekalov?"

"They were hunting you. You defended yourself." He spread his hands. "As far as the KGB is concerned the Washington police report has been accepted. Chekalov killed Naumov and blew himself up mishandling dynamite."

For a while the room was silent. All I could hear were the faint strains of music from a distant radio—Prokofiev or Khachaturian I thought.

Finally, General Kostikov spoke. "Why did you go to Paris? To kill Vasileyev?"

"I thought he must know who in the Firm was orchestrating this chaos. The murder of Dr. Cereza, a fine young woman with a useful life of healing ahead of her, old Monsignor Abelardo, Herbert Porter . . ." My mouth was dry. I drank from the chipped cup. "Apollo, he said. That was all."

Kostikov tossed the tape recorder on my bed. "Three Soviet agents are dead, can you be satisfied with that?"

"I suppose I should be."

"I think you should. You are an intelligent man with a considerable capacity to comprehend complicated situations. Honor has been satisfied through vengeance."

"I'll give a lot of thought to what you say, General," I said. "Does that lead to the main point? Negotiating over my life?"

"It does. Matters have so balanced themselves that the KGB is not your enemy. Accept that."

"Then why was I brought here, drugged and kept prisoner?"

"For two reasons. The first is that time was needed to establish a number of the things I have related to you. The solution was to confine you as painlessly as possible, allow you to dream the time away. The second reason is that you have knowledge—dangerous knowledge that could prevent ratification of the Treaty if you revealed it. Of course, I could simply have you injected lethally, but in reading reports of your activities I formed a certain professional admiration for you and was reluctant to see talent wasted. Accordingly, I ordered that you receive decent treatment during your confinement."

"How long will it last?"

"At least until the Treaty is ratified—and you know more about that process than I do."

"And after that, General?"

He sat down in the chair and gazed at me. "Beyond the KGB, Graves, you have a mortal enemy. I don't know if you could ever uncover Apollo—skilled men have tried—but as long as the two of you are alive, Apollo will be trying to liquidate you."

"I'm aware of that."

"So, what does your situation reduce to? What are your options? If I free you, Apollo will pursue you, and there is a limit to a man's luck, even yours."

"Do you know who Apollo is?"

He shook his head. "Only a few in his controlling section know his true name. In time you might be able to identify Apollo, but I doubt you could ever prove it. Already he has come close to destroying you. The position you occupied has disappeared. For all practical purposes, you have been discredited and isolated from your former colleagues, have you not?"

I nodded.

"You have no family dependent on you. You have private funds. You speak—to my knowledge—Russian, English, French and German. You performed hazardous work in Vietnam. You were trained by the American Intelligence Service, which has cast you out. I suppose you could go into some sort of business and add to your fortune, but I don't think money is important to you—or the uneventful existence of a businessman. I think you require more of life—matching wits, danger . . . am I right?"

"I guess that's the bottom line."

"There is another field in which you have obvious talent, Graves. I was well along the road to believing that drugs had deranged you. Then I read your all-source profile and realized how clever a dissimulator you are."

I said nothing.

"But even if I chose to protect you, I could not shield you from Apollo . . ." He leaned forward " . . . unless you agreed to work for me."

So that was it! The notion had occurred to me, but it seemed too far out.

"You weren't born in America," he said. "Basically, your education and inclinations are European. Why would you maintain your loyalty to an organization that has gotten rid of you, to a country that, in the long run, is destined to lose?" He stood up. "You are surprised by my proposal. Consider it a compliment, Graves. I don't require an answer now—I wouldn't be able to give one if you were recruiting me—but I will expect an answer when the Treaty is ratified."

"Would you expect me to work against the United States?"

"I was thinking of the China target. From Hong Kong, say. Or Japan."

"That would make things easier."

He nodded, and I saw a faint smile. "Still want a chaplain?"

"Since he's visiting his family . . ."

"Very well. I will come back—not to press you, but to exchange war stories. I have some interesting ones."

"I can imagine. Before I leave I'd like a tour of Leningrad. I've always wanted to see the Hermitage, the Kirov Ballet."

"National treasures," he said. "I can't promise, but in principle, everything is possible." He went out and I heard my door being locked.

I sat and smoked and began to consider his offer.

TWENTY-THREE

My next meal was a quantum improvement: two shoulder lamb-chops, parsley potatoes and a tomato-lettuce salad—with Russian dressing. And a cup of mediocre red wine. Close to five-star fare for Leningrad, I thought, and doubtless the best the clinic could provide.

Returning for my tray, the nurse—Katya, the SK informer—gave me two orange-colored pills and said they were vitamins. She waited until I'd swallowed them, then went away.

I read *Pravda* and leafed through *Izvestia* until my light went out. *Pravda's* Washington bureau provided a story about the pending Mutual Non-Aggression Treaty with the U.S. Its thrust was that although peace-loving peoples everywhere yearned for ratification, it was being opposed by right-wing militarist fanatics who preferred escalation and the threat of war, with the prospect of profits, to peaceful accommodation. Senator Frank Connors was quoted as saying he generally favored Treaty ratification, but was mindful of divided public opinion. *Pravda* praised the Senator for rejecting the outworn linkage principle and recognizing that the Soviet Union as a sovereign power was entitled to give assistance to its friends, whether in Afghanistan, Africa or Central America.

As I lay in bed, I wondered if Connors was the right man to take action on Sankov's confession. Toby Gerard thought so, and in my prolonged absence he might have breached our agreement and already delivered our material to the Senator. I hoped not. I was depending on his judgment.

According to Kostikov, my release depended on ratification, and I had no reason to disbelieve him. Therefore, the Treaty hadn't yet been ratified.

I picked up my small recorder from where Kostikov had left it and rewound the tape. As it played back I heard my questions and Vasileyev's answers: the three treacherous priests; how the Washington Embassy had spotted Sankov's location through signal intelligence. And the name Apollo.

I heard myself saying, *"Fini . . . Mort"*, the shuffling of the Algerians' shoes on the flooring and the click ending the recording.

Kostikov had known I would replay it because I had little else to do. And as an experienced KGB officer he probably thought it would aid my reflections on his offer.

I could understand his wanting to recruit me, for the reasons he'd stated. The sugarcoating was his suggestion that I work against the China target. But if Soviet policy changed, Kostikov could order me to work against my own country.

True, I was bitter over being ejected from the Firm, but I now believed it was Apollo's work rather than a concerted personnel decision. So my anger was more properly directed at the nameless traitor who conspired to kill Joann, Herb, Giuseppe Abelardo—and myself. Whoever Apollo was he had to be somewhere at a top level.

But if Angleton, with all his internal resources, had been unable to expose Apollo, how could I—working from outside and with no assets whatever?

KGB officers led privileged lives both within the Soviet Union and abroad. I knew it and Kostikov was aware that I knew. For that reason the West had had little success in inducing KGB defections. We couldn't offer anything comparable to what the KGB officer already enjoyed—except freedom. So we settled for walk-ins who'd screwed up and feared recall. Walk-ins like Sankov, who before his defection had been evaluated as a True Believer and invulnerable to inducements.

Kostikov was offering me a privileged position and steady employment against a major Communist target—initially, at least. He had implied he might free me even if I declined, but I couldn't believe that. The only other option was death. Refuse, and I would never leave the clinic alive. Poison by pill, food or injection would terminate me almost effortlessly. No one would ever know.

Because Kostikov was protecting me—if he was to be believed—he might be setting up a cell apart from the regular KGB directorates, a group of agents responsive only to him. As a Major General, Kostikov would be able to muster resources to develop his personal group of agents, and in any showdown with the KGB Chairman, their existence could provide Kostikov with life-saving leverage.

If by some miracle I returned to the States, what would be my position? Would the Firm try to prosecute me for alleged disloyalty? How could I prove a negative—that I *wasn't* disloyal?

The British system was far more favorable to traitors. Unless one confessed—as Blake had—prosecution was impossible. Which was why Philby, McLean and Burgess had been allowed to flee to Moscow, their treachery unpunished. Even Anthony Blunt, who confessed under a grant of immunity, was allowed to continue his career in the Royal Household until he was exposed by MI-5 interrogators disgusted at his refusal to abide by his bargain and reveal everything he knew.

During retirement and after his death, a damning case of treason had been built against Sir Roger Hollis, longtime head of MI-5. Even so, the smoking gun was lacking and Britain's Prime Minister, in a mealy-mouthed statement, defended Hollis's loyalty.

Without question, the British system was heavily loaded in favor of Soviet spies. In contrast, a number of disloyal American intelligence officers had been publicly tried and imprisoned.

I knew it, and Kostikov was aware that I knew it.

Leaving me what alternatives?

I visualized Leningrad's geographical location—on the Gulf of Finland about two hundred miles east of Helsinki. Even if I could get out of my locked room, how could I survive in the city and then get to Finland? I had never heard of a Russian escaping by the water route, how could I?

I might delay accepting Kostikov's offer to join his organization, but unless events intervened I was eventually going to have to make the choice.

I knew what my answer to Kostikov would have to be.

When Kostikov returned I complimented him on the improved cuisine. "Eggs for breakfast with bread and coffee. Pork, spinach and fried potatoes for lunch. With coffee."

"I thought you might prefer coffee to tea. Coffee makes my heart race—I don't drink it." He sat down and produced a deck of cards. "Rummy?"

"Why not?"

We tried playing on the bed, but the cards wouldn't slide, so he bellowed into the corridor for a table to be brought in.

It was old, wooden, badly made and much painted, but it provided a playing surface. Once I'd analyzed Kostikov's penchant for knocking early I took advantage of it to nail him three hands out of four. He liked to eye the discard heap, so I blocked it neatly, depriving him of that unfair advantage. I won the next two games by sizeable scores and Kostikov drew back his chair. "Enough. Keep the cards for solitaire. Vodka?"

"Sure."

The nurse brought it in two tumblers—his large, mine the two-ounce size. He lit a cigarette and told me he'd served a year in Afghanistan, managed to be wounded lightly and evacuated to Moscow for recovery. "Like your Vietnam troops, our Ivans became quickly disaffected. Malingering, self-wounding—defections were everywhere. Young boys smoked hemp and became addicted. And what was my responsibility? I was supposed to maintain the morale of a mountain regiment while acting as senior political officer for the entire command."

Angrily, he blew smoke across the table. "How was Vietnam for you? How did you like it?"

"I didn't like losing," I said, "but I got out alive. That was good. And I try not to think about the bad."

"We're much the same, Graves. Once a soldier, always a soldier, eh?"

"Always someone above you giving orders."

His eyes narrowed, and I sensed that he was thinking about the levels that separated him from Chairmanship of the KGB. Andropov had parlayed that position into the Chairmanship of the secret Defense Council, the Presidency, and maneuvered so skillfully that he became General Secretary of the Party. No KGB officer had climbed that high before, but with Andropov's precedent, why not Boris Kostikov?

He seemed to bring himself back from a reverie. "When Stalin died I was a young lieutenant, schooled to believe that he was the greatest wartime military leader. Then Khrushchev began systematically downgrading Stalin, revealing that he had been as mad and impulsive as Hitler. Stalin's insane directives prolonged the war, costing more thousands of soldiers' lives." He exhaled smoke across the gathered cards. "Did you know that two days after Hitler's attack, the Soviet Union had no air force? Stalin was warned of the onslaught but refused to alert our pilots." He shrugged. "What is the value of even the best intelligence if the leadership ignores it?"

He seemed in a revisionist mood, depressed. I knew the feeling. I said, "You were going to tell me about some of your professional triumphs, General."

"Yes . . . so I was." In earlier years, he told me, he had worked in the Balkans, kidnapped a Yugoslav cabinet member from his house and killed him. "As a warning to Tito," he explained.

In India he had agitated Muslims against Hindus and recruited the Foreign Minister. "He was ripe for recruitment, for he hated the British. At Cambridge he had been shunned and called "nigger,' so he was eager to work with us against the West. A spellbinding orator at the United Nations, he drew new, unaligned countries into an anti-Western voting Bloc. Until his death, that man really needed no direction from me. Once pointed in the correct direction he functioned automatically." He sipped from his tumbler. "I was in Cuba, too, setting up Castro's internal security service when our missiles began arriving. I warned Khrushchev against it but I was too late—the decision had been made. When Khrushchev was forced to back down he was like a madman in his humiliation. He remembered those who had warned against the move, and retaliated against us. Until his displacement I served in the Kuriles and felt myself lucky not to have been sentenced to mine gold in Kolyma. Then I was rehabilitated and sent to Ankara for a time. Not an easy post, because the Turks are implacable foes, with long memories. I had a hand in getting the English spies safely to Moscow, and later I was charged with getting George Blake out of Wormwood Scrubs." He sipped again, draining the last of his vodka. "The British thought Blake would never leave prison, but I managed the entire escape at a cost of less than ten thousand pounds. Even I was amazed by the corruptibility of British guards and officials." He smiled at the memory.

I said, "Did you have a hand in Vasileyev's attempt against the Pope?"

"Fortunately, no. A special group directed that, and in any case I was vacationing with my wife on the Black Sea."

"I've heard Sochi is very pleasant."

"Invigorating. I'll take you there one day, help you select a bungalow for yourself."

The casual commitment chilled me, because it meant I would never leave the Soviet Union. All the talk of Hong Kong and Tokyo was just careful misdirection. "I'd like that," I said, "if things should work out that way."

"And what have been your achievements in the clandestine world?"

"Nothing on the scale of yours, General. Mostly hunting Soviet agents and persuading host governments to help me."

"That's what you did in France?"

"Along with duplicating the Embassy's political reporting."

"And Spain? You were Illegal there?"

"I had contacts in Opus Dei," I said, "trying to prevent a Socialist takeover after Franco died. Obviously my trivial efforts were unsuccessful."

He slapped the table. "Ever since the Great War your country and the entire West has been in retreat from the forces of Communism, you agree?"

"I have to."

"Then you must accept the inevitability of Communist victory."

"I'm reaching that point," I said. "By and large, most of Europe prefers being Red to dead, and the infection spreads in my own country."

"It's so obvious," he said, "that people everywhere—government officials, business giants, scientists—are making private deals with us in the hope they'll be spared and permitted to live as usual." He grunted. "Lenin's useful fools. And as for this Non-Aggression Treaty, the Soviet Union will impose *its* peace, and friendship from the conquered will follow." He stared at me unblinkingly. "As night follows day."

"Well said, Comrade General. Historical inevitability."

"To me you don't appear to be a man who would cling forever to a losing cause."

"Until now," I said, "what options did I have?"

He got up and straightened his uniform blouse. "I'm gratified that you are beginning to think in sensible directions. I'll return tomorrow. You play cribbage?"

"Not well."

"Then I will bring a cribbage board. *Dosvidanya.*"

"*Dosvidanya.*"

He left the room and locked the door.

As I gathered the cards together I noticed that they had been printed in Barcelona. That started a train of thought.

I turned the wooden table on its side and knelt to study the unpainted underside. Stenciled there was a faded manufacturing marking: Lacombe Frères. St-Etienne—Loire.

The table had been made in France. Why would a cheap, French-made table be in Leningrad, USSR? The Russians made tables just as badly. Or Spanish playing cards? There was an answer, but I hardly dared believe it.

I tested the joints where the legs were nailed to the table. One leg was looser than the others. I pried and twisted until it came loose, straightened the rusted nails with my fingers and stood up. The leg was about three feet long, the nails looked menacing. I turned it over in my hands, gripped the floor-end like a baseball bat and swung.

I had a weapon.

TWENTY-FOUR

The weapon gave me hope. I replaced the table leg, righted the table and lay on my bed, heart pounding.

When my light went out I couldn't sleep and didn't want to. Adrenalin coursed through my bloodstream, honed my thoughts. I began forming a plan.

Either I was in the Soviet Union or I wasn't. The playing cards and table suggested the latter, but what if I was in Leningrad, as Kostikov said? I had to plan for that as well.

A high-speed hydrofoil operated over the waters between Leningrad and Helsinki. Two hundred miles, four to five hours travel. But how to pass Soviet emigration controls and board the hydrofoil? Without rubles how could I buy passage?

The alternative was a longer journey by foot through thick forests and chilly marshes around the Gulf's northern perimeter. Two weeks at best, dodging patrols, without food or weapons . . . Survival, facing very long odds. On the other hand, my prospects for survival at the clinic were doubtful. Once I accepted recruitment by Kostikov I would be more closely watched than ever. I was to be his latest prize; he wouldn't risk my slipping from his grasp.

General Boris Kostikov was my solution.

As promised, he returned with cribbage board and pegs. He took off his uniform blouse and we settled down to play. In 'Nam I'd had more pressing things to do than play cribbage, so Kostikov beat me three games running. I sat back, said I was hungry and wanted my meal, whatever it was. He pounded on the door, Katya came running and unlocked it. Curtly he told her to bring me food, and we played crib until she carried in a tray.

Not knowing how long it would be until my next meal, I drank the potato soup, wolfed meat chunks with boiled beans and ate the last crumb of bread. I sugared my coffee heavily—for energy—and when we resumed play I managed to glance at his wristwatch; 7:00 PM.

I considered my next move. Once committed, it was irrevocable. Either I succeeded or I would never leave the room alive. Kostikov would kill me and disembarrass himself of failure.

From this moment on everything depended on timing.

I decided not to wait for the end of the game, because I wanted Kostikov's gaze on the board, planning his next move. So I got up, opened my fly and went over to the commode. While urinating I watched the back of his neck. His hair was gray and white, like a badger's. After flushing the commode I walked silently to a position behind his left shoulder. Kostikov was still looking intently at the cribbage board as I swung my right arm downward. The stiffened edge of my hand struck hard above his collar. Without a sound his body collapsed against the table edge.

I didn't know if my blow had snapped his spinal cord, but my hand ached from the impact. As quietly as I could I dragged his body to the far side of the bed where it couldn't be seen from the door. I went through his trouser pocket and got out his billfold, stuffed it into mine. After turning him over I drew his wrists behind his back and knotted his belt around them as tightly as I could. I tore strips from a bedsheet and tied his ankles together. Then I went through the pockets of his military blouse. All I got from them was a package of cigarettes and a Swiss army knife.

I went back to Kostikov, pulled off his shoes, and got into them. They were a little large but they were better than the old felt slippers. While I was doing that his body twitched and he groaned. I jammed his handkerchief into his mouth and secured it there with another strip from the sheet.

That done, I took off his watch and put it on my own wrist. The time was 7:04.

I could wait for Katya to retrieve my tray or I could accelerate her arrival. While making up my mind I pulled off the loose table leg and felt its solid weight in my hands.

I was ready.

As Kostikov did, I went to the door, pounded on it and yelled, "*Katya*" imitating his deep voice. Then I stepped back.

Presently came the sound of the key unlocking the door. I waited until she was fully inside, kicked the door shut behind her and swung the club at her midriff. The blow drove her back against the door; her eyes rolled upward and she slid down. I opened the door far enough to retrieve her keyring, and locked the door from inside. Then I bound and gagged her with sheet strips.

My pulse was racing, my mouth dry. I gulped down a cup of water, took three deep breaths and unlocked the door.

Opening it slowly, I listened, heard no hostile sounds, then stepped out, quietly locking the door behind me.

I was in a dimly lit hallway. At the far end I could see a desk and a staircase. Someone was sitting at the desk, back to me. Club in my right hand, open knife in my left, I tiptoed the length of the corridor, came up behind the man at the desk and swung the club viciously against his head. With an *Oof!* breath left his lungs, and he began to topple sideways. I caught his body and let it slide down into the kneehole out of sight. Then I went to the top of the staircase and listened. There was light coming from below, but no sound.

For a clinic—and a mental clinic—it was a very quiet place. It seemed more like an old-fashioned rooming house than an institution, but then I'd never been in a Russian clinic before.

Kostikov's shoes felt strange on my feet, rigid, binding. How long since I'd worn leather? Ten days? Two weeks? Holding knife and club, I began going down the stairs.

Five steps and I saw a narrow lobby, a small registration counter by the wall. Beyond it a man's profile. He was sitting in a chair watching the screen of a small black-and-white television set. I could neutralize him or try to sneak past. If I attacked him successfully someone would notice his absence and pursuit would begin. I crouched as low as possible and started down one step at a time.

A riser creaked, my heart seemed to stop, but the sound was covered by a burst of laughter from the television set. The man was laughing, too, bending forward until his head was out of sight. I went down the last five steps as quickly as I could, looked around, saw no one and went out of the open entrance door.

I stood my club against the outside frame, gripped my knife and thrust my right hand in my pocket.

My ears, accustomed to silence, were so sensitive that the sounds of passing cars were almost painful. I looked right and left, saw passers-by and fell in behind two elderly women carring shopping bags. A lone car passed and I recognized it as a Peugeot. The next car a Citroën. I stared at it, because the license plate was long and narrow, black letters and numbers against a white background. Moscow tags, I remembered, were oblong and much smaller. Where were the Zils, the Moskvitches?

I stepped to the curb and looked back at the doorway that was my exit to the street. Above the doorway a flaking sign was lettered: Hôtel Duquesne.

Swallowing hard, I walked to the street intersection and stared up at a blue metal sign whose white letters read: Rue Meslay 2°.

Only then did I fit it all together. It hit me like a physical blow. I was dizzy with a surge of emotion.

I wanted simultaneously to sob and shriek hysterical laughter to the Paris skies.

Instead I turned and ran through the night.

The money in Kostikov's billfold was French, not Russian. Under a streetlight I transferred the bills to my pocket, changed one at the Laumière Métro station and used a coin to telephone the police commissariat of the Second Arrondissement. In an urgent, fearful voice I described shooting overheard at the Hotel Duquesne where a *patron* and his whore had argued violently. Then I hung up.

I would have enjoyed seeing the *flics* drag Boris and Katya from the hotel—assuming both were alive and able to walk—but it was a pleasure I had to deny myself. Instead, I relaxed in my seat as the Metro bore me southwest at high speed.

At the Hôtel de Ville stop I got out and climbed up to the brilliantly lit square. I sucked in cool night air that had never tasted so sweet, the air of freedom. On foot I crossed the short bridge to the Ile St-Louis and walked along the quai to my apartment building.

The concierge was having dinner in her apartment, so I lifted a key from the board and went up to my floor.

As usual the hall was dark, but I found the door lock and began inserting the key. Before I could turn it I felt something jab my spine. "Don't move. Where is she?"

Shit! I began raising my arms, spun around and kicked the man's belly. He yelped, bent over and tottered backward but stayed upright. I couldn't see a weapon, both hands were clutching his belly. I jerked his head back and saw the gaunt, bearded face of Raoul Boucher.

I opened my door, turned on the light and looked at him. He looked thin, wasted. This was the Latin lover my wife had left me for. I said, "If you mean Marilyn, she went back home."

"I want her," he bleated.

"Go get her," I said. "She's all yours."

He took a half-step in my direction. I said, "Forty-one Elm Street, Pottstown, PA. Keep her out of my life."

"You never understood. We were meant for each other."

"I believe it now," I told him. "Two sensitive souls struggling against an unfeeling world. Beat it." I closed and locked my door and set the snub chain, then headed for the cognac. I poured a stiff shot and gulped it down with a Perrier chaser. How long had Raoul kept his unrewarded vigil? I kicked off Kostikov's shoes and began going through his wallet.

A scrap of paper bore the scrawled inscription, Hotel Duquesne, rue Meslay 2º—old information. The principal find was a French diplomatic carnet in the name of Colonel Nikolai V. Kuzchin, Assistant Military Attaché, Union des Republiques Sovietiques Socialistes.

The photograph, though, showed the man who called himself Boris Kostikov, Major General.

Either name could be the true one. I suspected Kuzchin was the cover name, the lower rank allowing him more freedom to move about, get into things. Whoever he was, I hoped he would spend the night in the slammer, yelling about diplomatic immunity to indifferent guards. Tomorrow his Embassy would reclaim him and cool him off. Then would come a long period of unpleasant questioning . . . Tough tit, Boris, I thought, and went to my wall cache at the far end of the living room.

After pulling out a cabinet I slid molding aside and took out money, my Purdey passport and the HK .38. Kostikov/Kuzchin had its 9mm twin and I hoped he would use it to blow off his fucking head.

There was plenty of money in the envelopes: dollars and Swiss francs. Boris had my wallet, I used his to take a mix of currencies. I left his carnet in the cache and closed it.

At the Duquesne I'd had nothing but an occasional whore-bath, and I needed the real thing badly. Letting the shower run, I stripped off smelly clothing and laid out a change from my closet. Then I stepped under hot, refreshing water, soaped thoroughly and found myself humming "Rainy-Day Lovers" for no reason at all.

After shaving I dressed and packed the rest of my clothing, taped the pistol inside my ghetto-blaster and decided I was ready to move. I wanted to get back in touch with Toby Gerard, but not now. Wherever tomorrow found me I would put through a call.

After leaving money and key with the concierge I took a taxi to the Invalides Aero-Gare and went from one airline counter to another, looking for the next flight to Switzerland. The Sabena clerk told me I had just time enough to catch their flight to Bern—the airport bus was poised to depart for Roissy De Gaulle.

So I bought a first-class ticket and got aboard.

As the bus hummed south through the night I analyzed my situation. Kostikov and I knew that he had given me information about himself, Vasileyev and Apollo that he would never have provided had he thought I would be able to use it. Overconfidence had softened his judgment and now his position was endangered.

If he was alive he would be after me. Like Sankov, I had to be silenced. Apollo—whoever he was—would agree. So although I was free I was still the target of implacable forces. By leaving France I was throwing off pursuers while finding temporary haven in Switzerland. I needed time to organize my thoughts, to plan and develop countermoves. Kostikov didn't know I had copies of Sankov's filmed confession; only Toby did. The videotape was crucial to exposing the Kremlin's role in the conspiracy against the Pope. Properly used it could block the Treaty.

At Bern airport French-speaking Immigration officers stamped my alias passport and wished me a pleasant stay. I played my stereo while Customs officials went through my suitcase, and then I rode a taxi to the Zahringen Hotel, near the Bahnhof in downtown Bern.

Registering, I said I would keep the room two or three nights, bought London, New York and Zurich newspapers, and looked through them in my room.

On the plane I'd eaten a delicate chicken sandwich with a glass of champagne, but I was hungry again—not from physical exertion, but because my nerves were strung out. I went over to the Bahnhof's all-night cafe and ate a well-flavored veal ragout with fresh Swiss bread, red wine and coffee. There was still too much adrenalin in my system for sleep, so I walked through Old Town Bern, strolled cobbled streets past arcade shops on the Kramgasse. I paused before the four hundred-year-old Zytgloggeturn Clock Tower and reset Kostikov's watch to Bern time. From there I went down to the slow-flowing Aare and followed its horseshoe bend around and back toward my hotel. Lighted fountains were spouting, some of them decorated with brightly painted statues of notables.

One depicted blind Justice with sword and scales; at her feet an emperor, a sultan and a Pope.

Which Pope I didn't know, but his figure reminded me of John Paul II, and I thought again of Sankov, Ali Agca and Vasileyev as I passed near the solid Gothic form of the old Munster church.

My mother had recommended Dr. Walther Brock as an old family friend to whom I could turn for help. I searched the room telephone directory for his name, and not finding it, decided his permanent home must still be in Zurich. Mother had said Brock was science adviser to the Bundesrat. Under that listing I found his name.

It was more than twenty years since I had seen Dr. Brock. Younger than my father, he had been a dedicated skier and outdoorsman, a fair-skinned man with bristle-cut black hair, a thick mustache and penetrating eyes. By now, I thought, his hair would be silver gray, his face lined, glasses aiding vision.

Tomorrow at his Bundesrat office I was going to tell him about Sankov's confession and ask his help in staying alive. I knew he had resources that could be of use to me if he was willing to help.

TWENTY-FIVE

After a hearty breakfast of sweet rolls, sausage, chops and fried potatoes in the hotel grill I set out for the federal parliament building. An open-air farmers' market filled the Bundesplatz with shoppers seeking farm-fresh vegetables, cut flowers and cottage handicrafts. I went up the steps into the big lobby and asked the receptionist for Herr Professor Walther Brock's office.

"In the east wing," she said, "on the level below this. Take the first corridor on your right and his office will be found halfway along, to the left. If," she cautioned, "the Herr Professor is here today. You have an appointment?"

"If he's in I'm sure he'll see me. We're old friends."

I followed directions and entered an open doorway. The typist's desk was empty, and to its left I could see a man seated at a desk in the adjoining room. I walked toward it, rapped on the door, and the man looked up.

"Dr. Brock," I said, "I'm David's son, Brent."

He rose slowly, pulled off his spectacles and peered at me,

"Brent . . . Brent Graves. What an unexpected pleasure. Come in, my boy, come in." Putting on his spectacles he came from around his desk, took my hand and gave me a warm hug. Then he stepped back and we looked at each other.

There was more silver than gray in his short hair, and his face was leathery and wrinkled. The mustache was there, pure silver now, and he traced an index finger across it in a gesture I remembered.

"How long has it been?" he asked.

"Nearly twenty years."

"Your mother—she always remembers to send a Christmas card. She is comfortable, Brent? Well?"

"Some knee trouble, otherwise just the same."

He gazed at my face with the same penetrating, half-critical intensity I remembered from my Zurich childhood. Then he looked away and said, "Truly a cause for celebration. When did you arrive, where are you staying?"

"Last night, the Zahringen. I tried to call you but your number wasn't in the book."

"Ah, well, I keep a *pied-à-terre* in Bern to accommodate me when the Nationalrat is meeting. There is more than enough room for you. You'll stay with me."

"Gladly," I said. "I have much to tell you."

"I'm sure you do—and we'll have time."

On his desk a bell chimed and he shook his head. "I'm afraid I must leave for a conference. Here, take this key and move in, we'll lunch together." He wrote down the apartment address, pulled on his jacket and gathered files into a thick fiber folder. We walked up to the main floor, Brock waved and disappeared down a corridor.

The parliament building was filled with well-dressed, well-fed Swiss, and I could hear snatches of French, Schweizerdeutsch, Italian, and Romansh as I made my way outside.

By eleven-thirty I was moved into Brock's comfortable two-bedroom apartment on the tenth floor of a high-rise building two miles north of the city. From the balcony I looked down on the entrance garden. Cars moved along the tree-lined street. Here, outside Bern proper, there were other high-rises; Bern's building code limited all building to four stories. I could see the Aare River like a shimmering necklace around the old city. Looking west I could glimpse the distant Jura range beyond which lay the valleys and meadows of France.

I remembered how my father had crossed those mountains as his war was drawing to a close, leading his band of evaders into sanctuary from the Wehrmacht. He seldom mentioned the hardships they encountered, but I knew they drank melted snow and huddled together for warmth in the brutal cold. Any man, I thought, would be proud to have been my father's friend, and Walther Brock was one of his closest.

My memories of Zurich homes involved fumed oak, heavy drapes and dark Germanic furnishings. Brock's *pied-à-terre* was light and furnished with chromium chairs covered in beige leather and nubby cloth. Bright modern prints hung on the walls. There was a kitchen-breakfast nook with gleaming pans and cutlery hanging from the walls. It was a man's place, basic and efficient, and I wondered whether Walther Brock had ever married and if so whether he was a widower now.

Only one door was locked and I assumed it was his office. As science adviser to the seven-man governing council, Brock probably had to bring home sensitive documents from time to time. Switzerland manufactured precision ordance and sold it to whoever could pay their price. Moreover, the Swiss had developed miniaturized computers so advanced and specialized that the country was flooded with Japanese trying to steal or buy the superlative technology.

The telephone rang, and after I answered, Brock said we'd meet for lunch at the Zweizimmer Restaurant on Kramgasse. It was almost in the shadow of the old Clock Tower. I said I'd be there at twelve forty-five.

We lunched in a smoky, masculine atmosphere redolent of delicious scents and frosted steins, eating rump steaks with—what else?—Sauce Béarnaise, noodles and mixed vegetables. We talked about old times in Zurich when my father was alive, the skiing and skating, the toboggan slide I'd made of our slanting drive. Brock smiled. "Almost broke my wrist on it, Brent. Your ice was under light snow and I started for your doorway—almost didn't get there. You never knew that."

"Dad was pretty tolerant of my hobbies."

"And after your mother sent you off to a proper English school we rarely saw each other."

"I remember you at Father's funeral."

He nodded slowly. "A sad day for us all. Not even fifty and a life of great promise, only part of which he had fulfilled. But for David his family came first. I, on the other hand—well I tried marriage, but it wasn't for me. I had brothers and sisters and their families—and, of course, the family Graves."

He drained his stein and beckoned for another. "When you went off to your Asian war your mother was horribly frightened. She wrote from time to time—I was one of her few male friends from Zurich days—telling how greatly she feared you would be killed. Brent, I must tell you I could never understand why you went—in my eyes you were always Swiss. Have you thought of coming back?"

"Only recently," I said, "because Mother suggested it."

"And that is why you are here? I can put you in touch with—"

But I shook my head. "I'm here briefly," I said, "I hope. I'm keeping my options open. I have a strange tale to tell you, but not here."

"Then tonight at the apartment. I'd love to hear it. Behind thick lenses his eyes narrowed. "Some sort of trouble?"

I nodded.

"Don't worry. If I can't resolve it alone I have friends who can. Powerful friends, Brent, who respect me as I respected your father. The best kind of friends to have." He sipped from his stein. "Let me see, you survived the war, took graduate studies at—Columbia, was it not? And then"—he leaned forward—"your mother let me understand you'd taken up government service in some sort of intelligence capacity."

"That's true, but she shouldn't have told even you." I studied the

Venus reclining coyly on the wall behind the bar. "Now it makes no difference."

He motioned for the check. "Tonight we'll go into that—and other things. Meanwhile, use my telephone, and if you want to write letters there is a machine and paper in my little office. The door is locked but the key is in the kitchen." He smiled. "Behind the cuckoo clock. Nothing of value to protect, but I don't like Herta, my cleaning woman, disarranging my desk. Feel free to use it."

"I will."

We'd covered everything except the revelation I was going to make in private, so we parted outside the restaurant, Brock returning to his office while I taxied back to his apartment.

I found the office key in its hiding place, unlocked his door and sat behind his desk. For a while I considered phoning Toby Gerard—it was midmorning in Washington—but I remembered the Soviet capacity to intercept electronic communications, and the U.S. Senate was a natural target. Instead, I wound paper into the Olivetti and typed a long letter to Toby that updated him on everything that had happened since my note from Paris: Alekseyev, Kostikov/Kuzchin . . . the lethal hand of Apollo, my temporary refuge with Dr. Walther Brock. I asked Toby to lay everything before Senator Connors if in Toby's judgment Connors would make our findings public and not bury them in a circular file.

The essential question, of course, was Apollo's identity.

I'd formed some thoughts on the subject but saw no point in laying them before Toby Gerard. He had no experience in security investigations or CI work, and I had very little more. But I was at least familiar with the clandestine milieu and the workings of secret intrigues, as Toby was not. General Kostikov had been proud of Apollo, and with reason.

To me it was unthinkable that the Director was Apollo. The Soviet mole, however, had to be located within the Director's circle of close subordinates. Apollo couldn't be in the overt Directorate of Intelligence; he had to be either in the Operations Directorate, or so placed that he enjoyed an overview of the Agency's clandestine operations. Chief of Personnel was one possibility; Chief of Logistics another. Within Operations, the CI Chief knew almost everything that went on, but Herb Porter was dead, and his replacement—unknown to me—hadn't been in charge when most of the dirty work was done. The Chief of Security was a remote possibility—very remote—and I was willing to discard him from the list.

As for the Area Chiefs—such as Sandy Parton—their authority was limited geographically, as was the information that crossed their desks. So it would take a combination of Area Chiefs to make one Apollo, a practical impossibility. No, Apollo was a singleton agent working alone, exercising authority in plausible ways to serve Soviet ends. He had to be one of four or five officers who were the Director's immediate executives. The Executive Officer, Heydon Bissett, came to mind; I hadn't considered him before.

Realistically, the identification of Apollo was a task for inside investigators. I wasn't inside. Banished, in flight, I had to work toward Apollo with the slimmest of resources: knowledge of the Firm, operational intuition and a burning desire to save my own life. If luck stayed with me, one day we would converge.

I addressed the envelope to Toby's home and looked unsuccessfully for a stamp. I'd buy one later at the Bureau de Poste.

The office walls were lined with bookshelves containing mainly scientific and mathematical tomes. Whatever nonscientific books he possessed I assumed were in his Zurich home. There were photographs of Brock with other skiers at Davos, Appenzell and Buchs. Brock climbing the Matterhorn—his alpenstock and *piolet* were crossed on the wall like swords. Photographs of Alpine meadows; a younger Brock clownishly presenting edelweiss to a rather severe-looking woman. His wife?

On a shelf among his textbooks was a Philips multiband receiver, sponge-covered earphones atop the set. I could imagine him reading and writing at this desk while listening to the London Symphony live from Albert Hall.

I left the office and carried Toby's letter to a doorside table as a reminder to take it with me when I went out.

I lay on my bed, relaxing from the heavy meal and thinking about Ghislaine Sevier Mountjoy. Lainey. I missed her but hadn't had much time to think about her and our plan for joining our lives. In the "clinic" room I'd been too drugged or too distracted to imagine happier times.

I ought to write her now, I thought, and I would have—except that I was tired and sleep was coming over me.

It was after seven when Professor Brock woke me. He'd made a shaker of Manhattans and a fondue was bubbling in the kitchen. We used long spearlike forks to dip chunks of bread and cubes of beef into the creamy melted cheese. He made espresso and took our cups into the living room. Sitting in comfortable chairs we sipped coffee. Brock lit his pipe, I drew on a cigarette and Brock said, "Whatever you want to tell me, Brent, I'll hold in strictest confidence."

"I know that," I said, "and that's why I'm here." Then I began to talk.

TWENTY-SIX

Telling the tale took more than half an hour. When I sat back to sip coffee the dregs were cold. I lit my third cigarette and exhaled slowly. Brock said, "So they convinced you you were in Leningrad."

"Recognizing Katya from her DST photo gave me my first slight hope that I might not be. She was assigned to Paris, and though it was possible she'd flown with me to Leningrad, it was equally possible she hadn't."

"Then you noticed the Spanish playing cards and the French-made table," he said musingly.

"Even so it was a shock to find myself in Paris, welcome though it was."

"I can imagine. Coffee?"

He filled our cups and brought them back. "Like your father," he said, "you are extraordinarily resourceful. Still, you have no idea who Apollo might be?"

"Several candidates, but the names wouldn't mean anything

to you."

"So what are you planning next, Brent? How can I help you? You're welcome to stay as long as you want, you know."

"I need another identity. Perhaps your contacts could come up with a source."

He touched his white mustache. "It's possible, but I'll have to ask very discreetly, because of the illegality. That could take time."

"How long?"

"Three or four days." He knocked dottle from his pipe and began tamping fresh tobacco into the bowl. "How urgent is it?"

"I feel reasonably secure here, but there's not much I can accomplish from Bern. I was considering going to Rome to try learning more about the assassination conspiracy, but I'd be exposing myself without much offsetting chance of success."

"So you'll do—what?" He lit a match and applied it to his pipe. "Go back to the U.S. and look for Apollo?"

"Eventually. First, I think it's important I see Senator Connors, answer questions he'll have." I gestured at the letter on the table by the door.

"I'll mail that for you," he said. "Letters from Parliament receive preferred handling. Now, how many copies of the Sankov tape did you make?"

"Gerard has one, another is at my bank and the third is with my lawyer." I didn't mention the one at Lainey's house. It was reserve, and I didn't think it would ever be needed.

He said, "Very foresighted, Brent. Clear thinking under stress—a quality your father displayed." He sucked on his pipestem. "Doubtless you know he supplied technical information to your Government. Secret information from here."

"So I've heard. He told you?"

"More than that—I helped him from time to time. Today, of course, as a Government official I couldn't take such chances. Swiss espionage laws are very severe."

"But no death penalty." I stubbed out my cigarette. "I wonder if you're aware of a number of strange deaths in the European scientific community?"

"Such as?"

"Four in Britain, two in West Germany and one in Italy. That might not be unusual mortality except that all the victims were employed by companies performing subcontracted work on the U.S. Star Wars defense. Three suicides, three car accidents, one victim of an ostensible terrorist shooting."

"Incredible!"

"They were key scientists, Walther, close to irreplaceable. The Soviets selected them carefully and employed what they like to call 'active measures.'"

"That's shocking. I must issue a warning to Swiss firms involved in the project. I'll do so in the morning. But why haven't I learned of this savagery before?"

"The Brits aren't anxious to advertise their vulnerability, neither are the others. So it goes, eh? *Plus ça change* . . ."

He nodded. "But what about your own peril? Evidently those people stop at nothing."

"And they have long memories."

Brock gazed at me thoughtfully. "Are you sure you want to risk traveling on forged documents?"

"I don't have a lot of choice."

"I've heard—I mean it's been published that Austria—Vienna—is a large-scale source of forged documents for refugees from the East. Those who want to move on to Israel or Western Europe."

"I'd need false documentation to get into Austria—and if I had it I wouldn't have to travel to Vienna."

"Of course—what am I thinking of?" He ran one hand distractedly over his bristly hair. "I must have had a harder day with my politicians than I thought. And of course, the surprise of your arrival . . ." He sucked hard on his pipe, the scientific mind briefly off course. "Nevertheless, I will make prompt inquiries, depend on it. As for money I'm sure you can draw any amount to meet your needs."

"Least of my problems."

"Weapons? They're strictly controlled here, but I might—"

I smiled. "Finding handguns is much simpler than you could imagine. No, I won't need help for that. Just travel papers."

He sighed. "Everything you've told me is mind boggling. You've jerked me off my ivory tower and landed me on hard reality. If I didn't know you, I'd think you were spinning some drug-induced fantasy—but it's all dreadfully true. The Pope—think of it." He seemed sunk in reverie, then roused himself. "I keep early hours, Brent, hope you'll forgive me if I retire. You have a key and the whole of Bern is open to you. Cinemas, discothèques . . ."

"I'll read the evening paper and turn in."

Brock went off to his room. I washed our dishes and stacked them by the sink, read the *Berner Zeitung* and went to bed. Coming to Bern had been the right move, and our family's old friend would help me in any way he could.

Once during the night I woke, thinking I heard him moving around the apartment, but there were no further sounds to confirm my suspicion, so I went quickly back to sleep.

In the morning I got up after my host had left and was glad to see he'd taken my letter to Toby Gerard. I made coffee for myself, drank lingonberry juice and wrote short letters to Lainey and my mother saying I had recovered from my previous ailments but was continuing to travel for my health.

The building concierge directed me to a branch post office and offered to call a taxi. I said I preferred to walk for exercise, and strolled half a dozen blocks of tree- and flower-lined streets to the clean, efficient office, where I bought stamps and mailed both letters.

Around eleven Brock phoned to say he was going to work through lunch hour and suggested we spend the afternoon hiking the foothills around Biel. He'd show me one of my father's favorite trails and we'd take a picnic lunch.

If he'd made progress on finding a document source, he didn't say, but that might come later when we were alone.

Brock appeared at one-thirty, put chicken, cheese, bread and wine into a rucksack, put on climbing shoes and went into his office. He came out carrying alpenstock and *piolet*—a wood-handled ice tool that resembled a small pickaxe. I said, "I thought you said foothills, Walther, why the *piolet*?"

"Habit; these are my companions. I feel naked without them."

He handed me the sturdy four-foot alpenstock and we went down to his Ford Taunus.

The drive to Biel took twenty minutes. Brock detoured around the town and parked in a clump of leafy birch. Ahead of us lay a meadow, and beyond it the land sloped steeply upward. "Splendid view of Bern from the summit—worth the slight effort to get there."

It didn't look slight to me, but I didn't say so. By the time we got back to the car my leg muscles would be yelling for mercy. Brock tightened rucksack straps and we set off across the meadow. The ground underfoot was spongy and the waving wildflowers and unmowed grasses gave off a fresh, sweet perfume. The trail leading upward was pebbled earth worn from years of hikers' shoes, steep enough that I was glad of the alpenstock to help me keep up with Brock. My right shoulder started to hurt, then my forearms, wrists, thighs and finally my calves. From time to time Brock looked back, and called encouragement. Once he reminded me that my father was known to run up this very trail. I found it hard to believe.

The hillside was covered mostly with wild grass and scrub, but here and there stunted pines thrust awkwardly upward, trunks bent into strange, twisted forms. Updrafts from the warm meadow cooled my body; my shirt was soaked with sweat.

On I labored, keeping Brock in sight and wishing I'd declined his sporting invitation: he was accustomed to climbing, did it all the time. I reflected that it took a physical challenge like this to make me realize how badly out of condition I was. A good regimen would be climbing on my own while Brock was at his office, abjuring rich fondues and sauces and staying with salads and broiled meats.

Toward the summit the trail took a sharp twist into a rocky gully that was probably a watercourse for snow-melt and rain. The bank was eroded inward, forming an almost vertical face as far as the top. Brock said, "That's where we're going, Brent," and pointed upward. "Hungry?"

"I've worked up an appetite," I panted, and climbed doggedly on.

Another ten minutes and we were at the top, which proved to be a level area with another hill rising from the far side, and even steeper hills beyond. I rested on my back while Brock opened the rucksack and brought out our picnic lunch. He uncorked the wine bottle and handed it to me. I sat up to drink and the liquid was like the nectar of the gods.

Brock spread a large napkin between us and set out the food. I gnawed a chicken leg, sipped wine and stuffed down bread and Emmenthaler cheese. I was okay now, pulse and breathing normal, and I said, "I'm glad you brought me here, Walther, letting me follow in my father's footsteps. I'd have seen more of him, got to know him better if I hadn't been sent to boarding school." I drank from the common bottle. "Any results?"

"Results . . .? Oh, about your documents. Well, I've spoken with two men, discreetly, of course, and I think one will have a name and an address in the next few days." He took the bottle from me and drank deeply, offered me more chicken.

It was cool and pleasant where we were, the sun at its afternoon slant. Brock raised an arm expansively, shadowing the grass like a scythe. "Yes, I used to come here with David—often we had private matters to discuss."

"No microphones here. No eavesdroppers."

"I know you've had quite enough of that. I keep thinking of how you were confined in Paris. What was the place exactly?"

"A low-class hotel or rooming house catering to whores. The KGB has probably used it for years."

"Yet you managed to escape." He shook his head in wonderment. "Even though you were quite sure you were in Leningrad."

"I preferred dying with my boots on rather than in those damn felt slippers."

"Kuzchin's boots, too. Do you think you killed him?"

I kept my eyes down, startled by what he'd said. I had never mentioned the other name of the man who called himself Kastikov.

I chewed for a few moments before saying, "I don't know. At the time I didn't want to know." My body was cold all over, but not from mountain breeze. My fingers were stiff with tension as I picked up the bottle. I sipped and managed to swallow another piece of bread.

Brock said, "I'm not sure it was wise for you to leave behind that tape with Vasileyev's confession."

"I didn't. I erased it."

"I see . . . well, enough of what must be very unpleasant memories. So far you haven't seen that magnificent view your father was so fond of." He got up and walked toward the ledge.

I picked up the alpenstock and followed beside him.

Bern lay far away, much of it already in shadows. I could have admired the panorama but my mind was whirling with other things. I glanced down at the gully's rocky bottom a hundred feet below. Brock said, "I'll enjoy this view more fully with my pipe." He walked back, but his shadow stopped short of the picnic area. Stealthily, he came toward me from behind.

I watched his shadow near and then I turned around. There was no pipe in his hand but the sharp-edged *piolet,* and he was raising it to strike.

My muscles were already taut, expectant. I swung the alpenstock hard at his left side, but not soon enough to prevent the downward blow of his murderous weapon. It ripped my shirt before he tottered sideways. Again I slammed the alpenstock at him, but he managed to check it with his *piolet* and the alpenstock broke in half, free end spinning out of sight. Brock was staggering and groaning in pain but he still kept trying.

Another *piolet* slash and I jumped back. Before he could raise his arm for another blow I used the remainder of my club to strike at his head. The blow glanced off his shoulder and struck the side of his head. Brock yelled and lurched forward. I hit the back of his neck and he half dropped but kept stumbling on. I don't know if he thought I was ahead of him, but the *piolet* lifted again and swung, striking nothing.

The impetus carried him forward and in an instant he was off the ledge. I heard a shrill scream, then the sodden sound of his body striking the rocks below. There is no sound like it in the world.

Before looking over, I tossed the broken-off alpenstock after him.

Then with shaking hands I gulped down two mouthfuls of wine. After that I was ready to look down.

Herr Professor Doctor Walther Brock lay on his back in a twisted heap. Sunlight glinted from his bloody face.

I emptied the wine bottle on the grass and put uneaten food in the rucksack. The napkin fluttered in the breeze. I left it where it was and started down the steep trail.

Brock was barely alive when I reached him. His mustache was a painter's brush covered with shiny red paint. His lips moved and I bent over to hear what he said, if he said anything at all.

"Back," he whispered. "Spine broken." His face contorted. "Damn you, why did you have to come to me?"

"For shelter and friendship," I said, but I don't think he heard me, because he whispered, "You knew, didn't you—because of Kuzchin."

"Yes," I said. "I never mentioned that name."

"I—I'm glad you didn't give in to him. Once they get their hands on you it never ends." His body shivered like a dry leaf. More blood trickled from his mouth and nostrils. "My fault . . . my own fault." He was trying to lift the hand that had held his ice-axe. "Don't tell your mother about me."

"I'll tell everyone who should know."

His eyes closed. An immense shudder coursed along his body. A hand relaxed, opened. The bleeding stopped. He was gone.

My father's old friend and protégé, the man my mother said I could trust. The man who was going to help me.

I wondered how long he had been a Soviet agent.

Standing in shadows, I felt chilled by a rising breeze.

I picked my way down the trail to the meadow and got into the Taunus.

He'd left keys in the ignition—no one steals cars in Switzerland, just information. I started the engine and drove slowly back to the apartment.

Inside, it was like walking through a graveyard. I couldn't remain long because Brock's controller would be expecting a report confirming my death. When it didn't come, someone would try to contact Brock. The Soviets had me pinpointed, could take me whenever they chose.

I unlocked Brock's office and went in. The still air seemed heavy with the scent of death.

As I looked dully around I realized how isolated I was and helpless. Brock's bitter words echoed in my ears: *"Damn you, why did you have to come . . .?"*

Why indeed?

Refuge . . . succor . . . understanding . . .

Methodically, I began taking his office apart.

BOOK FIVE

TWENTY-SEVEN

Initially, I didn't know where to look because I didn't know what I was looking for. I wanted evidence of Brock's treachery—stolen documents, agent paraphernalia, perhaps a copying setup. They could be anywhere in the apartment, or nowhere.

My guess was that his covert activity was focused in the office for the sake of convenience. I glanced at the radio headset and noticed it had been moved since yesterday. Now I was reasonably sure I had heard Brock moving around late last night.

I began with his books, top level first, moving clockwise around the room. I opened each book and shook it out, replaced it and opened the next. I was also looking for a concealed safe, like the one I had, but found nothing incriminating in the first row of books. I worked along the second shelf, and while I was removing books behind the desk chair I struck gold.

One thick math volume was hollowed out, making a hiding place for four pads of thin paper, each with about a hundred sheets. Every sheet was printed with what appeared to be a crosshatched multiplication table, except that in place of numbers each small square contained a letter. A Cyrillic letter.

KGB code pads—one-time pads to the trade.

They were a prize for any intelligence service, including the issuing one. The science of cryptography had become immensely technical. In every capital computers work ceaselessly to devise breakproof codes, and to break the codes of other countries, especially their enemies. Here I had the raw material for decoding thousands of KGB radio messages. The top pad was open, a few sheets used. The other three pads were pristine.

A knowledgeable burglar might try to sell them. An inexperienced intelligence operative might steal them for his own service. But I had to consider the consequences of their disappearance.

After the KGB learned of Brock's death, someone would be sent to inventory and recover cryptographic and other materials he worked with. If the one-time pads were gone, the KGB would immediately change their system, rendering the pads useless for future decrypting. I didn't know if the National Security Agency had cracked the code Brock and his contacts used, but if they had and it were changed, a lot of U.S. time and money would have been wasted, and weeks or even months of computerized trial and error would ensue before the new system yielded. Meanwhile, intercepted agent traffic would yield nothing.

Reluctantly, I replaced the pads in their book-cache, and continued my search.

The sixth volume to the right included a radio transmit/receive schedule with frequencies linked to Greenwich Mean Time. One frequency was reserved for emergency contact. I moved over to the Philips set and turned it on. The dial was still set to that frequency. Brock had transmitted and received messages last night. I turned off the radio and looked for the third clandestine component.

I found it on the lowest shelf, directly behind the desk chair, also in hollowed-out book concealment. One part applied Morse dots and dashes to a metallic tape in the second unit, which resembled a TV remote control. Connected to the Philips transmitter by its patch cord the unit emitted a high-speed megaHerz burst that lasted only a few seconds. The minuscule duration prevented Direction Finding—the historic bane of agent radio operators—and receiving equipment could slow down the message for decrypting.

During training I had been shown a rudimentary model of the Soviet burst transmitter, but this unit compared to that exemplar as the Cadillac compares to Henry's Model T. It was a beauty, and I hated replacing it in its hiding place.

Like Colonel Abel's Brooklyn apartment, this place was turning into a clandestine treasure trove. Herr Professor Doctor Walther Brock must have been a loyal KGB servant for many years to rate their very best equipment.

I kept looking.

The penultimate volume on the lowest shelf was also hollowed out, and what it yielded surprised me—in a day full of surprises.

I drew out letters written on cheap five-by-eight sheets that were folded in half to fit their container. They were written by pen in Cyrillic script that covered both sides of each sheet.

Love letters.

I counted them carefully—thirty-two in all, their dates covering twelve years, the last written two years ago. The penmanship was delicate, the lines straight and level, as though the sheet had been placed over a line guide. I began reading the bottom letter—the sheet was stiff and smudged as though from repeated handling—and found it to be an amorous reminiscence of a lovers' night at the Moskva Hotel with the writer's hope of an early reprise.

It was signed: *Aleks.*

Succeeding letters developed a predictable scenario: Aleks had been detected by the KGB in communication with a foreigner. He would be allowed to live only if his lover cooperated with the KGB. As Dear Walther knew, the Soviet punishment for espionage was death. Don't let me perish, the letter cried; preserve our love.

Aleks.

So Walther had cooperated, thinking he was saving the life of his lover, who by then might have compromised another four or five Western scientists or diplomats.

I read on.

Walther had returned to Moscow for another idyll with Aleks, to be repeated two years later. Every other letter begged Dear Walther to continue cooperating lest Aleks suffer the consequence.

I wondered how many "Alekses" had composed the thirty-two letters to my dead host and why the letters had stopped coming two years ago. Had Walther balked? Tragedy was implicit.

I folded the letters and restored them to their dark place of concealment. Brock had been naive and foolish, but not uniquely so. I knew of at least three Western ambassadors who had been compromised into KGB service by male "sparrows" such as Aleks; they had all been repeatedly warned of that peril and should have known better.

Like Walther Brock, they didn't, and so their seamy dramas played out until discovery. Amazing how the Soviets could spot that weakness. Incredible how successfully they exploited it year after year after year.

I looked at Kostikov's watch and realized I had been searching for an hour. Darkness had fallen outside. Inside I felt a pervasive darkness of the soul.

I went to the kitchen and made coffee, laced it with Courvoisier and returned to Brock's spy center.

As I moved around the desk I noticed a wide-mouthed bronze urn in the corner. The interior bottom was covered with the black curled fragments of burned paper. Brock used it to dispose of used cryptographic sheets. I thought of adding his love letters to the ashes but decided against it. When found by federal police they would explain the roots of Brock's treachery in a way nothing else could.

All but one of the desk drawers was open, and in the locked one there was a key. I turned it and pulled out the drawer.

There lay the letter I'd typed yesterday to Toby Gerard. Parts of it were underlined, sections Brock had encoded and transmitted to Moscow Center. That was bad enough, but he must have added details I'd told him just twenty-four hours ago during my long confessional.

So I had to assume that the KGB knew everything. Including Toby's name. And the fact that he possessed a videotape of Filip

Sankov's confession.

I had to warn him.

Using the desk phone, I dialed Toby's home and asked for him. His wife answered, said Toby was working late and asked my name. John Smith, I told her, and read off Brock's number, asking her to contact him, urgently, on a matter of life and death. Before she could ask more questions I replaced the receiver. At least Toby was still alive.

To keep busy until he called, I pulled out every desk drawer and found a false partition at the end of one. From this space I drew out a sealed package, opened it and found Swiss and French passports in different names. Both passports carried Brock's photo. I stared at the face and felt my stomach contract. Despite our family friendship, despite having known me as a child who admired him, Walther Brock had done his best to kill me. But for his one discordant word I would be lying stiff and broken in the gully and Walther would be sitting here transmitting a message to Moscow.

There were large-denomination Swiss francs and American hundred-dollar bills in his evasion package, and I put them in my pocket. Both passports, I noted, bore Soviet, Austrian and German visas.

In death Walther Brock had provided me with the means of escape.

I replaced all drawers and sat at the desk, examining the Swiss passport under the glare of his typing lamp. The few items I needed for altering it were available in any office supply store and I'd find one in the morning. I'd also visit a photo shop for a substitute photograph. An hour's careful work and I'd be equipped for travel as Helmut Mollers of Seuzach, Zurich Canton, Schweiz.

I put the passport in my pocket and looked at the telephone. Where the hell was Toby? Why didn't he call?

To kill time I went through Brock's closets and helped myself to underwear, clothing and socks. All were Swiss made and consonant with my new Swiss identity. I packed them in his worn travel bag and left my Sea Island purchases in their place. Except for shoes. I had come to value shoes that fit me.

I sat at the kitchen table, staring at the wall phone, finally deciding to call Toby's office. A secretary said Mr. Gerard had left for an appointment, but refused to say where. "If you can reach him," I said, "tell him to get immediate protection. His life is in danger." I broke off.

If the Soviets intercepted my call, it concerned only what they already knew. Fuck 'em, as Herb Porter used to say.

Well, Herb would say it no more, nor anything else. I needed to return, do my best to get back at his murderers.

I got a frozen casserole from the freezer and heated it in the microwave oven. Drank wine and stared at the telephone.

I was washing dishes when it rang.

Grabbing it off the hook, I said, "*Toby?*"

No answer. The connection broke, the dead line hummed. My mistake. Wrong move, Graves. Careless. Now they know someone other than Brock is answering the phone. Very bad.

I knew his body couldn't have been discovered, just his absence from where he ought to be. I brought my radio to the kitchen and got out the HK .38. I jacked a shell into the chamber and set the safety feeling angry and aggressive.

The only fear I felt was for Toby Gerard.

I looked at my watch. Jesus, he should have been home long ago! I called his home again, the phone rang six times and when it was answered I heard a child crying. "Is your mommy there?" I asked as calmly as I could. The child wailed and I asked for Daddy. That brought more sobbing, and I felt my neck hairs prickle. "What's wrong?" I asked. "What's happened?"

"Daddy's hurt . . . in a hospital. Mommy's with him." The little girl sobbed brokenly. I gripped the phone. "Listen to me and do exactly as I say. If you're alone, lock all your doors and don't open them for anyone except Mommy, do you understand? Just Mommy. Tell me you'll do what I say."

"I . . . I'll do it."

"Good girl. Now be brave, and—"

"But I'm afraid for Daddy . . ."

So am I, I thought, and broke the connection. So am I.

My warning had come too late.

But I knew what I had to do.

I blocked both apartment doors with furniture and used Brock's disposal urn to burn my intercepted letter to Toby. It flamed, curled, turned black and broke apart. More ashes.

If Brock hadn't read it he wouldn't have known the Kuzchin name, wouldn't have made the fatal slip. That little blunder saved my life. I was lucky, I thought, that I had written the letter and Brock had opened it. Otherwise, I would be lying dead in that cold gully instead of the KGB spy.

In the bedroom I put on one of Brock's suits turned off the apartment lights and lay down on the living room sofa fully dressed, pistol by my hand, hoping someone would come for me.

TWENTY-EIGHT

During the night I woke twice, thinking I heard sounds at the door, but I didn't want to shoot through it until I was sure. After listening a while I went back to sleep.

Morning light woke me. A mist hung over the city.

I drank a glass of lingonberry juice, trapped both doors with paper scraps and left the apartment by the rear staircase. The building's garden gave out on a parallel street, and I walked toward the city until I found a taxi that took me to the Bahnhof restaurant. There I ate a large breakfast and lingered over coffee until I saw stores beginning to open for business.

The Brechtold stationery store had the materials I needed. The salesgirl wrapped them neatly and told me the location of a shop that made passport photos.

I was the first customer, so service was fast and efficient. I put the photos in my pocket and took a taxi to within three blocks of the apartment building, reaching it via the garden route.

The kitchen door's paper scrap was still in place. I walked

around to the front door and checked there. Also where I'd stuck it. I unlocked the door and went in, bolting it behind me and blocking it with a chair.

At Brock's desk I got out my purchases and began working on his Swiss passport, lifting his photo a millimeter at a time with a scalpel like tool until the photo was free.

I used a thin glass rod that came with the bottle of ink-eraser to bleach out Brock's date of birth, the colors of his eyes and hair. His weight was sufficiently close to mine that I left it. Immigration officers might shoot me, they weren't going to weigh me.

As I was leaving the passport to dry in the sun, the wall phone rang. I looked at it but didn't answer. It wasn't Walther Brock or Toby. One was dead, the other *hors de combat.*

After four rings the phone was silent. Presently it rang again. Twice. The four-two sequence was probably a prearranged signal: Meet me under the Old Clock tower in two hours, something like that. Well, the Herr Professor was not going to make the rendezvous. Not today, not ever.

But the call gave me an idea. I looked up Brock's Bundesrat office and dialed. When a male voice answered I asked for Dr. Brock. The man said he wasn't there but was expected later.

"Are you sure?" I asked. "We were supposed to take the Zurich train this morning. I'm calling from the station to make sure he's on his way."

Stiffly the man said, "If Professor Brock made that arrangement I have every confidence he will keep it."

"Thank you," I said, "Oh, here he comes!" I rang off. Brock's absence was now covered at the office; I didn't want the police banging on the apartment door.

When the passport page was dry I unstoppered a bottle of India ink and wet the tip of a steel-point pen. Carefully I filled in my own physical characteristics, then let the ink dry.

Next I brushed a small amount of white glue on the space where Brock's photo had been, blew on it until its sheen dulled. Then I set my photo in place and pressed it flat under the sugar jar.

While glue was drying I moved around the apartment, removing traces of joint occupancy; cigarette butts and used liquor glasses. I remade the bed I'd slept in, stretching sheets taut, army style. The French passport I left in the desk's center drawer where it would be found and raise the right questions.

The photo glue was almost dry. I placed the page in a shaft of sunlight and heard the lock turn in the kitchen door. It was bolted from inside; whoever was out there couldn't enter. I drew the pistol from my belt. Shoot through the door?

Rapping, then pounding. I sighted at the door, chest high.

A woman called, "Professor—Professor Brock—it's Herta—cleaning day."

I laid down my pistol and half-covered my mouth with a handkerchief. I spoke gruffly, trying to imitate Brock's voice. "Ah, Herta, forgive me—bad cold, very bad cold. Come back tomorrow." I coughed loudly.

Silence. Then, "But I can make you some hot tea."

"Done it," I said. "Tomorrow, Herta." I coughed again.

"Very well." I heard a long-drawn sigh, the sound of departing footsteps.

The telephone rang, I ignored it and collected my forgery materials and distributed them in separate desk drawers. I burned Brock's passport photo in the urn, plus three of mine, saving two for possible future use. I put my newly altered passport in my pocket, then made a final sweep of the apartment, ending in the bedroom. There I replaced my .38 in the stereo set and carried radio and packed bag to the kitchen exit.

I walked down the nine flights of stairs laden like a burglar. Out through the garden, then, and to the intersection, where I waited until a passing taxi picked me up.

At the Bahnhof I purchased a roomette ticket on the TGV to Geneva, and bought a flask of Martell before boarding.

The countryside was a blur out the window of the super-fast train. I sipped cognac and thought about what I was leaving behind.

If I hadn't discovered Brock's agent transmitter and Aleks' love letters I would never have been able to put him fully in focus. I might have found myself regretting that I killed him even while he was trying to kill me, glossing over his years of treachery and making excuses for the old family friend.

He hadn't lived long enough to plead the old Nuremburg defense, but I understood; he was only carrying out orders. I never thought it was his own idea. KGB agents don't form independent ideas.

It was within the KGB's power to frame me for the murder of Brock or someone else and let Interpol do their searching. But I was satisfied the KGB didn't want me arrested and put on trial—I could tell too much. The KGB wanted me dead—as dead as Sankov—and the sooner the better.

Could I reach Senator Connors before a KGB assassin silenced me? For the present, our courses of action ran parallel, but somewhere ahead they would converge.

And I had to take Apollo into account.

During the Lausanne stop I went into the dining car and ordered lunch. By the time I finished and paid the check the train was pulling into Geneva.

From the station I taxied to Cointrin Airport and checked flight destinations on the big data board. Montreal was one, but as I considered it the board flashed notice of departure.

A Lufthansa flight was leaving for Mexico City in a little under two hours. It was easier to cross into the U.S. from Mexico than from Canada. The clerk sold me a first-class ticket and copied down passport information on a Mexican tourist card. Good for ninety days, the clerk told me. I didn't even want to be there ninety minutes. I checked my bag through along with my stereo, packed in a strong cardboard container. I didn't expect to need my pistol for a day or so.

Before boarding the 747 I bought a mix of international newspapers, *Time* and *Newsweek*, and read until dinner was served over the Atlantic. During the JFK refueling stop several passengers left the plane, others boarded. Then we took off for Mexico City.

That night I slept at the Camino Real Airport and took a midmorning flight on a DC-9 to the border city of Reynosa. There the U.S. Consulate issued me a visitor's visa, and I walked across the international bridge to U.S. soil. Customs K-9s sniffed me and my baggage for drugs, a burly female inspector poked through my clothing and dismissed me.

A taxi took me to McAllen's Airport, where I found a feeder flight leaving for Houston International. From there I flew to Baltimore and registered as Helmut Mollers at the airport's Holiday Inn.

Unpacking, I reflected that I had come a long way by an indirect and complicated route. There was no possible way the Opposition could know where I was.

From a pay phone in the lobby I called Lainey.

Hearing my voice, she began to whimper. I cautioned her not to use my name, said I was in good health and wanted to see her. When she could control herself, she told me Peter was in London. "So why don't you come here? Stay with me?"

"Uh—not a good idea. Pack an overnight bag and drive my Porsche to the Baltimore train station. We'll meet at the newstand. Two hours?"

"Oh, yes, dear, I can't wait to see you."

An airport limo took me to the Amtrak station, and while waiting for Lainey I phoned Toby's Senate office, said I was an Amherst classmate and wanted to check out a disturbing rumor that Toby was hospitalized.

"I'm afraid that's true, sir, but I'm not able to give any details."

"I'd like to send flowers or something—what hospital?"

"You'll have to ask Mrs. Gerard."

"She's at the hospital; I'm asking you."

"That's all I can suggest, sir. If you care to leave your name and phone number, I'll see that it reaches Mrs. Gerard."

"That's exactly the right reply," I told her, "and I commend your caution. Keep it up." I rang off, got a handful of change at the newstand and fed most of it into the pay phone.

Dorsey Jerrault's secretary said her boss was in a senior partners' meeting. I gave her my name and asked her to root him out. Reluctantly, she said she'd try, and presently I heard Jerrault saying, "Brent, where in hell have you been?"

"Traveling, like you. What can you tell me about Toby Gerard?"

"Very strange—car jumped the curb and smashed him. Driver fled. Toby's been in a coma ever since, prognosis uncertain."

"Driver identified?"

"No, the car was stolen."

"It wasn't an accident, Dorsey. Toby was targeted because of something he's been involved in with me. Some weeks ago I left a package with your secretary."

"She showed it to me, said you'd provide instructions later."

"The time is now. I know you've got a VCR in your office, so I want you to watch the videotape, then put it securely away. I'll tell you more after you've seen it." I paused. "By the way, do you know Senator Frank Connors?"

"Fairly well."

"I may have to see him. Give me your home phone number and I'll call later."

When he'd done so I said, "Seeing the tape will put you at risk, Dorsey. As of now the body count is around fifteen, so if—"

"You're my client, Brent. How can I serve you if I don't know what it's all about?"

"Nevertheless, getting killed for a client is beyond the Bar's requirements."

"You let me worry about that. Just be sure to call."

I hung up, sat on the old-fashioned bench and watched the newstand. After a while Lainey sauntered in and began looking at the magazine rack. Just seeing her fresh, beautiful face put me among the living again. I went up behind her and whispered, "Don't turn around. Go out and get into a taxi. I'll join you."

Peter must have taught her something about clandestine discipline, because Lainey performed beautifully. Beside her in the taxi, I took her hands and kissed her forehead, cheeks and lips. She flung her arms around me and quietly began to sob. We didn't try to talk, just held each other close, touching, kissing.

In my room we tore off our clothing and made eager, passionate love, and I thought that she had never been more desirable, more completely abandoned. And I knew that I wanted her with me always.

She was lying half across me, head on my shoulder, when I said, "I can't tell you everything, because I don't want you endangered. If you love me you must trust me—"

"Oh, I *do.*"

So I told her that the KGB had been trying to kill me to suppress knowledge I possessed. I said an element within the Firm had been responsible for the death of Dr. Cereza and the attacks on my house. To survive, I'd gone to Europe. I told her about the Paris "clinic," my escape and refuge in Bern, where a man I'd trusted tried to murder me. Now I was back to try to pull things together so I could live peacefully with her for the rest of our lives.

Her face was pale as she said, "It's all so dreadful—and you're alone. Is there any way Peter can help?"

"I can't bring him into it—telling you is bad enough." I kissed her temple. "I wouldn't have, except that I felt you have the right to know the general picture." I paused and lit a cigarette. "How was the Anniversary party?"

"For me it was an ordeal, a sham. I never felt more guilty. And I missed you so much that I ached."

"Have you said anything to Peter about—?"

"No—I've been waiting for you to tell me to go ahead. Shall I, when he gets back from London?"

"We'll see." I told her about finding Marilyn in Paris and my brief encounter with her distraught lover. That made Lainey smile. "Such fidelity. Would you wait endlessly for me?"

"I have."

She said the insurance company had rehabilitated my house and that Salomé was there daily. I said I'd give her money for Salomé but my maid wasn't to know it came from me.

She licked my lips and touched my tongue with hers. We made love again.

After early breakfast I called a taxi for Lainey. We kissed ardently and I said I'd see her as soon as I could. I hated seeing the taxi drive away; she meant more to me than anyone ever had.

I packed, paid my bill in cash and taxied to the Amtrak station, where I put my bag and stereo in a locker. I found the address of a downtown theatrical supply house in the Yellow Pages. It was opening when I got out of the taxi. I told the driver to wait, went in and selected makeup items: beard, matching wig and mustache, spirit gum, solvent and horn-rimmed, non-refracting glasses.

I took the next train to Union Station in Washington and rented a dressing cubicle on the lower level. There I donned the wig and gummed the short beard and mustache to my face.

While the adhesive was drying I reviewed my second phone call to Dorsey Jerrault while Lainey was sleeping. Sankov's confession had stunned him, and he grasped its implications for the pending Mutual Non-Aggression once I'd made the connection. I asked Dorsey to see Senator Connors as soon as he could without letting the Senator think it concerned more than a lobbying matter; I asked him to show Connors the tape and if the Senator wanted to talk with me I would make myself available.

Dorsey agreed and suggested we lunch at a waterfront restaurant to review the situation.

Facial disguise in place, I rented a room in a no-star hotel on Vermont Avenue and bought a nylon shoulder holster for my .38. Back in the room, I tried it on, adjusted the harness and locked the holstered pistol in my bag. Then I flagged a taxi and rode along Maine Avenue to the seafood restaurant where Dorsey was to meet me.

I took a table, ordered Black Label and Perrier and watched arrivals until Dorsey appeared. He looked right at me without recognizing me—until I waved and beckoned him over. He slid into the opposite chair and pumped my hand. "Good God, Brent, this is *real* cloak and dagger!"

"Beard and pistol," I said. "For real."

"Well, after what I've seen and all you've told me I can understand why." He ordered a double vodka martini and leaned toward me. "The Senator didn't get enthusiastic until I said it had to do with the attempt on Toby's life. Then he watched the videotape—the two of us in his office. I told him a little about your struggle to stay alive and he said he wanted to see you. Not in his office, of course—at his house." He handed me a piece of paper with an address. "Chevy Chase, nine o'clock."

I folded the address in my billfold. "Any word on Toby?"

"Holding his own is all I know."

I told him how Brock had intercepted my letter to Toby and transmitted sections to his control, how I'd tried to warn Toby—too late.

"Wasn't your fault, Brent."

"I trusted Brock, had no idea he was a Soviet agent."

"How could you? There was every reason to trust the man." He drank deeply from his glass. "I must say the entire story is astonishing—that videotape is the convincer. I left it with the Senator, of course."

"Did he indicate what he plans to do with it?"

"Not in so many words, but he's very concerned, aroused. He doesn't want you in further jeopardy—he told me that.

"Glad he cares." I opened our menus and we ordered.

While eating, I described my Paris confinement, told Dorsey about General Kostikov's attempt to recruit me and how I'd managed to escape.

Dorsey said, "What interests me particularly is that Kostikov confirmed what Vasileyev told you about Apollo—that such a person exists."

"I have the scars to prove it."

"Better leave it to Senator Connors to take action against him, whoever he is. He's got the power and resources to do it. Subpoenas, marshals, the FBI . . ."

"And access to the media."

He nodded thoughtfully. "Connors has a dilemma. He's been shepherding this Treaty along, convinced it's in our best interests, and suddenly something crops up that shows him the Russians are up to their old tricks. I think he understands perfectly well that revealing Sankov's confession to the public would sink the Treaty. Yet I believe him to be an honest man and fundamentally patriotic."

"As politicians go."

He looked at me sharply. "Hey, wait a second!"

"Present company excepted." Dorsey had spent much of his

career in politics.

We ordered pecan pie and coffee, and when I called for the check Jerrault said, "I've got to be getting back, Brent. I want you to know that I'm in this with you for whatever it takes, as long as it takes. After your talk with Connors, why don't you phone me tonight?"

"I was planning to."

"I'm a semi-insomniac, so the hour doesn't matter."

We shook hands and he left. I paid our bill and used a wall-hung phone directory to search for three names. L. Windsor Warren had a house in McLean, Virginia; Sandor W. Parton lived in Old Town Alexandria. There was no listing for Merle Crosby, but I didn't expect there to be—COPS was too important a man to expose his abode to the general public.

I took a bus out Virginia Avenue, looking over used car lots. Most were auto graveyards surrounded by chain-link fencing, but one held several possibilities, so I left the bus and strolled in. I let the salesman-owner show me around, telling him I wanted a car with usable rubber and a reliable battery, year and model unimportant. A Pinto wouldn't start, but an old Pontiac Firebird did, and its tires looked okay for what I wanted. The whitewash price on the windshield was $850. I offered seven, cash, and the man licked his lips. After a few minutes' bargaining we settled for seven-fifty plus the tags from the Pinto. For temporary registration I used the Helmut Mollers alias and a phony address near Catholic University. I paid extra for two quarts of K-Mart oil, drove off the lot and filled the tank at the first gas station.

Not far from my hotel there was an all-night parking lot. I left my automotive prize there and walked to the hotel, pleased that I'd been able to use Brock's KGB-supplied escape money for my own purposes. Quite a lot of it remained.

My wig, false beard and mustache made me itch and perspire, so I used solvent to remove them. I cleaned my face with tepid water and a two-inch soap wafer, dried on a thin towel whose faded letters spelled *Niagara Falls*.

Then I stretched out on the lumpy bed and read The Washington *Post* until sleep came.

When I woke it was evening. I got up groggily, my body rhythms still recovering from jet lag. I used the tin-sided shower stall and shaved in front of the washstand's cracked mirror. Face smooth and dry, I applied my disguise and donned wig and glasses, put on a clean shirt—Brock's—and over it the nylon shoulder-holster. Then a coat.

Three hours until my meeting with Senator Connors.

I drove the Firebird into Virginia and located Wink Warren's house in McLean. At the end of his street, I U-turned and drove slowly back. One car in his two-car garage, nobody in the house.

From there I took the Beltway south and east into Old Town Alexandria, and found Parton's address on Wolfe Street. All the houses were old, narrow Georgian Colonial, and expensively reconditioned. Parton's resembled the others except for geranium boxes on both sides of the slate entrance walk. No garages visible. I drove past a second time to fix the location and turned up Washington and over Cameron to Gadsby's Tavern.

There I had a quaint early-American dinner served by girls in long, flouncy dresses and lacy, ribboned caps. The busboys wore knee-breeches and short waistcoats. I drank hot mulled cider to settle my stomach and ordered Virginia Ham Tom Jefferson.

What I got was a slice of boneless ham covered with raisin sauce, two sprigs of parsley, an overdone sweet potato, a popover and a bill large enough to refurbish Mount Vernon.

Still, I reflected, as I picked my teeth Franklin-style, someone had to support our historic eateries.

The Firebird started faultlessly. I took Memorial Highway into the District and drove out Connecticut Avenue to Chevy Chase for my meeting with Senator Frank Connors.

TWENTY-NINE

I found Connors' house on a dark side street in a quiet family neighborhood. An old three-story frame dwelling with tall trees bordering a well-tended lawn. I drove past to check for surveillance, saw none and parked around the block.

Before getting out of the Firebird I pulled out my .38 and stuck it under the seat. Then I walked through the late spring evening to Connor's front door. A porch light showed the bell button and an old-fashioned porch swing suspended by chains from the wooden ceiling. Potted ferns draped the railing. In Georgetown ferns weren't fashionable, but for old, settled Chevy Chase they were just right.

The man who opened the door was about five-eight, one hundred fifty pounds, with salt-and-pepper hair and a somewhat lined face. "You're Graves? Come in." He stood aside and I stepped past him. "We'll talk in the sun room." He led the way, and I saw a pitcher of iced tea and two glasses on the low wicker table. When we were seated he filled two glasses and gave me one. After sipping he said, "I've known Dorsey Jerrault a long time, Mr. Graves. Otherwise I wouldn't have seen him this morning. As you probably know, I'm almost completely occupied by Treaty hearings."

I nodded, and Connors set aside his glass. I sipped from mine although I didn't much feel like iced tea. He said, "I've seen the filmed record of your meeting with that defector—Sankov, is it?"

"Was. Killed the following night."

"So Dorsey said. And I understand that in some fashion my assistant, Toby Gerard, got involved with you in this matter."

"I involved him because I needed a trustworthy confidant and had nowhere to turn. He was to lay the whole conspiracy before you, Senator. Unfortunately, he's now unable to."

"It is your position that Toby was injured in an attempt on his life?"

"By inadvertence on my part, the KGB learned of Toby's involvement. He had to be silenced as they've been trying to silence me. As they silenced Dr. Cereza and Herb Porter."

"Maybe you'd better start from the beginning, sir, and give me more detail than I have."

"Gladly."

Each time I related the story it took longer. Connors interrupted now and then with questions. I answered them and continued through the Brock episode to the present.

When I finished, Connors refilled his glass and drank slowly. Finally he said, "It sounds quite incredible to an outsider such as myself, but I have no reason to doubt your honesty. You say you have the names of personnel at the Virginia clinic where you were treated?"

"A nurse was named Bailey, and the dietitian, Mrs. Simzak. I don't know who the orderly was but I could identify him in a lineup."

"And you say Toby was able to establish the existence of the house where all that killing took place?"

"He said he had. And it helped convince him I was telling the truth."

"And how were all those bodies disposed of? The incident kept out of the press?"

"I don't know, Senator. I don't have answers to a lot of questions. I hoped your investigators could wrap things up."

"Including the identity of this alleged spy, Apollo?"

"Isn't that a top priority?"

"You're sure he exists?"

"Aside from what Vasileyev and Kostikov told me, Apollo's existence is provable by applying logic. Certain acts could have been accomplished only by a penetration agent. The acts took place. Ergo, the agent existed."

"That's reasonable," he conceded, "but why haven't you taken all this to the FBI?"

"Because the Director would never grant the FBI authority to examine internal records, interrogate high-level personnel. Your Committee can require that access."

"That's so. Do you have a firm idea who Apollo might be?"

"No."

"Would you care to speculate?"

"No, sir. I don't want to compromise the investigation."

"I understand. But so little of what you've told me is provable by existing facts. Your case is mostly circumstantial."

"Nothing wrong with circumstantial evidence," I remarked. "And there's Sankov's confession."

"Which is—unsubstantiated."

"I was there, I'm on the tape."

"You're certainly the central figure in all this, and I appreciate you informing me so thoroughly. As you undoubtedly appreciate, I will have to proceed with a great deal of circumspection. Meanwhile, what do you intend to do?"

"What do you suggest?"

"I feel the most important thing is to preserve your personal security—and say nothing about this matter to anyone."

"Toby needs protection, Senator. I hope you'll provide it."

"Wouldn't guards upset his wife?"

"A dead husband would upset her even more, Senator. Anything else I can tell you?"

"Not until I've gone into it further. How can I contact you?

Through Dorsey?"

"That's best." I stood up. "Thanks for listening to me, Senator. It's in your hands."

"That's right. Leave everything to me." He went with me to the door, and when we were on the porch he stretched his arms and inhaled deeply. "My refuge," he said almost reverently, "where the problems of our country and the world seldom intrude."

"I envy you," I said and went down the dark walk, wondering to what extent he was letting my problems penetrate his sanctuary.

I turned around the corner, saw my car where I'd parked it and got out my keys. A car came down the street from behind and stopped beside me. I thought the driver was going to ask directions, but when I turned I saw the barrel of a gun.

"Get in," a voice ordered, and the rear door swung open.

I couldn't run because I was backed against the Firebird.

Nothing I could do but get in.

I sat between two men, my hands cuffed behind my back. They were both clean-shaven, suit coats square-shouldered in perennial Monkey Ward style that made me think they might be U.S. Marshals. "Got a warrant?" I asked.

The man on my left grinned, flashed what looked like some sort of official credential and put it away. "You're in custody," he announced.

"On what charge?"

"How's flight to avoid prosecution grab you?"

"Prosecution for what?"

The driver half-turned his head and said, "Don't talk to him, Ernie."

The man on my right said, "You're a security risk, Graves, haven't you figured it out?"

"What I've figured out," I said, "is that I'm being snatched by foreign agents or domestic white trash."

I grunted as an elbow rammed my ribs. Ernie said, "Shut up! That wig and chin whiskers didn't fool me."

"That's because you've had so much experience tracking desperate criminals. How about a closer look at that boxtop badge?"

"Fuck you."

"The Pep Boys—Manny, Moe and Jack. Book me and I get a phone call. After that you clowns head for Canada."

"Surprise," the driver said. "You're not gonna be booked."

"Terrific. That tells me what I'm dealing with." I sat back and saw that the driver was heading out toward Silver Spring. After a while he turned off Georgia Avenue and steered down into the underground parking area of a high-rise office building.

My two guards hauled me out beside the elevator, rang for it and waited while the car pulled away. We rode to the eighth floor and went down a long corridor that ended in double-width wooden doors whose only inscription was: DELIVERIES.

Ernie opened the door wide enough to shove me through and locked the door behind me. The room was dark. I moved slowly around until I collided with a chair. I sat in the chair. Waited.

When my eyes adjusted to the darkness I could make out a long conference table, chairs around it. There were bookshelves along the walls and a digital clock showing 11:52.

If this was execution eve I'd have been killed back in Chevy Chase, and I was still alive. That gave me hope.

At 12:11 I heard a wall door opening behind me. Lights went on and I turned, blinking at the sudden brightness.

Two men were staring at me. One said, "You're a hard man to find, Brent," and began walking toward me.

THIRTY

"I've been missing in action, Wink. Didn't know I was on your AWOL list." The other man pulled out a chair and sat at the end of the table. "Evening, Mr. Crosby," I said. "Keeping late hours?"

Merle Crosby looked at me unblinkingly. His pinched face was pale, his eyes large behind thick, rimless lenses.

Wink Warren said, "That's right, we all do—when there's reason. Here, let me get those cuffs." I sat forward, heard a key clink and grind. The cuffs opened, and I rubbed my wrists. Warren said, "Hope those soldiers didn't rough you up. I figured cuffs would protect them, and I didn't want you refusing the invitation."

"So the Senator fingered me."

Crosby said, "He summarized the situation for me and asked my advice on handling it. That told us where you would be and when. The Senator heard you out, did he not?"

"Reluctantly. What he believed he didn't like. The rest he discarded." I shrugged. "Back to square one."

"Perhaps not. Wink, why don't you stop hovering and sit down?"

"Right, Chief." Warren took a nearby chair, still watching me.

Crosby said, "To continue—things have reached a point at which, despite all you've accomplished singlehandedly, you need information to point you in the right direction."

"What I've accomplished is managing to stay alive."

"You also disposed of two extremely dangerous *spetsnaz* types."

"As you disposed of Herb Porter."

His expression didn't change. "I was afraid you might think that, Brent. The fact is Herb begged the Director for the Sri Lanka slot. That he wandered off into dangerous territory was his doing, not anyone else's."

"Who sent Jay Catini to Ethiopia?"

"We needed a talented man there who spoke fluent Italian."

"Who put Selwyn Bates in my slot?"

Crosby said, "That was my decision, too. Selwyn needed to feel he was doing worthwhile work. No one knew how long your recuperation would take."

"And my secretary's transfer?"

Crosby looked at Wink Warren, who said, "Shit, man, Mrs. Talman had a standing request to transfer to Commerce, for family reasons. A vacancy occurred, the personnel computer matched demand with supply and she left. We try to match employee's personal needs with those of the Firm."

"All right," I said, "allowing you the benefit of the doubt on those points, why was I treated as a prisoner in the Virginia clinic? My room bugged, no visitors?"

Crosby sat forward; it was the first time he'd moved. "At first it seemed too pat that you survived the shooting when so many were slaughtered in cold blood. Security raised questions about your possible role in setting the thing up. The office wanted you isolated while it vetted you further. Your building pass was removed, along with a reference to a Monsignor Abelardo. He was checked out, too."

"A rough vetting." I said, "He didn't survive. And how did I come out of all this special evaluation?"

Warren said, "No personal DI—but it was noted that an old friend from your Zurich past was an active KGB agent."

"How was the connection made? I never used Dr. Brock as a reference."

"Your father once tried to recruit him for us—without knowing Brock was homosexual. Your father was simply told Brock was not a suitable candidate. In rechecking you and your family, Brock's name appeared."

"He tried to kill me—I scored first."

"Good job," Crosby said approvingly. "We didn't know you were in Switzerland."

Warren said, "The Swiss police announced his death from a climbing accident. To our liaison they reported finding physical evidence of Brock's treachery. You're in the clear on that."

"No way I could be connected. But before Brock died he transmitted a long message to his Controller telling him a good deal about me and mentioning Toby Gerard as my confidant."

"Wink, who is Gerard?" Crosby said.

Warren shrugged. I said, "Assistant Counsel to Connors' Committee. He's in a hospital having barely survived a murder attempt disguised as hit-and-run. Abelardo wasn't so lucky."

"That was tragic," Crosby said. "The good man was once a source in the Vatican."

"Bringing us back to Filip Sankov's confession." I said. "I gather everyone regards it as an embarrassment."

Crosby coughed. "The Administration sees it as an impediment to ratification of the Mutual Non-Aggression Treaty. The White House prefers to hold it in reserve against some future need."

"That's Senator Connors' position, too, Brent," Warren said. "For political reasons he hasn't let it be known that he's working with the Administration on this one." He gazed at me and his face was stony. "Mighty sly of you to keep a private copy of that interrogation."

"You didn't ask me, Wink. At the clinic you told me everything had been destroyed in the safehouse fire. That was before I knew Herb was dead, before I decided the videotape had to be exploited."

Crosby said, "If we're ever going to clear up these misunderstandings and misapprehensions, Brent, now is the time. What you haven't understood until now is that after the massacre you came under suspicion. So you were isolated and watched. Normal procedure."

"If I'm cleared now, what cleared me?"

"Tell him, Wink," Crosby said.

Warren sat forward. "When the Sûreté cleaned out that whorehouse hotel they found a tape recorder with Vasileyev's voice on it—and yours. It stood to reason you wouldn't have been torturing Vasileyev for information if you'd masterminded the massacre." He shrugged. "That satisfied Security. You're fully cleared."

I thought it over. "Why did the Sûreté pass us the tape?"

"You worked Paris Station," Warren said, "you know the old rivalries among the Sûreté, DST, and S-Dec—like us and the Bureau. The Sûreté figured the tape was worth something to someone and they sure weren't going to give it to their competitors."

"My voice was on the tape," I said, "not my name."

"Voiceprint," he said. "We're all registered, you know that. Computer comparison."

I knew that, but it had never seemed important. I remembered telling Brock I'd erased the tape, but I'd lied. So I was indebted to the voiceprint register for my reinstated clearance.

Crosby said, "Most importantly, there's a final matter to be cleared up among us, and it has to do with what your attorney told Senator Connors. I refer to the alleged mole the KGB calls Apollo. On that subject we can help each other."

"I'm listening."

Crosby raised his head and I noticed that his Adam's apple was large and protruding above his collar and carefully knotted tie. It gave him the appearance of a minister addressing Vestry members of his church. He said, "Over the years the subject of penetration by a Soviet mole has been very carefully guarded. Publicly, the Firm could not acknowledge the possibility existed. Nevertheless, the ease with which MI-6 was penetrated and rendered impotent served as a precept and warning to us all. Defections from within our own family and the FBI heightened our concern that an active penetration of our upper levels might indeed exist. The Office of Security intensified its review of blown operations and information leaks. The Director placed Herb Porter in charge of a small Staff element to accomplish the same task. Security focused on the background and contacts of agents involved in failed ops. Porter's cadre examined the operations themselves for vulnerability."

"Anyone got a cigarette?" I said.

Wink Warren took one from a pack and gave it to me along with a pack of matches from the Palm Restaurant. Merle Crosby—COPS—watched until I exhaled smoke, and continued. "It was an ongoing search, Brent, one that keelhauled a number of individuals in the process of elimination."

"Not unlike the treatment I got."

"Yours was a special situation."

"Anything you folks missed, General Kostikov supplied."

"Yeah," Warren said, "you had a rough time, buddy."

"Much of which," Crosby said, "was your own doing, Brent. I hope you realize that now."

"Sure," I said, "with twenty-twenty hindsight. Would it have hurt someone to have told me then what you're telling me now?"

"It wasn't possible. Until recently you've been under suspicion." Wink Warren.

"So," I said, "after long and painstaking personnel review and ops evaluation, what turned up?"

Crosby glanced quickly at Warren, then his gaze settled on me. "I must have your word that you will not reveal what I am about to tell you. It's perhaps our most closely held secret; if breached, the impact could be devastating. Do you agree?"

I hesitated a few moments before saying, "I agree."

Warren said, "That includes your lawyer, your girlfriend, anyone you might normally confide in. Even Senator Connors. Understand?"

"Got it."

Crosby breathed deeply. "The lines of both investigations finally converged on one name, one man. Sandor Parton."

I stared at him. "Sandy? I figured it had to be one of you or the

Director himself."

"That was part of Apollo's genius—distributing clues pointing to others rather than himself. It's why identifying him took so long."

"Security checked back on how come Sandy missed being blown up in Beirut with all them other Arabists," Warren said, "He told everyone his flight had been delayed or canceled. Airline records showed the plane left Cairo on time. Why wasn't he on it? Because he'd been warned not to attend the regional conference."

"Warned—how?"

"About a month ago." Warren continued, "the Israelis picked up an Iranian defector—an intelligence type who had worked in Cairo while Parton was there. This particular rag-head had been co-opted by the KGB ever since his studies at Lumumba University. He reported the bombing plan to his Sov controller and a day later was ordered to tell a particular American to avoid Beirut." Warren lit a cigarette and blew smoke across my shoulder. "Guess who?"

I breathed deeply. "Leave it to the Israelis, eh?"

"Yes, indeed. And the Izzies loved telling us because they've always had Parton on their books as anti-Iz. His Soviet connection explains why."

"Going back to that old dispute over Sandy," Crosby said, "the Mossad was right about Parton, and our Director was wrong, unpalatable as it is. Also, we've learned that for years Parton has been hiding a fairly important fact, lying about it. Had he told the truth he would never had been cleared and hired." Crosby grimaced. "Parton swore he had no relatives behind the Curtain, said his mother had left Hungary after his father died. Turns out ma and pa were divorced and Sandy's father still lives there, an upper-level party official in Miskolc."

"Mossad turn that up, too?"

Crosby nodded. "During routine immigrant debriefings. We don't come out of this looking too well, Brent. Can't properly vet our own people without outside help."

"I guess the old Firm's not what it once was—or claimed to be. But the most important thing is finally identifying Apollo. How will the case be handled?"

"That's the current problem," Warren said. "A man as dedicated to the other side as Sandy can't be played back against them—he'd run just like Philby and the others did, so that's not an option. Publicizing his treachery would mean a major embarrassment to the Firm, and we've had enough of that in the past few years. Prosecute Parton? On what evidence? Mossad won't send an officer to testify to what the Iranian defector revealed—that's hearsay, anyway. And if by some miracle the Izzies allowed the Iranian to testify here, Parton's attorneys would shred him like a Cuisinart and Parton would walk. No longer in our employ, of course, but out there laughing and blabbing away about his years as a fuckin' mole." He tossed his cigarette at a brass spitoon. "I can see the book he'd write, the TV talk shows, the magazine articles making us look like assholes."

I nodded. "What I don't get is why you're telling me all this—an act of contrition?"

"In part," Crosby said. "But you've also shown yourself an extraordinarily resourceful man with uncommon survivability. I thought you might have ideas how to proceed and clear this up once and for all. Neutralizing Apollo without attendant publicity."

While I was pondering the deeper meaning, Warren said, "Parton set you and Sankov up, got all those people killed, sent *spetsnialny* against you—twice—and murdered Dr. Cereza. He's a Soviet agent who's done incalculable damage to us, but there's no legal way to get back at him."

I looked at both men. "Does Parton have reason to think he's under suspicion?"

"No," Warren said. "I see him as usual, talk with him, lunch with him, much as I hate it. Haven't tipped my hand. No way."

"Nor I," said Merle Crosby. "We've played it very, very cool. There's no way Parton could know." His expression was intense, eyes beady. For a while no one spoke. I said, "Suppose Parton were to be eliminated . . .?"

Crosby looked at Warren then at me. "The Firm's gratitude would be almost boundless."

"Yeah, bounty reward and job of choice," Warren said. "For the right man."

"My concern and the Director's is that the longer Parton's around the more damage he can inflict," Crosby said. "It has to end."

"He lives in Alexandria, on a quiet street," Warren said. "He suspects nothing."

"Just as Sankov and I didn't expect trouble. Strange how situations reverse themselves." I stood up and stretched. "Anything else?"

Crosby got out a scrap of note paper and wrote on it. "My private number. Call me any time." He got up and handed it to me. "Any questions, Brent?"

"You and Wink have painted a very full picture. I don't think there's more to be said." I smiled bleakly.

Warren said, "Your car's down by the elevator. Good luck."

I left the conference room and walked along the corridor to the elevators. One took me down to basement parking, and as Warren said, the Firebird was there. I got in, started the engine and reached under the seat. My HK .38 was there. I checked magazine and safety and fitted it into my holster. The ramp gave out on Georgia Avenue. The time was 1:04 when I turned south heading for Alexandria.

I understood the assignment.

Kill Sandy Parton.

BOOK SIX

THIRTY-ONE

By one-thirty I was at the corner of Washington and Prince. I parked and went to a phone booth, looked up Parton's home number and dialed.

The phone rang five times before I heard his voice.

"Night Duty Officer," I said, "an Urgent has just come in, sir."

"Can't my deputy handle it?"

"No, sir, it's slugged Immediate Action for you."

He groaned. "Very well. Half an hour, forty minutes." He hung up and so did I.

At an all-night diner I got a cup of black coffee and sipped it as I drove down to Wolfe Street. I parked at the end of the block where I could watch Sandy's flower-lined entrance walk.

In ten minutes his doorside bulls-eye lamps went on and I saw him leave. I didn't know where he parked his car, but he turned down the sidewalk in my direction. I opened my jacket and pulled out my pistol. When Sandy was abreast of me I got out and said, "Pardon me, can you tell me if there's a garage open?"

He stopped, turned and saw the pistol in my hand.

"Don't panic, Sandy," I said. "What's urgent and requires immediate action is that we have a talk."

Face taut under the streetlamp, he stared at me. "Jesus, Brent Graves!"

"Get in and drive."

As he slid behind the wheel he said, "Where are we going?"

"A quiet place—you know the neighborhood better than I."

As we pulled away from the curb he said, "Where the hell have you been, anyway?"

"Staying alive. Avoiding those unpleasant consequences you warned me about that time at the club. I should have taken the advice, Sandy. You said you were a messenger. Who originated the message?"

He looked away. "Wink. Wink Warren. He told me you'd been sniffing around my area, suggested I shoo you off."

"Been wondering about that sequence," I said. "There's a good place to park—over there by the HoJo." He turned into the motel lot and shut off the engine. I pocketed the keys and said, "Between midnight and one I was closeted with two of your close friends—Crosby and Wink Warren. I'll bet you can't guess what they suggested I do—for a big cash reward and a position of my choice."

"No."

"Kill you."

His face paled. "Are you going to . . . kill me?"

"Not unless you're Apollo."

"*Apollo?* Who the hell's Apollo?"

"The legendary Soviet penetration who's made so many things go wrong."

"You must be crazy."

"No," I said, but for weeks I've been running for my life. The experience tends to rid one of preconceived notions. They say desperate men don't think clearly, but this one did." I holstered my pistol. "Warren and Crosby presented a persuasive case against you. Want to hear it?"

Eyes round, anxious, he said, "I—I guess so."

I repeated what I'd been told in the conference room, and as he listened his face became even paler. Finally he said, "It's all a damn lie—fabricated. My father died in Hungary, and I never worked for the KGB in Cairo or anyplace else. I missed that Beirut flight because I'd stayed overnight with a girlfriend and had too much to drink. I overslept, Brent, and was ashamed to admit it. You've got to believe me."

I said, "I've heard so many lies, so many deceptions that yours could be just another self-serving tale. You know I can't verify your father's death or get your girlfriend's testimony. Not in the little time I have, Sandy. Crosby's waiting for my call."

"But, God, Brent, I'm not Apollo, whoever the hell he is, and you've *got* to believe me. Jesus, don't kill me. I'm not the man you want." His face was ashen, lips trembling.

"I know that," I told him. "But not because of anything you've said. Everything Apollo did, beginning with the safehouse massacre, had to be done by a man who could reach out anywhere in the Agency and have his orders obeyed. A man who could do things on his own, unquestioned. You've got rank, Sandy, and a degree of authority, but not the kind Apollo enjoys. There are maybe six men in the Firm with enough authority to do everything Apollo's done, but in the weeks since I last saw you I've had plenty of time to think things through. And I've narrowed it down to two."

His eyes glinted. "Two? You mean—?"

"Yeah. Warren and Crosby. For them everything was possible as it was for no one else." I looked at the dash clock. "Can you reach the Director?"

"He's in Belgium, NATO conference. No way I can contact him."

"Then," I said, "you'll have to disappear for a while. I mean totally, absolutely. No contact with your family or the office. Check into a motel and stay until you hear from me."

"I—whatever you say. God, I can't believe what's happening. It's like a nightmare."

"Give me your wallet."

Reluctantly, he dug it out and gave it to me. I checked his money—twenty-two dollars. I took three fifties from my billfold and gave them to him. "Pay in advance for your room. What name?"

He thought for a few moments. "Albert Waggoner." He looked at the Howard Johnson's entrance. "I'll stay here."

"Make damn sure you do. Your wife has to believe you've disappeared, met foul play, if she's to be convincing."

"I hate to do this to her. Isn't there—?"

"I'm trying to preserve your life *and* mine. There's no other way."

Another deep breath before he said, "I should be helping, Brent."

"Disappear. Stay in your room."

He swallowed. "What if—I mean, in the event you don't call . . .?"

"You'll be on your own."

He got out, stood for a moment, said, "Thanks"—and walked into the motor lodge. I watched him register, and after he disappeared down a corridor I drove around the block and watched the entrance long enough to convince myself he wasn't going to come out. It was well after two o'clock when I drove over to Washington Avenue and headed north for the District.

I was tired and tense. I needed time to think things through, and I didn't want Crosby and Warren to think I'd disposed of Parton too easily. What the hell had he ever done to them? Did COPS see Parton as a competitor? Did Warren? On the surface, the three of them had been convincingly clubby. Maybe because COPS and Warren knew Parton so well they'd decided he could be framed for the fall.

Along Vermont Avenue garish lights from rib-joints, blaring rock music, flashily dressed whores strolling back and forth. I steered into the parking lot and walked back to the hotel. From the lobby pay phone I dialed Parton's room and after the second ring he answered. "Just checking," I said, and hung up.

The desk clerk gave me an envelope and I sealed Parton's wallet in it. Then I went to my room and removed my facial disguise. I took a shower and lay on my bed in darkness.

Smoking.

From blocks away came the sound of screaming tires, a crash of metal against metal, and—silence.

I could barely see smoke rings drifting toward the dark ceiling. They spread and vanished, insubstantial as my thoughts.

Three hours until dawn. I dressed, fitted on my shoulder holster and released the pistol's safety catch. I put everything else into Brock's suitcase and carried it to my car. Then I drove to my house in Georgetown.

I hadn't been there since the night Chekalov triggered the booby-trapped safe. I remembered the stench of smoke and the dynamite fumes. Now the air was pure, my furniture replaced. In my library there were new bookshelves. Where the safe had been was plastered over and painted. I replaced the books and made myself a drink. Then I picked up the telephone and called Wink Warren. When he answered, I said, "I need to see you."

"Jesus, can't it wait until morning?"

"No."

"Ah—anything wrong?"

"Nothing," I said. "That impediment we were discussing has been removed."

"That's—great." He sounded less than enthusiastic. "Crosby know?"

"His line's been busy, but I'll try again. Meanwhile, get over to my house."

"What for? I don't get it."

"You will, because it concerns you. Vitally." I replaced the receiver and sipped more of my drink. My plan was about to take off.

The kitchen was clean and ordered and smelled very slightly of Creole cooking. One corner held a stack of newspapers Salomé saved for me; I hadn't thought to suspend delivery.

There was food in the refrigerator, but I wasn't hungry. I opened my wallet, looked at what Crosby had written and dialed the number.

Recognizing my voice, he said, "You have news?"

"Positive. I'm calling from Alexandria and I'll be leaving shortly for my house. It's best I leave the area for a while, but there are points that need covering. I want you to meet me."

"Yes," he said, "I believe that's a good idea."

"Unless you want me to come to your place."

"No, no, that's not . . . prudent. What's your address?"

I gave it to him and he said he would be there in forty minutes.

Wink Warren arrived in twenty-five.

Before letting him in I told him to park around the block, and when he returned I had a drink ready for him. I showed him to the library and turned off the living room lights. He wore a tieless shirt and a two-tone sweater under his coat.

Swallowing, he said, "So, Parton—?"

"Disappeared. Leave it at that."

He looked around self-consciously, until I said, "No body to be found—just this." I tossed him the envelope. He opened it and while he was staring at Parton's wallet I pulled out my .38.

"Hands up, Wink. You're next on Crosby's list."

He dropped the wallet and raised his arms. I crouched and patted him down, lifted his coattails and pulled a .38 revolver from a clip holster. Stepping back, I spilled shells from the cylinder and set the empty handgun on the coffee table. "I suppose," I said, "Crosby told you to eliminate me."

When he said nothing I said, "Hear the news, boychik. When I spoke with Crosby just now, he told me to dispose of you."

He stared at me, big mouth open. "*Whaaat?*"

"I don't have any problem with that—assuming you're the right man," I said. "Crosby says you were Sandy's accomplice."

"That's a damn lie!"

"There's been a lot of lying," I said, "and much of it in that conference room. How much of what was told me did you dig up on your own, how much was Crosby's information? About the Cairo flight, the Iranian defector and so on?"

"Crosby told me the whole story, said it came from his special source. Shit, man, I believe him."

"What did he tell you about me?"

"He said you had to be eliminated or you'd blackmail us the rest of our lives."

"Inasmuch as I'm the one responsible for Parton's disappearance, isn't it more logical you two could blackmail me?"

He thought it over. Grudgingly, he said, "Makes sense."

"He's been ahead of us all the way. I didn't fit it all together until Parton's last words denying he was Apollo." I looked at my .38. "Poor Sandy, I owe him."

Warren licked his lips. "You mean—?"

"Crosby laid his own guilt on Parton—with your connivance." I sighted down the barrel at his heart. "I'm in need of redemption, Wink. I'll start with you."

"Oh, God, Brent, don't kill me!" He sank to his knees, clasped his hands prayerfully. "Merle told me everything we did was right. I only did what he told me."

I heard a car coming down the street, approaching very slowly. "Think of this," I said. "Crosby didn't make you his accomplice because of your intelligence, he chose you for your stupidity, you cowboy asshole."

I couldn't hear the car any more. "Sit down," I said. "Don't move."

I went into the living room and peered outside. There was a black four-door on the far side of the street, no lights. When Crosby got out I unbolted the front door and went back to where Warren waited.

"You have a slim chance to save yourself," I said. "Keep your mouth shut and follow my lead. Understand?"

"Yeah." It was almost falsetto.

The doorbell rang. I called, "Come in and bolt the door."

To Warren I said, "Pick up your revolver, keep it in sight." The front door opened and closed. I heard the bolt slide home. Footsteps crossed the living room.

Merle Crosby appeared in the doorway, both hands jammed into the pockets of his loose-fitting black raincoat. My gun was out of sight. I picked up Parton's wallet and offered it to Crosby. With a smile he took it, fingered Sandy's building pass and said, "Good work, Brent. I won't ask how you did it, but I assume we won't be hearing from Sandy again."

"Not for a while." My hand tightened around the pistol grip. "There was talk of a reward . . ."

"So there was, and it's very much on my mind."

"Good. Because Warren says you ordered him to kill me—now you can clear that up."

"I will," Crosby said. "Wink, put down your gun, I'll handle things."

Relief on his face, Warren laid his revolver on the table and sat back.

From Crosby's pocket a silenced automatic appeared. It pointed at Warren and popped three times. Warren's head snapped back and I heard a long rattling sigh. Crosby's automatic swerved until it pointed at me. I said, "You don't want to do that, Merle, I've got Sankov's confession."

"Have you?" he said calmly. "I was going to ask about that, Brent, and to fortify my position I've taken something you want."

Very slowly, Warren's body slid sideways until it came awkwardly to rest on the sofa. There was a hole over his right eye, one in his throat, another where his heart should be. I imagined the widow would mourn him. I wouldn't.

To Crosby I said, "What is it you have to trade?"

"Your ladyfriend—Mrs. Mountjoy."

THIRTY-TWO

My body went cold. "Where is she?"

"Safe. Terrified, of course, and very confused." His smile was wolfish. "Blames you for everything."

"As well she might—having no idea about any of this."

Crosby's gaze traveled over to Warren's body. "So ambitious, so pliable—he'll be hard to replace."

"True. He had his uses, large and small."

"You, too." Crosby picked up Warren's revolver and pocketed it. "After we've made our exchange—assuming we do—I suggest you get out of the country for a while, quite a long while."

"I plan to. How do we arrange this trade?"

He sat down near Warren's body. "Let's count Sankov cassettes. You took the original videotape from the safehouse and had how many copies made?"

"Two. My attorney gave one to Senator Connors, and I gave one to Toby Gerard."

"The Senator will recover it for me. Leaving the original in your possession. How soon can you retrieve it?"

"Half an hour—after you prove Mrs. Mountjoy is unharmed."

Watching me, he picked up the extension phone and punched seven numbers. Presently he said, "Put her on," and handed me the receiver.

It was ice cold in my hand. "Lainey," I said, "I'll be coming for you. Are you okay?"

"Oh, Brent—please help me." Her voice was high, close to hysteria. I gripped the phone.

"Are you all right?"

"Yes—but I—" Crosby took the receiver from my hand and replaced it. "Satisfied?"

"The tape isn't here. While I'm getting it, have Mrs. Mountjoy brought here. When I'm satisfied she's okay, I'll hand over the cassette."

He thought it over. "After all you've gone through to preserve the tape, you're letting it go rather easily. I wonder why."

"Why not? Sankov's confession was only useful if it could be exploited. You've cut off every access I had—so it's worthless compared to Mrs. Mountjoy."

"All right. You have half an hour to bring the tape. If you're not here by then you'll find her body next to Warren's."

"One other stipulation—no goon squad on the premises. Just you and Lainey."

He looked at his watch. "Your half hour starts now."

I left him there beside Warren's contorted body. I started the Firebird and drove down to Canal Street, left the car and walked to the house.

It was dark inside. I got out my pistol, intending to break a finial window to unlock the door—and reconsidered. I turned the door handle and it opened. I went in.

Light from a table lamp was enough to show me the cassette shelves. I took out *Skiing-Gstaad* and fitted it into my left coat pocket. Then I drove partway back to my house and walked the rest of the way. Shrubbery gave me cover, so I could watch arrivals unseen. My watch showed I'd been away from Crosby for twelve minutes. In another hour dawn would gray the streets. The air was cold. My skin prickled.

Nine minutes later, a car arrived, pulled up in front and stopped, engine running. It was a black sedan like Crosby's. The driver stayed behind the wheel while a man got out, then a woman. I could see the glint of his pistol as he shoved her up my walk. The man—one of the three who had kidnapped me—opened my front door and drew Lainey in. I was pretty sure he'd leave her with Crosby because Crosby wasn't going to want witnesses.

It didn't take a genius to write his scenario. Take the tape, shoot Lainey and me, arrange weapons and rig the scene to show the men had shot each other and Lainey had caught a stray bullet in the gunplay.

My front door opened and the man came out. He looked left and right as he went down the steps. I wanted to shoot him in the belly, but he and the driver were low priority.

He got in beside the driver and the car pulled away. I waited until the engine sound faded and then I went around through the garden gate and peered into the library window.

Crosby was there, silenced pistol in hand. Lainey sat in a chair facing him, her face drawn, tear stains on her cheeks. I would have shot Crosby then if the angle had been right, but he was in profile. If I only wounded him he could still shoot Lainey.

I retraced my steps, entered the house noisily and found Crosby standing behind Lainey, pressing his pistol to her head.

"Please," she cried. "*Please,* Brent!"

Crosby said, "You're punctual. Put the tape on the table."

I took out the tape with my left hand. "Let her go."

"The tape."

Lainey screamed, "*Give it to him!*"

I looked at her tortured face. "I love you, but if we're going to leave here alive it has to be my way. Crosby, you want the tape destroyed, right?"

"Of course."

"I'll do it for you." From the table I took a lighter and carried it to the library's small, seldom-used fireplace. I ignited the lighter, touched it to a corner of the cassette's black plastic. Flame sputtered, spread. I bent over as though to drop the burning cassette in the grate. Instead, I flung it like a frisbee at Crosby's face. His head snapped aside, but the flaming cassette caught his temple and he released Lainey to swat it with his pistol. She dropped forward, falling on hands and knees as his pistol fired.

I had an unobstructed frontal shot with the .38, and before Crosby could sight on me I pulled the trigger.

The bullet caught him high on the right chest and spun him around. He howled in pain and his pistol fired again. I vaulted the table and kicked Crosby back, slamming him down across Warren's body. Lainey's open mouth was emitting high-pitched shrieks, but I ignored them and used my heavy .38 to batter Crosby's weapon from his hand.

For a small man there was a lot of fight in him. His left hand plunged into his coat pocket and came out with Warren's .38 revolver. Its muzzle was pointing at my belly when he pulled the trigger.

Click.

Pull again. Another click.

"Empty," I said. "It's all over." I pulled his coat open and saw blood gouting from the small entrance wound. The exit hole was the size of a baseball. Without emergency treatment Merle Crosby would bleed to death.

Lainey sat on the floor watching us, eyes large, mouth trembling, still on the knife-edge of hysteria. I knocked the revolver from Crosby's grasp and picked it up by the knurled grip. Crosby's face was twisted with pain, his breathing fast and shallow. I kicked the still-burning cassette into the fireplace and turned to Lainey. "Drink some liquor," I told her, "and bring some for me."

Her eyes regarded me dully. She didn't move.

"On your feet," I snapped.

That got her up. Wordlessly she went past me and out of the door. Still keeping my pistol pointed at Crosby I dialed the Howard Johnson motor lodge and asked for Room 219, Mr. Waggoner.

Four rings and I heard Sandy Parton's voice. "Things are smoothing out but I need your help. Get a taxi and come here fast." I gave him the address and had him repeat it, then broke the connection. Time for questions and answers later. Maybe.

Lainey appeared holding a bottle of Scotch by the neck. I made her drink from it, then helped myself. She stared at me uncomprehendingly, "Are you going to call an ambulance?"

"For a murderer?" I gestured at Warren's body. "The man who shot him happens to be a deep-cover Soviet agent. He would have killed us without hesitation." I stared at her eyes. "Without remorse."

When there was no reaction, I said, "Because of him at least a dozen people are dead—I was almost a victim."

"Oh, Brent," she said tonelessly. I caught her as she fell.

After I'd quickly massaged her wrists I looked over at Crosby. His face was fixed in a glare. "We know why Sankov defected," I said, "Why did you?"

The words bubbled from his throat. "There can never be world peace so long as . . . the superpowers contend." He coughed, and blood dribbled down his chin. "This country will lose. The sooner it . . . happens, the sooner . . . we have peace."

"So," I said, "you see yourself as a peace partisan. I wondered about that."

"Men like you," he whispered, "destroyers . . . all of you." His eyes were beginning to dull. I picked up Lainey and carried her to the living room couch, covered her with an Afghan my mother had knitted.

Crosby, I mused, actually believed what he'd told me. And he was going to find peace sooner than he ever thought . . .

At the window I parted curtains and looked out. Gray streaks of dawn lightened the eastern sky. Crosby's sedan was parked on the street. It was part of the problem I had to solve. I needed Parton's help.

When I left the window Lainey was sitting up. "I'm sorry," she said. "It's just that I'm not accustomed to violence." She smiled weakly. "I'd never been kidnapped before."

"It won't happen again." I sat beside her and kissed her cool forehead and salty cheeks, held her so tightly I could feel the beating of her heart. She whispered, "It's all right, now. After this I can take anything."

So while I waited for Sandy I told Lainey about the Sankov confession, the massacre, everything that happened to me in Paris and Bern, and how Crosby and Warren had hauled me in not twelve hours ago to feed me lies and set me after Sandy.

"But you didn't kill him . . .?" Her face was apprehensive.

"He's coming to help, dear. One good turn deserves another."

"Yes," she said, "it does. Peter called last night and—"

But Parton was pressing the doorbell. I let him in wild-eyed and disheveled, and introduced him to Lainey. Taking her hands, I drew her to her feet. "Can you make it home? If not I—"

She shook her head. "I'd like to walk. When will I see you?"

"I'll come as soon as I can." I kissed her and saw her down the steps. Then I came back to Parton and pointed to the telephone. "Call your wife, reassure her. Say you'll be home in two or three hours."

While he was doing that I went to the library.

Crosby had managed to shift around so that his head was lying on Warren's hip. His eyes were open and they stared at me as I picked up Warren's revolver and replaced the shells I'd removed from the cylinder. Before rigor set in I moulded Warren's hand around my .38, removed it carefully and tucked my pistol in his right-hand pocket.

Parton came in, saw the two bodies and went so white I thought he was going to faint. "Have a drink," I said, and handed him the bottle. He gulped a stiff jolt and shook himself. "I guess you'll tell me about this."

"Explanations can wait. Right now we're going to move these bodies. Wink goes first."

"But—Crosby's still alive."

I felt Crosby's pockets, found Parton's wallet and gave it to him. "He's surprised to see you, Sandy, having thought you dead."

"Son of a bitch!"

"Give me a hand with the big one."

Together we got Warren upright, and with his arms over our shoulders trundled him across the street to Crosby's car. I opened the trunk and we lifted the heavy body over the rim and down inside. Knee-chest position fitted best. I closed the trunk and wiped off my prints. "Just like Miami," I said. "Crosby shot him so quick I don't think Warren knew what hit him."

"God!"

We went back inside.

I set Crosby's silenced automatic on safety and stuck the weapon in the depth of his coat pocket. A lot of blood had seeped there, and I wiped my hands on the hem of his black coat. More blood spilled from Crosby's lips as we pulled him upright. "Must have hit that lung," I remarked.

"He's still alive."

"I want him alive—for a while."

As with Warren, we moved Crosby across the street and propped him on the passenger side of his car's front seat. I got behind the wheel and told Parton to get in the rear. I made a U-turn and drove back to where I had left the Firebird.

Parton got out and started the Firebird. He followed me out MacArthur Boulevard to the picnic area at Great Falls. There was plenty of gray light now, and I drove off the cleared area into tall grass, saw a good-sized pine ahead and braced myself for the crash. It slammed Crosby's head against the dash, and when I hauled his body across the seat and behind the wheel I realized he was unconscious. The car engine was still running, tires slipping on a bed of pine needles, grass and sand from the nearby river.

I wiped fingerprints from the steering wheel and clenched Crosby's hands where mine had been. I closed the door and polished prints from the handle. Crosby's eyes stared vacantly. I pushed his torso forward against the steering wheel and felt his carotid artery.

Merle Crosby—Apollo—was history.

I walked back to where Parton waited in the Firebird and told him so.

As we drove back to Georgetown I told Parton all he needed to know about last night and the long subterranean conspiracy that preceded it. He listened in silence, until we were at my house. Then he said, "I guess none of this will ever be known."

"No one will hear it from me—and I hope not from you."

He shook his head vigorously. "I'm just grateful to be alive, Brent. Thanks."

"I needed your trust, Sandy. I still do."

He nodded. "From now on maybe things will go better with our foreign ops."

"They should," I said, "and the Director will need a new Ops Chief—maybe you."

"Maybe." We shook hands.

"One last thing," I said. "Ditch this heap where it's likely to be stripped or stolen—leave the keys."

"Will do." He smiled bleakly. "By the old railroad yard."

I stepped back and watched him drive away. Then I went into my house.

In the library I found where Crosby's two wild bullets had impacted. One in the ceiling, the other just above the bookshelf top. I covered the holes with spackling paste and began wiping blood from the sofa cushions. Crosby's bullets hadn't passed through Warren's body, so they were where I wanted them to be for autopsy and ballistic comparison.

I burned bloody rags in the fireplace, where the remains of the videocassette were smoldering. Then I went upstairs, got under the shower and scrubbed blood from my hands. I was changing into fresh clothing when the telephone rang.

I didn't know who was calling but I knew who wouldn't be, so I answered, and it was Dorsey Jerrault.

"Brent—I waited all night for your call. What happened with the Senator?"

"Not much, he was pretty skeptical. I left the tape with him for further consideration but I think he's committed to the Treaty and doesn't want to make waves."

"Shit!"

"Well, I did what I could—and thanks for your help."

"You're just—walking away from it?"

"I have sense enough to know when I've lost. Anyway, I want a new life for myself, Dorsey, a different one. I'll be in touch."

I hung up, thought about it for a while, and continued dressing.

Then I turned out lights and locked the front door behind me.

Lainey's door was still unlocked. I went in, called, and heard no reply. I got the loaded revolver and tiptoed upstairs, found Lainey asleep in the bedroom. I put away the revolver and lay down beside her. After so much death I needed the warmth of life against my body. She moved against me, murmured in her sleep and relaxed.

It was nearly ten o'clock when she woke me, coffee cup in hand. Brushing a lock of hair from her forehead she said, "It was all a bad dream, wasn't it? A nightmare?"

"Just that," I said, "and *not* to be remembered." I sat up and sipped from the cup as she held it, remembering Dr. Joann Cereza helping me drink so many weeks ago.

"Did I tell you—I can't remember, so much was happening—about Peter's call?"

"You started to."

"Well, it was just before those men took me, Brent. Peter was mournful and hangdog and apologetic and said I should divorce him because he'd met someone he absolutely had to marry."

I took her free hand and kissed it. "Just like that?"

"Well, it's not as though he just met her and was swept off his feet—said he'd loved her years ago, dementedly, but she married a friend of his. Now, Lady Felicia Bournemouth is divorced and eager to marry Peter—they're very distantly related, by the way." She laughed very lightly. "The English always marry their relations, don't they?"

"With uncommon frequency."

"You haven't said anything—what do *you* think of it?"

"I think the timing couldn't be better. We'll get out of here today. Start packing."

EPILOGUE

By late afternoon we were in Santo Domingo, capital of the Dominican Republic. We stayed at the Hilton long enough to retain a lawyer and establish contact in London with Peter's solicitor. Then, while notarized documents were crossing and recrossing the Atlantic, we took a beach cottage down the coast near San Pedro de Macoris, and spent our time sunning on our stretch of white beach, snorkling for shells and lobsters and enjoying the cool refuge of our bedroom.

An airmail edition of The New York *Times* brought word of the Treaty's ratification by a vote of 62–34 with four abstentions. Senator Frank Connors voted with the majority. I put aside the paper and took a long walk down the beach.

Three weeks later we were married by the same judge who granted Lainey's divorce, and flew to Paris. For a week we did nothing but go to concerts and ballet, art galleries, the Louvre, afternoon racing at Longchamps.

I saw Freddy de Mortain, who told me that Colonel Nikolai V.

Kuzchin, the Soviet Assistant Military Attaché, had been recalled to Moscow following an embarrassing incident in a low-class brothel.

So much for Kostikov/Kuzchin, I thought. No longer a threat to me, or anyone else. The Soviets had their Treaty. They'd won all the marbles, they'd leave well-enough alone.

Lainey hired an interior decorator and began going through the apartment with pen and clipboard. Once she had issued all orders and established complete *entente* with Maurice, she announced that it was time we joined her parents in Epernay. I suggested she go ahead and pave the way while I looked up an old friend in Rome. She pouted and reminded me that I'd sworn to renounce my former ways. I said this was absolutely the last time I would travel alone and she agreed to my pleadings—with the understanding that I join her at the family château as soon as I could.

So I carried her bags down to the new Renault roadster I'd bought as a wedding present. I kissed my bride and watched her drive away.

That night I placed a phone call to Rome, and in the morning flew Alitalia to Leonardo da Vinci Airport, where Fred Jeffers was waiting to drive me into the city.

As we pulled onto the *autostrade*, he said, "Damn strange request, Brent, and damn little time to grease the way." He rubbed thumb and forefinger in the traditional Latin gesture. "I can't guarantee he'll talk to you."

"All I want is a face-to-face."

"Right. If you don't try, you never know." He was silent for a while until he said, "Couple of weeks ago Jay Catini flew in from Addis on R and R. We had dinner together, talked over old times, and he mentioned you were influential in keeping me here. I appreciate that, Brent, and so does my wife. *My* house is *your* house, as they say."

"How's Jay making out?"

"Surviving—only a two-year tour, hardship post benefits. But he misses Washington."

"I don't." My house was for sale, bank deposit box emptied.

He drove up to a high-walled building where we got out. I followed Fred inside. He stopped to talk with a uniformed official, pointed at me, and the man nodded. Fred came back to me. "It's okay. You're on your own."

I followed the official through a kind of lobby to a locked metal door. The man unlocked it, passed me through and showed me into a small, high-ceilinged room that held a wooden table and three wooden chairs. I lit a cigarette and put the pack on the table. I smoked a while and thought perhaps enough time had passed that the truth could finally be told. On that slim chance I had come.

A narrow side door unlocked and a man came in. He was wearing coarse, gray, prison garb and sandals.

I got out a cigarette and looked up at the still-youthful face and mad eyes of Mehmet Ali Agca.